LADY ROSAMUND
AND THE
HORNED GOD

LADY ROSAMUND AND THE HORNED GOD

A ROSIE AND MCBRAE REGENCY MYSTERY

BARBARA MONAJEM

Praise for the Rosie and McBrae Regency Mysteries

Barbara Monajem's *Lady Rosamund and the Poison Pen* is a delightfully spicy mystery, peppered with sharp wit and memorable characters, especially the titular Lady Rosamund. Rosie is a woman who seems to know her own mind…or does she? Battling her greatest fear, Rosie must discover the true identity of the mysterious caricaturist Corvus, and outsmart the author of the poison pen letters before it's too late. Indifferent to the tongue-clucking of her peers, Rosie is full of surprises. Fans of historical mystery are in for an entertaining treat. – Kelly Oliver, Award-winning, bestselling author of the Fiona Figg Mysteries.

Lady Rosamund and the Horned God is an excellent historical mystery—well researched and well written! As a psychotherapist, I was particularly intrigued by Lady Rosamund's OCD tendencies (accurately presented, by the way), and her realistic terror of being locked away in an asylum as mad, should others become aware of her behaviors. OCD and most other psychological disorders have existed for centuries. Portraying how one suffering from it might have coped in a society unforgiving of "oddness" gives the Lady Rosamund stories a unique twist. – Kassandra Lamb, author of the Kate Huntington Mysteries and the Marcia Banks & Buddy Cozy Mysteries.

Chapter One

Be careful what you long for—better yet, be realistic. That should stop the longing cold.

—From the diary of Corvus

Summer at my father's estate in Westmoreland was bliss. Far from my mother and her strictures, I could do as I pleased. I dipped my toes in the lake. I tramped through the wood to the moor. I scrambled to the top of the fell and admired the view....

I found myself wishing for a corpse.

Allow me to explain. I am not naturally of a macabre frame of mind. I don't wish a gruesome death on anyone. My previous encounter with a corpse, when I'd found a dead footman on the service stairs of my London house, had set in motion a series of unpleasant events.

Interesting ones, mind you. Frightening, too, but I'd been forced to think and act in ways I had never done before. Now I was back to the usual ladylike occupations, which lack almost entirely in intellectual stimuli. I am bored by needlework, I cannot draw, and one can only spend so much time reading or clipping the roses. I found myself imagining a corpse hidden behind the cairn. Or tangled in the water lilies. Or simply blocking the path, tripping us up, bringing something *different* into our lives.

So, I could scarcely contain my delight when we were invited to a fortnight-long party at the house of Sir Alphonse Lewis.

I had met Sir Alphonse once years ago. An eccentric patron of the theater, he was known to frequent the green rooms, but not solely to ogle the actresses. He was genuinely interested in the plays. Imagine that! But I couldn't claim more than the barest acquaintance, for we don't move in the same circles. Even those theater people who may claim a degree of social status—such as Sir Alphonse—are known for their lack of refinement and loose morals. They are simply not our sort.

"I can't think why he's invited us." My father, the Earl of Medway, wandered into the breakfast parlor, waving a sheet of foolscap with crossed lines in a flowing hand. "The last time we met, he swore never to speak to me again."

"Heavens, why?" I asked. It should have been the other way around. Sir Alphonse's antecedents are far from exalted; he should treasure the friendship of an earl.

"A disagreement about the horned god of the Celts." Papa set the letter down to open the covers of various dishes on the sideboard. "Bacon and onions. Ah!" He served himself a heaping plateful, along with two poached eggs.

"Perhaps he has forgiven you," I suggested. "Or now agrees with your point of view."

Papa snorted. "Not likely." He took a seat, and I poured him a cup of coffee. "It's for a Lammas festival."

"How marvelous!" I cried. "Maybe he just wants good company." Which was my oblique way of complaining about the lack of it in Westmoreland. My father is a darling, but I craved excitement.

"Won't there be a Lammas festival here?" asked my dearest friend, Cynthia Benson.

Trust Cynthia to pour water on newly-kindled flames. She used to be much more fun. I love her dearly, but since she became *enceinte*, she won't go anywhere or see anyone except the vicar's wife, and that is only because that kindly woman is gullible enough to believe the lies we have told her.

I quite understand Cynthia's reluctance. She is expecting my deceased husband's illegitimate child. She was his mistress for years, and before that she was Lord Benson's wife. She assumed she was barren, so the pregnancy was quite a surprise—and, because she is unmarried, must be kept secret. Here in Westmoreland, Cynthia is going by the name of Mrs. Horsham, and pretending to be a widow of only a few months rather than over five years.

"Yes," I huffed, "but it'll be a bunch of rustics vying with one another. *Such a bore.*"

A few days earlier the vicar's wife had rambled at length about the upcoming Festival of First Fruits, where villagers brought loaves of bread to the church. "Instead of an offering of thanks for the first harvest of the year—not that we have much of that sort of harvest here; I can scarcely grow cucumbers—it has become a competition between housewives to produce the most beautiful loaves." She sighed. "And beautiful they are—all shapes and sizes, often in the form of birds and animals, but the acrimony between the various women completely negates the spirit of gratitude, which is the reason for the festival in the first place."

Since London society is one monstrous competition for most fashionable gown, outlandish hat, outrageously expensive ball, et cetera, my mother would at this point have quipped about the small, in their meager way, aping the great. I must admit, my first thought was precisely that.

Thought number two, hard on the heels of number one, was *Don't say that aloud, for you never know who may be listening.* So, I hadn't until just now, with that snide remark about rustics.

Not that there was the slightest chance that Corvus, the well-known caricaturist, was eavesdropping nearby in the guise of a footman, but what of the servants? One thing I learned from the unpleasantness a few months earlier was that servants and other members of the lower orders do not appreciate being looked down upon.

Thought number three was *It's probably a faulty notion anyway.*

This is a remarkable admission on the part of the daughter of an earl, granddaughter of a marquis, and cousin of a duke. I have been taught from the cradle that the nobility and gentry are far superior to everyone else—rightly and necessarily so. The lower orders are, according to my mother and many like her, stupid, immoral, and lazy. It is only thanks to the firm guiding hand of the upper classes that England is not in perpetual chaos.

I'm not so sure of that anymore. Truth to tell, I'm not sure of much at all.

However, enough of that. I didn't mean to digress from the point of this tale, which is that I longed for a diversion and it had now been offered. "How kind of him to invite us. It will be such fun!"

"But, Rosie dear," Cynthia said, "you're in mourning. You can't attend a house party!"

"Nonsense," Papa and I said in unison, and we exchanged grins. "I have no patience with the custom of sitting about and moping when one is bereaved," he added. "Far better to be out and about, keeping oneself busy."

I agreed with him, although I couldn't add that I didn't feel the least bit bereaved. Saddened, yes, but not for the usual reasons. I had not confided the truth to Cynthia. She had been Albert's mistress for years and was now expecting his child, and felt his loss far more than I. Nor had I told my father the whole story of the aforementioned unpleasant events.

"I should love a change of scene," I said. People might decry my inappropriate behavior, but with my father's support, I needn't fear much beyond the occasional tut-tut from some disapproving matron. "Does Sir Alphonse say who else is invited?"

"The usual odd sorts," Papa said. "Alphonse's latest fancy is Druidism, which attracts fools and eccentrics. He mentions something about play-wrights, too. A fellow called…Bellevue?"

"Harold Bellevue?" I made a face. "He's large, with untidy tow-colored hair and a great deal of money. He considers himself Shakespeare's equal."

Papa chuckled. "By your expression, I infer that his plays are tripe. How promising."

"Not if he insists on reading them to everyone." I shuddered, recalling an evening of poetry at the house of a friend, where Bellevue would have read his entire play if our hostess hadn't stopped him after the first monologue.

"That's precisely what is promising, Rosie," he said. "It will spark rude comments, or more likely downright venom, a shouting match or two, and if we're lucky, a bout of fisticuffs."

I gave him a reproving look. "That's not the sort of excitement I want." A dead body is one thing; two fools bloodying each other's noses another entirely.

He laughed. "Theater people are notoriously volatile. I'm surprised that Corvus fellow hasn't satirized them more often. A very talented man, that caricaturist. I should like to meet him someday."

And I would have been happy to introduce them, if not for two facts: 1) I had promised to keep Corvus' identity secret, and 2) I didn't expect to see him again, except perhaps as the merest nodding acquaintance.

"Did I show you his latest?" Papa asked. "It arrived yesterday."

"Yes, Papa," I sighed. It was a mortifying drawing in which Corvus twisted about, trying to birch his own bare buttocks. Why did that embarrass me, you ask? I'm not such a prude that I blush at the sight of a naked bum, but this caricature recalled an earlier one where I was portrayed birching a much aroused Corvus. In the new one, Corvus was bemoaning the fact that doing it to oneself wasn't anywhere near as much fun.

Well! I knew he was alluding to the fact that I was leaving Town and was therefore unavailable to punish him (not that I had ever done such a thing; let me make myself clear), but there was more to it than that. Later, I consulted Cynthia, who laughed and explained that he was also referring to a man's need to satisfy himself sexually in the absence of a woman.

I had grown accustomed to the earlier print, but this one infuriated me. I'm not sure why—it was crude (no surprise), but no more lascivious than the previous one.

Perhaps it was because Corvus had kissed me, and I had almost—almost, I repeat—enjoyed it. How could I possess even a shred of attraction to such an abashedly vulgar man?

"I don't fancy that sort of excitement either," Cynthia said. "I'm glad I won't be able to come."

"What?" Papa said. "Of course you'll come."

Cynthia sighed. "My dear Lord Medway, surely you see it's impossible. One does not appear in society when *enceinte*."

"Sir Alphonse and his sort do not bother with such foolish notions," Papa said.

They also don't bother with propriety. Everyone knows what actresses are like. Shamelessness seems to be a matter of pride with them.

But, you ask, wasn't Cynthia's liaison with my husband equally shameless? Yes, but she is respectable, whilst actresses are not. Surely you understand.

"I dare not display my shame for all to see," Cynthia said. "Every day, I dread that the vicar's wife will learn that I am unmarried, and she is a relative nobody whose opinion matters not a whit. What if someone at Sir Alphonse's party recognizes me from London? I know of him only by reputation, but I'm sure we share acquaintances. The same applies to Mr. Bellevue. Someone is sure to know me or guess who I am. Corvus' prints made both Rosie and me notorious. Someone will see my belly and begin to whisper, and soon all the world will know."

She is correct. Respectability can be somewhat precarious, and although I shall always stand her friend, others might not.

"I can only be thankful Corvus is nowhere near. He would delight in making matters worse," she said.

Corvus will not mock Cynthia, for I asked him not to—but needless to say I couldn't reassure her on that score.

"And what about my poor unborn child, branded as illegitimate?" she said. "Imagine how horrid for him!"

Why does everyone assume an unborn child is male until proven otherwise? So unfair. If I ever have children—which I most definitely will not, for the thought of marital congress utterly revolts me—I shall assume they are all girls, just to even out the balance a little.

"It will be whispered about anyway," I told her. "You can't come back with a baby after a long absence without provoking gossip. What if the poor mite looks exactly like Albert? Then everyone will know for sure."

"Yes, but as long as one maintains a polite fiction, it doesn't much matter."

"As for the house party, you needn't worry," Papa said. "Alphonse's guests are usually the literary sort, promiscuous by nature and not in the least inclined to judge others harshly, except with regard to their respective endeavors. In that respect, they can be damning—and most entertaining, as I just said." He bent a sympathetic gaze on Cynthia. "You must cease to consider it shame, dear child. Pregnancy is merely nature taking its course."

Do you see why I adore my father? He is so pragmatic about the consequences of carnal folly—no blighting pronouncements or grim disapproval. He never questioned my friendship with Albert's mistress—thank God, because I couldn't possibly explain the terms of my marriage, even to him.

"Naturally, it's preferable if it takes place within wedlock," he went on, "for purely practical reasons, such as providing the child with a male parent, a means of support, and so on. Fortunately, you have plenty of money."

This was followed by a ghastly silence on Cynthia's part, and a tense one on mine. Then my father, who is a stranger to *gêne*, asked, "Why, Cynthia, are you so unwilling to consider poor Sir Roderick Whatshisname?"

I was surprised he hadn't posed this question earlier, for he could hardly have failed to notice the weekly arrival of letters to Cynthia from Sir Roderick Frockmartin. I expect Papa was preoccupied with tales of pixies and hobgoblins, but eventually he had asked me why Cynthia was throwing her correspondence unopened into the fire.

"I've met him once or twice," Papa said now. "He's a member of my London club. Seems a decent fellow, and by what Rosie tells me, he's desperately in love with you. It's a rare man who is willing to stand by while his beloved is the mistress of a married man, and then, once he's dead, to take on the child of his rival."

Cynthia glared at me. "Have you been gossiping to your papa?"

I shrugged. "Dearest, he asked, so I had no choice but to satisfy his curiosity. Much as I dislike Sir Roderick, I am not unaware of his good qualities. He has been extraordinarily faithful to you."

"If there is something seriously amiss with the man," Papa said, "let me know and I'll write to him myself, ordering him to cease and desist."

For a long moment, Cynthia was silent. Then she dropped her gaze to her hands, which lay perfectly still in her lap—too still. I wondered then, as I never had before, if perhaps her habitual composure was a mask for something far less tranquil deep inside. "No, I cannot lie about Sir Roderick. He is a—a very good sort of man, but the fact remains that—that I don't wish to remarry."

"Why not? Is the fellow a fortune hunter? A libertine? Seems unlikely, if he's so very faithful."

"He's not a fortune hunter," I said, "nor a libertine, as far as I know. But if Cynthia doesn't wish to remarry, surely that is her choice."

"Yes, but such a choice, now that she is expecting a child, requires a reasonable explanation." Papa frowned at her. "What is it, girl? Are you afraid he'll beat you? Or…ah, perhaps he has unorthodox desires, which you prefer not to satisfy."

Cynthia blushed. "Lord Medway, this is a most improper subject!" She glanced at me. "Think of Rosie's feelings."

"Rosie's not embarrassed," Papa said. "You are."

This was unusual. Cynthia is habitually poised and cynical about worldly matters, but pregnancy had changed her. She was gloomy at odd moments and prone to tears.

"What is it, birching? Playing pony?"

How I wished I could ask what the latter was, but Papa wouldn't discuss that sort of thing with me, and Cynthia wasn't in the mood.

"No, no!" Cynthia flapped a hand. "Spare *me*, then. Please."

"Orgies?" Papa said, and poor Cynthia went from embarrassed to aghast, but my father was oblivious. He frowned down at the invitation from Sir Alphonse. "Deuce take it! I'd forgotten about that."

"About what?" I asked.

"Orgies. When Alphonse was dabbling in witchcraft, he and some other fools danced nude in a clearing under the full moon, which led to a full-blown orgy. Perhaps we shouldn't accept the invitation after all."

"Oh, Papa, don't say that. I'm longing for some excitement." Then I blushed too, for he was frowning at me over the top of his spectacles. "Not an orgy, Papa. Heaven forbid!"

"I should hope not," he said, suddenly severe.

"I'm sorry, Papa, but I do miss…crowds of people. Balls and musicales. The play and the opera." London, in fact, which was foolish and ungrateful of me, because in Westmoreland I was safe. No one could drag me away to an asylum. No one even wanted to. Mother was content to leave me be if I stayed far, far away from society and its gossipy ways.

"Maybe Druidism doesn't include naked rituals, but I wouldn't put it past Alphonse to add one," Papa said. "However, you'll be perfectly safe, Rosie. And you too, Cynthia. I'll see to that."

"Thank you, Lord Medway," Cynthia said, "but I shan't attend the party. I'll go straight to Ireland as planned."

Both Papa and I protested, for this was *not* what we had intended. Cynthia and I were to go to the wilds of Ireland at the end of August, to stay with a distant cousin for a year or so. Papa would accompany us, remain for a short visit, and then return.

"I don't like it," Papa said. "Ladies should not travel alone."

"I shan't be alone," Cynthia said. "My maid will accompany me. I'll write to let my cousin know I'll arrive earlier than expected, and that you and Rosie will follow later." She bit her lip. "I'm sorry, but I simply cannot risk being recognized at the house party. Not only that, Rosie, you know I'm not the least bit interested in the theater or plays or anything of that sort. I'm sure I'll be bored to tears."

This was true. I attended the theater often when in Town, but Cynthia never accompanied me.

Papa pondered but at last acquiesced. "Very well. My coachman and groom will leave me and Rosie with Sir Alphonse and continue with you to the coast. The groom will accompany you to Ireland and see you safely to your cousin's house, and then return to me."

"Thank you! That is *most* kind of you, my lord." Cynthia hurried away to write the letter.

Papa frowned at me. "I am rather displeased with your friend. She seems to have less than commonsense."

"She's not usually like this, Papa. Only since she got in the family way."

"Yet another reason she should not travel on her own. I'm not sure a groom is sufficient escort. Perhaps I should…" He wandered away, muttering to himself, leaving me to finish my breakfast in a leisurely fashion. A footman took Cynthia's letter to the village to catch the mail coach, along with Papa's correspondence, which was frequently voluminous and this time included an express letter to London. I wondered which rival he was so urgently lambasting, but thought no more about it.

About ten days later we set out. As the crow flies, it wasn't more than ten miles to Sir Alphonse's estate, but one had to go down to the foot of our lake, over a bridge, through a valley, over a pass between two fells, across another bridge, and most of the way down the next lake—a long, tedious drive on poor roads.

Cynthia and I and our two maids suffered in the carriage, while Papa rode alongside. He had given his valet a fortnight's leave, as Sir Alphonse's valet would take care of his needs, which would be limited in such an informal gathering. We expected to arrive by late afternoon, after which Cynthia would continue for a few more hours toward the coast.

Except that Papa fell ill partway. We had stopped for a change of horses in the village in the valley. Papa declared that he was famished and ordered a delightful nuncheon – oat bread, local cheese, and raspberries and cream. I couldn't imagine what made him ill, for Cynthia and I ate a great deal and were perfectly well. Groaning, Papa asked to be conveyed to a bedchamber. Braxley, the rubicund landlord, and his garrulous wife obliged him with a maximum amount of fuss and bother.

To pass the time, Cynthia and I took a walk along a pretty little beck that gurgled and spun over gleaming stones. We drank tankards of small beer. We used the necessary (which Cynthia requires far too often nowadays). We went for another walk. I peeked in on Papa—he was fast asleep. We sat on a bench in a little garden outside the taproom, shaded by the wall, and read the novels we had brought along to beguile the ride—or rather, I did.

Cynthia stared at the page, gazed into space, sighed, and clutched her shawl about herself. The climate of the north of England didn't suit her. After several years in India with Lord Benson, she'd become accustomed to a warm climate and often felt chilled even in London. Poor dear, she did not look forward to a year or more in a village in northern Ireland which would be just as cold, but in the interest of remaining respectable, she had little choice.

As the day wore on, she became more and more restless, and finally frantic.

"What am I to do?" she whispered. "At this rate, I'll have to spend a night at Sir Alphonse's before continuing to Ireland."

I shut my book. "Unless Papa is too ill to continue." I was more concerned about him than about Cynthia's reputation. "But he has a strong constitution and will probably wish to go on, so…maybe we should disguise you. An ugly bonnet, perhaps, and a pair of spectacles."

She made a moue of distaste. "I'll look frightfully dowdy."

"That's the point," I retorted. "No one will equate a dowdy widow six months gone with beautiful, fashionable Lady Benson. Oh! Better yet, you'll be a wife, headed to join your husband in Ireland. Morning sickness made travel impossible until now, et cetera, et cetera."

"You have a most fertile imagination, Rosie," she said. "Very well, needs must, I suppose."

I jumped up. "I'll go see what we can borrow from the landlady." She's right, I do have a fertile imagination, and lately it had been causing me a great deal of trouble—as it did that very minute.

A chaise rolled to a stop in front of the inn, and a footman leapt down from his post at the rear to open the door for his master. A gentleman jumped out before the footman had a chance to put down the steps, and strode toward the inn door, shouting, "Braxley, you fat wretch, broach a keg. I'm parched!"

However, it wasn't the gentleman who caught my eye, but rather the footman.

Who was *not* Mr. Gilroy McBrae.

He had the same black hair, but so do hundreds of other men. He was of middle height, but ditto. When he shut the door and headed around the back of the coach, I glimpsed his face.

Which was, admittedly, similar to McBrae's—but not his.

I heaved a sigh, mostly of relief. Ever since leaving London, I often thought I saw or heard McBrae, but soon realized it was someone else altogether. They say that after a loved one dies, it takes time to become accustomed to that person's absence. One tends to see the dearly departed on every street, hear the loved one's voice. Most disconcerting, I'm sure, but Gilroy McBrae was alive and well, far away in London, while my husband, Albert, was dead. So why was I 'seeing' McBrae?

He certainly wasn't a loved one. Nor was Albert, admittedly, but I hadn't 'seen' hide or hair of my dead husband lately, except in a few unpleasant dreams. McBrae and I had been the merest acquaintances in London, and—

No, I'm being unfair. McBrae was a Scottish gentleman, a nobody in Mother's estimation, but he had been kind to me, and I was almost certain he had saved my life. I also suspected that at times he masqueraded as a footman. Nevertheless, I didn't expect to encounter him anytime soon—or even wish to after seeing Corvus' latest effort.

So why, again, did I seem to find him around every corner, so to speak?

It made no sense at all, and to tell the sad truth, it frightened me. Anything that smacks of madness does. My peculiar quirk of checking things over and over had improved since I'd come north, but this incessant glimpsing of McBrae wasn't helping in the least. One form of madness was difficult enough to control, but *two*?

I clenched my fists and shut Gilroy McBrae and his 'appearances' out of my mind.

"What is it, Rosie?" Cynthia asked. "Oh, was it that gorgeous gentleman?" She snickered. "He's so gloriously handsome that he affected even you!"

I turned. She must mean the man who'd gone into the inn. I'd scarcely noticed him, but he was a good enough excuse. "Handsome indeed," I replied. "I'll go find Mrs. Braxley."

I was about to march into the inn, when Cynthia said, "Wait, let's go by the kitchen door."

"By the *kitchen*?" What an appalling idea. It is far beneath the dignity of the daughter of an earl, et cetera, et cetera, to enter by a servants' door. "For heaven's sake, why?"

She grabbed my arm and tugged me toward the back of the inn. "What if that gentleman who just arrived is headed for the house party? This isn't exactly a bustling post road, Rosie, so it seems highly likely. I must assume my disguise immediately."

I resisted. "Then let's send your maid or mine in the back door." Neither maid would like to follow such an order, but they usually did what they were told.

"No, because they're sitting in the coffee room, so to get to them we have to go by the front door," Cynthia groused. "Come *on!*"

Well! Cynthia is only a baron's daughter, so not raised in such a rarified atmosphere as I, but never before would she have plunged through a yard, circumventing wilted cabbage leaves and shooing away the chickens, to get to a kitchen. Quite a measure of her desperation!

It was a warm day, but the kitchen was frightfully hot and redolent of preparations for the evening meal. Mrs. Braxley stirred a pot, whilst a boy turned a spit on the hearth. A scullery maid chopped leeks on a deal table. They all looked up at our entrance. The maid dropped her knife with a tiny shriek. The boy stopped cranking and gaped.

"Mercy me!" cried Mrs. Braxley. "Dear ladies, is something amiss?" A logical question, for we wouldn't enter by the kitchen if it weren't.

Time for more quick thinking. I put my fingers to my lips and beckoned her forward. She wiped her hands on her apron and obeyed. "We wanted to speak to you, but not in the hearing of that gentleman who just arrived. Who is he, by the by?"

"Oh, him!" She flapped a hand. "That's Master Lance, it is, although he's not a child anymore. Must be thirty if he's a day, but I still think of him as a naughty little boy playing at knights in shining armor. Because of his name, you see." Seeing our complete incomprehension, she added. "Sorry, my lady. I forgot, what with his lordship being so familiar with the gentry hereabouts, that you might not be also. He's Lancelot Lewis, Sir Alphonse's son."

"Ah," I said. "Then he's going home for the house party at his father's estate."

"I suspected as much," Cynthia said.

"Handsome as an angel, isn't he?" the landlady said, a dreamy look in her eye. "He never was an angel and never will be. He surely does love the ladies, and they him." She recalled with whom she was speaking. "Begging your pardon, I'm sure."

"We must avoid him," I said, "for we're planning a play for the house party at Sir Alphonse's, and he mustn't see what we are doing. Might we beg or borrow a few items?"

Mrs. Braxley sneaked us into her private parlor off the kitchen, where we waited, drinking more small beer, while she produced a slightly tattered poke bonnet (which would help conceal Cynthia's features), an old-fashioned overskirt that would hide the expensive fabric of her gown this evening, a violet shawl, and a mobcap.

The instant the landlady returned to the kitchen, Cynthia hissed, "I refuse to wear that thing!" I wasn't sure whether she meant the bonnet or the mobcap, but I wasn't about to let her refuse such an excellent disguise.

"It's perfect for a play," I said. Mrs. Braxley had no spectacles to lend us, so I decided to borrow Papa's, as he only needs them for reading. The instant Lancelot Lewis and the footman who was not McBrae drove off again, I hurried upstairs.

Papa was sitting up in bed sipping tea and looking perfectly well. "Thanks to Mrs. Braxley's cowslip wine," he said, when I commented on his improved appearance. "Helped me sleep it off. Dash it all, it's getting late. We'd better hurry if we're to arrive at Sir Alphonse's before dark."

I proceeded to tell him about Cynthia's plans. "We'll keep the name Horsham, but we've decided to make her a wife traveling to join her husband in Ireland, not a widow. She's rather impoverished but with some small claim to gentility. Hopefully, people will feel free to ignore her. She'll stay the night at Sir Alphonse's but leave first thing tomorrow."

Papa sighed. "All this subterfuge is folly. Fortunately, it's not my business—but she must retire to bed early, as I read at night and need my spectacles to do so."

There should be no difficulty about that, as Cynthia would wish to stay out of sight as much as possible. Fortunately, malaise of pregnancy was the perfect excuse.

Papa was so much recovered that he continued to ride beside the coach. It was nearing sunset when we finally arrived at Lewis Grange. Dinner was probably long since over if our host kept country hours. I hoped his cook could drum up something for us, as I was famished. We rumbled slowly along the road, the lake vast and quiet to our right, shimmering in the last rays of the sun.

We approached a quaint stone bridge over a tinkling beck—pretty and idyllic—and came to an abrupt halt. Shouts and swearing arrested me in mid-yawn. I let down the window and craned out. In the shallows at the lakeshore, two men grappled in combat. One man slipped and fell, and his opponent immediately took advantage, shoving him beneath the water. Under our horrified eyes, he tried to drown the poor man.

No, no, I didn't really *want another corpse!* Frantically, I yanked open the door, and would have tumbled out if Mary Jane, my maid, had not forcibly held me back.

"Wait, my lady," she said. "Some men are coming to the rescue."

Lancelot Lewis and the footman who was not McBrae bounded past us. Shouting at the aggressor to stop, they slipped and slid down the shingle towards the shore. Mary Jane let go at last, and I sank back against the squabs.

Perhaps I should have reprimanded her for taking such a liberty—my mother would have been furious at being restrained by a servant—but Mary Jane has been with me forever, and I think perhaps she actually cares about me. Or maybe she just doesn't want me to embarrass her, in which case she is doomed to disappointment.

Lancelot grabbed the would-be murderer's arms from behind, whilst the footman knocked his faltering grip free and dragged the coughing, sputtering man to his feet. My father by this time had dismounted and hastened to offer assistance.

More curses erupted from both combatants, one struggling in the combined hold of Lancelot and the footman, the other retching up water between curses.

"Goodness," whispered Cynthia. "What do you suppose they are fighting about?"

"Perhaps they are rival playwrights," I said. By what little one could catch between imprecations, the wet man was a jealous, interfering bastard, whilst the dry one stank like a pile of horse manure and lacked any of the qualities of a gentleman.

"Enough!" my father bellowed. "Ladies present!"

Rather absurd in its way, for I was familiar with all their bad language, and my father isn't always careful to moderate his speech in my presence, but it did the trick.

Apparently the mostly dry combatant was a gentleman in at least one respect, for he glanced at our carriage and immediately collected himself. Well, almost immediately, for he snarled at the footman, who let go, and snapped at Lancelot to release him. Now I recognized him: it was indeed a playwright, Harold Bellevue. The wet fellow composed himself as well, but continued to glare at the other with narrowed eyes whilst wringing water from his coat.

I sat back, relieved. No murder, no corpse, and despite my father's crossed arms and austere frown, I knew he was enjoying himself. He waited as the men passed the coach in a sorry procession, Lancelot Lewis hustling the wet, shivering fellow up the slope, while the other stomped arrogantly behind. The footman retrieved his cap, which had fallen at the water's edge, and shook it out while following respectfully in their wake.

As I turned to watch their progress through the opposite window of the coach, I spied a young woman above them on the rise. She watched their approach, eyes wide, hands covering her mouth. Like a startled deer, she turned and fled ahead of them through the heather. After a long moment, my father remounted and gestured to our coachman to continue.

It took us a good five minutes to reach the house, by way of a long, winding drive bounded by unkempt shrubs. A cormorant flapped down to perch on a lone pine. The vista opened, and before us stood a rambling stone manor house, the sort which started as a keep in the middle ages and ended up a hodge-podge: wings at odd angles, turrets, competing styles of chimney pots and gables, mullioned windows here, casements there, and ivy crawling up the walls.

"What a jumble!" Cynthia peered over the top of Papa's spectacles, which sat awkwardly on her delicately-featured face.

"A haunted house," I said.

I had left the window down, so Papa heard this and chuckled. "Not that I know of. There's a resident hobgoblin, but I've never had the good fortune to see him. Mrs. Alderthwaite, the housekeeper, leaves milk and cakes out for him at night."

I knew better than to scoff at this. I don't know what Papa actually believes, but he never disparages the lower orders for their credulity.

We drove slowly up the last stretch of the drive and came to a halt before the massive oak front doors, open under an archway of stone. Papa's groom opened the coach door and put down the steps, and Papa dismounted to help me out, and then Cynthia. Sir Alphonse, tall and thin with fading fair hair and side whiskers, strode out of the house, a table napkin tucked into his cravat, crumbs cascading onto his waistcoat.

Ah, I thought, perhaps they hadn't quite finished dining. My stomach growled happily.

"Welcome!" Sir Alphonse shouted. "Welcome, Medway, you old rascal. It'll be like the old days, drunken revels and futile discussions. And such lovely ladies you have brought with you!" His protuberant eyes were on me, which just goes to show what an excellent disguise a mobcap and a pair of spectacles make, for Cynthia is far prettier than I.

"My daughter, Rosamund," Papa introduced me. "In mourning for her late husband, Albert Phipps, but I dragged her along anyway."

"Yes, yes, well done, Medway." Sir Alphonse beamed at me. "We've met, haven't we, my dear? Quite some time ago, I fear."

Papa went on before I could respond. "And this charming lady is a friend for whom we beg your hospitality—"

But he didn't complete the introduction, for just then a rider galloped up the driveway, his mount all a-froth, and leapt from the saddle. "Excuse me, pray, whilst I greet my wife." He dashed forward, pulled Cynthia into his arms, and kissed her on the mouth.

He drew back with a slight frown and removed the spectacles from her nose. "Your eyes been bothering you again, darling? We really must get you some eyeglasses of your own."

Cynthia paled. She stood utterly still and said not a word.

Papa moved forward and took the spectacles. With a grin, he thrust out a hand. "Sir Roderick. Well met!"

Sir Roderick grinned back at Papa. This in itself was extremely odd, as I had never before seen even a hint of a smile on his dour face. He loathes me, though, so that may explain it.

He shook Papa's hand vigorously. "So kind of you to escort Lady Frockmartin thus far, Lord Medway. I am forever in your debt."

"Not at all, dear fellow," Papa said without a blink. "Happy to be of service."

Chapter Two

She is an observant woman. My powers of concealment will be taxed to the utmost, complicated by the fact that I hope she will unmask me again—whilst I dread her inevitable repugnance.

—From the diary of Corvus

Well! Now it was obvious what Papa had done—taken matters into his own hands. That express letter ten days earlier had gone to Sir Roderick.

I was brought up to behave with ladylike restraint—in other words, to display only the mildest of emotions—and I did my best not to glare at Sir Roderick. I dislike him intensely, mostly because of his unfair opinion of me. In London, he had berated me often for not making an attempt to win my husband back from Cynthia. He wasn't to know that Albert and I had agreed not to have carnal relations, and I couldn't possibly explain it, but it still hurt to be so maligned.

Needless to say, Sir Alphonse invited Sir Roderick and his 'wife' to remain for the party. "The more the merrier!" He shouted to his hovering housekeeper to prepare another bedchamber.

Cynthia continued to say nothing at all.

"My wife is fatigued, as you can see," Sir Roderick said tenderly, and Sir Alphonse, all solicitousness, nudged them indoors, sending a servant scurrying for tea and wine while the maroon bedchamber was prepared for them.

Which meant not only was Sir Roderick pretending poor Cynthia was his wife, but he fully intended to share a bed with her. How dare he? Outraged, I began to say something about how poorly Cynthia slept, thinking to secure her some privacy, but Papa put a hand on my arm.

I scowled up at him. I am rarely at odds with my father, but this was simply too much.

"Not now, Rosie," he murmured.

"But—"

"Come in, come in, Medway," cried Sir Alphonse. "Still dwelling on our little disagreement, are you? It's an argument you'll never win."

"It's not even an argument, my dear fellow," Papa drawled.

Usually, I would have had to muffle a snicker, but I was far too angry to be amused.

"I'll just show my daughter the view, and then we'll be right in." He nodded to Sir Alphonse—which might be taken as either a polite gesture or a subtle dismissal—and turned to me. "Let's stroll about and admire the sunset before we are obliged to meet and converse with the other guests."

Perforce, I went with him—for it would be the worst of bad manners to make a fuss in public—but I intended to give him a piece of my mind. Or at least as much of one as I could without being rude or disrespectful.

Before I could get a word out, he said, "It's none of our business, Rosie."

"You seem to have made it yours," I retorted hotly, and immediately regretted my loss of temper. "I beg your pardon, Papa," I muttered, "but, how *could* you?"

He tucked my hand in his arm, and we walked slowly along the front of the house. The sun was dipping below the fells on the far side of the lake, and the sky was a wash of pink and gold. "Because it was plain to me that Cynthia is not indifferent to him. I thought it best that they be thrust together to sort out whatever the problem is."

"But what if Cynthia doesn't want to be thrust together with him? What if she doesn't want to share his bedchamber?" I shuddered at the thought of such an intrusion.

"He's a gentleman. He won't force himself on her. Isn't that a beautiful sunset?" When I didn't respond—I was far too anxious for Cynthia to appreciate the view—he added, "But she will have no choice but to talk to him. That was what was required, and therefore I did my best to make it happen."

Even to the extent of delaying our journey. "You weren't feeling poorly at the inn today, were you?"

"No, merely somewhat anxious that Sir Roderick mightn't arrive in time. I didn't want him to follow her to Ireland, because I wouldn't be there to keep any eye on things." We turned the corner and ambled along the side of the house. The scene was truly picturesque, but I couldn't bring myself to care about the folly down by the lake, or the island topped by a stand of pine, or the path leading, Papa said, to a very tolerable waterfall.

"How," I asked, trying to remain calm, "can you keep an eye on what goes on in their bedchamber?" Judging by what I've heard from time to time, often by way of Cynthia, carnal pleasures take many disgusting forms.

"Actually, I believe there's a peephole from the broom closet. Or was the last time I visited, for I slept in the maroon room." He chuckled at my face of horror. "One of Sir Alphonse's ancestors was what the French call a *voyeur*.""

I moaned. The more I hear about this sort of thing, the more confused and appalled I become.

"You needn't worry about your bedchamber. Miranda wouldn't put a lady in such a room, and moreover, I expect she has had all the peepholes plugged up. I made quite a fuss last time."

"Miranda?"

"Alphonse's mistress." He paused at my evident incomprehension. "The actress, you know. Miranda Tyne, embellished to Miranda of the Tyne during her years in the theater. She left the stage to live here with him."

I'd heard of her, of course. Born in the North, she'd taken the London stage by storm, but she'd left before my first season. "What about his wife?"

"Died long ago. Miranda's much more fun, I promise you."

How frightfully improper of Sir Alphonse to set his mistress up as his hostess, particularly when inviting respectable guests—and thoughtless of Papa to expose me to such an immoral household.

Very well—I admit I asked for it.

"I see you're shocked, my dear. It never occurred to me… Absent-minded as I am, and since you had what amounted to a *ménage à trois* with Cynthia and Albert, I assumed…"

"We had no such thing," I retorted.

"Close enough." He shrugged. "Well, it's no matter. There is a touch of your mother in you, which is natural, but I'm sure you know better than to betray your disapprobation in any manner."

"Yes, Papa," I said, belatedly realizing that I shouldn't have come to this party. There is plenty of improper behavior in the beau monde, but at least we do our best to appear to be respectable—unlike theater folk, who are unabashedly immoral. The guests would think I was just as bad, because of a ménage that had never existed but was made all the more believable thanks to Corvus' naughty caricatures, drat the man.

"Or to show in any way that you consider yourself superior to your host and hostess or the other guests."

"No, Papa." I *did* consider myself superior, for how could I help but do so? (Daughter of an earl, et cetera, not to mention certain of my moral uprightness.) I hoped he didn't mean I had to be truly friendly with any of them. Politely cordial, certainly. In my attempts to differentiate myself from my mother, I had become quite adept at genuine cordiality while maintaining an appropriate distance. I would never wish to be deliberately unkind.

Unfortunately, as I discovered to my dismay a few months earlier, it is far too easy to slight someone without in the least intending to.

"You needn't fear for Cynthia," he said. "If I sense that she is truly distressed by Sir Roderick's presence, she shall share your bedchamber whilst I deal with him."

"How do you propose to do that?" I demanded.

"I am not nobody," Papa said austerely. True, and he'd dealt with the combatants easily enough. But Sir Roderick was a middle-aged widower, not a callow young man.

A footman emerged from a side door, carrying a bucket. I started, which was absurd, because I had already seen and decided that he wasn't McBrae. He pulled his forelock without raising his eyes and hastened away.

I shivered. And sighed. Sooner or later, I would stop imagining that the disconcerting Scotsman was nearby.

"What is it, Rosie?" Papa asked, as we retraced our path. "Don't worry about Cynthia. I promise you all will be well."

I hadn't been thinking of her for the last few seconds, but I wasn't about to admit to my problem with imaginary McBraes.

"I'll try not to." Thinking to distract him, I asked, "Tell me, who was right, you or Sir Alphonse?"

He laughed. "Either, neither, or both of us: who knows?"

"Sir Alphonse seems to think he does."

"That's because he cares whether he's right, whereas I merely enjoy the disputes." He chuckled. "That's why your mother and I could never get on."

That I understood. Mother believes there is only one way to think, one way to act, one way to speak, and so on.

"She's afraid of anything she can't control," he said. "A fearful woman—unlike you, my dear Rosie."

Unlike *me*? Granted, I'm not fearful in social situations, but why the deuce do I have such a stupid urge to check things over and over, if I'm not fearful? I was too flabbergasted to speak.

"There are always a number of viewpoints to any argument. Why settle on only one? Think how tedious. And now," he said, "I don't know about you, Rosie, but I'm ravenous."

I couldn't decide whether to be flattered or annoyed, for although I didn't doubt Papa's sincerity, I suspected he had chosen to compliment me as a distraction from my indignation at his treatment of Cynthia. However, I had changed the subject first, giving him the opportunity to do so.

Regardless, I intended to speak to her the first chance I got.

Sir Alphonse was just inside the doorway in a Great Hall lit by flaming sconces. A massive curved oaken staircase, which split to serve the two main wings, detracted somewhat from the medieval effect, although three stuffed stags' heads on the narrow landing joining the wings definitely did not. The center trophy, hanging somewhat askew and sporting a massive rack of antlers, eyed us balefully.

A tall woman with glossy chestnut hair glided forward with an elegance and poise equal to my mother's. Don't tell her I said that, though. An actress and abandoned woman to rival a countess? Horrors!

"Here's my Miranda," Sir Alphonse said as we entered. "My love, you're already acquainted with my friend Medway, and how kind of him to bring his daughter, Lady Rosamund Phipps." He grinned at me. "Yes, *the* Lady Rosamund of caricature fame."

Which was not at all a proper introduction, but I already knew this was not a proper sort of place.

"For heaven's sake, Alphonse, don't embarrass the poor girl." Miranda of the Tyne had a rich contralto voice and a warm, all-embracing smile. "Please accept my condolences on your loss, Lady Rosamund. I hope our festivities will help raise your spirits."

"I trust they will." It had become second nature to play the grieving widow. "It's frightfully kind of you to have me."

"We don't stand on ceremony, so no need to change for dinner,' Sir Alphonse said. "Matter of fact, if you do, you might not get any. Our cook's a Tartar when it comes to late arrivals." My startled dismay must have shown, for he laughed.

Miranda rolled her eyes (a sign of vulgarity but very welcome to me at this point, which just goes to show I am not a high stickler, whatever you may think), just as Lancelot Lewis clattered down the stairs, saying, "Pay no heed to my father."

We were duly introduced, properly this time. Lance was indeed a handsome man, annoyingly so. Certain kinds of beauty are distracting. One feels compelled to stare, despite not wishing to in the least. No doubt he had a flaw or two, if one looked closely enough, but I would not be caught dead doing so.

"You are so very like Corvus' drawings, Lady Rosamund," he said, eyeing me appreciatively. "But even prettier in the flesh."

Good God, the man was flirting with me. "You'd best take care, Mr. Lewis. One never knows when Corvus may be listening, and he might take your flattery of me amiss."

"Corvus? Here?" He snorted. "It's not flattery, but sincere admiration. One cannot help but hope to rival him."

"Even worse," I said. "He will surely choose you for his next victim."

"Hmm. I wonder how he might caricature me."

"By choosing a subject that will mortify you and amuse everyone else," I said.

Lance raised his perfect brows. Everything about his physical being was beautiful, but I had no reason to suppose that his character was anything other than ordinary.

"And did he mortify you, my lady?" he asked.

"No," I said, "he amused me, but he had misjudged my character."

"Then I must hope he will misjudge mine as well, for I do not intend to withdraw from the lists."

Drat. The last thing I wanted was an admirer.

"I regret that you were obliged to witness that contretemps by the lake," he went on. "It was naught but a bit of foolishness."

"More than foolishness," I retorted. "A man almost drowned."

"Two young men, too much wine, and a pretty woman." Sir Alphonse beckoned to a footman waiting at the foot of the stairs. "Up you go and refresh yourselves. You'll find us all in the dining room."

My bedchamber was next to my father's. It was spacious and tastefully decorated, and even in the gathering dusk there was a delightful view of the lake.

Mary Jane was there waiting, torn between satisfaction with the room allotted to me and disapproval of the household in general. "Such goings-on," she muttered as she quickly brushed my hair and put it up into a topknot. "Not dress for dinner! Whatever is the world coming to?" She sighed heavily. "But what can one expect when an actress is expected to play hostess to the nobility?"

"She has better manners than Sir Alphonse," I said. "Did she provide adequate accommodation for you and Lady Benson's maid?"

"Yes, my lady," she said grudgingly. "Agnes and I are to share a room. I am not looking forward to that silly girl nattering on and on about Sir Roderick's unexpected arrival. It matters not a whit what she says to me, but what if she blabs to the other servants? Think of the gossip!"

"Lady Benson's maid is accustomed to keeping her mistress's secrets."

"Humph," Mary Jane said. "It is for the best that we are to share. I shall do my best to advise her." She draped a light shawl around my shoulders. "There will be gossip anyway in the end. Sir Roderick will be laughed at and called a cuckold for taking on another man's child, but it will be even worse if people learn he had to chase Lady Benson to the end of the earth to do it." She sighed again. "And yet, how daring of him to come to her rescue like a knight in shining armor!"

My mother would never have put up with this chatter. According to her, servants are not permitted to have opinions of their betters, much less to express them.

I wasn't surprised that Mary Jane approved of Sir Roderick, but I'd had enough. Knight in armor, indeed. A bully, more like. "What if she doesn't want to be rescued?"

"Come now, my lady, indeed she does. If you haven't noticed how quiet and thoughtful her ladyship has been for the past month, I certainly have. Regretting her folly, she was."

I didn't bother to enquire which folly, for to Mary Jane's mind, Cynthia had committed a whole string of them: becoming a man's mistress instead of remarrying, and then repeatedly refusing Sir Roderick's offer to make an honest woman of her. (What a horrid description that is! And so unfair. In this particular case, I should say my husband was the far more dishonest.) Then falling pregnant out of wedlock, which she had no reason to expect after years of barrenness both with her husband and then with mine.

I was too hungry to listen to what would doubtless prove to be a scold. "Then why did she refuse to read Sir Roderick's letters?" I stood, shaking out my skirts. I checked the contents of my reticule only once rather than the usual several times, for I could return upstairs if I needed something—f ortunately, for I dare not check anything while my maid is watching. She worries about my foible, so I do my best to make her believe I have overcome it.

Let me make myself clear: it wasn't that I disapproved of Sir Roderick. He was wealthy and eligible, and although I didn't like him, that hardly mattered. I understood all the arguments in favor of a hasty wedding for a woman in Cynthia's situation.

No, it was the thought that she was being *forced* into marriage that infuriated me so. She was well able to support herself and her child, so why must she allow a man to run her life?

I was scowling as I left the room, and whom should I encounter coming along the corridor but Cynthia herself on horrid Sir Roderick's arm. No doubt he thought the scowl was for him, and rightly so. Cynthia looked rather more herself now, in a fresh gown and a cap edged with lace, but she had no expression—or perhaps the slightest suggestion of a pout.

"How are you, dearest?" I asked. "Not too tired after the long drive, I hope."

"Frightfully so," Cynthia said, scarcely above a whisper. "But I couldn't bear to be cooped up in my bedchamber."

Cooped up with Sir Roderick, that is. She'd planned on retiring to her room as soon as she arrived, and now she was obliged to do exactly the opposite to avoid him. I was right, and Papa was utterly wrong. "You needn't come down to dinner," I said. "I'd be happy to keep you company upstairs." I paused. "We can eat together in *my* bedchamber, for privacy."

There was a fraught silence as we continued slowly down the corridor. It wasn't a narrow passageway, but it was crowded for three people walking abreast. I didn't like the feeling of being *de trop*.

"Is that what you wish, darling?" Sir Roderick asked at last.

"No," she whispered, "but thank you anyway, Rosie dear."

He smirked, and I longed to slap his smug face. I went down the stairs ahead of them, fuming. Was she frightened of him? She must be to acquiesce so easily.

What could I do to help her? Papa would be no use, or at least not yet. He intended to give Sir Roderick a chance.

The same footman who'd conducted us upstairs—not the one who resembled McBrae—was waiting in the Great Hall to show us to the dining room. We hardly needed his help, for the hubbub of conversation indicated the way.

It was easy to see why there was no need to stand on ceremony. Both gentlemen and ladies were seated around the table, but most had finished their meals. Instead of withdrawing properly, the ladies had stayed while the gentlemen enjoyed their port. And shared it, by what I could see.

At least there are no cigarillos, I thought with a shudder. Disgusting enough when a man indulges, but imagine a woman doing so!

"It's your own fault, Harold." The speaker was a young woman with a sizeable bosom almost spilling out of her decolletage and the sort of husky voice which is almost always feigned. "You drove poor little Miss Gardner away. Perhaps you thought fighting for her would excite her, but violence frightens her sort." She pouted as if considering. "I haven't the slightest notion what *would* excite her." She batted her eyelashes at Mr. Bellevue.

"A marriage proposal," said a middle-aged man with protruding teeth and a loud, nasal laugh.

"Rightly so," Miranda of the Tyne snapped. "She's a respectable girl."

"If she's so respectable, what is she doing here?" The nasal man laughed again, and a few others snickered. A grey-haired lady with the air of a bluestocking, seated beside my father, pursed her lips.

Next, I spied, to my astonishment, a retired military man and his wife who were longstanding acquaintances from Kent. Colonel Wendell looked irritable and Mrs. Wendell frankly uneasy—no surprise, as this wasn't their sort of society at all. How strange to encounter them here.

Miranda turned and saw us hovering in the doorway. "Do come in, Lady Rosamund, and forgive this foolish talk. And Sir Roderick and his good lady—how delightful that you are recovered enough to join us."

"Not just any Lady Rosamund, but the famous one, come to liven up the party," Mr. Bellevue said, a hint of a slur in his voice.

My father, who was at the far end of the table carving himself a slice of roast beef, turned and fixed Mr. Bellevue with a blighting stare. The playwright subsided, muttering an apology. Heaven knows what Papa would have done if Bellevue had added something genuinely annoying, such as *Brought your switch, love?*

I couldn't help imagining a caricature by Corvus with exactly that caption. I pondered my probable response.

"Sit down, sit down, and pay no heed to Bellevue," Sir Alphonse cried. "He's drunk."

"On love and chagrin, as well as wine." Lancelot pulled out a chair for me, so I had perforce to sit next to him, when I would have preferred to be near Cynthia.

"Do introduce us all, Lance darling," the voluptuous young woman said.

"I expect I must," Lance said, "although one never does remember so many names, particularly when the possessors are not in the slightest way memorable." He watched hopefully, head cocked, for a reaction, but got none. The woman was far too full of herself to let a jab disturb her—in fact, I think she rather liked it, for it meant, to her at least, that she was the sole memorable one.

He proceeded to introduce the various guests. I am good at names, thanks to my mother's insistence. However, I shan't list them at the moment, but rather mention them as they play a role on the stage of this tale, so to speak. My greatest concern was that someone might recognize Cynthia, but no one blinked an eye when she was introduced, and although Sir Roderick received a few nods, no one commented on his sudden acquisition of a wife.

Which would have been fairly normal in polite society—most gossip being the backbiting sort—but judging by what I'd seen so far, these people knew no such restraint.

Lance introduced the voluptuous woman last of all. "Miss Ellis is Miranda's niece, and seeks to follow in her footsteps."

"Indeed, she does," Sir Alphonse said. "Excellent stage presence. She would make a perfect Druid priestess."

I suspect Miss Ellis would have preened, but for the fact that it would make her look too young and eager. She yawned, as if such compliments were common as lice.

Lancelot snorted rudely, and although I tended to agree with his assessment, I glanced at Miranda, wondering what she thought of her niece's talents. I spied a narrow-eyed frown, but immediately she turned away, solicitously suggesting tisanes to Cynthia, who looked utterly miserable, as if she regretted coming downstairs. Caught between two horrid alternatives, poor dear.

"Why a priestess?" Harold Bellevue complained.

"Consort of the priest who plays the horned god in my play," Sir Alphonse said.

"Which is to be *your* part, I assume," Colonel Wendell said.

"Not necessarily." Sir Alphonse turned to Papa. "Perhaps you'd like the part?"

"Spare me," Papa said around a mouthful of beef.

"Why not offer it to someone who actually wants it?" the colonel pursued.

"Do you wish it, Colonel?" Sir Alphonse raised incredulous brows.

"Dash it all, of course not," the Colonel said. "I'm no actor, but there are plenty of lusty young fellows here who would like to play opposite a beautiful female. Be the sportsmanlike thing to give them a chance."

"Now, now, darling." His wife patted him on the arm. "We don't want to foment discord."

He barked a laugh. "Foment it? Don't need my help for that. The place is seething with it."

"Nonsense. Everything is perfectly fine," Sir Alphonse said. "A little friendly rivalry never hurt anyone."

Since one man had almost drowned, I couldn't agree—and I hadn't seen much friendliness displayed so far. However, it behooved me to play a neutral role. "Do I understand that there is to be a performance as part of the Lammas festival?"

Sir Alphonse turned eagerly. "The local festival, although amusing, lacks entirely in sophistication, so we're having a private competition for the best play. We'll read them all and vote on which to perform."

I caught Papa's eye. He winked.

Well! That gave me a brilliant notion. I had been rather frustrated ever since I was—as I saw it—summarily dismissed from reading my stories aloud to the orphans at the Home for Indigent Female Orphans. Not that anyone less than royalty would dare to dismiss outright the daughter of an earl, cousin of a duke, et cetera, particularly not the mere matron of an orphanage, no matter how much she disliked my little tales.

But by hiring a schoolmistress to read to the children, no doubt at Mrs. Brill's instigation (she is my mother's enemy and a loathsome woman), she got rid of me most tactfully. I expect she was quaking in her boots for fear I would wreak some dreadful vengeance, but I am not that sort of person. At least I don't think I am, although I wouldn't have minded a bit of revenge on Mrs. Brill. However, my muse had deserted me at the time, due to far more urgent concerns.

Writing plays is not a ladylike occupation. Yes, there have been some very good female playwrights—most recently Elizabeth Inchbald, who lives retired now—but I have no ambition to associate myself with the stage. Thanks to Corvus, I (along with my mythical switch) am already far more notorious than one would ever wish to be.

And yet, my muse was now prompting me most urgently. Why not amuse myself by penning a little play? I needn't enter it in the competition.

"What sort of play?" I asked, lightly I hoped.

"A tragedy," Mr. Bellevue said. "The life and death of Boudicca."

The man with the nasal laugh, whose name was Fence, made a rude noise. "We'll all be dead of boredom by the time that's over."

"I suppose you have a better idea?" Mr. Bellevue said.

"A ritual," retorted Mr. Fence. "Praise of the Goddess Summer, culminating in—

"An orgy!"

Laughter and commentary broke out, and the one who'd suggested the orgy, a thin youth with a prominent Adam's apple and a wispy beard, grew quite pink. The bluestocking, a Mrs. Holloway, muttered, "Humankind hasn't a hope if that's what we're begetting nowadays."

Sir Alphonse put up a hand. "Sorry, Johnny, but we're to have no more orgies. Miranda's orders. Once was enough." He grinned at me. "Do we shock you, Lady Rosamund?"

Honestly, so very annoying, and yet I mustn't show it. "My dear sir," I said in my best languid tone, "I have navigated London society for years." And participated in a *ménage à trois,* if others assumed the same as my father. How ghastly that people believed me to be as amoral as they. Even McBrae assumed the worst, which for some reason bothered me. Perhaps because he liked me, and because I didn't want him to like someone I wasn't, if that makes any sense at all.

Well, no matter. I couldn't do anything about what people thought, but if I acted jaded and blasé—which I am not—I was as bad as Miss Ellis. "That said, I believe I should prefer…" I pretended to consider—again, just as much for effect as she. I don't enjoy being a hypocrite, but one must maintain appearances. "A moral tale."

This evoked more laughter and an appreciative glance from Lancelot. I sighed, wishing I had someone to confide in, someone to whom to confess that I was far from jaded. That although widowed, I was an untouched virgin, rather disturbed by what I knew of carnal pleasures, and therefore not available for a light-hearted *affaire*—which is doubtless what Lance was pondering.

I applied myself to my dinner, sampling the remains of a baked carp, some cutlets of veal, creamed spinach and various salads. Now I was all the more determined to pen a play. A moral tale indeed, in the manner of one of Corvus' caricatures. What fun! It almost took my mind off Cynthia. She was seated beside Miranda, with Sir Roderick on her other flank. She wasn't saying much, or eating much either, merely huddling in her chair, looking queasy. Miranda received a teapot and cup from the housekeeper, and poured for Cynthia.

"This will ease your queasiness and help you sleep," she said kindly. I nodded my gratitude at her, and received a smile in return. I decided, immoral actress though she was, that I quite liked her.

Harold Bellevue stood suddenly, knocking over his chair. "Where the devil is Miss Gardner?"

"In her bedchamber, of course," said Mrs. Holloway.

"With Powers, one supposes," the nasal Mr. Fence said.

"It seems likely," the husky-voiced Miss Ellis said. "She prefers the hapless sort."

"Kindly refrain from speaking nonsense," Mrs. Holloway said. "That bout of fisticuffs frightened her, and she needed time to compose herself."

"With the help of Mr. Powers," Mr. Fence prodded.

The bluestocking shot him a glare, at which he giggled. How ghastly; his nasal laugh was bad enough, but he was far too old for such a childish sort of laughter. Pointedly, she returned to conversing with my father and Sir Alphonse.

Bellevue took a swig of wine. His fingers clenched around the cup. "I'll kill him. Would have done it earlier, if not for Lance's damned interference."

"Sit down, Bellevue," Colonel Wendell said. "If the lady prefers Powers, it is her business. Let us hope he has made her a happy woman."

Bellevue tossed his wine across the table at the colonel. "Unsay that, you dastard!"

The older man stood as well, roaring. "Stupid pup! I'll thrash you within an inch of your life!"

"Now, now, dearest." His wife tugged at his sleeve. I looked to Sir Alphonse, expecting him to intervene, but he was deep in conversation with my equally oblivious parent.

Lancelot stood with a sigh. "Do forgive him, Colonel. Bellevue is drunk and unutterably vulgar. No doubt it never occurred to him that you hoped Miss Gardner had received a proposal of marriage." He shoved Bellevue back into his chair, and the colonel subsided, grumbling. His wife took a napkin and attempted to mop him up.

"Powers is no suitor," Mr. Fence said. "Too poor, for one thing, and too caught up in his bloody poetry for another, but poets are the worst sort of lechers. He just wants to tup the chit."

Bellevue had been muttering into his cravat, but at this his head came up. Lancelot put a hand on his shoulder and kept him in his chair. "Ignore him."

"I'd like to tup her, too," Fence said, although he used a much more vulgar word to describe the act, which I shall not repeat here.

"Ladies present!" the colonel barked.

Johnny-of-the-Adam's-apple rolled his eyes. Fence grinned at him. "I think an orgy with these ladies would be fun."

A spasm of disgust crossed Sir Roderick's features—the first sign he'd been paying attention to anyone but Cynthia—and then he turned back to her, patting her hand and murmuring. He was doing an excellent job of playing the solicitous husband, which made me loathe him all the more.

"No one wants to know what you think, Fence," the colonel said.

Fence raised an unpleasant eyebrow. "No?"

The older man's face darkened, but he said nothing, merely pushing his wife's hand away. "Let be, my dear. It's only a cravat."

"And a waistcoat," she fluttered. "One of your best, and—"

"Let *be*," the colonel snapped, and she subsided, red with chagrin.

What a merry party this was proving to be!

I gave poor Mrs. Wendell a commiserating grimace. The Colonel was always a gruff sort of man, but how unlike him to scold his wife in public.

"Tea!" cried Miranda. "And no more port." She directed a footman to remove the wine and have tea brought to the drawing room, and then grimaced. In the doorway stood Mr. Powers, his hair still damp.

He was of more than medium height, not quite as tall as Mr. Bellevue but more sturdily built. A lock of dark hair fell over his forehead. He directed a fearsome glower at Fence, and his fists clenched. He must have heard the man's offensive remarks.

Our hostess rose to the occasion. "Here you are at last, Mr. Powers. We're all concerned for Miss Gardner. Will she come down to take tea?"

"I doubt it," he said stiffly. "She abhors violence and is most distressed."

And embarrassed, no doubt, and dreading the inevitable commentary from this vulgar group of people.

"Tsk," Miranda said. "I'll go to her. In the meantime, don't let these drunken fools tempt you to another fight. Alphonse, I expect you to exert yourself a little. You too, please, Lord Medway. I count on your wiser heads to prevent further foolishness."

My admiration for her grew. Not just anyone dares to order an earl about, and she, an actress and mistress, was far down on the social scale. However, my father only takes offense when it serves a purpose. He grinned at her and winked at me. With palpable reluctance, Mr. Powers uncurled his fists and ceased glaring at Fence. Apart from Mr. Bellevue grabbing a bottle of wine from the footman and the boy with the wispy beard attempting the same and falling flat on his face, everyone settled down.

Soon we withdrew to the drawing room, and after a few desultory games of whist, we all trooped up to bed, Sir Alphonse refusing to permit the inebriated gentlemen to ruin his billiards table. I dismissed Mary Jane and blew out the candle, but I couldn't sleep for worrying about Cynthia. How sickening to be obliged to share a bed with a man one disliked—worse, a man whom one had spurned over and over! Would he take her by force? Perhaps not, due to her condition. How I wished I could go to her, but I had promised Papa that I would not.

After tossing and turning for an hour or more, I decided to go to the kitchen for a cup of milk, my tried-and-true method of overcoming sleeplessness. I lit a candle, donned my wrapper and a pair of slippers, opened my door and headed toward the stairs.

The candles in the sconces had been extinguished, but on a table at the head of the staircase a lamp glowed dimly. The Great Hall below was in darkness. Unfortunately, I had only the vaguest notion where the kitchen might be, based on the direction from which the footman serving us dinner had come.

"Lady Rosamund! Is something amiss?"

Thank heavens. Miranda Tyne came up behind me, carrying a tray with a small coffeepot and two cups. The delightful aroma of coffee wafted to my nostrils.

I couldn't imagine drinking coffee at this ungodly hour—I should be up all night if I did—but to each her own.

"I couldn't sleep," I said. "I should like some milk, as it sometimes helps, but I prefer not to disturb the servants. They are obliged to wake early, whilst I am not."

"How thoughtful of you." Doubtless she was surprised—the aristocracy are not known for consideration of their servants—but she was far too competent an actress to let it show. She set the tray down on the table by the landing and picked up a lamp burning low there. "Come with me." She headed in the direction from which we both had come.

"Your coffee will grow cold," I said.

"Two minutes won't make a difference. Not only that, you really should not be out of your bedchamber alone at night. *Some* of our guests are as likely to accost a well-bred lady as a servant." She strode down the passageway past my bedchamber.

I took a guess. "Such as Mr. Fence?"

At the end of the passage we rounded a corner and halted before a door. Her expression was pure disgust. "Yes, Fence and that idiotic pup who takes his cue from him."

"The one called Johnny?"

"Johnny Beaver. By what Mrs. Holloway tells me, he began frequenting the theaters recently, and seemed a decent sort until he started following Fence about. He's a budding playwright, hoping to eclipse Sheridan, whilst Harold Bellevue…" She opened the door. "Be careful on the stairs. They're rather steep but by far the quickest way to the kitchen."

I ventured to finish her earlier statement. "…Sees himself as the new Bard."

She choked on a laugh. "Precisely."

Perhaps it wasn't two minutes, but it couldn't have been more than ten before I was back in my bedchamber with a cup of milk. I drank it, snuggled back under the coverlet, and fell immediately into a deep sleep.

From which I was awakened by a terrified shriek.

Chapter Three

I could leave almost immediately, if I chose, as the identity of the thief is obvious. However, revealing it requires some thought—which gives me the perfect excuse to stay.

—From the diary of Corvus

I sat up in bed, heart battering my chest. By the grey light in my room, I surmised it was almost dawn. Had that shriek been merely a dream? The house seemed enveloped in silence.

And then came more screams, ghastly and chilling, one after another after another.

I leapt out of bed, crammed my feet into my slippers, donned my wrapper once again, and rushed into the passageway.

It was cloaked in gloom, but faint light from the Great Hall filtered up. It was from there that the screams came, now dissolving into hoarse sobs. A door opened behind me across the passage, but I was first to the stairs.

Which you no doubt think was foolish of me, but I couldn't help myself. Although I have had many small brushes with supposed insanity, I'm not a complete idiot. I peered over the bannister before starting down.

Below me, flat on the floor, was a man. All I could discern was his head and feet, for something huge and unidentifiable lay atop him. As I stared, a woman appeared and glanced about. She bent over the huge something, grunting…and then with a swish of skirts, she vanished.

Meanwhile, a sobbing girl stumbled up the stairs toward me. She tripped on her gown and fell, crying out, and I helped her up. "What happened? What's wrong?"

"He's dead." She swayed. "Oh God, he's dead. He murdered him!"

I feared she would faint, so I kept a firm hold on her. "Who?" A stupid question, I realized. In the first place, I didn't specify whether I was asking for the identity of the victim or the murderer. In the second place, she was hysterical and unable to speak coherently. I could very well go see for myself, once I got rid of her.

"It's all my fault," she whispered, clutching my arm. "I wish I had never come to this horrid place."

An understandable sentiment, but she couldn't have predicted this…could she?

"Helen! Miss Gardner, that is." Mr. Powers hurried up, clad only in shirt and breeches. This utter disregard of the proprieties, coupled with his use of her Christian name, seemed to indicate that his relationship with the young woman might be as close as Harold Bellevue feared. "What happened?"

"He's dead!" she wailed, and cast herself upon his breast.

"Hush," he said. "Who's dead?"

"How *could* you?" she cried, and sobbed into his shirt. She, at least, was fully dressed, making the embrace less improper than it otherwise might have been.

I left them to it and hastened down to see the body for myself. Obviously, it behooved me to determine first of all whether the man on the floor was indeed dead.

It was the unpleasant Mr. Fence, but looking unlike himself—tranquil and at peace. With a shudder of revulsion, I realized that what lay atop him was a huge rack of antlers. I glanced up at the wall of the landing: sure enough, the largest stag's head I'd seen there last evening was gone.

I knelt beside him and felt for his pulse—a waste of time, for even if he still lived, he wouldn't for long. Two prongs of the antlers had pierced his chest.

There was not even a flutter of heartbeat.

I stood and took a deep breath, trying to shove away the thought that ran over and over through my mind: you wanted a corpse, and you got one.

Fine, I should be careful what I wish for, but I couldn't stand like a stock, doing nothing. I was dithering about where to go for help when it arrived from all sides at once.

Miranda emerged through the servants' door followed by Wiggs, the ancient butler, who was tugging on his waistcoat in an attempt to appear properly attired. "There seems to have been an accident," she said. At the same moment, Lancelot thumped down the stairs, and the footman who was not McBrae came into the Great Hall through another door.

"Lady Rosamund!" Lance said, after taking in the ghastly sight. "Are you... ? Was it you who screamed?"

"No, of course not," I retorted, annoyed to find that my voice was trembling a little. I am not the sort of ninny who dissolves into shrieks of hysteria, and even a shaking voice seemed an intolerable weakness. "It was Miss Gardner. Mr. Powers came and took her upstairs."

"How dreadful for you to encounter such a sight." Lance was quite a sight himself in a red and blue banyan open at the throat, his golden hair tousled from sleep.

"Dreadful for anyone," I said. He was handsome as ever, but I couldn't keep my eyes from the body—or perhaps I was drawn, as ever, by the appearance of not-McBrae. He knelt next to the corpse and shook his head.

"Nothing to be done for him, sir," he said in a soft Scottish burr. I had only heard McBrae speak with a Scots accent once. This man's speech was slower and far more comprehensible. Definitely not the same.

But I already knew that. It wasn't he.

He examined the dead man's temples and crown, then lifted Fence's head, slipped his hand underneath, and laid it gently down again. Was he checking for blood? Seemingly, he found none, for his hand emerged clean.

"We'd best get him out of here." Distaste suffused Miranda's voice. "Where shall we put him?"

"Not in the scullery," I said. Unsurprisingly, both Miranda and Lancelot stared. I hastened to explain. "When our footman fell down the stairs and broke his neck, the kitchen maid wouldn't work with his corpse nearby."

Lance laughed. "You certainly are an original, Lady Rosamund." He sent Wiggs doddering away for some men and a hurdle.

It had grown slowly lighter as dawn advanced, which is perhaps why I glimpsed Miranda, on the other side of the body, nudging it with her shoe. I couldn't see the expression on her face.

"It must have fallen on him." Lance glanced up at the wall. "But why? It wasn't loose, was it?"

"It was slightly askew," I said. "I noticed when we arrived last night."

"It's been askew for years," Lance said. "Let's get it off him. Come, Mac." He and not-McBrae took one side each and tugged on the massive rack. It came out of the corpse with a slick, sucking sound and a soft pop. I shuddered again as they laid it on the floor beside him.

Mr. Fence's corpse was fully dressed. So, I realized, had been Miss Gardner.

"She said it was murder," I blurted.

They stared at me—Lancelot, Miranda, and, for the briefest flick of an eye, not-McBrae.

"Who?" Lance demanded.

"Miss Gardner."

"Pooh," Lancelot said. "She was hysterical. Why would anyone murder Mr. Fence?"

From behind me came the slightest huff of a laugh from not-McBrae, but when I turned, startled, he was contemplating the bare patch high on the wall.

I returned my attention to Lancelot. "Judging by what I witnessed this evening, I should think the question would be, why *wouldn't* anyone do so? He was disgusting."

Lancelot chuckled. He had a charming smile. "True, but—"

"What was he doing down here fully clothed at this time of night?" I asked. "Miss Gardner seemed to think—"

"Yes, yes, she said it was murder. We understand that," Lance said.

That wasn't what I'd intended to say. I try to avoid repeating myself. "But—"

"Whisht, lassie."

It was not-McBrae again, and although I am in general a considerate mistress, I cannot tolerate being ordered about by servants, particularly when they give me the sensation of encountering a ghost.

Well, not precisely a ghost, for McBrae wasn't dead, but he was no longer present in my life. I swiveled to give the footman my most blighting stare—the one perfected through generations of earls—but Lance forestalled me. "As I told you before, Mac, Scottish customs are not the same as those prevailing here. You will henceforth treat Lady Rosamund with proper respect." He gestured. "Take that disgusting thing away. The stag's head, not the remains of Mr. Fence."

"Where shall I put it, sir?" came that soft Scottish burr, sounding not the least bit chastened. I couldn't bring myself to look at him, for I would have stared. I could easily keep myself from gazing at handsome Lance, but I was tempted to really *look* at not-McBrae. Perhaps he was a cousin of sorts, or even a brother of McBrae. He was so very like, but something in the expression, in the lines of the face, was not the same.

"God knows," Lance said. "My father likes the bloody thing, which really *is* bloody at the moment. Ah, here he comes at last."

Sir Alphonse came down the stairs, accompanied by, of all people, Sir Roderick Frockmartin. As they bent to examine Mr. Fence, exclaiming and speculating, I had a brilliant notion. This was my opportunity to speak to Cynthia alone.

Without a word, I slipped up the staircase. At the landing, I paused and glanced back. Sir Roderick was examining the stag's head. Perhaps he hadn't noticed my presence at all. Not-McBrae saw me, though—his eyes caught mine for an instant before he returned to gazing at the empty space on the landing wall.

Why had he told me to hush?

There was no time to think about that now. I flew down the corridor past my room. Cynthia and Sir Roderick had been put in a bedchamber near the end of the passageway, next to a broom cupboard. (I had made a point of learning who was housed where when we went up to bed.) Had the screams pierced that far?

I listened for a second at Cynthia's door. Silence. Gently, I opened it.

Cynthia was sitting up in bed, a book in her hands, looking weary and vulnerable in the light of a small branch of candles.

"Dearest!" She closed the book. "Do come in. Whatever is going on? Sir Roderick and I heard a woman weeping in the corridor, and a man's voice comforting her. I thought perhaps it was Mr. Powers."

"It was, and the woman was Miss Gardner. There has been a dreadful accident." I had already decided not to call it murder. I had no proof of that, and before I considered such a shocking possibility, I must carefully ponder all I had seen and heard. Besides that, Lancelot had pooh-poohed the idea, and not-McBrae had told me to hush…

Which just goes to show I am not above taking the advice of a servant. Just because he was impertinent, it didn't mean he was wrong.

But about what? About suggesting it was murder? Or that even if it was murder, one would do better not to say so. In which case, why?

"Mr. Fence is dead, and poor Miss Gardner saw the body and became hysterical."

She paled in the candlelight and put a hand to her mouth. After a long moment, her voice trembled. "An accident befell him? What happened?"

Hurriedly, I explained about the stag's head, for I didn't wish to waste what little time I had alone with her. "Yes, a horrid accident, but listen, Cynthia-love, how are you? I've been so worried. You needn't stay with Sir Roderick if you don't wish to. I'm furious with my father for being so underhanded, but I'll stick by you. We can leave if you like. Papa can't prevent me, and nor can Sir Roderick."

Actually, they probably could, for between an earl and said earl's daughter, people will invariably obey the earl. Also, I didn't wish to become estranged from Papa—but how dare he interfere in such a highhanded way in a matter which was none of his business?

Nor is it mine, you might say, but Cynthia is my dearest friend. I consider it my duty to take care of her.

Cynthia broke into the jumble of my thoughts. "Your father meant well, and so does Sir Roderick."

"In what possible way does forcing himself on you constitute meaning well?"

"He hasn't forced himself on me," Cynthia said. "He has been extraordinarily considerate, considering how unkindly I have treated him."

I was dumbfounded at this statement. It seemed to me that Cynthia had been ridiculously patient with Sir Roderick, for he had pestered her with his attentions for over a year, despite the fact that she was my husband's mistress and wanted nothing to do with him. Not only that, the way she turned the book over and over in her hands proved she wasn't as calm as she claimed.

"He forced you to pretend to be his wife!"

"Yes, because it was the only way to get me to talk to him." She sighed. "I can't help but admire his persistence. He loves me, you know. He wants to take care of me and the baby."

"Despite the fact that it isn't his child?"

She shifted against the pillows. "Truly, Rosie, you mustn't worry about me. He can't force me to marry him."

Perhaps not, but he could make life impossible for her. He could, for example, claim that the child was his and that she was an unfit mother, and take the baby away if she refused to marry him. No one would dispute his claim. Except perhaps Papa, if he thought such an action justified, but naturally he believes in a man's right to his children.

"Sir Roderick would never do anything unkind," she said, as if she had read my thoughts. But she didn't sound completely sure—and rightly so. "Stop fretting. If worse comes to worst, I'll run away with you."

I can tell when Cynthia has made up her mind—in this case to talk to Sir Roderick, about what I hadn't the slightest notion. It sounded to me like a waste of time.

"Everything will be fine," she said, "but in the meantime, do try to be civil to Sir Roderick."

"Very well," I said begrudgingly, "but it would help if he were civil to me in return." He loathed me because I hadn't tried to lure Albert, my husband, away from Cynthia, which was completely unfair, for my marriage was based on Albert's promise to stick to her and leave me alone. But that was a secret I would take to my grave—and I trusted Cynthia to do the same.

I scowled, suddenly not so sure. "You won't tell him about us, will you? About Albert and so on."

"Definitely not, dearest. It's none of his business, and in any event, he wouldn't understand. I'll suggest that civility toward you would please me. That should do it." She gave me a wan smile. "Now, go back to bed and get some sleep. That's what I mean to do." She set the book aside and lay down under the coverlet. "Blow out the candles, will you? It's light enough now for Sir Roderick to find his way to the sofa."

I now noticed what had escaped me when I entered—a pillow and a rumpled blanket on the sofa. He really wasn't forcing himself on her, at least not in a carnal way. How astonishing—but perhaps only because she was with child. I knew nothing of such matters.

Accepting defeat, I kissed her goodnight and returned to bed.

I couldn't sleep. Once I had dismissed the ridiculous notion that I had caused the appearance of a corpse simply by wishing for it, I went on to ponder who might actually be responsible.

Miss Gardner seemed to think she was—and, if I had understood her wailed *How could you?* that Mr. Powers had committed the dreadful deed.

From jealousy? Not likely, for why would an innocent miss choose the nasty middle-aged Fence over a decent young man? From offense? It seemed an extreme reaction to mere insults, which litter the ground of society, so to speak.

Fine, but why had Miss Gardner been fully dressed at the crack of dawn, which comes in the wee hours during the northern summer?

The same applied to Mr. Fence. Had he come down to meet someone? If not Miss Gardner, then whom?

I got out of bed, crossed to the dressing table (for there was no *secrétaire* as in my boudoir at home), took pen and ink, and opened my diary. I call it that, but I would never confide my secret thoughts where any nosy person—such as my mother—might chance upon them. Those I record elsewhere in a code that looks as if I am practicing my copperplate.

I considered putting my questions and observations in this code, but decided against it as too time-consuming. I would tear the pages out and hide them, once I had organized my thoughts.

First of all, accident or murder?

I completely understood why not-McBrae had gazed so contemplatively at the wall. It was hard to imagine such an accident, for it involved various coincidences. For the death to be accidental, the stag's head must have fallen off the wall, bounced off the baluster rail, and landed rack down on top of Mr. Fence—who just happened to be directly under it at the time. The stag's head was huge and the landing was narrow, but would it have hit the baluster rail, had it fallen? Perhaps, but I had my doubts about whether it would fall with the rack down. Which was heavier, the head and neck or the antlers? The head must be stuffed with something. Straw? Sawdust? Rags? I had no idea.

Apart from that, even if it had bounced off the rail, wouldn't it have landed on Mr. Fence's head, if he'd been standing under it? As far as I could recall, his head had shown no sign of injury. He looked fine from the front (more so than usual, since his corpse wasn't sneering), and not-McBrae hadn't found blood anywhere on his head.

He might have been on the floor already when it fell…but why would he lie down in the Great Hall at this time of night—or at any time, for that matter?

Murder, then.

I am ashamed to say that I felt a thrill of excitement. (But not, perhaps, as ashamed as one should be.) Just think—a murder, right here under our noses! I didn't care one way or another about the man's death, and if anyone mourned him, it would probably be for appearance's sake or for mercenary reasons, such as a bequest.

But I couldn't help but be alarmed by the thought that one of the guests was a murderer. Or, though I hesitate to suggest it, one of the servants. Not that I believe servants are incapable of murder, but I would not wish you to think I am firmly prejudiced in favor of the ruling classes. I am indeed biased in many instances, but I do try to examine my motives and feelings—at least whenever it occurs to me to do so. It's surprisingly tedious to question oneself constantly, and sometimes I forget.

Motives, then. Who might want to kill Mr. Fence, and why?

First, the gentlemen.

Mr. Powers, whose motives I indicated above. His aggressive mien last evening supported this possibility.

Mr. Bellevue, because of rivalry, or because Fence had insulted his proposal for a play.

Johnny of the wispy beard, whose surname I had forgotten, also rivalry.

Colonel Wendell, to rid the world of a blackguard. He was a starchy old gentleman with rigid notions of fair play, but I couldn't quite imagine his going to such an extreme.

Lancelot Lewis, out of annoyance.

Motives were very thin on the ground. I couldn't think of any reason Sir Alphonse might have wanted Fence dead. Far better to just not invite him to the Grange.

That left Papa, whom I would never suspect of such a dastardly deed, and Sir Roderick. Much as I wished I could dispose of him by way of the hangman, he hadn't even been invited, and had come only because of Cynthia.

The women, then. Neither Cynthia nor I, for obvious reasons.

Miranda of the Tyne. I had no idea why she might want to kill Fence, but three facts contributed to my suspicion of her. 1) Upon reflection, I knew it was she I had glimpsed in the Great Hall. 2) That grunt as she leaned over the stag's head… Had she pushed down on the antlers to ensure that Fence was indeed dead? This possibility was reinforced by 3) the way she'd later nudged the body with her foot. A gesture of derision, or maybe even hatred. Perhaps she would have liked to kick his corpse, but that would have given her away.

I hoped I was wrong, for I liked Miranda best of everyone I'd met there.

Next, Miss Ellis, Miranda's niece. Apart from her vulgarity, she reminded me of young ladies on the marriage market who preen and pose, proud of their beauty or wealth. She was quite a pretty woman, but… Ha!

I had noticed, despite her distress, that Miss Gardner was also very pretty—in fact, when not disfigured by fright or tears, she must be astonishingly beautiful. Definitely a cause for rivalry. Perhaps Mr. Fence had been in love with Miss Ellis, and then switched his allegiance to the more beautiful Miss Gardner.

So why wouldn't Miss Ellis kill her instead?

Next, Mrs. Holloway, who had an air of intelligent competence, and, I had learned last night, was Miss Gardner's godmother and had brought her here. I couldn't imagine a motive, unless to protect Miss Gardner from Fence's lechery.

Lastly, Mrs. Wendell, but she was the least likely of the ladies—a kindly individual without apparent motive or the strength required.

In fact, strength was a significant concern. I doubted I, or any of the other ladies, would be able to heft that stag's head 1) off the wall, and 2) over the balustrade.

Onto a man lying cooperatively below. Absurd!

Onward to the servants. The butler, Wiggs, was elderly, and the housekeeper middle-aged and plump. How about a maidservant to whom Fence had made improper advances? Female servants were frequently stronger than their mistresses, because of doing manual labor. Alternatively, the footman, to protect said maid's virtue.

I hoped not-McBrae wasn't the culprit. Why, I'm not sure, for I had no reason to either like or dislike him, apart from his brief foray into impudence. But I did have questions about him. Why he had been downstairs and fully dressed? (In fact, far too many people were up and dressed in the middle of last night.) And why had he warned me to hush? Because it would be better by far if everyone believed Fence's death an accident?

That would certainly benefit the murderer, while on the other hand, if he were suspected of murder, he might kill again to protect himself.

Why had not-McBrae been staring up at the wall? If he were innocent:

perhaps to work out how the stag's head had fallen or been thrown. If he were guilty: to ensure that no evidence of his perfidy remained.

I had to see for myself. The culprit might have already dealt with any evidence—but on the other hand, he might not. It was full daylight now, but although servants were up and about, the guests were likely still abed. Now was my best chance.

I pulled on my wrapper, knotted it about my waist, and opened the door. After a quick glance up and down the passageway, I hurried toward the head of the stairs. The Great Hall appeared to be empty.

Perfect. I scuttled—an undignified sort of progress—onto the narrow landing joining the two wings, and stopped. A man stood there, sketching on a scrap of paper.

He looked up, and it was McBrae.

Chapter Four

I am rarely anxious. My concern about how she would react to my presence is a testimony to the depth of my feelings.

—From the diary of Corvus

"Och," he said, very Scottish, and then, "Damnation," in Eton-and-Oxford, and then with a sigh, "This was inevitable." He folded the paper and tucked it into his pocket, but not before I glimpsed a rough image of a crowd of people gaping at Fence with the stag's head atop him.

"It *is* you!" I cried, scarcely able to believe my eyes. "But *how?*"

"Hush, my lady." He picked up a crowbar from the floor.

"What are you playing at?" I demanded. "Why didn't you identify yourself to me earlier?"

"I'll explain later." He glanced about. "Go back to your bedchamber, Lady Rosamund, and be quiet about it." He turned from me and swiftly dented the balustrade with the crowbar.

Meanwhile, he wanted *me* to be quiet? Oh, very well, he'd made little noise, but how dare he? He advanced towards me, making shooing motions.

I retreated, still furious. "Did you follow me from London?" I was panting with rage, but I kept my voice down—from habit, for a well-bred lady must never cause a fuss. "Have you been hovering about ever since then, pretending to be someone else? An ostler, perhaps? Or a tapster?"

He looked at me as if I were mad. It is an expression with which I am familiar. "No, I did not," he said softly. "I was in London until a week ago."

"Oh." Blood rushed to my cheeks. I wasn't about to admit to all the not-McBraes who had haunted me these past two months—although knowing McBrae, he would work that out for himself.

"Please return to your chamber." He lowered his voice still more. "And for God's sake, don't bring up the possibility of murder. We'll speak later." He followed me into the passageway and bowed. In the soft Scots accent of earlier, he said, "It's t'other way, my lady, but if you ring, your maid will be sent to you."

I returned to my room in a dudgeon and rang for Mary Jane. I was battling so many conflicting thoughts and feelings that I almost forgot to tear the pages from my diary and hide them.

Don't bring up the possibility of murder, McBrae had said, and that included concealing my written musings. No matter how baffled and enraged I was, instinct, coupled with previous experience, told me to trust McBrae's judgment. He was clever and discerning, and a few months earlier, he had saved my life.

But he was covering up a murder—for I was sure he had whacked the balustrade to make it appear as if the falling stag's head had damaged it, thereby reinforcing the appearance that the death was an accident. What a despicable course of action—the sort of thing no self-respecting Englishman would do!

But McBrae wasn't English, and one never knew when it came to the Scots. I tried not to think of what he had done to save me, for there was no proof... My husband's death had seemed to be an accident... Logically speaking, it *must* have been, and yet...

I sank onto the chair before my dressing table, reeling—and meanwhile taking reluctant note of the fact that I was far more affected by McBrae's possible perfidy than the sight of a corpse.

I tore the pages from my diary. My reticule is not the sort of hiding place I prefer, but I wasn't at home where I have a multitude to choose from—in books, under floorboards, in the pockets of cloaks out of season, and so on.

Even at Papa's house I have places, although I don't need them as much, for with him I'm comfortable and therefore less likely to conceal things and then check them over and over. Here, I had nowhere, so at the first opportunity, I would transcribe my thoughts into code and burn the originals.

Mary Jane bustled in. "Oh, my lady, it's dreadful. There was an accident, and a gentleman was killed!"

"I know." Hurriedly, I tightened the strings of my reticule. "I was wakened by screams and went down and saw the body."

She gasped. "My lady, you shouldn't have! I heard he was impaled upon the antlers of a stag. Gored to death! I wish we hadn't come to this house."

I was too tired to protest at this foolish comment. She also wished we hadn't come to the North and never tired of saying so. She preferred London, with its shops and fashionables, where she got to dress me three or four times a day. At Papa's, I often wore the same gown from morning till night, thereby enduring her laments that I do not behave according to my God-given station in life.

"Not that I'm surprised," she said. "This is a house of sin, and by what I hear, the man who died was one of the worst sinners of all."

My ears pricked up. "Really? What are they saying about him?"

She pursed her lips. "That he fondled the maids in the passageways and tried to pull them into his bedchamber. They say Mrs. Tyne threatened him with a fate worse than death if he didn't leave them be."

"Well, he's dead now, so she needn't worry about the maids anymore." I frowned. "What, I wonder, could be worse than death?"

Mary Jane didn't reply immediately. I recognized her silence as a struggle with her conscience. She considered me an innocent. Although we never discussed it, she knew I had never shared a bed with my husband. Therefore, certain kinds of carnal matters—don't ask me how she decides which are which—should never be commented upon in my presence.

Which is absurd. She is not so very much older than I and was married for a mere six months before her husband died, after which she came to work for me.

"For a man, some fates are worse," she said darkly.

"I suppose you mean castration," I said, to get it over with. I didn't truly understand, for seeing as I have no interest in sexual pleasures, I assume anyone can live a useful and contented life without them.

I shouldn't know about human castration (although one cannot help but be aware of the gelding of stallions), but thanks to my father I have a basic education in history, music, and the classical world.

"She's an immoral woman with a vulgar mind and tongue, but I cannot fault her for protecting the maids," Mary Jane said.

"I rather like her," I said. "She is an excellent hostess, far better than one would expect in a fallen woman. Mr. Fence proved to have a far more vulgar mind and tongue last night at dinner. You would have been shocked beyond measure."

"It is the judgment of the Lord that he died, my lady. If he were alive, I would fear for your safety."

"No, he wasn't interested in me," I said. "He lusted after Miss Gardner."

"So do all the others, by what I hear. They say she's very beautiful." Pause. "And that Miss Ellis is jealous. No better than she should be, that one. She paints her lips!"

So did many ladies, but to Mary Jane's mind, this was a sign of immorality. She had certainly gathered plenty of gossip in the short time since we had arrived at Lewis Grange.

It was useful to receive confirmation of some of my surmises, but it didn't help me decide what to do. McBrae's request not to mention murder was entirely unacceptable. It is the duty of every law-abiding citizen to do his or her best to see that justice is done.

Not that justice actually *is* done much of the time. I am not so naïve as to believe that all judges are impartial. Even my mother doesn't believe that—but she assumes, on the other hand, that every accused criminal is guilty of something, if not that with which they are charged, and therefore punishment is well-deserved. I might have agreed with her at one time, but no longer. I have become wary of assumptions, for all too often they prove to be wrong.

Regardless, I must confront McBrae so I could make up my own mind about what to do.

It is not a simple matter for a lady to speak privately with a male servant who works for someone else. Pondering how to go about cornering McBrae, I went down to breakfast—but not before surreptitiously making certain that the folded pages of my diary were indeed in my reticule. Yes, I knew they were there, but I felt compelled to see them again with my own eyes. I don't suppose that makes any sense to you. It is as if by repeating an action several times, I can be sure I have done it—when I already know I have.

I was greeted in the dining parlor by the roar of my father's voice.

"This is unacceptable! Not at all what I expect in a gentleman's house—even yours, Alphonse."

My father is usually even-tempered, so something must have upset him severely. I glanced about; only Papa, Sir Alphonse, and Miranda Tyne were at the table.

Our host was the picture of chagrin, so I hastened to intervene. "Please don't blame Sir Alphonse, Papa! He can't help what happened. This wretched mu—man's death is extremely awkward for him, too."

"Death? Oh, that fellow Fence. Irrelevant." He scowled. "My diamond cravat pin is missing."

"Are you certain you brought it with you?" I asked.

He huffed. "I saw it in my dressing case whilst I was putting on my rings last night."

In other words, before dinner. "Did you lock it before leaving your bedchamber?"

"Lock it? Why would I? I never lock it at home, and I assumed—" He turned his scowl in the direction of our host. "That in my friend Alphonse's house, I had no need to do so. Certainly didn't the last time I visited."

"So sorry, old fellow," Sir Alphonse said. "We've had a bit of a pilfering problem lately, you see."

"Pilfering?" Papa cried. "It's not an old penknife. It's a diamond pin!" He stabbed his fork into a morsel of ham.

"Theft, then, if you must. I would have told you last night, but I had already informed the other guests, and what with your tardy arrival, and all the talk of Lammas and moral tales and such, it slipped my mind." Sir Alphonse winked at me. "I should dearly love to see a moral tale, Lady Rosamund. Shall you write one for the competition?"

'Heavens, no." I fear I blushed. "I was jesting." I nodded to the footman hovering nearby to serve me some shirred eggs.

"What a pity," Sir Alphonse said. "The others are certain to be a dead bore. You've heard Bellevue recite, I expect. His attempts at blank verse make one queasy. Beaver's practically a babe in arms—if he's written anything, I've never heard of it—and Powers is a romantic. All daffodils and sunbeams, like that fellow Wordsworth."

I'm not a great admirer of Wordsworth, but not only was this an unfair assessment of his poetry, it didn't fit my impression of Mr. Powers. "Truly? He seemed to me an angry, even violent, sort of man."

"He has a bit of a temper," Sir Alphonse said, "but his sonnets—"

Papa spoke over him. "Who gives a hedgehog's arse for sonnets when my diamond pin is gone? I demand that a search be done at once!"

"We shall, my dear fellow, but I'm afraid we won't find a thing. We've had the same problem before. Some of my fellow Druid-fanciers came for Beltane this spring, along with assorted wives and children. The children had great fun collecting birds' eggs and caterpillars, but their parents each lost a small item of value. Frightfully embarrassing, I must say. The same happened last month, when friends from Lance's Oxford days visited. All the servants' belongings were gone through each time—most inconvenient, I assure you—but nothing was found."

The footman, stone-faced, served me several slices of bacon. I thanked him with a smile. In past years, I wouldn't have noticed his expression, or wondered how he felt about the accusations against him and the other servants.

Not that they were definitely unfounded. Just because I have recently become more aware of the injustices perpetrated on the lower classes, it doesn't mean they're all honest and upright, and some of them are indeed lazy.

"For naturally the servants were obliged to do the searching, and unless they are all in it together, which is impossible given the jealousies and rivalries servants are prone to, it has caused a great deal of resentment below stairs," Sir Alphonse said. "I'm surprised we haven't all been poisoned in our beds."

I glanced at the footman again. If possible, he was even more like granite than before. I knew what I should say at this point, or rather, what McBrae would want said. What a pity he wasn't in the room to hear me say it.

"It's unfair to assume a servant is to blame," I said, "particularly since there is no proof whatsoever."

"My dear girl, who else could it be?" Sir Alphonse paused. "Perhaps the gardener is the thief, and is burying the items under the shrubbery." Another pause. "But he doesn't even come into the house, so how could he get into the guest bedchambers? There are a few maids who come from the village daily, but where would they hide the purloined items? I fear Mrs. Alderthwaite will give notice if I ask her to search the girls again."

"Mrs. Alderthwaite may go to the devil," Papa said. "I want my diamond pin."

Miranda, who had been silent and preoccupied until now, said, "Fortunately, since we would be lost without Mrs. Alderthwaite, it can't be the dailies, for they had gone home before you arrived last night, Lord Medway. I sent them away early because of Fence pawing them in the corridors."

"One shouldn't speak ill of the dead, Miranda," Sir Alphonse said.

"Stuff and nonsense," she snapped. "He was a lecher. I don't know why you invited him."

"Because he praised you so highly, my dear. Said Beaver was an aspiring playwright who longed to worship at your feet, and could they both come along."

Miranda glowered. She didn't seem at all flattered—but perhaps she was so used to compliments that she disdained them, at least from such as Johnny Beaver and Mr. Fence.

"What could I do but agree? We were already acquainted, since he frequents—frequented—the theaters." Sir Alphonse turned to my father, spreading his hands. "We shall do our best to find your pin, but in the meantime, you must simply lock up your valuables when you're not wearing them."

"This," my father said, "is the last time I accept an invitation from you, Lewis. Slapdash research was bad enough, but now thieves running about day and night…" He spread marmalade on a slice of toast with bitter strokes of the knife.

"Not to mention murderers," a husky voice cooed. Miss Ellis posed dramatically in the doorway.

"Murderers?" Sir Alphonse cried. "Whatever can you mean, dear child?"

Miranda Tyne narrowed her eyes at her niece. Miss Ellis caught the glance but lifted an indifferent shoulder.

"Whoever killed Mr. Fence," she said with a tiny moue of her tinted lips. "Miss Gardner said so." She paused, turning her head. "Here she comes. She'll tell you. She practically saw it happen!"

"Saw what happen?" Miss Gardner tripped hesitantly into the room, followed by an uneasy-looking Mr. Powers. She was indeed beautiful—golden hair, cornflower-blue eyes, et cetera—but traces of the puffiness due to weeping remained on her face.

"The murder." Miss Ellis drew the word out long and eerily, widening her eyes.

"I didn't!" Miss Gardner was more composed than earlier, but just barely. "I didn't see anything."

"Miss Ellis is jesting," Mr. Powers said.

"No, I'm not," Miss Ellis said. "Think how enthralling to witness a murder!"

My first thought was, *Good God, what a fool.* My second: *You're the fool, Rosamund, for wanting a body in the first place.* Isn't it strange how one actually believes, at least a little, that one's wishes might cause something dreadful to take place?

"I didn't!" Miss Gardner repeated. "I was merely coming from the drawing room, and there he was, dead!"

"The drawing room at four o'clock in the morning?" asked Sir Alphonse. "Whatever for?"

"I couldn't sleep, and I'd—I'd left my book there," she said. "I *promise* I didn't see a murder, just a horrible dead man."

"We believe you," Miranda Tyne said. "You couldn't have seen a murder, for there wasn't one."

"Precisely," Sir Alphonse said.

"Then why did she say so?" Miss Ellis demanded. "I heard her in the corridor, whining and crying to Geoff about murder." Judging by the direction of her glance, Geoff was Mr. Powers. He had progressed from uneasy to aghast.

"Surely you're imagining things, Miss Ellis." Lancelot Lewis appeared in the doorway. Mr. Powers let out a relieved breath. Lance to the rescue once again?

"No, I did not imagine it." Miss Ellis put her hands on her hips and arched a brow at Miss Gardner. "I *heard* you."

The poor girl shrank, and her eyes filled with tears. "It was because—because—"

"Because he *looked* murdered," I interposed, for Mr. Powers was dithering between the two ladies (not that Miss Ellis merited that description), while Lancelot frowned as if he would like to slap them both but unfortunately was too much of a gentleman to do so.

"He was like something in a dreadful novel," I went on. "His eyes were open and staring, and his mouth wide with shock." Which wasn't true at all—he'd merely looked asleep—but I continued to embellish the image I'd created. "As if he'd seen a seven-foot-tall Viking brandishing a stag's head. Or maybe just a stag about to gore him. Something terrifying, in any event. Isn't that so?"

I smiled at Miss Gardner, hoping she had the sense not to contradict me. "I understand completely," I added. "It gave me quite a start, too."

Sir Alphonse broke into indulgent laughter. "A start, she says. A start! Fortunately, there are no seven-foot Vikings in the house, and that stag died years ago. It was just an accident, my dear Miss Gardner."

She slumped, dabbing her eyes. "I'm frightfully relieved to hear that." She seemed disproportionately so, as did Mr. Powers—with good reason if in another fit of temper, he had murdered Fence.

Why, I asked myself, had I just denied it was murder, when I was so certain of the contrary? To my dismay, I realized that McBrae had entered with a fresh pot of coffee. Had he heard my blatant untruth?

Lancelot certainly had. He was no longer frowning, but watched me with a quizzical expression I wasn't sure I liked. Meanwhile, Miss Ellis flounced to a chair, pouting. After a few seconds' more dithering, Mr. Powers sidled over to sit next to her, and Lancelot wandered to the sideboard to examine the various dishes there.

"Which reminds me," Sir Alphonse said, "I'll have to contact Johnson, the coroner."

"The coroner?" Miss Gardner asked, a tremor in her voice. "Why?"

"Required for any unexpected death," he sighed.

"But aren't you the magistrate, sir?" she asked.

"Yes, and if Fence were someone of no account, I could declare it an accident and bury him speedily. However, since he was a gentleman, I have no choice but to call Johnson in." He grimaced. "Can't stand the fellow, and the feeling is mutual. We'll have to put him up while he summons a jury, but if he thinks I'm going to leave the body *in situ* for days, he has another think coming. I've had it put in the icehouse. Nowhere else cool enough in this heat."

There was a short silence, while we all (I assume) pictured the corpse on a slab in the icehouse, hopefully far away from pails of milk, crocks of cream, and so on. Fortunately, the building was a little way distant from the house, near the path to the lake.

"Knowing Johnson," Sir Alphonse said, "he'll demand the stag's head as deodand."

"Surely you don't want to keep the horrid thing?" I asked.

"No, but Johnson's been ogling it for years, and I took great pleasure in refusing to sell it," Sir Alphonse said grumpily. "Now, I'll have to either give it to him or ransom it back for some absurd sum."

I was aware of the law of forfeiture, thanks to the accident which befell my husband. He was killed when he ran in front of the coach of a London merchant, and the coroner tried to demand both the coach and horses as the cause of death. This seemed dreadfully unfair to me, but in the end, thanks to my father's intervention, they settled for the value of one of the horses, which the merchant could well afford. It still wasn't fair—but I could hardly say what, or rather who, I believed to be the true cause of the accident.

I introduced myself to Miss Gardner, since no one else seemed likely to do so, and offered her a seat next to me at the table. She was most gratified—understandably so, for not only had I rescued her and Mr. Powers from a most unpleasant situation, but I am far, far above her on the social scale. "Thank you," she whispered.

Papa gave me an approving glance, but I must admit that this kind gesture on my part was not entirely due to good breeding. I'd caught her hesitation about fetching a book. If she were comfortable with me, she might let slip something significant—if not now, then hopefully later.

Soon the Colonel came in, saying he for one wouldn't miss Mr. Fence, and Mrs. Wendell, who begged Sir Alphonse to remove the rest of those dangerous trophies from the Great Hall. Then Mrs. Holloway arrived, rosy-cheeked and cheerful in hobnailed boots, carrying a walking stick.

"Luckily I took my constitutional this morning, as I always do," she said, taking a cup of coffee and beckoning to the footman to serve her a heaping plateful of eggs. "If I'm not mistaken, we're in for a storm later."

Papa nodded. "Yes, indeed. I sensed it on the breeze last evening."

"Those who want a walk had best take it now." Lancelot finished his plateful of ham and eggs. "You must come with me to the fairy well this morning, Lady Rosamund. It's *de rigueur* for anyone who visits Lewis Grange."

Miss Ellis pouted. "Don't go. It's a boring trudge with nothing to see at the end."

"I rather liked it." Miss Gardner seemed to have summoned up some spirit.

"A complete waste of time," scoffed Miss Ellis. "Isn't that so, Geoff?"

Mr. Powers, if not precisely between Scylla and Charybdis, nevertheless did his best to placate both ladies. "It's rather a long walk," he said, "and tiring in the heat, but the well is quaint. I'm thinking of writing a poem about all the wishes hanging from the trees."

I caught a soft snicker from Lancelot, but his father said, "As long as it's respectful, my boy. One mustn't offend the fairies."

Miss Ellis made a rude noise.

"Wishes?" I asked in a bright, enquiring voice, although I didn't need an explanation. People go to fairy wells to ask for help—with love, with money troubles, with ill health, and so on, and they leave kerchiefs, embroidered squares, even rags as tokens for the fairies. But a question seemed a good way to divert the conversation.

Not for long. Sir Alphonse had barely managed a few explanatory sentences when Miss Ellis interrupted. "If there really were fairies, they would take the disgusting rags away. They look so ugly, all bedraggled and dirty on the trees."

Despite her bad manners, I didn't entirely disagree with her.

"My dear child," Sir Alphonse said, his tone unexpectedly indulgent in the face of her rudeness. "Don't speak such sacrilege! You can't play a Druid priestess if you don't believe."

She hunched a shoulder. "Oh, very well. But in any event, I loathe walking."

Papa snorted. "I expect you're jealous because young Lance didn't invite you to accompany him." Before the astonished girl could do more than gape, he turned to me. "Run along then, Rosie, and be quick about it, for you'll be stuck indoors later because of the rain."

I could hardly refuse, could I? Besides that, my father had just made an enemy for me. Miss Ellis might resent his remark, but henceforth she would hate me.

What a bore, as if one doesn't get enough of that in London.

"Don't make any wishes when you're near the well, and you'll be fine," my father said.

This produced a few snickers, as well as a sullen huff from Miss Ellis.

"Yes," Sir Alphonse said, "for you never know when the fairies are listening, and they may grant your wish and then make you pay the price."

"Dear me," I said. "I'd best keep my wishes to myself, then."

"Unfair," Lancelot said. "I'll have to coax them out of you."

I almost rolled my eyes. (I should have, for I rarely get to do so in London;

it's a vulgarity, which would have been entirely appropriate amongst this company.) I was not thrilled at Lancelot's offer, for he seemed in a flirtatious mood. How annoying. I wanted to corner McBrae and demand an explanation.

However, short of suffering a sudden migraine, I had no choice but to accompany Lance.

Chapter Five

To my great dismay, it seems that I have figured in her nightmares.

—From the diary of Corvus

I hurried upstairs, where Mary Jane whisked me into a grey walking dress and my sturdiest boots. I donned a light pelisse and bonnet, verified that the pages were still in my reticule (while asking Mary Jane for a clean handkerchief, to disguise my real reason for checking), and returned to the Great Hall—to see almost-McBrae coming out of the servants' quarters, carrying a jug and a sack. That is, it was the real McBrae, of course, but with his counterfeit face on.

I hesitate to admit it, but that face made me feel rather ill. It wasn't an ugly face, nor even an unpleasant one…but it wasn't quite *his*.

I had no idea how he did it. I merely knew that I disliked it very much.

He set the jug and sack down and doffed his cap. "Good morning, Lady Rosamund." He spoke in that soft Scots burr and didn't meet my eyes, which was entirely proper in a servant, and exasperating because he was merely playing at being one, when he knew perfectly well we needed to talk. He had *promised* we would do so.

I glanced about. No one seemed to be nearby. Dare I confront him here and now?

He shook his head ever so slightly and muttered, "Patience, my lady. And discretion, I implore you."

Lancelot ambled down the stairs. "Now, now, Mac. You know better than to accost the guests."

McBrae stepped back with a mumbled, "Sorry, sir."

"I apologize for keeping you waiting, Lady Rosamund." Lance offered me a blinding smile and tucked my hand in his arm. We made our way outdoors.

"A perfect day." He indicated the prospect with an elegant wave of the hand. The lake shimmered through the trees. A cormorant flapped overhead. Clouds sailed in a brilliant sky. Et cetera.

I did my best to admire the view, but how could I possibly appreciate the natural beauty of the world with a corpse in the ice house, a murderer running loose, and worst of all, McBrae seeking to shield him?

I must have scowled, for Lance asked, "Something amiss?"

"A man just died," I retorted. "Have you no sensibility?"

"None. It's a glorious day, and I'm about to spend a few hours with a beautiful woman. What more could I ask?" He truly did have a dazzler of a smile. It made me quiver inside—an experience I disliked greatly.

I said in a businesslike manner, "Very well, then. Let's go." I wanted to get it over with, but despite the double aggravations of McBrae and Lance's grin (not to mention that absurd compliment, for while some consider me pretty, I am not a beauty), I summoned a remnant of good manners. "We'd better hurry—not that I see the slightest sign of rain, but my father is always right about the weather."

"Oh, we have plenty of time. It's naught but a mile or so each way. Mac, where the deuce are you? Shake your stumps."

McBrae came down the steps, carrying the jug and sack, and we set off around the house, McBrae a respectful distance behind.

"Your footman is coming with us?" I asked, surprised.

"Mac? He's no ordinary footman," Lance said. "He's also valet, butler, groom, coachman, steward…anything that's required. A versatile fellow, is Mac. I found him at Oxford, where he was a scout for a short time."

"I see," I said, but I didn't. I found it believable that McBrae could fill many of the above-mentioned roles, but I also knew he wasn't Lance's servant. McBrae was a gentleman, albeit a Scot and far beneath me socially. He was a close friend of some peers with whom he had attended university, and had lived in London for more than a year with a servant of his own, producing caricatures of the beau monde.

He might have been employed by Lance at some time in the past, but it seemed unlikely. McBrae wasn't a rich man—he'd told me the caricatures were a source of necessary income to him—but servants are paid very little. "Has he been with you long?"

"On and off," Lance said vaguely. "On and off." His eyes twinkled merrily. "Good thing he's here now, for it's thirsty work walking up to the well, and *someone* has to carry the ale."

At this, I had to stifle my annoyance even more. Not that I had the slightest objection to McBrae acting as a beast of burden, for he deserved it (catty of me, I know), but I *wished* I knew what was going on.

He had asked me to be discreet, but about what? Were he and Lancelot together in wishing to conceal the murder? That thought rather frightened me, for although I trusted McBrae or at least wanted to, I had no such confidence in Lance.

Setting aside questions about the murder, did he know McBrae was a gentleman? That he possessed a strange ability to alter his facial expression to look much less like himself? (On this score, I wondered if I were 'seeing things,' as my mother would put it—a sign of madness. Not that I've ever had that sort of problem, but Great Aunt Edna did, so Mother fears the tendency will one day surface within me.)

There were further questions: did Lance know McBrae was an accomplished artist? That he published caricatures under the pseudonym Corvus?

I had to be extremely careful what I said, for I might reveal something I shouldn't. I was obliged to play along. To wait and see. To be patient, as McBrae had just said.

I didn't feel patient. I felt confused, aggravated, fretful, unsociable, and more than usually disinclined to flirt.

Fortunately, we were soon walking up a steep path through the wood, which meant single file, less conversation, plenty of huffing and puffing, and no flirtation. A little choir of siskins, with their upward and downward trills, accompanied our trek. A rabbit, feasting on clover at the edge of the path, vanished into the wood at our approach. Soon the gurgle of water greeted us, and emerging from the trees, we followed a charming beck up the side of the fell. At last, Lancelot halted and turned with a wave of the hand.

"The view—another obligatory sight for visitors."

McBrae set down his burdens with a thump.

The view was indeed splendid. Far below us, the lake sparkled in the sun, but in the distance, dark clouds built. "Here comes the rain," I said.

"We'll beat it," Lancelot said cheerfully. "It's only a few more steps to the well."

Soon we plunged into a small wood and reached a clearing. A quaint structure of stone, too tiny for anyone but fairies to inhabit, stood over the well. Every tree round about was festooned with cloths in various states of griminess and decomposition. A little stone bench nearby was equally filthy, so although I would have liked to sit, I remained standing.

"Much as I would rather not, I can't help but agree with Miss Ellis' opinion of those dirty rags," I said.

From behind me came a distinct "Tsk."

Lance snorted. "Mac disapproves, but it is rather ugly, isn't it? Still, one must put up with the beliefs and customs of the lower orders."

Which was rude of him, if he didn't know McBrae for a gentleman. Some evil demon prompted me to answer in kind. "And the Scots."

Lance burst into laughter, and belatedly, shame washed over me. Even if I harbor certain prejudices against the Scots, Irish, Americans, et cetera, it is ill-bred to give voice to them. Why had I done so?

Because I was upset with McBrae, and when one is upset, one does and says stupid things. I hastened to add, "And one's superstitious fathers."

Lance grinned. "Which I am usually happy to do, but this business of Druids is a bit much. As for choosing that trollop for the priestess, it's a travesty. Miranda is the obvious choice, particularly if my father means to be the Horned God, which I assure you he does. One can only hope people don't vote for his play."

He pulled a handkerchief from his pocket, flicked it open, and set to wiping the stone bench.

"Perhaps Miranda doesn't wish to play the priestess," I suggested.

"So she says, more credibly than my father's offer of the Horned God role to other comers. Miss Ellis played with a traveling company, but she aspires to roles on the London stage. Miranda invited Harold Bellevue in the hope of giving her another useful London contact, but he seems fixed on Miss Gardner instead."

"Is she also an actress?"

"Not unless she's a particularly bad one. She came with Mrs. Holloway, but she doesn't seem much of a bluestocking, either. Meanwhile, Powers cannot decide which woman to pursue. What a parcel of idiots my father gathered here this time." Lance finished wiping the bench and offered it to me with a sweeping bow. He dropped the handkerchief onto the path.

McBrae picked it up and knelt to rinse it in the well.

"My dear Mac, you needn't go to such lengths to prove your servitude if, as you assure me, Lady Rosamund knows it's a ruse," Lance said. "I don't want that rag back."

"Someone else will find it useful," McBrae retorted in the Eton-and-Oxford accent he used in London society.

"I daresay." Lance sighed. "I suppose I'll have to pour my own damned ale, but I'll pay you back when we return to the house." He paused. "Unless you plan to revenge yourself by putting a frog between my sheets."

"Why harm an innocent frog? Perhaps an adder—although one corpse is plenty."

Meanwhile, I said nothing, for although it was now clear that they were friends rather than master and servant, I still didn't know how much Lance knew about McBrae. Evidently, McBrae's practice of taking on the role of a servant wasn't a recent one. If Lancelot was to be believed, he'd done it whilst attending university at Oxford...

Suddenly, I knew. "You're playing at being a servant to find the thief."

"Aye." McBrae met my eyes. He looked like the real McBrae now. After that brief glance, he looked away and said nothing more. I expect he was as annoyed as I was—with far less reason, in my opinion. He knows about my prejudices and puts up with me despite them, while I know far too little about him. He wrung out the handkerchief and draped it across the roof of the well.

After a brief silence, Lancelot roused himself. "Mac informed me you are intelligent and discreet. I am duly impressed."

Which made me feel even worse for making that snide remark about the Scots—while at the same time I bristled at the thought that the two of them had been discussing me. Why that should bother one, I don't know. People talk about one another all the time, and in this instance, it seemed McBrae had complimented me.

Ah, well. I had best stop being annoyed and get down to business. McBrae set about uncorking the jug and pouring ale for everyone, while I pondered how discreet to be and about what. Not about my certainty that murder had been done, but until I knew more, I must maintain my silence about McBrae's alter ego, Corvus.

"It's kind of you to consider me discreet, Mr. McBrae, and so far, I have remained so, but I cannot keep silent about this business of murder without a very good reason."

"To prevent injustice being done," he said.

I let out a breath of relief, for I had anticipated an argument. Thank heavens he wasn't trying to pretend it wasn't murder. I glanced at Lance, who proved to be watching me with prurient interest. (Despite my virgin state, I recognize lust when I see it.) How exasperating—I hoped I wasn't blushing—but given his silence, it seemed he too believed murder had been done.

"Allowing a murderer to…remain at large is *causing* injustice," I retorted. I had almost said "go scot-free", and judging by the narrowing of McBrae's eyes, he knew it. So unfair, because that phrase has nothing to do with the Scots. It's a medieval usage to do with not paying one's taxes.

(It doesn't matter how I know this obscure fact, and I don't mean to tell. I should loathe to be thought a bluestocking.)

In any event, if people *think* it is a slur against the Scots, it doesn't matter what it really means. Tedious, isn't it? But I didn't wish to cause any more offense, so it behooved me to avoid using it.

"To convict an innocent man of murder is far worse," McBrae said.

"I suppose you mean one of the servants," I said, which was utterly idiotic. McBrae would never automatically assume a servant was to blame. However, once I'd started down such a stupid path, I felt obliged to continue. "Perhaps Mr. Fence caught one of them stealing from him."

"Who then killed Fence immediately and set up that absurd tableau?" Lance, who was lazing against the trunk of a fir tree, cocked his head. "It's not such a bad idea, Mac."

"Except that the culprit isn't a servant," McBrae said stonily. "Neither the thief nor the murderer."

"That sounds like something you would say," Lance said.

"I have no choice, seeing as no one else will stand up for them."

"Yes, but standing up for servants doesn't mean they're never guilty. You mustn't let your partiality for the lower orders blind you to their faults—or your dislike of your social equals blind you to their virtues."

"It so happens my concern this morning was to protect one of my so-called equals—Mr. Powers." He turned to me. "As you did when you rescued Miss Gardner this morning, Lady Rosamund."

"I felt sorry for her, not him," I said. "Thank you both for not contradicting my description of the corpse."

"Why would I?" Lance said. "Miss Ellis deserved a put-down, and your flight of fancy was most entertaining." He shrugged. "I doubt Powers is guilty."

"Given his previous behavior, Miss Gardner's outburst, and Miss Ellis's spite, he is at risk of arrest if there is talk of murder," said McBrae.

"What previous behavior?" I asked.

"He threatened Fence about making advances to Miss Gardner, and it was he who started the fight with Bellevue, not the other way around."

"He does seem rather a murderous sort," I said, and flushed, for who was I to judge? I didn't think of McBrae as murderous, but since the death of my husband, I wasn't so sure. Did I sense a slight paling of the natural color of

McBrae's cheeks? He gazed about the clearing, his eyes following a squirrel as it scampered from one larch to another.

I hastened to explain. "However, Mr. Powers' hasty temper probably means he lacks the self-control and forethought to plan a murder. Our culprit cleverly disguised this murder as an accidental death."

Lancelot widened his eyes at me. "My dear Lady Rosamund, I hope you will never have reason to murder me."

"That is entirely within your power," I retorted.

McBrae grinned. Perhaps he wasn't upset with me after all. "I agree, Lady Rosamund, but officers of the law usually seek the easiest explanation."

"Powers couldn't plan a cold-blooded murder if he tried," Lance scoffed. "He can't even make up his mind between two women—whom he wants for entirely different purposes. He could have them both if he played his cards right." He paused. "Although not at the same time." Another pause. "Pity."

"Forgive Lance's crude remarks," McBrae said. "The company at the Grange is so far from select that he forgets his manners."

"Not at all," Lance said. "Lady Rosamund is a woman of the world. A woman who dared to participate in a *ménage à trois*. Who bore the opprobrium of caricature by the dreaded Corvus with grace and good humor. I would scorn to treat her like a silly little innocent."

For many intents and purposes, I *was* an innocent, but I could hardly say so. Where did people get such odd ideas about me? Cynthia, Albert, and I never shared the same house, much less the same bed.

"Or ask her whether she brought her switch with her." Lance grinned.

"Obviously not," I retorted. "Haven't you seen the caricature? Corvus kept it to use on himself."

"I wonder why he never drew the three of you together *in flagrante delicto?*" Lance said.

Because it never happened! But much of what McBrae portrayed in his caricatures wasn't true either, and society believed it anyway. I frowned at Lancelot. Was that gleam in his eye still lust, or was he hinting mischievously that he knew the identity of Corvus?

I dared not risk a glance at McBrae for some sign, so I attempted to set the conversation back on the proper path. "May we return to more important matters? How can justice be done if a foul killing is masked as a mere accident?"

I sucked in a breath. So much for minding my tongue. In my concern to avoid revealing his alter ego, I had struck right at the heart of the estrangement between McBrae and me.

Not that it was an estrangement, exactly. We had never been close, but I liked him, and he had helped me and saved my life. I blew out the breath again, wishing I could apologize, but it was neither the time nor the place. It might never be.

"Justice," McBrae bit out, "is rarely done. Every year, dozens of innocent people are hanged or transported on the word—the mere, worthless word—of their so-called betters." He marched to the edge of the path, gazing into the distance. His fists, I saw, were clenched.

Lancelot roused himself to push away from the tree. "Mac and I are often at odds, but in this instance, we are entirely in agreement. We cannot let Powers suffer due to the folly of two useless females."

Not useless for everything, I thought darkly, judging by his earlier statement. However, I let the insult to my gender roll off my back. One can only expect so much from men—and evidently, they feel the same about women.

"If it rains as much as seems likely..." Lance motioned with his chin at the approach of dark, lowering clouds. "The roads will become impassable, and we shall have a day or two to determine who killed Mr. Fence and why, along with sufficient proof to present to Johnson and his jury."

"Very well," I said, more concerned, to my discredit, with McBrae's feelings about my outburst than about the murder. It's both fascinating and appalling how one's priorities can shift in the blink of an eye.

McBrae returned, reached into the sack, and pulled out a little tin cup. He filled it with ale and set it on the lip of the well.

"For the fairies?" I asked inanely. I had to say *something*.

It was Lance who replied. "Custom requires us to leave a cup of ale after each visit. And yes, it is invariably gone by the time one returns."

"The cup as well as the ale?"

He made a droll face. "Yes, but now and then a number of cups appear at the kitchen door overnight. We never question how they got there. It simply wouldn't do. Let's go, shall we?"

My priorities shifted back with a rush. "But we haven't discussed what we're going to do. When neither man responded, I said, "To unmask the murderer!"

"My dear Lady Rosamund," Lance said, "you needn't trouble yourself about that. Mac and I shall take care of it, I assure you."

I wanted to glance at McBrae to estimate his response, but I lacked the courage.

"That doesn't reassure me in the least," I said. "There is a murderer at large in the Grange."

"Ah, you are afraid. I understand completely, but you need not be," Lance said. "No one wishes to harm you."

I gripped my reticule with its folded pages inside. "You don't understand in the least. I am not afraid. It is simply that we must make some sort of plan before returning to the house. For example, someone should search Mr. Fence's belongings, as they may give us a clue to his murderer's identity."

Lance blinked at me, as if astonished at such a suggestion from a mere female. So much for admitting that I was intelligent only a few minutes earlier. "A good notion, but Mac already took care of that."

I turned to McBrae. "You found nothing out of the ordinary?"

McBrae shook his head. "Most likely the murderer got there before me and removed anything incriminating."

"And destroyed it if possible, or hid it if not," I mused, for that is exactly the sort of thing I do when I don't want people to know my secrets. "As I was saying, we must make a plan, for it is almost impossible for all three of us to gather to discuss the murder if we are stuck indoors while it rains."

Lance gave me the half-pitying, half-coy look of a man being kind to that inferior member of the species, a woman. "You need not be privy to our discussions," he said gently, "for there is nothing you can do to help."

I was tempted to stomp away in a tantrum, but that would have strengthened his assumption of my uselessness. I took a deep breath. I am accustomed to being considered foolish and even mad by some of my family members, so I have had practice weighing my words. I wasn't doing so well today. Due to my unguarded tongue, McBrae was unlikely to side with me, despite the fact that I had unmasked Corvus.

With help, I admit that, but I had hired and directed the help.

"Come now, let's go." Briskly, Lancelot waved me toward the path. "Mustn't risk a drenching. Lord Medway would never forgive me if I let you come to harm."

I doubted he would let my father's opinion stop him from seducing me. Fine. If these stupid men refused my help, I would just have to look into this dreadful business myself.

"I disagree," McBrae said suddenly.

"About what?" Lancelot said, still encouraging me to leave, whilst I remained stubbornly still, arms crossed.

"Lady Rosamund can do much that we cannot," McBrae said. "In fact, if we are to identify the murderer swiftly, we *need* her help."

Now my gaze flew to him of its own accord.

He wasn't looking at me. "You and I cannot easily glean information from the ladies," he told Lancelot. "Yes, you wish to dispute with me about this, but you are a flirt, too easily distracted from important matters, and I am a mere servant. Lady Rosamund can gossip with all the ladies."

"And find out what? None of the ladies could have heaved that stag's head over the balustrade."

"Perhaps not, but our first task is to find out who hated Fence enough to kill him. The ladies may have something to say about that." He turned to me, his gaze cool. "Are you willing to undertake this task, my lady?"

"Yes, indeed," I said, grateful and much abashed—but unwilling to acknowledge either emotion. "I was already planning to do so."

Chapter Six

Jealousy threatens to consume me.

—From the diary of Corvus

We descended the path quickly and in silence, for the dark clouds had begun swiftly to gather overhead. It didn't occur to me until I was in my bedchamber, with Mary Jane helping me change out of my walking dress, that I should have given McBrae what I'd written down earlier this morning. My fault entirely, for with my careless words I had plunged myself, and perhaps McBrae too, into a morass of emotions. I couldn't identify his for certain—for all I knew, he didn't care what I thought of him—but I felt something akin to despair.

Why? Because I had made an unkind comment about the Scots? Yes, but that wasn't all.

To my shame, I realized I was feeling sorry for myself. He was a friend of sorts, someone I liked to talk to, someone with whom I felt comfortable.

Not anymore.

Be that as it may, I certainly did not intend to share my thoughts so far with Lancelot—for it must be done in privacy, and I didn't trust him not to try to seduce me with that smile of his.

He wouldn't succeed, but I loathe scenes.

"I've locked all your jewels up good and proper, my lady," Mary Jane said. "But if you want to know what I think—"

I almost snapped at her. I stopped myself just in time. I had already made more than one stupid, thoughtless remark today.

"That we should leave this house of sin?" I asked. "Unfortunately, we can't. Even if his lordship would agree to go, it's pouring rain and the roads will be mud." Not only that, I had a responsibility to Cynthia.

And to the principle of justice, which sounds frightfully hypocritical of me. I hadn't worried much about justice when it came to the death of my husband. Not that anything could have been proven, and I'd believed it an accident until a few weeks later… And even if his death wasn't the sort of accident it seemed, it could hardly have been planned…

I did my best to banish these fruitless reflections. Not only that, McBrae's explanation made sense: he wanted to prevent injustice, a noble goal.

Very well. I must find a way to pass my assessment so far to McBrae. In the meantime, I would transcribe it into code. I asked Mary Jane to have tea sent up and then dismissed her, as this work must be done in private. It is often a slow, painstaking process, but my list was relatively short. I added a few notes about Mr. Powers' evident tension—not surprising, for whether innocent or guilty, he was a likely suspect—and about Miss Gardner's explanation that she'd gone to the drawing room for a book she'd left there. But she hadn't been carrying a book, nor had she dropped one in shock, or I would have seen it on the floor.

Not only that, I didn't recall her reading a book the evening before. She'd played whist and perused the *Ladies' Monthly Museum.*

Now to find a way to pass this information to McBrae. I stowed the coded pieces in my travel desk, where they would look entirely innocent if a servant succumbed to curiosity, and put the originals in my reticule again. And yes, I checked them twice before leaving my room.

A cold collation had been set out in the dining room for those who wished to take refreshment in the middle of the day. I am one of those, particularly after morning exercise. My mother wouldn't approve—she does her best to starve me into the placid obedience that is her notion of a dutiful daughter—but I eyed the cold meats and salads with glee.

At the moment, only Mrs. Holloway was there. I pounced upon this opportunity. "I am relieved to see another lady with a healthy appetite. I don't suppose walking to the fairy well compares with your morning exercise, but I am definitely peckish."

She regarded me warily before responding. Did I seem too friendly? I'd been distantly polite so far, but now I was supposed to invite confidences. I didn't think I could be coyly inquisitive even if I tried. I wished I possessed my father's friendly cordiality towards all and sundry.

Perhaps she was wary because of my social status. Or because of my notoriety. Or because she was a murderess. She was vigorously healthy, and therefore perhaps strong enough to lift the stag's head.

After that brief pause, she nodded amiably enough. "Yes, Lady Rosamund, I walked about thrice as far up one of the steepest sections of the fell. I walk at least twice a day whilst here, as it is far more strenuous and healthful than in London. Vigorous, solitary exercise is beneficial to the mind as well as the body."

Which seemed a slightly snide comment on my stroll in the company of a flirtatious man with designs on my virtue (or supposed lack of it). How exasperating to have the reputation of a racy widow when I was as untouched as a girl in her first season. Most girls, that is. I have become sadly cynical of late.

"Handsome gentlemen are all very well, but they do get in the way of rational enjoyment," I said. "I indulge in a great many long, solitary walks when residing with my father."

I served myself ham and bread, a couple of slices of the delicious local cheese, and several leaves of lettuce. Now to business. "Tell me, who *was* this Fence person?"

She made a face. "Didn't he make that entirely clear last night?"

"Rude and vulgar, agreed, but seemingly born a gentleman," I said.

"Of a sort. He was a minor civil servant in India until his return to England some months ago. He has the entrée in certain circles." Her nose twitched. "Not your rarified sort."

Despite this dig, I became even more determined to remain cordial. "That would explain why I've never met him or even heard of him. I must say, though, I'm surprised Sir Alphonse invited such a man, particularly one who wanted to meet Miranda of the Tyne."

"Considering the way Mr. Fence behaves—behaved—in the London theaters, it does seem odd," Mrs. Holloway said. "Perhaps he agreed because Fence was bringing Johnny Beaver. Alphonse encourages youngsters who show interest in writing plays." She paused. "Not that he's done much since he arrived but drink too much and echo Fence's disgusting suggestions."

"It's hard to imagine how anyone would choose to emulate such a man."

She grimaced. "Agreed. Fence was known for seducing young, gullible actresses who believed his lies about money and influence."

"He was not well off?"

"I know nothing of his family, but he didn't throw money and gifts about as wealthy men do to tempt beautiful mistresses." Was that bitterness in her tone, or merely disapproval? "In any event, Sir Alphonse had nothing to fear. Miranda would never have welcomed Fence's advances."

"According to my maid, she threatened him with castration if he assaulted her servants."

Mrs. Holloway's stern face became almost friendly as she laughed. "That sounds like Miranda."

"She seems an estimable woman." I fear I didn't quite mean it, for how can an immoral actress be estimable? And yet she did seem admirable in her way. "And an excellent hostess."

"Luckily so, since Alphonse is far too eccentric to be a good host. Did you and Lance leave a cup of ale at the well?" A flicker of her eyelashes seemed to indicate that she disapproved of such nonsense.

I answered in the affirmative while helping myself to another slice of bread. "My father's housekeeper leaves milk and oatcakes for a hobgoblin, so I am used to such customs."

"And do you approve?"

"I don't think I have the right to approve or disapprove."

"Very diplomatic." She seemed to be assessing me, which had begun to rankle. I'm accustomed to others passing judgement on me in the privacy of their minds; it's the consequence of 1) exalted status and 2) notoriety. But at the moment I was supposed to be assessing her, not the other way around.

"Naturally, you don't wish to offend your father by saying fairies don't exist," Mrs. Holloway said.

"Nonsense!" Papa strolled into the room. "My Rosie would be happy to believe in fairy creatures, but she hasn't actually met any, so she wisely reserves judgment."

I couldn't help laughing, for he was absolutely correct.

"But don't tell her mother that," he said.

My appalled agreement must have shown on my face. That I would even consider believing in fairies would constitute proof of madness, in my mother's view.

McBrae came into the room, carrying a jug of lemonade. He sketched me a wink.

I felt my color rising—so annoying—but hopefully no one had noticed such audacious (not to mention highly improper) behavior on the part of a servant.

"You are acquainted with my mother?" I asked Mrs. Holloway, to cover my confusion.

"Hardly. One glimpses her at the theater." Her face darkened. "And hears her comments about the plays, which show a complete lack of imagination and—and charity." Heavens, what a heated response!

"There, there, Mrs. Holloway," my father said. "Don't let it vex you. My wife can't help who she is, but I assure you, Rosamund has inherited her imagination from me." He beckoned to McBrae. "We'll all have some of that lemonade, thank you. This fine young fellow," he told us, "has been regaling me with stories of the fae in the highlands of Scotland. Quite extraordinary! I shall make a point of traveling there one of these days. What say you, Rosie, to joining me on such an adventure?"

I glanced at McBrae's impassive face and away. He wore his altered features again, but now that I had recognized him, I saw right through the disguise, so to speak—but not to what he was thinking. I quite desperately wished to avoid offending him again.

"I fear I should lose my maid if I agreed to such a journey," I replied. "I am already in her bad graces for coming this far north. She misses the London shops and the opportunity to change my clothing three or four times a day."

"And you do not?" Mrs. Holloway said.

"I miss the theater, the museums, the musical entertainments. I'm not much interested in clothes." Although I was already sick and tired of mourning attire—so dismal. I longed to wear colors once again.

"We'll find a brawny Scot to flirt with Mary Jane," Papa said. "That should reconcile her to the journey."

Anyone less flirtatious than Mary Jane I couldn't imagine, but I smiled obediently. I was surprised to find, deep within myself, a seed of curiosity about McBrae's homeland. And McBrae's relations too, although they were beneath me socially.

I shook off these uneasy reflections. I really must get down to business—which included giving those pages to McBrae.

"What say you, Mac?" That was my father again.

"Aye, we've plenty of brawny flirts in Scotland, my lord," he said in that soft burr.

My father chuckled and waved him away. Drat! I'd hoped to give McBrae a speaking glance to let him know I needed to talk to him.

"That was a feeble excuse, Rosie," Papa said. "Mary Jane would follow you to the ends of the earth, which she no doubt believes Scotland to be."

"It wasn't an excuse, merely a statement of fact. I should love to visit Scotland with you."

Oh *God*, why had I said that? Just because I was mildly curious, it didn't mean I intended to do any such thing.

The answer was painfully obvious: because McBrae was still within hearing distance, and I didn't want him to think I was prejudiced against his country. Absurd, because he already knew I was. I expected, but unhappily accepted, his disdain—while at the same time, I appreciated his friendly winks. I didn't understand his kindness to me. Perhaps I never would.

"And that young footman," Mrs. Holloway said disapprovingly, "is one of them."

"One of what?" Papa carved himself a thick slice of ham.

"Brawny flirts. He winked at Lady Rosamund!"

I blinked. "Surely not." Thank heavens McBrae had now gathered some dishes and left the room. "He doesn't look particularly brawny, either."

"He's compactly built, but that doesn't mean he's lacking in strength." Mrs. Holloway spread goose liver paste on her bread. "However, if you're not offended by him, I have no reason to be."

"No, why would I be? Maybe what you saw was only a tic, but even if it was a wink, it did no harm."

"Are you sure you're your mother's daughter?" she quipped.

Papa laughed. "Perhaps you should put my Rosie and her mother in a play—after altering the names, needless to say."

Relieved at the change of subject, I asked, "You write plays, Mrs. Holloway?"

"Yes," she said shortly, and then, perhaps not wishing to sound rude, "I dabble."

"Come now, Mrs. H," Papa said. "Don't hide your light under a bushel."

Her brow furrowed, and at the same time, I heard approaching voices. "Perhaps Mrs. Holloway doesn't wish it to be known."

"Generally, yes, but you're entirely trustworthy…" He slewed around, to see the Colonel and Mrs. Wendell, followed by Sir Roderick and Cynthia. "Ah, perhaps not."

"Thank you," Mrs. Holloway said softly.

The newcomers seated themselves, and in the flurry of passing dishes back and forth, I took the opportunity to study Cynthia closely. She seemed much the same as the last time I'd seen her—tired and resigned. Sir Roderick, however, didn't glower at me, which perhaps reflected her influence on him. Or maybe it was only because Papa was there.

Conversation became general, on such tried-and-true subjects as the weather (coming down buckets and unlikely to stop anytime soon) and the beauties of the Lakes (when it wasn't pouring). I excused myself, rather glum about my lack of progress. McBrae had entrusted me with a job to do, and—

Heavens! How had such a reversal come to pass? How dare I see myself in a subservient role, as if McBrae were the master and I the servant! Such a notion contradicts all that keeps English society stable and orderly. Besides, I had decided what to do before he'd even suggested it, and I didn't quite accept his assumption that Mr. Powers was innocent. Baffled and appalled at myself, I made my way through the Great Hall to the massive staircase.

Not that McBrae was really a servant, I reminded myself. As the son of a Scottish laird, he was a gentleman of sorts. Nevertheless…!

Speak (or rather think) of the devil, and there he was—standing on a battered step stool in his shirtsleeves, removing one of the remaining trophies from the wall. And looking unexpectedly brawny, I must say. Although I have no interest in the marriage bed, I am not unappreciative of a powerful male form.

Quickly, I mounted the stairs, for regardless of my scattered thoughts, this was my chance to speak with him alone.

He lifted one of the trophies and set it down. There were patches of perspiration under his arms. "She's Umberto Fulsome," he said softly, adding after a second, "Mrs. Holloway, that is."

Belatedly, it sank in. "She writes those brilliant farces!" I saw why she didn't wish it known. The farces, which are performed in the intervals or after the plays, are scandalously bawdy.

I wasn't surprised that McBrae knew about her. As Corvus, he made a point of knowing a great deal that he shouldn't.

"I see. I'll not mention it to anyone." I lowered my voice even more. "Lancelot Lewis doesn't know about Corvus?"

He shook his head. "I appreciate your continued discretion."

"Of course," I murmured, relieved that he still trusted me. This situation—his lack of a coat and our low-voiced conversation—felt strangely intimate. I glanced about. "I have written down my observations about the various guests and their possible motives." I removed the pages from my reticule and held them out.

His brow furrowed, and suddenly I felt stupidly awkward, remembering my attempts only a few months earlier at solving a mystery concerning myself. "The last time I gave you a list it was utterly useless, so perhaps I shouldn't have bothered."

He snatched the pages. "The list wasn't useless. You weren't to know what was what." He looked as awkward as I felt at this discussion. "Sometimes it is impossible for one close to a problem to see what is plain to an outsider." He retrieved his coat from the floor and stuffed the folded pages in a pocket. "You must be more careful, my lady. Don't write anything down. What if the murderer saw this?"

"I was careful. I copied it in code. Now *you* must be the careful one."

"Code?" His eyes brightened with interest, but all at once he reassumed his role of footman, Scottish burr and all. "Mrs. Wendell begged that they be removed, my lady, for fear of another accident."

"What a pity," I said at my most supercilious. "I rather like such trophies." Which wasn't strictly true, for although stags' heads are magnificent to gaze upon, I always feel sorry for the poor beasts who die to decorate a wall. I put my nose in the air and glided away.

A throaty giggle greeted me as I headed toward the corridor to my bedchamber.

"Flirting with the footmen?" It was that ghastly Miss Ellis, with Mr. Powers following her like a faithful hound. Or perhaps a guard dog, ready to snap and snarl at the slightest provocation, although at the moment he seemed immersed in some happy daydream—of carnal pleasures with Miss Ellis, no doubt.

"Your reputation precedes you, Lady Rosamund," she tittered.

Allow me to explain. The unpleasant events of a few months earlier had begun with the body of a footman on the stairs. Corvus, who wasn't properly acquainted with me at the time, published a print suggesting that I, a scorned wife, had been spurned by the footman and pushed him to his death.

I fancy I handled that absurdity rather well, but by now I was fed up of such remarks. "My dear Miss Ellis," I said, "now that Mr. Fence is gone, what else can one do?"

Which was a horrid insult to footmen everywhere. I hoped McBrae knew I didn't mean it. In any event, it shocked Miss Ellis out of her pose of sophistication. She burst into raucous laughter. Mr. Powers winced, startled out of his daydream. There is something to be said for my mother's insistence on prim, ladylike titters, if the alternative sounds like the bray of a donkey.

She gazed past me at McBrae, her eyes alight with prurient interest. "Please don't push this one down the stairs. It would sadden the staff. The maids say he flirts with anything female, without the slightest discrimination."

Well! This was a new side of McBrae—and he accused Lancelot Lewis of being too flirtatious!

"How thoughtful of him," I replied. "No one feels left out, not even poor little me."

I returned to my chamber, pondering what little I had learned. I already knew Miranda disliked Fence—but enough to murder him? Mrs. Holloway also disliked him, but she was too old for such a man to seduce. She was Miss Gardner's godmother, but not particularly protective, for she 1) had brought the innocent girl to this den of iniquity and 2) seemed unalarmed by the prurient interest shown by both Powers and Bellevue. I knew nothing of Powers, but I doubted Bellevue, who prided himself on his wealth and ancestry, would marry a beautiful nobody. Perhaps, in theater circles, one's standards necessarily became lax.

As for Miss Gardner herself, if she hadn't been retrieving a book, why was she wandering the house, fully dressed, in the small hours of the morning? A tryst? I didn't like to think so.

In any event, it would have been difficult for a woman to get that huge stag's head off the wall. It was heavy and unwieldy, and she would have needed a ladder or a step stool like McBrae, or at the very least a chair. I didn't remember seeing any such item last night on the landing, and the chairs in the Great Hall were monstrous Elizabethan oak pieces which I doubted anyone ever used, unless as thrones in a play. It would take two burly footmen to carry one of those up the stairs.

So much for the women. However, Mr. Fence might easily have made any number of male enemies in theatrical circles.

At dinner that evening, the play-writing contest came up for discussion again.

"We must set the rules," Sir Alphonse said. "For one thing, each play must take no longer than a half hour to perform."

"Half an hour!" cried Mr. Bellevue. "That's nowhere near long enough for a life of Boudicca."

"Yes, it seems rather short, but do recall that each of us has to read all the entries," Sir Alphonse said.

"Most of which are likely to be tedious," Lancelot drawled. "Luckily for us, you'll only have time for Boudicca's tragic demise."

That evinced several chuckles. Mrs. Holloway's laughter was rightfully smug, for her farces are short and perfect.

"Considering we had a tragic demise in this very house only a few hours ago, you're rather lighthearted about death," Mr. Bellevue retorted.

"Nothing tragic about Fence," Colonel Wendell said. "Good riddance, if you want my opinion."

Various grunts and murmurs signified agreement. Which reminded me… What had the Colonel said to Mr. Fence last night? Something rude, I recalled… Ah, he'd told Fence that no one was interested in what he thought—and Fence's response had been brimful of mockery. Heavens, what was *that* about?

I was startled from my reverie by a soft Scottish voice beside me. "More salmon, my lady?"

McBrae was assisting the genuine footman with serving the guests. I wondered if I should ever become accustomed to dealing with him in his various roles.

"A small amount," I replied. He served me and moved on.

"Half an hour is just right." Mr. Powers turned the topic back to the play (and also, perhaps purposely, away from discussion of the murder). "It requires skill to bring a play to a satisfactory conclusion in such a short time."

A dig at his foe of yesterday; one couldn't help but appreciate that.

"Perhaps we could define the subject matter," Powers went on. "Mythology, perhaps, as it is the great interest of our host, as opposed to present-day politics or society."

Since Mrs. Holloway's farces center on just those topics, I wondered if Mr.

Powers knew and hoped she wouldn't enter the contest—as her sardonic expression seemed to say.

"Not everyone is interested in myths," my father said. "Better to choose a theme which can be treated in an infinite variety of ways."

"Carnal passion," Johnny Beaver said, to snorts of laughter. Was that all he thought about? I glanced at him. To my surprise he looked neither smug nor embarrassed, but slightly green. Too much wine, no doubt.

"Well then, fatal beauty." Miss Ellis primped. "They say Boudicca was beautiful."

I couldn't help but wonder if Tacitus, the Roman historian, had actually said this, or if her beauty was merely one of those qualities which are *de rigueur* in any heroine.

Miss Ellis sent a sly glance at Harold Bellevue. Unfortunately, he was gazing like a mooncalf at Miss Gardner, who shrank into herself. She had a lot to learn if she wanted to survive in the world of the theater.

"She was also spirited," Miss Ellis added nastily. "Lively and fearless."

"Quite right," Sir Alphonse said. "You would make a perfect warrior queen, Miss Ellis." God only knew what he saw in the chit.

"Jealousy," Miranda said tartly. "Rivalry. Betrayal."

"Plenty of that about," Sir Alphonse said cheerfully. "So many excellent themes to choose from."

"Unrequited love." My father cocked his head at me. "What say you, Rosie?"

This was rather fun. "How about blackmail?" I said.

Chapter Seven

She blushed when I winked at her. And she uses a code! Fortunately for what conscience I possess, I shall have little opportunity to decipher it. I would be unable to resist.

—From the diary of Corvus

Complete and utter silence fell. I gazed about me, mildly surprised. Miss Gardner had clapped a hand over her mouth, but everyone else seemed frozen in place. I spied Lancelot's raised brows and a trace of some unidentifiable emotion on McBrae's altered features. Belatedly, I realized what all this might mean. "That does seem to have hit the mark," I added brightly, and Colonel Wendell began to cough.

And cough and cough, half-rising from his chair. Mrs. Wendell patted him on the back. "Dearest, what's wrong?"

He was too busy coughing to answer. "He choked on his wine," I lied.

"'S right," he said, between gasps and coughs. "Exactly so."

He sat again, and a babble of relieved voices broke out.

"Why not true love?"

"Desperation."

"Madness."

"Mediocrity."

"Who would want to see a play about mediocrity?" Lance drawled. "I rather like Lady Rosamund's notion."

The frantic chink of cutlery on china plates met his remark. Meanwhile, despite the obvious implications of this conversation, I was dithering about the word *madness*. Who had suggested it? Mrs. Holloway.

I let out a sigh of relief. Mrs. H knew nothing about me. Her suggestion was a coincidence, nothing more, but it did raise a question: Would I be willing to commit murder if someone were blackmailing me?

Definitely not, but I had other ways of dealing with awkward problems, such as an influential father. And McBrae.

I didn't want to think about McBrae's protective instincts. Besides, he'd probably lost all respect for me by now. In fact, although his features were properly impassive, his eyes, as they met mine, held a warning.

About what? The gall of the man. Didn't we want to identify the murderer? Admittedly, I'd mentioned blackmail purely by chance, but the shocked reaction of too many people meant I'd hit the nail on the head. He should be pleased with me.

"Blackmail could apply to almost any theme," Lance said. "A secret passion, secret jealousy, secret rivalry, ouch!" He glared at McBrae, who was offering him parslied potatoes. "Clumsy oaf!"

"Beg pardon, sir." McBrae moved to the next guest.

Lance picked up where he'd left off. "Secret desperation, secret madness…"

"Secret mediocrity?" Papa said to roars, titters, and all-round relieved laughter.

Eventually they settled on, would you believe it, a *ménage à trois*! This was Lance's notion. I found myself possessed of an urge to strangle him.

No, not literally, but he was the most annoying man, the sort who pokes and prods at one's sore spot. I was tempted to throw something across the table at him, as I might have done to one of my teasing brothers when we were children.

"I shall wait with bated breath to see how Lady Rosamund turns *that* into a moral tale," he said, which made me all the more determined to do so. "One…of them…shall die!" he added in an eerie voice.

"Very poor taste, Lance," Sir Alphonse said. "Lady Rosamund is in mourning. Apologize at once."

Lance smirked but bowed his head, a hand to his heart. "So sorry, my lady. I couldn't resist."

"You're not the least bit sorry," I said. "I must think of an appropriate punishment." Yes, that was flirtatious, but it was expected of me. It provoked more merriment, for of course everyone had seen not only the recent print, but the one of some months ago in which I was portrayed birching Corvus's bare bottom.

The very idea! But McBrae scarcely knew me then, and at the time, he'd been attracted to me. Carnally, I mean. Yes, it all seems rather odd, doesn't it? I'd had no notion what that atrocious print signified until Cynthia explained it to me.

"I can't wait," Lance murmured appreciatively. An unpleasant expression flickered across McBrae's face. Disgust at me, no doubt, but how else was I to deal with such innuendo? I couldn't turn all starchy and insulted. That would have made this rather risqué set uncomfortable—or they simply wouldn't believe it. My response was in character, at least as people saw it.

Notoriety is such a bore.

I glanced down the table at Cynthia. Hopefully, with all the attention directed at me, no one would realize that not one-third, but two-thirds of the supposed ménage were here at Lewis Grange.

She gave no sign of discomfiture, but she must know that she didn't look much like her fashionable self. Her face was pale and puffy, and her golden hair was almost entirely hidden under a cap. She and Sir Roderick sat side by side near the foot of the table, where he and Miranda did their best to tempt her appetite. She seemed resigned, and…almost contented.

How disconcerting. Pregnancy had stripped away some of her composure, but her uneasiness of the past few months was largely gone. This was not the proper outcome of a moral tale. In my version—in which one person of the ménage would be Sir Roderick—he would pay dearly for his persecution of my closest friend.

I would have loved to retreat to my bedchamber, there to start on my little story—for that's what it would be, not a play. Let the playwrights compete; mine was a private sort of tale, one I didn't wish to expose to the world.

But if we were to unmask the murderer, I must get on with my task. The ladies removed to the drawing room—except Cynthia, who went early to bed—and when the gentlemen joined us, I agreed to play whist again. Miranda set up the tables, partnering me with Miss Gardner. "The poor child needs a kind-hearted partner," she whispered.

Fortunately, we were playing for chicken stakes against Colonel and Lady Wendell, but he seemed distracted, causing his wife to exclaim over and over that he was not at his best, whatever was he thinking, and so on, until he erupted and told her to leave him be. She subsided, as close to pouting as made no odds.

Despite his mediocre play, we lost, for Miss Gardner's was worse. When at last a tea tray appeared, I suggested we give our places to others.

She accepted with relief. "Thank you, my lady," she said when we were seated cozily on a sofa with recent numbers of *The Ladies' Monthly Museum*. She flipped immediately to a fashion illustration. "I'm sorry I played so poorly. I don't care for card games, but one has no choice."

I felt like saying, *I don't care for fashions*, but in the interest of detecting a murderer, needs must. "Believe me, I've had enough of the Wendells. Do they always carp at one another like that, or was he just not paying attention tonight?"

"I don't know them well enough to say," she said, which was proper and polite but got me nowhere. I hadn't seen the Wendells in several years, but I remembered her as a pleasantly chatty lady. Maybe she was anxious about her husband. Maybe Fence had been blackmailing the Colonel—but about what? He'd always seemed a bluff, harmless sort of man.

Miss Gardner flipped through a few more pages with scarcely more attention than she'd shown in the game. Was she worried about Mr. Powers? Why did she think he might have murdered Fence?

I was about to attempt a delicate probe on the subject when she closed the periodical with a sigh. "I wish I could retire to my room and write my play."

This was a surprise. "You intend to enter the contest?"

She flushed, then stuck out her chin. "Why shouldn't I? England has had many great female playwrights!"

"True, and I wish you the best of luck. How marvelous if you were to win, confounding all the men."

"Wouldn't that be wonderful? But I don't see how, when I know nothing about the theme they chose." She gnawed her lip. "This is frightfully forward of me, but…could you enlighten me a little?"

So that was what she'd been stewing about. Good Lord. No, I couldn't.

She flushed a pretty pink, which accentuated the pale perfection of her complexion. "I'm so sorry. I shouldn't have—"

"I'm not offended," I said, "and please don't apologize. It puts you at a disadvantage." To my mother, apologies are anathema, and to a great extent I agree, which is why I make most of my apologies silently—acknowledging my fault, but only to myself. Which is unfair, I suppose, but the daughter of an earl, et cetera…

(For some reason, I lose sight of my ancestral dignity when I'm speaking to McBrae. I have to bite my tongue not to apologize for every misstep. I made a promise to myself to think about why that was so, once this murder business was out of the way.)

"As for the ménage, that's nothing but a myth. My husband's relations with his mistress were carried on at her house. The three of us never shared a dwelling."

She blinked. "I must say, that sounds only slightly less dreadful to me."

"I daresay it does." I understood perfectly. If I'd been having carnal relations with Albert, I wouldn't have appreciated him trotting off to another woman almost every night.

Or perhaps I would have, if he'd been that insatiable. I suppressed a shudder.

"Weren't you jealous?" she asked.

"Not in the least. I was only too happy to share." Let her make what she would of that.

She brightened. "A play about that would certainly be different. No bitter rivalry, but instead some amusing sharing of confidences about the gentleman's…" She flushed again. "Although I haven't the slightest notion about that, either." She paused. "Despite anything Mr. Fence may have said."

She gave me a desperately inquiring look. The last thing I wanted was to repeat his vile remarks. On the other hand, it might invite more confidences.

"I'm so sorry," she blurted before I could respond. "I shouldn't ask, but no one else will tell me what he said. You seem unafraid to speak your mind." A contemplative pause. "Perhaps that comes of being an earl's daughter. You can say and do precisely what you like, and no one dares criticize you."

I suppressed a snort at this absurdity. "They draw caricatures of me instead."

"I'm sure that's horrid," she said. "I'm *frightfully* sorry."

"Didn't I tell you not to apologize? I found the caricatures rather amusing."

"How astonishing." Visibly, she gathered her courage again. "Please tell me. Did Mr. Fence say anything about me when you were at dinner last night?"

"He implied that Mr. Powers was visiting you in your bedchamber."

She whimpered. "I feared as much."

"Nobody believed it, I assure you, except perhaps Mr. Bellevue, because he's jealous."

"I'm not at all interested in Mr. Bellevue, and Geoff, Mr. Powers, that is… He's my friend, nothing more, and everyone knows he's madly in love with Miss Ellis."

Across the room, Miss Ellis was playing whist with three gentlemen—Powers, Beaver, and Bellevue—and flirting with all of them at once. Mr. Bellevue kept glancing our way.

"She's jealous of you," I said. "You're very beautiful—far more so than she."

She grimaced. "Being beautiful is a dratted nuisance. I wish Mr. Bellevue were enamored of her. She can have him, and welcome."

"But not Mr. Powers?"

"How he can be such an idiot? Can't he see she's toying with him?" For a mere friend of the man, she was certainly up in arms—and Powers had picked a fight with Bellevue over her. Something was amiss, but what?

"And with every other male in the house," she added. "She wants to get Sir

Alphonse in her toils, too."

"Why? He's helping her get roles in London. Isn't that enough?"

"Not for her," Miss Gardner said. "She's perfect for a character in a play—but not about a *ménage à trois*. No other woman would put up with her."

A masculine voice behind us said, "Two men might."

I ground my teeth. The poor girl beside me blushed to the tips of her ears. Lancelot Lewis chuckled and came around the end of the sofa.

I huffed. "Is that *all* you men ever think about?" Across the room, McBrae set a used cup on the tea tray with a clatter. His eyes blazed for the briefest instant, as if he were furious with me, before he bent to his work again.

Well! I sniffed imperiously. He would have to learn to control his emotions if he wished to play a convincing servant. My mother, and many like her, would dismiss a footman whose expression did not remain properly impassive.

Lance's grin was decidedly less charming when so liberally laced with lust. "When in the presence of beautiful women, what else is there?"

"It's frightfully unkind of you to embarrass this innocent girl," I managed, still wondering at McBrae. What had I done to merit that glare? He had agreed that I should mine information from the ladies.

Lance chuckled. "My apologies, Miss Gardner, but we're a tawdry bunch here."

Yes, and I had begun to feel tawdry by association. I didn't like it, but at least half of my reputation was McBrae's fault. To Hades with him.

"Perhaps you can put Mr. Lewis' vulgar suggestion to good use," I said. "How about a play about a woman who is being pursued by two men, one a legitimate suitor and the other a masked interloper?"

"About whom she has erotic fantasies," Lance interposed.

"Hush," I said, but it was a good suggestion. "She's caught between the two of them, wanting both the respectable suitor and the dashing seducer. Then the masked man suggests they all get into bed together."

Miss Gardner made an unhappy mew.

Lance crowed. "Now who's embarrassing her?"

"Wait till I finish," I said, but suddenly McBrae filled my vision. He'd come up on soft feet to gather our cups. "More tea, ladies?"

"No, thank you," Miss Gardner said. I merely shook my head and glowered at him. Did he think I was enjoying this folly?

Actually, I *was* rather enjoying it. I like making up stories. "But she's not as foolish as she seems, and before she can do anything so utterly stupid as agree, she realizes that her two paramours are one and the same man. The suitor was testing her moral fiber."

"That dastard!" At last, Miss Gardner got into the spirit of things. "She sends him to the rightabout and marries a man who trusts her from the start."

Lance made a face. "Too obvious. Why not end it with a punishment scene? She gives him a good birching. Everyone will love that."

"Are you volunteering for the part?" I snapped. I'd had enough for now of both Lance's innuendo and McBrae's whatever it was. Maybe he was a rigid Calvinist and found this conversation morally unacceptable.

No, impossible. His caricatures overflowed with immoral allusions. He was no prude.

Colonel and Mrs. Wendell rose from the card table and headed for the Great Hall—and their bedchamber, I assumed. Excellent; here was something useful for me to do. I stood as well, using one of the time-honored excuses for escaping unpleasant company. "I believe I shall retire, as my head is beginning to ache. Write it all down, Miss Gardner, and don't let Mr. Lewis's vulgar notions prevent you from ending it as you choose."

I hurried away and reached the foot of the staircase soon after the Wendells. I paused, pretending to adjust my shoe.

McBrae appeared beside me, proffering an empty lemonade glass, no expression at all on his counterfeit face. "This might prove useful." Before I could say a word, he was gone again.

I supposed that meant he was annoyed but still willing to accept my assistance. How had he known what I intended to do? Perhaps eavesdropping at closed doors was a common practice for Corvus.

Not for me—let me make that perfectly clear. However, as the youngest child, often excluded from the activities of my elders, I had done so often.

At the head of the stairs I paused again, for my bedchamber wasn't far down the corridor. I mustn't appear to follow the elderly couple.

"Whatever is wrong, Owen?" Mrs. Wendell said. "You haven't been yourself all day."

The Colonel muttered something.

"Don't tell me it's nothing. After thirty-two years of marriage, I know very well when you're upset."

I followed them as quickly as I dared, thankful for the candles in sconces on the wall. Mrs. Wendell scolded and pleaded while the Colonel growled at her repeatedly to hush. They passed the broom closet and Cynthia and Sir Roderick's room, and turned the corner at the end.

I hastened after them, ears a-prick.

"Whatever it is, don't bottle it up," Mrs. Wendell said. "I know it has something to do with that man Fence, because—"

"Shut your damned mouth!" he roared. "Do you want to get me hanged?"

She shrieked. A door slammed just as I reached the corner. Fortunately, there were only three doors to choose from, left, right, and straight ahead.

Which door went to the service stairs? I fancied it was the middle one, but I hadn't paid attention when Miranda brought me this way last night.

Luckily for me, Mrs. Wendell burst into horrified sobs. "Wendell, what have you done? Did you—did you..." Her voice dropped too low for me to hear. I crept closer and put the lemonade glass against the door on the left.

"What? No, of course I didn't murder him," the Colonel said.

"Then why are you so upset? It *does* have to do with Mr. Fence, doesn't it? Please don't deny it."

"Oh, for God's sake!" A pause. "I had a—a sort of run-in with Fence years ago in India. Nothing important, but if it got out, people might think I had good reason to kill him."

"That's absurd! You would never kill anyone."

"One never knows what the coroner and jury will decide. Best not to give them any ammunition."

"But Sir Alphonse said it was an *accident*." Her voice quavered. "Do you mean it wasn't an accident at all?"

"I mean nothing of the sort. Stop blubbering. Nothing dreadful will happen if you keep your mouth shut and behave as usual."

"But, Owen…"

"Damn you, stop whimpering and go to bed. I'm going down for a drink."

At the sound of his footsteps, I whisked around the corner, but I would never reach my bedchamber in time to avoid being seen. I must appear to be in the corridor for an innocent purpose—which, fortunately, was right to hand. I had come to see how my dearest friend was doing.

I put my ear to Cynthia's door. Complete silence, so I tapped softly and opened it—to find Cynthia in a passionate embrace with Sir Roderick!

I gasped. They broke apart, and Sir Roderick descended upon me in a fury. "What the devil are you doing here?"

Chapter Eight

She is an excellent conspirator with a quick and clever mind. How can I not adore her?

—From the diary of Corvus

I couldn't find my tongue. Sir Roderick is tall and broad, and his expression was menacing. "Stay away from my wife," he snarled.

That damnable lie restored my courage. "She is not—"

He grabbed my arm and dragged me through the doorway. Out of the corner of my eye, I spied Colonel Wendell coming around the corner and decided not to struggle.

Sir Roderick shut the door, but before I could manage a wrathful, "Unhand me, you cur!" he let me go. I set the lemonade glass down on a table, rubbing my arm indignantly, and feigned indifference, when I was actually rather frightened. I didn't think he would strike me, particularly not with Cynthia there, but my heart pounded against my ribs nonetheless.

He breathed down his nose like an angry bull. "How dare you burst into our private chamber?" His gaze lit on the glass, and he loomed over me. "Were you *listening at the door?*"

I backed away. "Not at all," I retorted, but my voice trembled—how mortifying. Thanks to my mother's rigid tutoring, I summoned haughty indignation, an excellent method of recovering self-control. "How dare you suggest that I would stoop so low as to *eavesdrop?* And I didn't *burst* in. I wanted to speak with Cynthia. I thought you were still downstairs."

"You came to make trouble," he growled. "You've made trouble from the start, and your husband's dead now, but you just won't let go, will you?"

"I—"

It was no use trying to defend myself. Sir Roderick *wanted* to rant. He had always blamed me for not luring my husband away from Cynthia, which was unfair, but he didn't know the true circumstances. Now he lambasted me for trying to keep her safe from his odious advances, which she'd been refusing for years.

Judging by the embrace I had just witnessed, his advances weren't so odious anymore.

I glanced at Cynthia, who mouthed, "Sorry!" but she didn't try to defend me. That hurt a little, but protesting my innocence and good intentions wouldn't have done any good, and we both knew it. "Talk later," she mouthed.

Sir Roderick tore my character to shreds. I shan't repeat his words here. Suffice it to say he completely discarded all pretense of gentility.

Fortunately, I don't care what he thinks of me, but it is nevertheless unsettling to be the object of hatred. Loath as I am to admit it, my mother's tutelage stood me in good stead. I found myself repeating two of her dictums over and over in my mind: *A true aristocrat maintains an attitude of superb indifference. A descendant of the House of Medway must never give way to fear.*

At last he wound down. "…If it weren't for you, she would have become my wife years ago."

This was nonsense. Cynthia had remained my husband's mistress to *avoid* Sir Roderick. However, I said nothing, merely sighing as if I were remaining only to humor him.

He sneered. "I have no choice but to mention this unforgivable intrusion to Lord Medway. I hope he takes a switch to you."

"No fear of that," I retorted, goaded into speech. "My father isn't a bully like *you*."

I picked up the lemonade glass, turned on my heel, and left, hoping he didn't realize that his Parthian shot had hit home. (I hoped my return shot had done so.) Papa wouldn't beat me, but he would be dismayed at my seeming disregard of his instructions. I couldn't explain that I'd been hiding from the Colonel after eavesdropping on him and his wife. What was I do to?

I would have to say I had come to ask Cynthia how she was doing, assuming Sir Roderick was still downstairs—and hope Papa couldn't tell I was lying. How horrid, for 1) I prefer to be truthful with my father, 2) I was already keeping far too much from him, and 3) what if he believed Sir Roderick's version? My father's regard is worth more than anything in the world to me.

Glumly, I made my way to my bedchamber, where I found Mary Jane waiting for me. "Oh, my lady, I was so worried! I was told you had a headache." She indicated a steaming tisane on the dressing table. Judging by the odor, I wasn't going to like it. "But when I came upstairs, you were nowhere to be found."

"Who told you I had a headache? I didn't ask to have you summoned."

"It was Mr. Lewis' man, the one who calls himself Mac."

That explained it. How thoughtful of McBrae, but unexpected, for 1) he was out of charity with me, and 2) hadn't he realized that the headache was an excuse to follow the Wendells?

"I ask you, what sort of name is Mac?" Mary Jane began swiftly to undo the hooks on my gown. "I don't even know if it's a surname or a Christian name."

"Why not ask him?"

"That dreadful Scottish flirt? Called me Mary Jane, bold as brass, he did! Mrs. Smithson to *you*, I told him. I don't know why Mr. Lewis puts up with his antics."

I removed the only ornament I wore during the early months of mourning, a gold cross on a chain. It conveyed the right sort of message, according to Mary Jane—not that it had the appropriately daunting effect on Lancelot.

"Like master, like man," I said. "Mr. Lewis is just as bad." Except that I could easily dismiss Lancelot's flirtatiousness as irrelevant, but the news that McBrae flirted with the help annoyed me for no apparent reason. I certainly didn't wish to discuss it, so I changed the subject.

"It's nothing but a headache. Why were you worried?" I asked.

"In this house of sin, how could I not fear for your virtue? Not to mention stags' heads falling off the walls wherever you turn."

"Mac took the other two down before they had a chance to fall," I said.

"He escorted me here and told me not to worry, that he would see to your safety." Pause. "Raise your arms, please, my lady." She removed my gown and swiftly untied my laces. "As if the word of a rascally Scot would reassure *me*."

"I'm sure he meant well," I said into the fabric of the nightdress she had tossed over my head.

"Humph." She shook out the folds of my gown and laid it over a chair. "I informed him that you had doubtless gone down the passageway to enquire after Lady Frockmartin's health. He said he would ascertain if you were indeed there."

It took me a second to realize whom she meant—for I did *not* think of Cynthia as Sir Roderick's wife....

Good God. Surely not. What if McBrae had overheard that ghastly rant?

"Yes, that's where I was." To my horror, my voice shook.

"What is wrong, my lady?"

I managed to blurt, "My head aches quite *dreadfully*." In truth, I was well-nigh faint with chagrin. First that dreadful scowl from McBrae when I was doing my best to get information, and now this!

"My poor dear. Lady Frockmartin shouldn't have kept you when you're so ill. I should have come to fetch you instead of sending Mac."

"It's only a headache, Mary Jane. I got here perfectly well without an escort."

"Mac didn't wait?"

"No, I didn't see him." I shivered, thinking, *unless he includes invisibility in his accomplishments.* What nonsense one imagines when overset.

She shook her head. "So much for protecting you." She plumped up the pillows and settled me in bed with a cup of the tisane, then set about tidying the room.

Usually, I avoid feeling sorry for myself, but in one blow I had lost both Cynthia and McBrae. Not that McBrae had ever been more than an acquaintance, but Cynthia was my closest friend. If she married Sir Roderick, he would forbid her from associating with me. We would be reduced to polite nods in public. Tears sprang to my eyes, and hurriedly I gulped some of the tisane. As I suspected, it contained valerian, which tastes even worse than it smells.

"Horrid stuff," I griped. "It never does the least good."

"Now, now, my lady, it's just what you need. Nerves are what's ailing you, and no wonder. Finding dead men is more than enough to make a body ill."

No, losing one's best friend is. But whenever Mary Jane starts talking of nerves, I know she's thinking about my peculiarity. "Nonsense," I grumbled. "*I* wasn't the one who screamed and ran sobbing up the stairs."

She tsked. "No, but you've been uneasy ever since, my lady, and you were not yourself after you found that footman on the stairs. Enduring those disgusting caricatures, and then becoming so pale and wan…"

"Enough!" I said. "It's bad enough having a headache without you scolding me."

At last she curtsied and left. She means well, but she doesn't know what really went on after I found the dead footman. No one does, except McBrae, and he—

I refused to think about him. Just because he despised me even more by now, it didn't mean I should shirk my responsibility to seek out motives for murder.

I got out my diary and recorded the conversation between the Wendells. Had the Colonel done something illegal or unsavory whilst in India? He didn't seem the sort.

Miss Gardner's possible motive was malicious gossip on the part of Fence, but that seemed insufficient for so dreadful a crime. Not only that, she'd been truly aghast at finding the corpse. Perhaps she still feared that Mr. Powers was guilty—but would he kill Fence to stop him from gossiping? It wasn't enough of a motive. Jealousy seemed more likely, or fear that Fence would ravish Miss Gardner.

But what about the ambiguity of her relationship with Powers? Was he merely a friend (close enough to use Christian names), as she claimed? The obvious alternative was that she loved him, but if he didn't love her back, he had even less motive to kill for her sake—or to pick a fight over her, for that matter. Also, she'd seemed more indignant than jealous about his infatuation with Miss Ellis.

I was getting nowhere, so I put my diary under my pillow, blew out the candle, and lay down. Sleep refused to come—with good reason! I should tear the latest page from my diary and record it in code. No, I was too tired. Well then, I should at least hide the page somewhere safe.

No, I told myself. It was perfectly safe in the diary until morning. Nevertheless, I stupidly felt under my pillow to verify that my diary was still there.

I stared into the darkness, listening to the rain, whilst my mind went in circles, worrying about Cynthia, fretting about my father, and purposely not thinking about McBrae.

There was nothing for it but to go to the kitchen again for a cup of milk. Fortunately, thanks to Miranda the previous night, I knew how to get there.

I crept into the passageway, then remembered my diary and returned to my room. I should hide it immediately—or at least the page on which I had just written. It's more than my life is worth to let anyone read my true thoughts, so my diary is tedious in the extreme—filled with innocuous entries about places visited, people met, birds sighted, gardens admired, et cetera.

But where to hide it? I hadn't the time to search for loose boards, and...

No! I told myself sternly. I would be gone five minutes. It was the middle of the night, so no servants would enter my room. I slipped the diary under the coverlet and left.

And returned to check. To check what, you ask? That I had indeed put the diary under the coverlet. So yes, perhaps I was uneasy, as Mary Jane suggested. (I'm not above considering the opinion of my maid, although frequently I dismiss it. I hope and pray she doesn't realize that my peculiarity tends to become worse at times of uneasiness.)

I checked it again, twice—it was precisely where I'd put it, needless to say—and then forced myself to leave. I tiptoed along the passageway, not for fear of Sir Roderick, who could go straight to the devil as far as I was concerned, but so as not to disturb anyone's sleep. Around the corner, I paused at the door to the left, in case the Wendells were arguing again, but no such luck. I listened at the other two doors—silence. Slowly and silently, I tried the one on the right, which proved to be a lumber room.

That left the door in the middle. The stairs were cloaked in gloom, and my little candle didn't give much light. I gripped the baluster and tiptoed carefully down. It was frightfully dark…and then, as I reached the first landing, it wasn't. A dim light shone from below.

"Let me be! I didn't touch the girl. Came to apologize." A man's voice, somewhat familiar, drawled from the effect of drink. "I wanted him dead, y'know."

"Come now, Beaver." That was Harold Bellevue's proud tones. "You followed that bastard about like a puppy."

"A ruse," Johnny Beaver said. "Clever one, too. Everyone thought I admired him, but I hated him."

"If that's true, it would be wise not to say so." That was Lance. "Let's bundle you off to bed before someone hears you."

I realized where they were—in the passageway leading from the foot of the stairs to the kitchen in one direction and the Great Hall in the other. If they meant to bring him up these stairs, I should retreat in a hurry. Instead, I listened.

"Believe in speaking the truth," Beaver said. "Duty of playwrights, y'know."

"Stuff and nonsense," said Bellevue. "Plays can be utter bollocks, as long as they have profound meaning. Think I know the first thing about the real Boudicca? No one does, so I'll make up her life from start to finish."

"In blank verse," Lance said dryly.

"Yes," retorted Bellevue, "in blank verse, like the Bard himself. A tried and true poetic form, and—"

"Now that he's dead, I can say what I like," Beaver said. "Wish I'd been the one to kill him. Needed satisfaction, y'see."

"What, he insulted your writing?" Lance laughed. "Get used to it, Beaver."

"One never does," Bellevue said mournfully, in unexpected support for his fellow playwright. "The utter lack of appreciation is torment. However, what else can one expect from small minds? One must persevere." I suspected he had drunk a little too much as well.

"My play will be about the murder," Beaver said.

"Heaven preserve us from idiots," Lance said. "There was no murder. It was an accident. A fortunate one, no doubt, but an accident all the same."

"A lucky one," Bellevue said. "Beaver's foxed."

"So are you," Lance said, "but not too foxed to help get this fool upstairs. Come on, Mac."

I jerked back as if stung. I did not want to see McBrae just now. Or anyone, for that matter.

"I'll light the way," Lance said. His voice was closer, and I retreated hurriedly up several stairs.

A few thuds spoke of an attempt to get Beaver moving. "Not that way, sir," Mac said. "Too steep; one misstep and we'll all break our necks. Best to take the main staircase."

"Good thought," Lance said. "Or…perhaps we should lay him out in the Great Hall with a stag's head atop him, like another corpse."

A feminine squeak greeted this suggestion. "No, Mr. Lance, you mustn't!"

"I took the other trophies down, sir," Mac said. "They're in the cellar."

"Pity," Lance said. "You take his left, Bellevue, and Mac will take the right. As for you, girl, go back to sleep and keep your mouth shut. This man is drunk and talking nonsense."

"I won't say a word, Mr. Lance, sir. Upon my honor, I swear."

"I daresay, but if I hear that it's got about, it'll be the worse for you."

"She won't gossip about it, sir." McBrae took his typical stance in favor of the lower classes, but I wondered if he was thinking the same as I—that Harold Bellevue was far more likely to talk. If he had been blackmailed by Fence (for what reason I had no idea), he would be eager to shift the suspicion elsewhere, whether or not he'd killed the man.

Footsteps receded into the distance. I waited until the light vanished and ventured down.

I opened the kitchen door, and a face loomed up. I gasped, and the maid yelped. She clapped a hand to her ample breast. "Oh, miss, I mean my lady. You gave me such a start."

I moved past her into the kitchen. "I should like a cup of milk."

"My lady, you should have rung for me. It's not safe to wander about at night."

"Why not? You mustn't believe this foolish talk of murder."

"No, my lady," she said obediently. Being a servant and therefore bereft of a rational mind, she would believe any tale she was told, the more frightening the better. (The fact that murder had indeed been committed was irrelevant.) She lit a candle and disappeared into the pantry.

A pallet lay by the hearth, a rumpled blanket atop it. "Surely you don't sleep here?" I asked when she returned. There had been no maid in the kitchen last night.

"I walk home most nights, my lady, but it's two miles, so Mrs. Alderthwaite let me stay because of the weather. If I'd known Mr. Beaver would come in here, I'd have gone, rain or no rain. Shall I warm the milk for you, my lady?"

"If it's not too much trouble." Such courtesies make servants feel they have a choice, when of course they do not. However, it obliges one to reward them suitably.

"Won't take but a minute. The stove is still warm." She poured the milk into a pan, opened the stove, and ran it back and forth over the coals.

Why not try for more gossip? "Mr. Beaver tried to take advantage of you?"

"Not this time, my lady. He said he'd come to apologize for trying it on before, but you can't trust a drunken man."

"I hear Mr. Fence was even worse."

"Aye, he was always lurking about, trying to paw us. Mrs. Tyne quarreled with the master something dreadful when she heard Fence was coming. 'Don't you know what he's like in the theater?' she says. "Chases every skirt in sight. I won't have it. We'll have to lock him up at night.'"

"Lock up a guest?" I said. "That seems a rather extreme measure."

"That's what the master said. 'He's not a prisoner,' he says, and Mrs. Tyne says, 'He should be. I'll warn him,' and warn him she did." The girl giggled.

"You don't want never to get on the wrong side of Mrs. Tyne. My mum don't like me working in an immoral household, but Mrs. Tyne is ever such a good mistress."

"A good hostess, too," I said.

"She won't let none of the men bother us." The girl paused in her back and forth motion of the pot. "Though if that new man of Mr. Lance's were to want me, I'd be hard put to say no. Ever so kind, he is." She sighed.

This was true with regard to servants (for his caricatures were notoriously unkind to the beau monde). McBrae knew this girl couldn't resist a gossip, and yet he'd stood up for her. "And flirtatious, I hear."

"Aye, but 'tis nowt but funning. He's faithful to his lady love, he says. Can't even spare a kiss for another woman."

This was sheer nonsense, for McBrae had once kissed me. Still, I couldn't resist a chance to learn more about him. "He loves a girl in Scotland?"

"I reckon so." She withdrew the pot from the coals and poured me a cup of steaming milk. "Shall I carry it up for you, my lady?"

I am quite adept at climbing stairs with various encumbrances, but she was hoping for a sixpence. "Yes, please. Tell me your name."

"Lil," she said. "Short for Liliana, but nobody calls me that."

When we reached my bedchamber, I gave her a shilling, at which her face lit up with delight. I wished I could be so easily pleased. I was feeling rather melancholy about losing my best friend. I went to the window and opened it, drinking my milk while listening to the soothing sound of the rain.

Ah, well. I do my best to banish melancholia, as it accomplishes nothing. (My mother forbids it utterly.) I would pass what information I had to McBrae tomorrow. He disdained me, so he wouldn't be surprised at how little I had done.

I drew back the covers to get into bed.

My diary wasn't there!

Chapter Nine

I wish she wouldn't leave her bedchamber at night. It's not safe.

—From the diary of Corvus

Frantically, I flung the covers wider, and there it was—but *not* where I had left it. I knew precisely where it had been, for I had checked three times. (Evidently, there are some advantages to my peculiarity.) It was farther from the edge of the mattress, and a little closer to the foot of the bed, too.

Someone had been in my bedchamber whilst I was gone.

Someone had seen my diary.

The murderer? I flipped through the pages. The one on which I had written my notes only a short while ago was still there, but that didn't make me feel safe. He would have had no reason to take it. It gave him valuable information—that I knew Fence's death was no accident—whilst I remained unaware of who he was and whether he'd actually read what I'd written.

A descendant of the House of Medway must never give way to fear. All very well to say, but I trembled as I lit a branch of candles. I shook out the sheets and coverlet. When one has brothers, one learns not to panic when finding a frog in one's bed. However, an adder would be a handy way for a murderer to rid himself of an inconvenient someone.

Next, I searched the room. No one lurked behind the curtains, under the dressing table (which would be a tight fit for anyone but a child), or under the bed. I was alone, but that didn't make me feel safe either.

There was no key in the door, so I piled various items against it—a chair, a valise, a bandbox, and three books. If someone tried to open the door, the tower would topple, alerting me.

On the other hand, if Mary Jane came in to wake me—which she might, if she was worried about my health, or if I slept late—she would fear that my peculiarity had gained control of me again. I am terrified of being thought insane—even more so than of chance murderers returning to finish me off in the middle of the night.

Needless to say, I didn't get much sleep. I woke hourly. At some point during the night, I tore the page from my diary and put it in my reticule, so Mary Jane wouldn't see me do it and wonder why. When at last I heard the sounds of servants stirring, I dismantled the tower and fell properly asleep. It felt like I'd barely dropped off when Mary Jane bustled in.

"Before you start fussing about nothing," I said, "The headache's gone. I'm fine."

She took offense immediately—but that didn't stop her from sniffing when she saw the cup that had held the milk. She didn't ask when or where I'd got it, and I didn't offer to explain. Not that she couldn't guess perfectly well for herself, since at home I often go to the kitchen for milk in the middle of the night, but I let her wonder if perhaps I'd rung for someone who wouldn't fuss over me.

The advantage of having offended my maid was that she didn't comment on my appearance. After one glance, I avoided the looking-glass, too. Two nights without enough sleep, a murder, a horrendous rant, and an intruder in my bedchamber had all taken their toll, but I refused to go to breakfast looking the picture of woe, for that would give Sir Roderick the satisfaction of thinking he had upset me.

What I needed was fresh air and exercise. I opened the window. The rain had ceased for now, but dark clouds hovered, and thunder rumbled not far away.

"The grey walking dress," I said, "and quickly."

"But, my lady," Mary Jane began, and then wisely refrained from objecting.

From then on, she worked efficiently and in blessed silence. Seven minutes later I was dressed, gloved, booted and bonneted. Ready to go. I picked up my reticule—

Damnation! Strong language, yes, but my mania had struck suddenly—and unsurprisingly, I admit, for it tends to rear its ghastly head when I'm worried or afraid, and now I was exhausted as well.

I shooed Mary Jane from the room and began frantically to check and recheck my reticule. For what, you may ask? Mostly for the paper on which I had written my notes last night. The reticule didn't contain much else—a handkerchief, hair pins and a few coins; one never knows when one will come across a beggar. I counted the coins and added more—which was foolish, as I wouldn't give a beggar more than a penny and quite possibly less, depending on his or her story—and then counted them again. And unfolded and refolded, unfolded and refolded again the page with my notes.

At last I got ahold of myself, pulled the drawstring of my reticule firmly shut, and hurried down the stairs to the Great Hall. Luckily, no one was about, although cheerful voices drifted from the dining room. I let myself out the front door and strode briskly downhill, following the path Miss Gardner had taken in the opposite direction on the night we arrived. I passed the fork that led to the ice house (refusing to think about its ghastly inhabitant), crossed the drive, and arrived at the lake.

Usually, water calms me. I stood on the shore, breathing in the fresh, moist air. Ducks dipped for food and squabbled in the reeds. Lapwings circled and called, and a curlew picked amongst the shingle with its long, curved beak. It was so very tranquil by the water. So quiet and solitary and out of view from the house—

Perfect for a murder. I whirled. Not five yards behind me stood McBrae.

I gasped, swaying, and he leapt forward to steady me. My heart thudded violently, but his hands were warm and strong. I closed my eyes and a let out a long breath of relief.

"Lady Rosamund?"

"I'm well. You startled me." I opened my eyes, and he released me.

He stepped back and bent to pick up an umbrella, which he must have dropped when he grasped me. "I beg your pardon. I wished to speak privately, but you appeared so peaceful here by the shore that I hesitated to disturb you."

I made a tiny sound of dissent. Peaceful? How I wished I were.

Momentarily, I'd forgotten about Sir Roderick's scold, but now it all returned. Why was there such concern in McBrae's gaze? If he'd heard it, he should despise me.

"Evidently, appearances can be deceiving," he said, with a twist of a smile. "If you're fretting over what Sir Roderick said last night, don't."

"I'm not," I retorted. "He has loathed me for years. I couldn't care less what he thinks of me." Now, another complication occurred to me. "Please don't tell anyone that his so-called wife is really Lady Benson."

"I shan't, lassie. Sir Roderick's not such a bad fellow. A man in love may be forgiven for losing his temper."

Indignation surged within me. "In *love*? He doesn't love her. He's nothing but a bully. Lady Benson refused to read or reply to his letters, so he came here to force her to talk to him. To force her to share his *bedchamber*." Between anger and mortification at discussing such a subject, I began to pace. "Do you know how difficult it will be for her to shake him off, to claim that she isn't his wife, that the baby isn't his child? Meanwhile, my father is aiding and abetting this travesty."

"I doubt Lord Medway will continue to aid Sir Roderick if he feels Lady Benson does not wish for the match—"

I interrupted. "So he says, but how can he *know*?"

"—But I believe, deep down, that she does wish it."

Another typical man, thinking he knows everything.

"That makes no sense at all. She has avoided him for years." Oh, how I wished I could explain, but that was impossible—and yet I wanted, however unworthily, to exonerate myself. "She wasn't obliged to remain as my husband's mistress. She *chose* to." For a horrid second, I wondered if she'd done it because of her arrangement with me, but no. She'd become Albert's mistress months before our marriage, and I had always known there was a risk they might part someday. I'd hoped he would simply find someone else to satisfy his animal urges.

"There might be any number of reasons, some tragic, some amusing…" McBrae cocked his head, no doubt regretting his earlier promise not to mock her. "You believe her liaison with your husband was an excuse to avoid marrying Sir Roderick…" He didn't wait for me to confirm this statement. "I wonder how long they have known one another, and what her life was like with Lord Benson."

All I knew was that she'd married Lord Benson and gone with him to India, where he had died some years later. She had returned to England a widow, but she'd never spoken of the past, and I didn't ask. Unlike Corvus, I believe in allowing people their privacy. McBrae's blatant nosiness made me determined to avoid this subject.

"Sir Roderick intends to take care of her and his child, and one cannot help but honor him for it," he said.

"*His* child?"

Again, that twist of a smile. "It's almost certainly his."

I stopped pacing to stare. "You mean—she was unfaithful to my husband?"

"Indeed, she was." I didn't ask how he knew. Corvus made a point of nosing out scandal. It must be easy to do when one can alter one's features and accent, one's stance and manner, one's very class. No one would have taken him for a footman now, clothed as he was in confidence and authority. "Even if I didn't know that for certain, consider the fact that she didn't fall pregnant during the years with Mr. Phipps, and nor did you."

I felt myself reddening. I hoped he took it for chagrin at my supposed inability to bear children. The real reason was far more embarrassing.

"But she did so after succumbing to Sir Roderick," he went on. "It stands to reason that the fault was with Mr. Phipps."

"She didn't fall pregnant with Lord Benson, either. She thought she was barren."

"True, and that is a mystery to which I don't have the answer. Perhaps she knows and will explain it to you someday."

"Not likely," I muttered. "Sir Roderick will forbid her to associate with me."

McBrae shook his head. "No, he loves her too much to deny her your friendship. I expect she gave him a good scold last night after you left." He paused. "However, I suggest that you avoid trying to speak with her for now."

"I wasn't," I protested. "I didn't intend to go there at all. When I was eavesdropping on Colonel and Mrs. Wendell, the Colonel suddenly decided to return downstairs, and I had to find someplace to hide in a hurry. If I'd known Sir Roderick was there, I would never, ever have opened their door." I shuddered with mortification at the memory. "They were embracing."

"Awkward." He chuckled. "It explains his fit of temper."

"Yes, I suppose." How kind of McBrae to make light of it. Why was he so easy to speak to? So blessedly safe? He shouldn't be safe company. He was an avowed seeker of gossip who made a mockery of the cream of society, to which I belonged.

A gust of wind arose, and a few fitful drops of rain presaged another downpour. Time to go back to the house—and yet I wished I needn't. I would far rather stand there on the shore with McBrae.

He put up the umbrella and held it over my head. "Did your eavesdropping produce any results?"

I dug into my reticule and passed him the paper. "This is what little I have, not only about them but about Miss Gardner and Mr. Powers."

"What did you think of Beaver's maundering last night?"

How had he known I was on the stairs? "I am inclined to believe him, but I should like to know *why* he hated Fence."

"I suspect Bellevue hated him, too, although he hides it well." A tiny smile curled his lips. He enjoyed this process of investigation.

I wasn't sure whether I did. I certainly felt obliged to continue, in the interest of justice. Meanwhile, a question nagged at me, but how to ask it without seeming vulgarly inquisitive?

"It was kind of you to vouch for the maid, Lil—who could not hold her tongue if you paid her to."

He shrugged. "No, but she means well."

I couldn't resist probing. "She has quite a *tendre* for you."

"She wouldn't if she knew my flirting is a means to get information. None of them know what I'm really like."

Implying that I did know, which was nonsense. I knew next to nothing, whilst he always seemed to know everything.

Fine, but I had something to say that he *didn't* know.

"I couldn't sleep, so I went to the kitchen for a cup of milk. When I returned to my bedchamber, I realized that someone had been there in my absence."

"What?" He rapped the word out. "The devil you say."

I explained that I had concealed my diary. "It seemed a foolish precaution at the time. I knew where the kitchen was and where the milk was kept in the pantry, for Miranda had shown me the night before. I didn't expect to take more than five minutes."

"When did you go to the kitchen, and how long did you spend there?"

"Directly after you all got Mr. Beaver out of the way. I was there at least ten minutes, maybe more, as Lil offered to warm the milk for me. I don't usually bother warming it, but she wanted to help." I needn't have said that; it was one of my stupidly obvious attempts to prove to McBrae that I do care about the feelings of servants. "I gave her a shilling." That was an even stupider thing to say.

Fortunately, his mind seemed to be elsewhere. "You're sure the diary had been moved?"

"Yes, I'm sure. I know exactly where I put it." *And don't you dare disbelieve me or ask how I can be so sure.* "After that, I scarcely slept a wink."

"That explains why you're so pale this morning, and so easily startled."

This remark annoyed me (unreasonably, I am aware). "I went for a walk in the hope that a little exercise would put a bloom in my cheeks." I gritted my teeth. "I shan't be able to *bear* it if Sir Roderick thinks I couldn't sleep because of his horrid harangue."

He tsked. "Decide whether or not you care what he thinks of you, and then put your decision into practice."

I shut my eyes and took a deep breath. This was sound advice, but the situation wasn't as simple as he imagined. "You don't understand."

"It would be my privilege to listen, if you wish to explain."

I shook my head, and he didn't persevere, although his interest was only too evident. He liked digging into people's deepest thoughts—a practice which I found repugnant.

Perhaps he didn't pester because of the fat drops of rain plopping here and there on the path. The wind had picked up, and although the umbrella protected me for now, he would soon be soaked. Frowning, he asked, "There's no key for your door?"

"Not that I saw. I set a trap of sorts—various items piled before the door—so that anyone attempting to enter would cause it to topple. But it didn't help me sleep, because I feared my maid would come to wake me and…and ask awkward questions."

I could put up with his advice, his nosiness, his intolerable self-control, and his unwarranted kindness to me. I could *not* explain why I cared what my maid thought of me.

"Yes, servants can be the very devil if you don't think of them as furniture," he said.

Too true. My mother is oblivious to servants except when they inconvenience her. My father is more considerate… I sighed, remembering Sir Roderick's threat.

"It's not so much what Sir Roderick thinks." I brushed tendrils of hair from my face. "I'm used to being the object of his hatred. It's what will happen when he speaks to my father."

"You'll get your revenge," McBrae said. "If he has the gall to complain to Lord Medway about the apple of his eye, he will regret it for the rest of his days."

"Apple of his eye?" I blurted.

"Your father adores you," McBrae said with a grin. "I assure you, the Earl of Medway can make life difficult for mere Sir Roderick. That was an empty threat if ever I've heard one."

"I hope so." His kind words cheered me a little, but I still had to find out who had been in my bedchamber. I dismissed the impossible candidates: McBrae himself, as well as the three gentlemen with him that night. That left all the ladies and only a few gentlemen: my father (highly unlikely; he wasn't a surreptitious sort of person), Sir Alphonse, Colonel Wendell, Mr. Powers, and Sir Roderick, who had been far too occupied with Cynthia to sneak into my bedchamber.

Sir Alphonse might well have been blackmailed by Mr. Fence. Perhaps he'd been forced to invite him to the party. Or perhaps he'd invited him with foul play in mind. Mr. Powers might also have been a victim of blackmail. But none of this gave either of them a reason to enter *my* room.

Colonel Wendell was a more likely candidate. What if he'd spied me as I hurried away from his door? If he knew I had overheard, he might be desperate to silence me—permanently. I shivered.

"Don't worry about the intruder," McBrae said. "I'll ensure that you are safe."

It was all very well to say he would protect me, but I didn't see how he could do so. I was about to say so when he cursed softly and lowered his gaze. A few seconds later my father appeared with Sir Alphonse.

When McBrae raised his eyes, his features had shifted. He had become the respectful servant once more. I shivered, swallowing down my uneasiness at this sight.

"There you are, Rosie," Papa said. "Are you chilled?" He took the umbrella from McBrae and dismissed him with a word of thanks. "But worth it, perhaps. I well understand the temptation of fresh air, and walks can be delightful on a rainy day."

"I don't like being cooped up in the house," I said, as McBrae strode away up the hill. "Where might I find an umbrella to take with me next time?" Which was my awkward way of pretending the umbrella was the sole reason for McBrae's presence by my side.

"There are quite a number in a stand near the door," Sir Alphonse said.

I thanked him and pondered taking one to my bedchamber as a weapon. What if a murderer crept in as I slept?

I couldn't go without sleep—after two disturbed nights, I was well-nigh dropping already—but nor did I wish to order Mary Jane to sleep on a pallet at the foot of my bed. It would require either 1) a truthful explanation, or 2) a false one, such as fear that a drunken man might enter my chamber, or 3) no explanation, in which case she would wonder if I were succumbing to madness again.

Occasionally, I consider developing a reputation for eccentricity. Certain great ladies drive their servants to distraction with illogical and contradictory commands. However, such behavior breeds discontented servants, and think how exhausting to maintain a maddening persona merely to avoid being thought truly mad.

No Mary Jane, then. I could ask for a key, but that would raise eyebrows—again, as if I had a fear of lecherous men. Which, deep down, is perhaps true, but not something I wish the world to know. I would have to think of a way to barricade my door whilst not appearing to do so.

In the meantime, I would persevere with observing the guests and gossiping my heart out. In the interest of fairness, I made a point of considering the ladies, one by one, as possible intruders.

Motives were very thin on the ground. Why would a lady go to my bedchamber—and not finding me there, just happen to notice my diary under the coverlet, which, incidentally, was thick enough and rumpled enough not to indicate it concealed a slim book?

Very well. Mrs. Wendell, to protect her husband, if she knew I'd been eavesdropping. Might he have realized it and told her, after which she came to confront me—or plead with me to remain silent? But if so, why lift my covers?

Miranda, if she wished to speak to me for whatever reason. Miss Gardner, ditto. Mrs. Holloway, likewise. But none of these ladies would have a reason to lift the coverlet, either.

Miss Ellis… To put a toad between my sheets? No, she wouldn't touch a toad in the first place.

I discarded my pelisse and wet shoes, tidied my hair, and went down to breakfast, taking a seat next to my father. Apart from him and Sir Alphonse, the company consisted of the younger guests. It was later than my usual breakfast time when in the country. I am naturally an early riser, but when in town, one's social schedule forces one to sleep late.

"Have you begun to write your play, Lady Rosamund?" Sir Alphonse asked coyly.

Oh *God*, not the play again. "My dear sir, with such a louche subject, how can one possibly write a moral tale? It could only be a tragedy. Everyone would die, most likely unrepentant, and suffer eternal fire. Think what a bore."

Lancelot eyed me like a cat anticipating a visit to the cream pot. So annoying of him, for I was definitely not his tasty treat. "I daresay *ménages à trois* are all the rage in Hell," he said. "Just what you've always longed for, Beaver."

Johnny glared. "You have no idea what I long for."

Miss Ellis gave her unpleasant bray. "You'd better hope to die young, Johnny, for it's the only way you'll ever participate in one."

"Tsk," Lancelot said. "Those whose vaunting ambition o'erleaps itself shouldn't throw stones."

Everyone laughed at this delightful mixture of quotes, except Miss Ellis, who speared him with malicious eyes, and Mr. Powers, whose chuckle rapidly became a cough.

What charming company for breakfast!

Next, who should appear but Cynthia and Sir Roderick Frockmartin! He bade us all a cheerful good morning—which in itself was strange, for he is naturally rather taciturn—but when his eyes met mine, they were cold as ever. I stared haughtily back. Cynthia smiled at me, which was kind of her, but their arrival reawakened my *gêne* from the previous night.

I turned resolutely away and addressed Miss Gardner. "How is your play progressing?"

"Wonderfully well, thank you, my lady. You were most helpful last evening." Her smile dissolved into a worried frown. "Perhaps you should abandon the moral tale and write a frivolous adventure story. You had such wonderful ideas for mine."

What a sweet girl. "As it happens, I do have an adventure in mind."

"Frivolity has no place in art," Harold Bellevue pronounced.

Lancelot gave a crack of laughter. "You would change your tune if you'd heard Miss Gardner's plot last night."

She blushed. "Art doesn't always have to be serious. It can be entertaining and fun. What about Shakespeare's comedies? What about Molière? Susannah Centlivre? Elizabeth Inchbald?"

Bellevue tutted. "Comedies and farces are all very well, but if a play doesn't convey a serious message, it's not true art."

Dear me. Bellevue had chosen a thorny path to Miss Gardner's heart.

"Serious messages are too, too tedious," Lancelot said.

Bellevue sniffed disdainfully.

"Sometimes, serious messages are *necessary*," Beaver said. "As in my play."

Bellevue made a dismissive noise. Such a rude man. Isn't it strange how some people think wealth gives them the right to denigrate others?

Oh, drat. I suppose that applies to me lately—for I have both wealth and birth—but I wasn't rude to McBrae because I feel superior. Obviously, I don't, or not entirely, or I wouldn't feel ashamed.

"My play is about a man who deserved to be murdered." Beaver's Adam's apple bobbed.

"Spare us." Lancelot turned to me. "Tell us about your play, Lady Rosamund."

"I'm not sure playwriting is my forte," I said. "I may write a novel instead… about a bully, the helpless woman he persecutes, and—I'm not sure whom. A lover from the past, perhaps."

I ventured a glance at Cynthia. She clutched a knife in one hand and a slice of toast in the other, shock on her already pale face. McBrae, behind her with the coffee pot, frowned at me.

Oh, no! Did she think I was telling her story? "But I haven't worked it out yet," I said hurriedly. "Whatever it is, it will be entirely frivolous. But do tell us about yours, Mr. Beaver. I do adore a serious work."

I dared not glance at Cynthia again, but I hoped she realized from this comment that I wasn't writing a novel about her.

Very well, it was about her in a way, but not really. Admittedly, her situation had inspired the part about the bully and the hapless woman, but Cynthia's past was 1) a husband dead many years, and 2) a lover (my husband, also deceased) who could not by any means be termed a romantic hero. Quite different, you see.

As for McBrae... I was tired of trying to understand him. Tired of caring whether he approved or disapproved of me. I must continue to do my best according to my own beliefs and standards.

"There's a bully in my play, too," Beaver said, "a villain through and through, driven only by his base desires."

That caused a spate of laughter, at which poor Beaver turned a dull red. "I'm not as debauched as you all think."

Miss Ellis snorted. "You're not debauched at all. You just wish you were."

"I do *not*," Beaver retorted, "and if you keep on acting like a strumpet, you'll end up with the pox."

She gasped, going red with rage. "How *dare* you?"

"Serves you right," Lance said. "I can't think why my father bothers with you."

"Mind your manners, Lance," Sir Alphonse said, and his son subsided, looking unexpectedly annoyed. Was the presence of Miss Ellis a point of contention between them?

"Do go on, Mr. Beaver," I said, to fill the uneasy pause.

Beaver was gratified by my interest, which just goes to show that wealth and status can be put to good use. "The heroine is an innocent maiden cozened by the villain, who whisks her away to his estate with false promises. When she realizes he means to ruin her, she chooses to stab herself rather than give in to him."

"How frightfully sad," I said, surprised that in spite of this trite theme, I meant it—because *he* clearly did.

His Adam's apple bobbed again. "However, I prefer not to write a tragedy. The hero, a valiant knight, arrives and snatches the dagger from her hand in the nick of time."

I clapped a hand to my breast. "What a relief."

"But the villain, whose infamy knows no bounds, offers to share the heroine with him in a *ménage à trois*." He reddened again, perhaps thinking of my history. "The heroine faints at the thought."

"The dastard!" I cried. "Does the hero confront the villain in mortal combat?"

"He wants to, but there are dozens of men ahead of him who seek revenge. He has to defeat them first to gain the right to kill the villain."

Men just love fights, don't they?

"But he prevails in the end," I suggested.

"Not really. One of the other men goes behind his back and kills the villain, so he doesn't get the satisfaction he deserves."

How too, too transparent. He'd really meant what he said last night—that his admiration of Fence was a ruse. Now, he resented the fact that someone else had killed him.

"What a stupid story," Miss Ellis muttered.

"I quite liked it," Miss Gardner said shyly. "I think the hero—if he's truly heroic—will be relieved that he didn't have to commit murder."

"You're entirely correct, Miss Gardner," Beaver said. "He dismisses resentment in favor of relief. Now he can love the heroine without a stain on his conscience."

"Mawkish," Lance said.

"Hush," said his father. "Now let's hear about Lady Rosamund's play." He gestured to me. Good, another chance to prove to Cynthia that I wasn't writing about her.

"It won't be a play, as I said before, but a novel." I risked another glance at Cynthia. She was carefully buttering the piece of toast. Sir Roderick's arm was about her shoulders. "The lover from the past—"

"Her lover or his?" Lancelot asked.

I was about to answer the obvious—hers—when I thought of a better way to cover up my mistake. "His lover, who comes to rescue the hapless woman from his clutches and reclaim him for her own. She will be a Druid—a present-day warrior priestess, I believe."

"There are no Druids anymore," Harold Bellevue said.

"Don't be so sure of that," Sir Alphonse said. "They're amongst us in disguise, biding their time."

"Just like the fairies," Papa said with a grin.

Another furtive glance at Cynthia showed she had recovered her equanimity. She finished buttering the toast and passed it to Sir Roderick with an adoring smile.

I had never before seen her smile like that. I didn't know what to think. Maybe McBrae was right, that Sir Roderick wasn't the fiend I believed him to be. Perhaps Cynthia cared for him, judging by last night's embrace.

I'd had enough of the emotions circling the room. I motioned to the footman to serve me some fresh coffee, then helped myself to ham and cheese and buttered a roll.

Fortunately, before another quarrel could break out, Sir Alphonse signaled to the servants to leave and close the door behind them. Then he stood and motioned us all to silence.

"The coroner, Mr. Johnson, will arrive soon. I hope he will get a jury together quickly and bring in a verdict of accidental death, but most likely I shall be obliged to invite him to dine and spend the night here."

He paused, his stern gaze alighting on each of us in turn. "There has been some foolish talk of murder. Kindly do not mention such a possibility, whether in jest or in relation to plays you are working on. You will not only endanger yourself, but everyone else if you do so. Johnson takes himself far too seriously. Once an idea enters his head, it's impossible to dislodge it."

Lance grimaced. "Such as his absurd longing for your trophy."

"Yes, damn the man." Sir Alphonse glowered. "Therefore, without precisely lying, we must collectively give the impression that although none of us knew Mr. Fence well, we are shocked and saddened at the loss of a fellow enthusiast of the theater." His stern gaze traveled from one person to the next in a schoolmasterish way. "Miss Ellis, as one of the genuine actresses amongst us, I count on you to set an example. Think of this as an opportunity to display your considerable skill."

Miss Ellis preened, and I gained a new respect for Sir Alphonse. What a clever way to bend the odious girl to his will. She'd likely been plotting revenge against Beaver, but now she had a more important task.

"As for the stag's head..." Sir Alphonse sighed heavily. "It goes against the grain to put it in Johnson's greedy hands, but I fear I shall have no choice."

"Won't he be obliged to sell it and give the proceeds to a worthy charity?"

I asked.

"That won't stop him from selling it to himself for much less than he offered me."

"Think of it as a weapon," Papa said. "If this fellow is sufficiently puffed up at his supposed coup in gaining the trophy, he won't start wondering about murder."

"True." Sir Alphonse sighed again.

Yes, but what if it was *murder?* Perhaps many of the guests believed the accident story, but did my father? He is an intelligent man. I didn't like to think he was part of a conspiracy to hide the truth. It offended my sense of justice and undermined my confidence in my father's essential probity.

And yet I also understood McBrae's point of view. One couldn't wish a miscarriage of justice. Was it better to let a murderer go free than to convict an innocent man?

Yes, obviously. And yet, what if that emboldened the murderer to kill again?

Fortunately, since I was becoming more and more mired in philosophical questions, the dining room door opened, and Miranda and Colonel Wendell came in, followed by McBrae with fresh coffee.

"Ah, Miranda, there you are. And Colonel Wendell. I hear Mrs. Wendell is unwell."

"She's resting comfortably," Miranda said. "I expect she'll be fine before long and well enough to join us for dinner."

"Not so sure about that," Colonel Wendell said. "She's had one of her spasms. Needs to be left alone."

"How tedious for her," Miranda said. "Perhaps if someone were to read to her this afternoon?"

The Colonel shook his head. "Her spasms are invariably followed by a migraine. Quiet and darkness is what she needs."

If I hadn't heard them quarreling last night, I might have believed him. Lance caught my eye and raised a brow. Evidently, McBrae had told him about the conversation I had overheard.

What if the colonel was forcing his wife to stay in their bedchamber, for fear that she would blab?

Well. I would do my best to make her do exactly that—to me.

121

Chapter Ten

I hope I am mistaken, but I know Lance all too well.

—From the diary of Corvus

Sir Alphonse had given his little warning address just in time, for a few minutes later Wiggs announced the coroner. A sharp-nosed man with sandy hair marched into the dining room and halted, frowning at the guests from under bushy brows.

"Johnson!" Sir Alphonse cried. "There you are, old fellow. Thank you for coming so promptly. Care for some breakfast?"

"I breakfasted hours ago," Mr. Johnson said. "And although *I* am prompt, *you* took a whole day to let me know about the sudden death of this...er..." He consulted a folded paper in his hand. "Mr. Fence."

"Because of the storm, dear fellow. Think of the hazard to my horse and groom in all the rain and mud! Bad enough with one man dead—and haste on my part wouldn't have made him any less so."

"Humph," Mr. Johnson said. "That's all very well, but what about leaving the body *in situ?*"

Heavens, what a fussy sort of man. I considered him and found McBrae's eye on me. How dare he despise the advantages of rank, and then silently suggest that I make use of them!

"The rules must be followed," Mr. Johnson said, "and—"

Sir Alphonse interrupted as McBrae approached with the coffee pot. "Have

122

a cup of coffee, then, and allow me to make a few introductions. I am entertaining some most distinguished guests, the Earl of Medway and his daughter, Lady Rosamund Phipps." That startled the man into silence. "Lord Medway, Lady Rosamund, allow me to present Edgar Johnson, the coroner."

Mr. Johnson bowed respectfully at my father's genial nod, but blinked uneasily as he turned to me.

I smiled at him. "Yes, I'm *the* Lady Rosamund of caricature fame, but it's all nonsense, I assure you. Thank you so much for braving the weather to come help us."

"Indeed, my lady," he said eagerly, "I never believed a word of it."

"So very kind of you," I said. "It was a frightful shock to come upon a corpse so soon after my bereavement..." I whipped my handkerchief from my sleeve and dabbed at my eyes.

"My condolences upon your recent loss, my lady," he said, and after a suitable pause, he asked, "You found the gentleman's body?"

"No, poor Miss Gardner did." I indicated her with a flutter of my handkerchief, as Sir Alphonse hadn't attempted any more introductions. "She was wakeful and had gone to the drawing room to fetch her book. While crossing the Great Hall, she saw him lying there and screamed. Luckily, I was wakeful as well—I seldom sleep soundly since the loss of my dear husband—and rushed to her aid." I shuddered. "Horrible, horrible! I daresay we shall both of us dream of it for the rest of our lives."

Miss Gardner said in a tremulous voice, "It was ghastly. I have never been so terrified in my life." Unlike me, I don't think she was feigning fright. She managed not to glance at Mr. Powers, for which restraint I admired her. She needn't have worried, though; Mr. Johnson was smiling at her in blatant admiration.

So far, Miss Ellis had remained silent and almost demure. Perhaps she, too, was exercising restraint...

No such luck. She couldn't bear that the coroner's attention was on Miss Gardner. She took a deep breath, gave a tiny sob, and tears began to roll silently down her cheeks. She said not a word. Impressive!

Fine, but best to get this display over with. "My dear Miss Ellis, please don't weep." A feeble comment, I admit; I would rather have said sarcastically that red, swollen eyes would mar her perfect beauty, but she would have taken it amiss. Which under ordinary circumstances hardly mattered, but not here, not now.

Miss Ellis dabbed at her tears with her table napkin. "Mr. Fence was… he was so *kind* to me. And so patient! He helped me practice my lines over and over. He was even writing a little monologue for me to perform whilst here."

"A tragedy indeed." Did I detect a hint of irony in Mr. Johnson's voice?

Evidently, Lancelot did too, for he snorted. "Doing it a little too brown, love. There was nothing kind about it. He just wanted to tup you."

"That is the fate of actresses, alas." Miss Ellis passed a languid hand across her brow.

"For God's sake, girl, *stop* it," Miranda snapped. She turned to Mr. Johnson. "Miss Ellis is my niece and shows great promise, if only she will confine her propensity for drama to the stage."

Miss Ellis narrowed her eyes, and hastily I intervened. "Sir Alphonse kindly ordered the body removed, for as you can surely see, we ladies couldn't have borne to pass it again and again. Gentlemen have stronger stomachs than we do." I grimaced. "Please say we needn't look at it again."

"There, there." If Johnson had been sitting next to me, he would have patted my hand. "You needn't worry, Lady Rosamund. No one would dream of obliging you to view the corpse."

He accepted a cup of coffee and added a liberal amount of sugar. Sir Alphonse introduced everyone else, and after savoring a slice of plum cake, Johnson got down to business. "I'll take a look at the deceased first of all. Then I must go to the village to see about summoning a jury."

"If there's anything I can do to help…" Sir Alphonse murmured. "You are of course welcome to put up here for the night. We're rather full, but…" He looked to Miranda for inspiration.

"Mr. Johnson may take Mr. Fence's room," she said.

Sir Alphonse made a face. "That's rather macabre, although he didn't actually die there." He turned to Johnson. "I quite understand if you'd rather stay at the inn."

"Not at all, Sir Alphonse. I don't anticipate meeting a ghost." Johnson laughed heartily at his own jest. "I'll hold the inquest tomorrow, here in the Great Hall. We'll reconstruct the scene as it was—that's as close as we can get to leaving the corpse in situ."

There was an awkward, not to say anxious, silence. He added, "We'll need someone to play the deceased."

"My man will do it," Lancelot said. "He's an excellent fellow, jack of all trades. He'll make an excellent corpse."

Sometimes I rather liked Lancelot—he was both capable and witty—but this callous treatment of McBrae annoyed me no end. "Not if you mean to put that horrid stag's head on top of him."

"Nay, my lady." McBrae said softly, approaching me with the coffee pot. "Never fear for me."

Johnson brightened. "Stag's head?"

"A huge trophy that was on the wall above the staircase," I said. "It fell on poor Mr. Fence."

"Well, well." He rubbed his hands together. One could see the clockwork ticking happily in his brain. "That explains why I didn't see the trophies on my way through the Great Hall."

"One of the ladies asked to have the others removed, for fear of another tragic accident," Lancelot said.

"Quite right, quite right. Where is the trophy that fell?"

"In the cellar," Sir Alphonse said grumpily.

Johnson gulped down his coffee and stood. "Excellent. We'll need it at the inquest tomorrow."

My father stood as well. "We'll view the corpse, and then I'll stroll down to the village with you. Do me good to stretch my legs." He turned to the Colonel. "Come along with us, Wendell. Always good to have another mature man about. Anyone else? How about it, Sir Roderick?"

Colonel Wendell agreed with alacrity—no doubt he was flattered—but Sir Roderick demurred. Perhaps Papa was trying to give me a chance to speak with Cynthia, which was kind of him but useless, judging by Sir Roderick's hard face.

However, my father had provided me with a far more important opportunity—to speak to the Colonel's hapless wife.

The instant the men were out of the way—Lance and McBrae went as well—I raced upstairs, tapped on Mrs. Wendell's door, and didn't wait for her to bid me enter. Which was impolite, but I wanted to catch her as she really was, not as her husband had ordered her to be.

I needn't have bothered. She was sitting up in bed, looking perfectly healthy and extremely annoyed. "Owen, I—Oh, it's you, Rosie. I thought it was my husband, come to check on me again." She put a hand to her lips. "Oh, dear, I hope you don't mind me using your nickname. Rosie was what we all called you as a child, although I'm sure your mother would say it was entirely improper now. She didn't like it much back then."

I wasn't sure I liked it now either, but needs must; my goal was to induce her to confide in me. "It's perfectly fine. My father still calls me Rosie, and I like it very much." I smiled and closed the door behind me. "I hear you're feeling poorly, Mrs. Wendell."

She pursed her lips. "That depends on whether my husband is about to come check on me."

"He's gone with the other men to view the body of Mr. Fence, and I believe he intends to accompany them to the village inn." I cocked my head. "You don't look as though you have a migraine coming on."

She huffed. "Is that what he said?"

"Yes, that your spasms invariably lead to a migraine, and that you need darkness and quiet."

"Spasm? What nonsense. I merely told him off, which he rightly deserved. He doesn't want me to go downstairs, for fear that I shall talk too much. I ask you, what else is a woman to do, but needlework and gossip?"

Too true. "Indeed, the life of a gentlewoman is far too restricted—such a bore."

"Please do sit and chat with me for a while. It's lonely all by myself."

I sat in a pretty Hepplewhite shield-back chair by the bed. "Perhaps he is worried that the word *murder* will accidentally slip out. There has been some little talk about it, absurd of course, for Fence's death was obviously accidental, but Sir Alphonse begged us to take care what we say. Apparently, the coroner is the sort of man who will make trouble if he gets the wrong idea in his head."

She pouted. "My husband takes me for a fool. Why would I mention murder?"

"You wouldn't—for it was you, wasn't it, who asked to have the remaining trophies removed for fear of another accident?"

"Precisely," she said, crossing her arms.

"I wonder what the Colonel was worried about, then—so worried that he would order you to keep to your bedchamber, all alone?"

She was silent for a long moment. At last she said, "Just because it wasn't murder, it doesn't mean there weren't people who wished him dead."

I feigned surprise. "Such as who?"

"Mr. Bellevue, for one."

"Heavens! I wonder why?"

Her eyes sparkled. "Mr. Fence tried to blackmail Mr. Bellevue. I overheard them!"

"Blackmail—how horrid." I lowered my voice to a conspiratorial tone. "About what?"

"Paying someone else to write love poems for him."

It wasn't unheard of for gentlemen to hire a poet to write amorous verses to woo a prospective bride or mistress, but Bellevue was a serious playwright who should be able to compose verses of his own. "How mortifying for him."

"Mr. Bellevue denied it and refused to pay him as much as a farthing. 'Go to the devil and stay there,' he said, which he wouldn't if he'd known I was nearby." She paused. "I must have made some small noise, for he turned and saw me. He was positively livid, but he controlled himself and apologized for his bad language." She rolled her eyes. "As if we ladies have never heard our father and brothers swear."

I stopped myself just in time from rolling my eyes in agreement. If I did not take care, I might find myself doing it without thinking. Horrors! Not that she would have noticed one way or another, for although she is a lady, she is not quite our sort, and known to us only because of being a near neighbor in Kent.

She prattled on. "Mr. Fence laughed and said, 'It'll be all over London now without my help.' So horrid of him, for to whom would I gossip about a poet, of all uninteresting people? But then he said, 'And I have the proof that will clinch it.'"

Which seemed to indicate that Mr. Bellevue's denial was a lie, and that he therefore had good reason to wish Mr. Fence dead.

"And *then*," she went on, "he turned to me with a positively *evil* grin and said, 'Everyone has secrets. Have you asked your darling Colonel about his?'"

"What a ghastly man he was," I said.

"I wonder how many people he blackmailed." She seemed lost in thought, so I restrained my impulse to ask the obvious: *Did you ask your husband?*

At last she said softly, "Rosie dear, may I confide in you?"

I gave silent thanks and moved my chair closer to the bed. "Indeed, you may."

"I wouldn't say this to any other lady, but—I know you'll understand."

I knew what was coming. Not precisely, of course, but something to do with my dubious reputation. A tiny spark of annoyance flared, which I tamped down in a hurry.

"My husband has not always been faithful," Mrs. Wendell said.

I gave the long-suffering sigh of a cynical spouse. "Gentlemen have needs," I said, infusing weariness into my voice, "and seemingly a wife is not always sufficient to satisfy them."

"Exactly so," she said, "but at least your husband did not try to pretend otherwise."

"No, indeed; he was very open about it." I paused. "I gather Colonel Wendell is not."

She scowled. "He thinks I know nothing of it. That I am ignorant of such matters. What does he think ladies gossip about? Recipes for asparagus pudding?"

I laughed. "No one can make asparagus pudding palatable, so that topic is over and done with. I'm not too fond of hearing about preparations to loosen the bowels, either."

She chuckled. "Nor to stop them up. How can we help but prefer to discuss infidelities? He thinks I don't know about his mistresses."

I blinked at that. "He has more than one at a time?"

She snorted. "No, he's not that, ah, energetic, but from time to time he dismisses one and takes another. He doesn't go to common prostitutes, so I have no cause for complaint. I even called on one of them. She was rather hostile, until I explained that I simply wanted to be sure he treated her well."

A better excuse than I had come up with when visiting my brother's mistress a few months ago. But that was a different story entirely.

"That was a lie, for it is not in his nature to be unkind. It was curiosity that drove me, nothing more. It must have been simpler for you, Rosie, for you were already acquainted with your husband's mistress, were you not?"

"Yes, much simpler." I stopped there, for she would find plenty to gossip about without me adding to it, and besides that, what if she realized that selfsame mistress slept only a bedchamber away? "What does the Colonel fear you will say?"

"It's completely stupid, Rosie. It seems Mr. Fence knew about my husband's mistresses and threatened to tell me."

Was that all? "That's not much of a motive for murder."

"I challenged him with it this morning, and he flew into a rage. He was embarrassed, poor lamb, which he doesn't handle at all well. He ordered me to keep to my chamber, for fear I might blab to everyone. As if I would!"

I didn't entirely blame him for fearing she would be indiscreet. She'd grabbed the first opportunity to get it off her chest.

I made my way downstairs. I had done my best to convince Mrs. Wendell to come with me to the drawing room, but she'd refused, saying there was no point in upsetting her darling Colonel any more than she already had. "I'll send someone to rescue you in time for dinner," I told her, and she thanked me, saying she had plenty to read for the moment and felt sure she could pacify the Colonel by then.

Lancelot Lewis had returned from viewing the body and was alone in a corner of the Great Hall. The huge stag's head lay there now, and Lancelot was examining the wooden board that had attached it to the wall. He looked up and saw me.

"We're going to dent it a little and then put it back in the cellar," he said. "Make it appear to have been damaged when it hit the balustrade."

I pursed my lips.

"You don't agree?"

"I dislike the idea of falsifying the evidence of a crime," I said softly but firmly. "Naturally, I don't wish anyone to hang for a murder he didn't commit, but nor do I wish the actual murderer to go free."

He eyed me. "I never imagined you would be the idealistic sort."

My blasted reputation again. "It has nothing to do with idealism. Like anyone, there are certain things I cannot or will not do."

He eyed me again, his charming, devilish grin adding a lascivious sense to his words. "And certain other things you can and will."

I was becoming accustomed to his excessive good looks, if not enough to remain entirely unaffected by his smile. However, I am used to concealing my feelings and shrugged off this impertinence.

Or tried to, because then he said, "Which of the not-at-all-charming guests at my father's house has caught your eye, my dear Lady Rosamund?"

"I *beg* your pardon?" How dare he assume I had a prurient interest in anyone? Perhaps it was because I hadn't fallen instantly in lust with him, conceited ass that he was.

Well! He didn't deserve to learn about my recent findings, but McBrae materialized silently out of nowhere, carrying a crowbar.

At which I scowled, but I might have no other chance to speak to McBrae, with or without Lance, and immediately launched into my news. I repeated my conversation with Mrs. Wendell, adding, "Mr. Bellevue may have a motive for murder, but I find it hard to believe the Colonel does."

"Rather a waste of your eavesdropping last night." Lancelot grinned. "I do believe you're enjoying some aspects of this unidealistic process, Lady Rosamund, and why not?"

McBrae narrowed his eyes at Lancelot. After a strange, drawn-out silence, he said, "It was in no way a waste. Each small discovery leads to another."

"Exactly so," I said. "If I hadn't overheard their conversation, I might have believed the Colonel's nonsense about spasms and migraines." Such ills were common enough amongst ladies of the nobility and gentry. My mother would have it that we are more delicate and easily exhausted, due to sensibilities that females of the lower orders are too coarse to understand.

I'm not sure whether this is true. For one thing, the only time I feel delicate and easily exhausted is when my mother deprives me of nourishing food. On the other hand, one does tend to dismiss the loud, vulgar, often hysterical emotions of female servants as mere playacting.

I should probably spend some time pondering this, for fear of doing or saying something offensive to a member of the lower orders without in the least intending to. I had done that in McBrae's presence a few months earlier and subsequently endured a horrid scold from him. I still shudder to think about it.

Drat, I was fretting about his opinion of me *again*. Surely my reasons for examining (and possibly adjusting) my beliefs and behavior should be due to a desire to be an honest, upright, compassionate human being, and not because I want to impress—

No. That is entirely wrong. I did *not* seek to impress McBrae and never shall. For the daughter of an earl, etc., etc., such an ambition is, quite simply, impossible. Not only that, he is substantially below me on the social scale.

But that wasn't right, either. Where he is on the social scale in comparison to me does not determine the validity of his views, nor whether I should consider them.

McBrae interrupted my confused thoughts. "Please carry on. Your assistance is invaluable, and we don't have much time to come to a conclusion, one way or the other."

"Or no conclusion at all." I frowned at the crowbar.

"Unfortunately, yes. Now, if you don't wish to be party to deception, my lady, I suggest that you leave."

I stormed away.

Chapter Eleven

I'll kill him.

—From the diary of Corvus

My fit of temper did not last long. I was determined to pursue my inquiries despite the dishonest behavior of Lancelot and McBrae (who was clearly unfit to teach me about uprightness). The brief shower was over, so I went outdoors to walk and think. The sun shone through the wet trees, and a fresh breeze tugged at my bonnet. This time I took an umbrella, just in case—whether of rain or a stray murderer, I wasn't sure—and made my way towards the lake again, intending to follow the shore to the gazebo and back.

Stonechats conversed cheerfully in the trees edging the path. I passed the fork to the ice house (where the corpse still reposed, but from which the milk and cream, Miranda assured us, had been removed). The lake soon came into view. A heron posed on a rocky spit and watched for foolhardy fish. Far away, a sailboat sped down the lake, its brown sail taut in the wind. I trod slowly along the shingle, glad of my sturdy boots, and pondered whom to work on next.

Gossiping with Mrs. Holloway wouldn't get me far—she was too clever to let anything slip—and the same went for my hostess. I didn't think I could lower myself to Miss Ellis' catty level. Not only that, she was an attention-seeker whose violent impulses emerged via her mouth, not by dropping a heavy trophy atop a prone man.

Why, I wondered again, had he been lying there in the first place? He might have passed out from drink, I supposed, but…he'd looked too tidy for that. Not that I know much about how drunken men fall, for my father and brothers have always taken care to do their carousing elsewhere.

I was concerned for Mr. Powers, for Miss Ellis' uncertain temper put him in danger. (It put Beaver in danger too, but he'd brought that upon himself.) If she became annoyed and repeated what Miss Gardner had said after finding the corpse, the coroner would have no choice but to suspect Powers of murder.

I saw it as my duty to clear his name in advance, just in case. Time for a little talk with Miss Gardner.

It took place much sooner than I expected—for as I neared the gazebo, I realized someone was already there. Two someones, judging by the voices…

"Geoff, I don't like that coroner." Miss Gardner's sweet voice was unmistakable. "He's suspicious. I could tell by the way he looked at me."

"That was admiration and nothing more," Mr. Powers said. "He seemed a decent fellow."

"But what if he finds out?"

"He has no reason to find out, or even to question anything. Don't worry, love. Just write your play and stop fretting…" His voice petered out, and an instant later he plunged out of the gazebo, swearing.

"What is it?" Miss Gardner followed suit.

"I do beg your pardon," I said. "I didn't like to interrupt."

They gaped at me: two pairs of alarmed blue eyes, two mouths a-cock in blatant dismay, expressions startlingly alike.

"Oh, my heavens," I blurted. "You're brother and sister!"

"Shhh!" Mr. Powers said, glancing about. Miss Gardner paled, and for a second, I feared she would faint. Then she burst into tears.

Mr. Powers glared at me in a rather frightening way. I gripped the umbrella, realizing why he had looked about us. No one else was nearby.

His fists clenched, and a muscle twitched beside his eye. "What do you mean to do about it?"

"Oh, no, Geoff," Miss Gardner sobbed, "Please don't!" She tried to take his arm, but he shook her off.

"Well?" he demanded. I am not accustomed to such treatment—but nor am I accustomed to rude, angry males. Even my brother Julius, who is forever berating me, never looks as if he wished to kill me. (To shut me away, though…far too often.)

"About what?" I asked, wishing I could reassure Miss Gardner, yet not daring to move while her brother looked ripe for murder. "It's none of my business. I wouldn't have said a word if I hadn't suddenly seen the resemblance."

"We share a father," Mr. Powers said, "but it must remain secret at all costs."

"Including murder?" Stupid of me, yes.

"No, no!" Miss Gardner shrieked. "He didn't, I swear."

"Hush!" I put up a hand. "If you wish to keep your secret, you must be quiet." That calmed her a little, and I forged on. "I believe you, Miss Gardner, because despite Mr. Powers' horridly menacing expression, he is far too hasty-tempered to engineer a scene such as we found in the Great Hall." Fervently, I hoped I was correct.

Mr. Powers slumped. "My apologies," he muttered. "But Helen *would* come here amongst these dreadful people, and although Mrs. Holloway was to give her countenance, what if people found out what sort of woman *she* really is? Her plays are *not* the sort a lady should write." He gulped. "I shouldn't have mentioned—"

"I already know about Mrs. Holloway," I said. Considering the number of people who knew her secret, I found it progressively more difficult to believe she had a motive for murder.

"Then you understand that close acquaintance with her cannot reflect well on my sister—and nor does the play Helen is writing now. We shouldn't have come here."

Miss Gardner wiped her eyes. "Why not? They're a louche set of people but otherwise quite interesting, and if I'm to be a playwright, I must learn to—to navigate the theater world. What else could I write but an improper play, after being given such a subject? I do believe it will be quite funny."

"No doubt, but if you pursue this course, you must resign yourself to being an outcast. Sooner or later, your secret will out, which won't matter much amongst these people, but what of your prospects for marriage? I wish we hadn't come."

"I'm glad we did," she retorted, "and if you had controlled your temper yesterday, we wouldn't be in a fix now!"

If I hadn't already believed they were siblings, this squabbling would have convinced me.

Miss Gardner put her hands on her hips. "If I can't find a husband who will take me as I am, I shan't marry at all. Papa has settled an annuity on me, so I shan't starve—and perhaps I'll earn a great deal from my plays."

"You'd be safer with a husband," her brother said. "Someone to take care of you despite your unfortunate origins."

Unfortunate origins? How typically stodgy! I know, I know, people set great store by birth within wedlock, for which I can see the advantages—but why punish a child for its parents' folly? That makes no sense at all. I opened my mouth to object, but Mr. Powers hadn't finished his lecture.

"A husband will safeguard you from the lecherous sorts who would pursue you otherwise," he said.

"And prevent me from writing plays. And expect me instead to do needlework and bear his children."

"At least they'd be legitimate ones," he growled. "It's exactly as Miss Ellis said—the fate of actresses, and doubtless that of illegitimate, unmarried, stunningly beautiful playwrights, is ruin."

"No thanks to men like you," she flashed. "How *could* you fall for such a harpy?"

"A temporary aberration," he said, not at all abashed. "Besides that, she's no better than she should be, while you're an innocent in need of a minder."

"I am not a child," she cried. "It's not my fault that I'm beautiful."

"Nor that you're illegitimate," I interposed. "I have no patience with the foolish notions of society. For what it's worth, you may count me your friend."

She smiled shyly. "Thank you, Lady Rosamund. It's worth a great deal."

"As for you, Mr. Powers, for your own safely, I suggest you continue to flirt with Miss Ellis. She is a vengeful sort of person, and if she feels you have lost interest, she may bring up Miss Gardner's unfortunate comment about murder."

He made a face. "If I must."

"And make it appear that you have lost interest in Miss Gardner, too. Meanwhile, I shall do my best to—"

Heavy footsteps crashed through the underbrush. We all swiveled as Harold Bellevue blundered from the wood onto the shingle, shaking his fist.

"You blackguard!" he shouted. "Trying to steal a march on me? You're a dead man, Powers."

Then he noticed me and stopped, taken aback just long enough to allow me to get in his way, brandishing my umbrella.

"Don't be idiotic, Mr. Bellevue. Mr. Powers is enamored of Miss Ellis. All men are fools, but surely he would not be so stupid as to court two women at once."

He made a rude noise. "Then what is he doing here with *her?*" His eyes narrowed. "Tattling on me, that's what it is. That stupid old busybody couldn't keep her mouth shut. Whatever she said, it's not true."

If I'd had any doubts about Mrs. Wendell's tale about Bellevue and Fence, I had them no longer.

There was a brief, bewildered silence. "What's not true?" Miss Gardner asked.

Mr. Bellevue reddened. He opened his mouth and shut it again. At last he said, "It doesn't matter, since it's nothing but a pack of lies."

"Heavens!" I prompted. "Did Mr. Fence threaten you, too?"

"How did you—" he began, then clamped his mouth shut again.

"He seems to have had his hooks into a great many people," I said.

"Maybe, but their dirty secrets are real, while mine isn't. What about Alphonse, Miranda, Lance, the Holloway woman? I'll wager they have secrets. Even Beaver, who made it completely clear that he wanted Fence dead." He glowered at the other man. "What's your secret, Powers?" He clenched his fists and tried to push past me.

I jabbed him in the chest with the tip of the umbrella. "Go away, Mr. Bellevue. Mr. Powers and I were helping to work through a scene from the play Miss Gardner is writing." I paused for emphasis. "In what little privacy we could find down here on the shore."

"I daresay," he said with a bit of a sneer, and veered toward Powers again. "Thought you could bring her around by admiring her little play, did you? You don't fool me."

"You certainly won't bring her around by insulting her play," I said, earning a grateful glance from Miss Gardner.

He huffed. "Very well, I should humor her, but at least my intentions are honorable."

Perhaps they were, but I doubted they would remain so if he knew she was illegitimate.

He glared at Mr. Powers again. "If you're not in love with her, why are you so damned protective?"

"If you must know—" Miss Gardner began furiously.

I interposed, fearing she would betray her secret in a moment of anger. "Mr. Powers is an old friend of Miss Gardner's family. As a gentleman, it behooves him to protect her from insult and injury." I jabbed him again. "She is also a friend of mine." Therefore protected to some extent by my father—or that was what I hoped he would conclude.

I turned away as if in utter disinterest. "Come, Helen," I said. My use of her Christian name should put the cap on it. "Mr. Powers, kindly escort us to the house."

At last the wind dropped out of Mr. Bellevue's sails, and he trudged behind us up the path.

I remained somewhat miffed with McBrae; nevertheless, I knew I must relay this new information to him as soon as possible, whilst begging him not to disclose Miss Gardner's secret to Lance, whom I did not trust in the least.

But McBrae was nowhere to be seen, and a wave of fatigue overtook me. I desperately needed some sleep. I doubted anyone would accost me in the daytime, but I carried the umbrella upstairs all the same.

As I approached my bedchamber door, I was brought up short by a flurry of grunts and curses. What in heaven's name?

Cautiously, I opened the door upon an astonishing sight. Lancelot and McBrae struggled in close combat in the far corner of my room.

"You dirty bastard," McBrae grunted, his Scots accent to the fore. "Frightening a lass like that."

"How was I to know she would realize I'd been here?"

"Because she's clever and observant. You deserve a whipping."

"Think you'll give it, you uppity little Scot?" He heaved, but McBrae, although a bit shorter, didn't give an inch. Brawny indeed.

And quick! McBrae twisted suddenly and jabbed an elbow into Lancelot's nose. "So much for red-blooded Englishmen."

"You're jealous," Lance snarled, "because she doesn't fancy you." Blood bubbled out his nostrils.

"Not looking quite so handsome now, are you?" McBrae scoffed.

"She'll never fall for a grubby Scot," Lance retorted.

I had had enough. "What," I demanded, "is the meaning of this?" I expect I sounded just like my mother. It certainly had the same effect. The combatants ceased on the instant and broke apart.

I shut the bedchamber door and stood against it, wondering what to do next. My mother would have demanded an explanation, but if what I had just heard meant what I thought it did, we would all be embarrassed. Well, McBrae and I would be—I for obvious reasons, and McBrae because he was attracted to me. He had made that clear a few months ago, while knowing perfectly well that a liaison between him and me was out of the question.

On the other hand, I couldn't allow Lance to think I would prefer him, or that what he'd done was acceptable.

I pulled out my handkerchief and pushed him towards a chair. "Sit down and put your head back to stop the bleeding."

"Yes, ma'am," he said meekly.

"You two should be ashamed of yourselves." I marked off their offenses with my fingers. One. "Brawling." Two. "Using foul language." Three.

"Entering a lady's bedchamber uninvited."

Lance chuckled.

I rounded on him, embarrassment be damned. "Twice, in your case," I said. "How dare you come to my bedchamber last night? How dare you lift my covers, as if…" I couldn't bring myself to say it and made an infuriated sound instead.

"As if I expected to spend the night in your bed," he said. "Why not?"

"Because I didn't invite you to do so!" I cried. "Have you no shame?"

"None," he admitted. "You don't by any chance have another handkerchief to spare?" He dropped the blood-soaked one to the floor.

I grabbed another from my dressing table and tossed it at him. "For one thing, I'm in mourning. For another, I'm not interested in taking a lover." I almost blurted I would never take one, but although it was the truth, he would see it as hysteria. "If and when I do, it will not be a man I had met only a few days before." That reminded me of something he'd said. "You thought I'd gone to the bed of some other man last night, didn't you? That's what you meant with your snide remark this morning."

"I beg your pardon," he said, not at all abashed, "but it seemed a logical conclusion."

"It was a stupid conclusion," I retorted. "Those caricatures about me were sheer nonsense."

"Perhaps, but do please look at it from my point of view," he said, wincing as he dabbed at his nose. "Considering who else was on offer, most available women would opt for me."

"Yes, you're handsome and charming and so on, but I'm not available, and I don't wish to go to bed with you."

He shrugged. "Far be it from me to take an unwilling lover."

I turned to McBrae, who during this exchange had stood utterly silent and still save for the slow uncurling of his fists. "Thank you for…" I didn't quite know what to call it, and settled on, "defending me."

"I'm ever your servant, my lady," McBrae said, and I knew he meant it, and it brought tears to my eyes. Hastily, I blinked them away.

Lancelot withdrew the handkerchief from his nose. "Fine words, Mac, but you can pack up and leave for all the use you've been in catching the thief."

Oh, no you don't! I thought, wondering frantically if I could hire McBrae as a footman. He mustn't leave *now*. The thefts hardly seemed to matter, what with a murderer about.

"I identified the thief the moment we arrived," McBrae said, unperturbed. "As a matter of fact, I had already guessed—correctly—before we got here."

Lancelot stared. "Who is it? Tell me!"

"Not until I have proof," McBrae said. "We've been otherwise occupied, so I set it aside for the moment. I'll get what I need in the next day or two."

"Who, damn you?"

"Use your brain, Lance. It's obvious, but you'll deny it if I tell you. Even when I give you proof, you won't know what to do with it."

"What the devil are you talking about? The thief must be dealt with and punished by the law."

"Think it through," McBrae said. "I'll give you till the inquest is over. Once things calm down, you can consider what to do."

"Damned show-off," Lance said, but in a grumpily good-natured sort of way. I had to give him credit for that. He seemed to have lost all prurient interest in me. How disconcerting to find that a man's attraction to one is so ephemeral—here one second, gone the next—but since I didn't want him or any other man, it was also a relief.

He didn't seem about to throw McBrae out of the house, either.

"Curse you, Mac," he said. "How did you know it was I who sneaked in here last night?"

Did I detect a smirk on McBrae's lips? "I suspected immediately, but I became certain when you knew about the eavesdropping before either Lady Rosamund or I mentioned it. Therefore, you must have read about it."

"Fair enough," Lance said. "I suppose you know the identity of the murderer, too."

McBrae shook his head ruefully. "Not yet."

"Mr. Bellevue seems to think Fence was blackmailing almost everyone," I said. "When challenged about his own secrets, he all but accused Sir Alphonse, Miranda, Lancelot, Mrs. Holloway, and Mr. Beaver."

"Me?" Lance grinned. "How exciting, but unfortunately my life, as they say, is an open book."

"You challenged Bellevue?" McBrae asked. "Please don't endanger yourself, my lady."

I didn't want him worrying about me. "I believe I was helpful in preventing further violence. I was on the shore, chatting with Mr. Powers and Miss Gardner about her play, when he suddenly appeared, claiming that Mr. Powers was stealing a march on him."

"And was he?"

Now I had a bit of dilemma—for I didn't wish to reveal Miss Gardner's secret to Lance. That would have to wait until I could speak privately with McBrae.

"I don't think so. Mr. Powers claims to be an old family friend, and he doesn't seem amorous toward Miss Gardner—who, in any event, wants nothing to do with Mr. Bellevue." I paused. "They are both typically male and rather stupid in their attitudes towards women, so I am undoubtedly biased against them in return. I shall try to speak to Miss Gardner again—alone, this time."

I shooed them out the door, after checking to see that the corridor was empty. I had enough problems with my reputation as it was. I rang for Mary Jane to undress me and requested one of her soothing tisanes—without valerian. She fussed over me and helped me to bed.

I lay under the covers, feeling more and more annoyed at myself. I should have known it was a man with prurient interest who had come into my bedchamber. Why would a so-far-nameless murderer sneak in and look under my covers? I must learn to think logically and not allow foolish fears to influence me.

Which led me to more important matters. How had McBrae identified the thief before he had even arrived here? What was so obvious to him and so utterly unclear to Lance? (And why did I unquestioningly believe that McBrae's conclusion, whatever it might be, was correct?)

I could at least answer that last question. McBrae had a brilliant mind. He considered me observant, but he noticed everything and drew conclusions while I floundered in mental mire. Lance, although quite witty, was in other ways rather ordinary.

But it couldn't be as simple as brilliant versus ordinary minds—for why, I wondered, would Lance be unwilling to believe McBrae without proof?

I fell asleep pondering and woke refreshed but none the wiser. Meanwhile, a sense of urgency gripped me—for if we did not uncloak the murderer before tomorrow morning, he might go free. I must tell McBrae about the relationship between Miss Gardner and Mr. Powers, when I got the chance, but that information seemed to bring us no closer to an answer.

Dinner was an uncomfortable sort of affair, for we were all trying to keep our mouths shut, so to speak, except for Miss Ellis. As we gathered in the drawing room before the meal, she maundered on and on to anyone who would listen about dear Mr. Fence and her broken heart and chances lost forever (an insult to Sir Alphonse, who was far more her patron than Mr. Fence ever was or could have been). Unfortunately, no one *wanted* to listen to her. Even Mr. Powers, who was obediently doing his best to appear to admire her, had to stifle his yawns.

Thank heavens, our host nobly ignored the insult, stepped into the breach, and invited her to sit next to him at the head of the table. He spoke at length of great roles she might play. (Shakespeare? Ha!) Miss Ellis simpered and preened so idiotically that I couldn't help an involuntary glance at Miranda, seated at the foot of the table.

And encountered a look of...was that *anguish*? It vanished so suddenly that I wondered if I had even seen it, for it was replaced by a tolerant sort of scorn. I rolled my eyes (quite a concession from such as I), and she rolled hers in agreement, but immediately turned away again.

What an agreeable woman she was! Despite her evident disgust at her niece's behavior, she remained composed and cheerful, the perfect hostess, seeing to everyone's comfort.

She and my father together did a magnificent job of occupying Mr. Johnson. They discussed the upcoming Lammas festivities, which included a great number of sporting events, such as footraces, archery, wrestling, and a hound trail in which Mr. Johnson had entered a prized dog. Johnson was entirely happy to go on and on about his hounds, and suddenly decided to postpone the inquest until the afternoon. The trail, which ranged ten miles across the moor, would end just short of the nearby village, and he didn't want to miss cheering his dog on if the inquest took too long. Sir Roderick and Cynthia were at that end of the table, too, and Sir Roderick eagerly expressed a wish to wait with him at the end of the trail. I had never seen him so enthusiastic and—heavens!—almost happy.

Well, why not? Cynthia had accepted his presence in her bedchamber. Meanwhile, Papa's glances in their direction showed his satisfaction with his strategy in throwing them together.

I tried to stifle my distress over that whole business—for there was absolutely nothing I could do about it—and applied my mind logically to the question of the thief. If McBrae could guess the answer easily, so could I.

1) McBrae wasn't previously acquainted with any of the people here except Lance, nor did they know him. This was a reasonable assumption, for how else could he successfully play the part of a footman? His 'disguise' was useful, but not perfect. A person who knew him well—or at least had conversed with him frequently—might see through it, as I had.

2) Who was at Lewis Grange at the time of all the thefts? The servants, but McBrae was convinced none of them were to blame. Who else, apart from Sir Alphonse, Miranda, and Lance? The three groups of guests seemed to be quite different sets of people. Was someone else, someone I didn't know of, at all three gatherings? Perhaps, but if so, how would McBrae know? Had Lance given him a list?

Maybe…but McBrae's suspicions had been confirmed once he arrived here. Therefore, this other person must be here, too.

I let my gaze roam around the table. None of the guests seemed to be Druid-fanciers; they were more inclined to scoff. Nor were Lance's friends from his Oxford days here.

With increasing unease, I considered the too few possibilities. Not Lance, for he had asked McBrae to find the culprit. Not Sir Alphonse—for why would he steal from his guests? He didn't seem to be suffering financially. The house was in excellent repair, most of the furnishings in good taste, the meals excellent… Would Papa know if his friend was in difficulties? He would surely have said something…

That left the one person whom I admired most. Whom I didn't want to suspect.

Miranda Tyne.

Oh, *dear.* I glanced at her again, and quickly away. Thank heavens, McBrae was serving braised trout to the Wendells, or he might have noticed my gasp of horror. As it was, I took a hurried gulp of wine.

Miranda was a mistress, not a wife. At any time, Sir Alphonse could send her away and replace her with someone younger, such as Miranda's own niece. Did she fear that Sir Alphonse would turn from her to that tedious child? Impossible; he was only making much of Miss Ellis to prevent her from saying something stupid about murder.

But…older men often indulged their desires with young, nubile women.

How sickening, but although Sir Alphonse seemed to think Miss Ellis had promise as an actress, he didn't seem disenchanted with Miranda. He spoke highly of her, relied on her to play hostess…

And yet, one never knew what went on between a couple. Miranda was an accomplished actress, capable of appearing entirely composed despite turmoil in her heart. And the unpleasant reality was that Sir Alphonse hadn't married her. She had no financial security but what she could take for herself. She might have some savings, but not enough—so she had chosen to augment them by theft.

This made complete sense and also explained McBrae's conviction that Lance would deny it. Sir Alphonse may or may not have tired of Miranda, but Lance liked her very much. He was courteous and considerate of her, almost as if he was her son.

Now that I knew the truth—what should I do?

Chapter Twelve

She had to hold back tears. It is my hope—futile, no doubt—that more than relief and gratitude lie behind those tears.

—From the diary of Corvus

It is not easy to ride the horns of a dilemma while at the same time pretending interest in a bunch of vulgar plays about *ménages à trois*. On the other hand, the louche subject matter held Mr. Johnson's attention. The more wine he drank, the more he sent sly glances at me, but I fended those off easily enough whilst trying my best to work out my next step.

It was a glance at my dear father's face that showed me the way. Except when he was conversing, his expression told me that something preyed on his mind. It might be Cynthia's problems—but I didn't think so. Was he as perturbed as I about covering up for murder—or did he truly believe the trophy had fallen by accident? I dared not ask, for fear of disturbing a hornet's nest.

Or…perhaps the loss of the diamond cravat pin had upset him rather more than one would expect. It was an old piece of jewelry, passed down from his grandfather. Perhaps he valued it for that reason.

Therefore, I would get it back for him.

With this plan in mind, I waited impatiently for the evening to end. So preoccupied was I—and increasingly drowsy—that I couldn't concentrate on the rousing tale in *The Ladies' Monthly Museum*. I didn't notice McBrae until he said in my ear, "More tea, my lady?"

I started violently. "Must you sneak up behind me like that?" Immediately, annoyance at myself washed over me, which was bad enough, and then I caught Papa's incredulous expression, which made it worse. Such snappish behavior was unpleasantly reminiscent of my mother, which he would deprecate, but in this instance, I had complained more as if to a friend than a servant—which might lead to an unwarranted suspicion on his part.

After all, I'd been caricatured as a scorned wife repudiated by a footman. What if Papa believed that to be true, and that I now had this footman in my sights?

I sucked in a worried breath—not because of the suspicion, which was absurd, but because I would rather not lie to my father. Nor did I wish to reveal McBrae's true purpose here.

"Beg pardon, my lady," McBrae said in that soft Scottish drawl.

I flapped my hand. If he weren't so dratted soft on his feet, I wouldn't be in this fix. "Perhaps some coffee," I said coolly. Despite my afternoon nap, I was frightfully weary, but I had to stay awake until Miranda went upstairs to her chamber.

"Of course, my lady." McBrae glided away.

The coffee, hot and strong, helped a little. We dispersed to our various bedchambers earlier than usual because of the busy day ahead. I'd had no chance to speak with McBrae about Miss Gardner and Mr. Powers, but hopefully it didn't matter. I hoped he had unearthed some more useful information, for time was swiftly running out.

I let Mary Jane undress me and dismissed her, assuring her I didn't need warm milk or a tisane. That might prove to be untrue, but I had to reach Miranda before she went to sleep (or worse, if Sir Alphonse joined her. I shuddered at the thought of interrupting another moment of passion). I donned my dressing gown and slippers, picked through my jewelry box, and left.

The corridor was quiet and dark, save for low light from the sconces below. I tiptoed across the narrow landing, now denuded of trophies, and crept along the opposite corridor to Miranda's chamber. A dim light showed beneath the door. I hesitated, listening, then scratched on the panel.

"Who is it?"

"It's Rosamund Phipps," I said softly, not wanting to advertise my presence to the entire house. A second later, the door opened.

Miranda was already in nightclothes, her hair in a braid down her back. She peered at me. "Is something wrong, my lady?"

That was one way of putting it. "I'm afraid so, Mrs. Tyne. May I come in?"

She beckoned me inside and closed the door. Now that the moment was upon me, doubt suffused me. What if my conclusion was entirely wrong? I would feel an utter fool, and she would think I was mad, and…

No. I could not afford to dither. I had to surprise her, before she had a chance to put on an act.

"I have come to ask you to return my father's cravat pin."

She watched me in utter silence—and growing dismay. After a silence that stretched too long, she sighed wearily and said, "How did you know?"

"By a process of deduction. If the only three people apart from servants who were at this party and the two previous ones were Sir Alphonse, Lancelot, and you…" I stopped, unable to continue. How embarrassing for both of us if I had to explain why. One simply doesn't discuss certain subjects, particularly with a mere acquaintance.

Kindly, Miranda forestalled me. "I am the logical choice, for I have no means of support except Sir Alphonse. I must provide for my future."

"How dreadfully unfair," I said inadequately, adding, "I understand…and sympathize." Maybe she believed me; supposedly, I had been a scorned wife. A misleading reputation certainly has its uses.

I opened my hand, which was sweaty from gripping my diamond ear drops. "Therefore, I wish to offer an exchange—these ear drops for my father's pin."

She gaped. "You're not going to tell Alphonse what I have done?"

"No, for it's none of my business. But my father values that pin, and I don't give a fig for these drops, and their value is perhaps comparable."

Miranda shook her head. "That's most kind of you, my lady, but unnecessary. I'm ashamed of what I've done, but I felt I had no choice." She smiled sadly. "You'd best return them to your jewelry box, or your maid will notice they are missing and cause an outcry."

This was true. If I really wanted to give them to her, I would have to allow her to win them at piquet or some such. But using one's jewelry as a stake is either 1) vulgar or 2) a sign of desperation, neither of which apply to me.

She opened a drawer in her dressing table, reached into the back, and brought out my father's pin. "How do you plan to return it without betraying me?"

"I don't know," I said truthfully, stowing both the pin and my eardrops in the pocket of my dressing gown. "I'll think of something. If worse comes to worst, I'll say I found it someplace."

"I hope that will fool Lord Medway," she said. "He is an observant man. Perhaps that is where you came by that characteristic, Lady Rosamund."

"Perhaps." Certainly not from my mother, or if so, in a different way. She notices a great deal but understands very little. My father may misunderstand or misinterpret one's actions from time to time, but he doesn't refuse to be put right.

Miranda motioned to a sofa over by the fireplace. "Come, please have a sip of brandy with me."

I wanted to leave, but it would be impolite to refuse her hospitality under these already mortifying circumstances. Noting my hesitation, she asked, "Or coffee? I noticed you took some earlier this evening."

"Yes, but I'd best not risk drinking more." I took the proffered seat.

"Understood. One doesn't wish to lie awake all night." She moved gracefully to a table in the corner, which held a decanter and two crystal glasses.

"Just a small amount," I said—too late, for she had already poured more than I would care to drink. I thanked her and took a tiny sip, pondering how much good manners required me to consume. One must take particular care when in the company of a social inferior; it is much easier to cause offense, however unwittingly, than with one's equals.

She seated herself at the other end of the sofa. "I shall leave the Grange forever as soon as this dratted party is over. I wish I could depart now, but it would mortify Alphonse, which I couldn't bear."

"And yet you suspect that he may dismiss you? Isn't that an excessive degree of loyalty?"

"No, it's an excessive degree of *love*," she retorted, tossing back half the brandy in one swallow. She must be both upset at the prospect of leaving the man she loved, and unnerved by my visit.

"Drink some more, Lady Rosamund," she urged. "It will help you sleep. It certainly works for me."

She was drinking to drown her sorrows, poor thing. This interview was becoming more awkward by the second, and then she made it worse.

"Didn't you love your husband?" she demanded, unabashedly inquisitive now. "Didn't you care that he betrayed you?"

It had become clear to me what a brilliant actress Miranda was. She played the lady well, but now, under the influence of brandy and unhappiness, her facade had fallen away and her ungenteel origins were revealed.

"No, I didn't love him," I said. "I held him in affection, certainly, but he was an, er, excessively virile man." This explanation usually served me well as an excuse, for I couldn't disclose the unusual conditions of our marriage.

She laughed mirthlessly. Her response to my polite reference to marital relations was so very vulgar that I couldn't possibly record it here. Suffice it to say that she mentioned the conjugal act in the crudest of terms and downed the rest of her drink.

"Sharing him made my life more comfortable," I said.

"Got him off your back, did it? And your front." She snorted. "Drink up, my lady. The night is young." Her dark, haunted eyes bored into me, deep with some emotion I couldn't quite read. I took another tiny sip.

A profound uneasiness, which had been growing within me, now assailed me full force. Something disturbed me, although I couldn't say quite what. I only knew that I wanted to leave—immediately.

I set the glass down and stood. "You're most kind, but thank you, I'd rather not. If you change your mind about the ear drops, let me know."

I hurried to the door, turning on the way out. "Thank you for the brandy,

Mrs. Tyne," I said politely, and left.

I shut the door and almost bumped into Lancelot Lewis. He must have been hovering in the passageway—eavesdropping? Good Lord, I hoped not.

"Good night, Mr. Lewis," I said briskly and hurried away. I prayed he wouldn't follow.

"You've a visitor waiting," he said. Who in God's name…? Hesitant now, but mistrusting him more than ever, I continued down the corridor, across the landing, and turned the corner…

To find McBrae lounging against the railing, paring his nails—both his attitude and occupation entirely improper in my presence, whether or not he was playing footman. It spoke of an intimacy which simply did not exist.

On the other hand, I did wish to speak to him. On the table sat a small covered pot and a cup. He dropped the scissors into his pocket and straightened his stance.

"Thank heavens it's only you," I whispered. "Mr. Lewis told me I had a visitor. I swear he said it to frighten me."

"Perhaps," he murmured. "He's not in the best of moods."

"Because he realized the identity of the thief?"

"Indeed." McBrae picked up the tray and opened my bedchamber door.

I entered, and without asking my permission, he followed and closed the door. We were alone together in my room! I shuddered at the impropriety, but needs must.

"I've just been to see her," I said. "She gave me my father's diamond cravat pin, and I promised not to betray her." I set the ear drops on the dressing table but put the cravat pin in my reticule, thinking to find a way to return it to my father.

"Lance won't betray her either." McBrae set the tray on my bedside table. "This is milk to help you sleep."

How thoughtful of him. "Thank you. I may need it after drinking the coffee." And after the unhappy scene with Miranda. "Mrs. Tyne is planning to leave Sir Alphonse once the house party is over."

He had made his way toward the door, but at this he turned. "Is that so?"

"She seems frightfully upset," I said. "She's drinking brandy and talking rather...crudely."

"Does this evidence of her vulgar origins bother you, my lady?" The sardonic note in his voice irritated me, but I refused to let it show.

"Only in that it reveals how unhappy she is, I assume because of his affectionate treatment of Miss Ellis."

McBrae made a rude noise. "Sir Alphonse isn't in love with that trollop."

Annoyance washed over me. I did not wish to make excuses for Miss Ellis, but I simply cannot tolerate such wholesale disparagement of my gender. "How dare you dismiss her as immoral, when most men are much worse? If he turns from Miranda to Miss Ellis, he's far more at fault. She's a foolish young woman, but he should know better."

He raised his brows, and I reddened, realizing that this moral tirade must seem at odds with my somewhat tawdry reputation—much of which was his fault. No one had paid much attention to my relationship with my husband and his mistress before he published those horrid caricatures.

I reminded myself severely that I could do absolutely nothing about that with regard to the opinion of society or of McBrae himself. I didn't care much about society, but it hurt, deep down, that McBrae so misjudged me.

I didn't consider him a friend or even a social equal, so why should I care? And yet I did.

I took a deep breath and set my irritation aside in the interest of getting at the truth. Or maybe, if I am being genuinely truthful, I was just curious. "Why wouldn't Lance betray her? Won't he tell his father?"

"Miranda has been more of a mother to Lance than his own ever was." He lounged against the door, arms folded across his chest—another disrespectful stance. Perhaps he was doing it on purpose, in which case I must ignore it.

"His mother left Sir Alphonse when Lance was a child of ten. She was an actress, too, but unlike Miranda, she'd insisted on marriage. When she realized Alphonse's interest was waning, she ran off with a German count."

"For heaven's sake, why? She was Alphonse's wife, not a mistress who could be dismissed at any moment."

"Perhaps she couldn't tolerate a rival for his affection," McBrae said sardonically. "Or perhaps love mattered more than anything else."

"You sound like a romantic novel," I retorted, for I knew full well his remark was directed specifically at my marital relationship in which love had clearly played no great part. Why must that stupidity butt its way into everything? I planted my hands on my hips. "She abandoned her son. That doesn't seem like love to me."

"Now we're discussing two different sorts of love," McBrae said, "and well you know it."

"You don't know anywhere near as much about love as you think you do," I retorted.

He shrugged, and I took another deep breath. How dare he remain so calm while I grew steadily more aggravated!

"Miranda took Lance under her wing," he said. "He will be devastated if she leaves—as will Sir Alphonse."

Well. The logical solution was for Sir Alphonse to marry Miranda, but how might one bring that about?

"Good night, Lady Rosamund," he said. "Sleep well."

Little chance of that, with the risk of someone coming in to murder me. Or just seduce me, take your choice.

"There's a key on your dressing table," he said. "Lock the door."

I should have thanked him, but I was so taken aback that I couldn't say a word. One moment he criticized me with the mere lift of a brow; the next he did me a great kindness.

He was almost out the door when I remembered. "Wait." I hurried toward him. "Shut it again. One never knows who might be listening."

He closed the door and waited, eyes half hooded, smiling faintly.

"I didn't want to tell you this when Lance was there, for it's none of his business."

He eyed me quizzically. "Tell me what?"

"Mr. Powers and Miss Gardner are brother and sister," I whispered. In my haste to detain him, I had approached him far too closely. I retreated a little. "They share a father."

His quizzical expression faded. He didn't shrug this time, but looked as if he were doing so in his mind.

"They hope to keep the secret of her illegitimacy—or rather, he does." I was determined to explain, whether or not it mattered to this vexing man. "She doesn't care quite so much, as in the world of artists, playwrights, poets, and such, it doesn't seem to matter."

He nodded, again giving the impression of a shrug.

"It explains his protectiveness toward her," I added.

"So it does."

"Perhaps Mr. Fence knew their secret and had threatened to reveal it."

"It seems likely."

"Which in turn explains Miss Gardner's fear that Mr. Powers might have killed him, but I'm almost sure he didn't."

Another nod. Evidently, he had reached this conclusion without even knowing the facts.

Fine, but I intended to continue doggedly until I was done. "I suggested that he stay away from Miss Gardner and renew his interest in Miss Ellis until the inquest is over, for safety's sake."

"Wise." Politely, he added, "Thank you for clearing that up, Lady Rosamund." He opened the door again, and this time I let him go.

Chapter Thirteen

So much for my fond and foolish hopes—but as that pompous ass
Bellevue says, one must persevere.

—From the diary of Corvus

The morning dawned clear and bright—perfect for the Lammas fair.
Cynthia declined to attend, saying the heat would be too much
for her. I don't think Sir Roderick would have attended either,
despite his interest in the hound trail, but she persuaded him to go. His
reluctance to leave her seemed so full of genuine concern that I found myself
actually approving of him.

What nonsense. He wanted to continue pestering poor, beleaguered
Cynthia to marry him. Perhaps he thought more of those passionate kisses
would do it. I can't imagine anything less likely!

However, I've done enough complaining about Sir Roderick, so onward
to the day's event. After breakfast, we trooped less than half a mile to the
village green to watch wrestling, archery, rowing matches, and sundry races.
There were booths with items for sale, ranging from perfumed soaps to
ribbons to jams, pickles, and other preserves. There was also judging of
flowers, vegetables, and some absolutely gorgeous examples of first fruit
loaves. I crossed my fingers and hoped Sir Alphonse's cook would win—and
she did!

All in all, very lively and entertaining, but I couldn't stop thinking about the upcoming inquest and our failure to identify the murderer. McBrae gave no sign of having reached a conclusion. Worse, he seemed entirely carefree as he participated in the archery (second place—impressive!), and a sack race, in which he did well until suddenly he slipped, fell, and rolled out of the way of the rest, laughing. What an excellent sport he was—and what a completely unconscionable way to behave while a murderer was about to escape justice.

Lance strolled about with Miranda—being protective? Or simply taking his father's place while Sir Alphonse presented various prizes. She was putting a good face on it, but she didn't look at all well. Miss Ellis, meanwhile, had commandeered Powers, as there was no one else to be had; she was at daggers drawn with Beaver ever since his remark about the pox. Miss Gardner resignedly allowed Harold Bellevue to squire her about, chaperoned closely by Mrs. Holloway and the Wendells.

McBrae was helping to set up another race when Lance left Miranda with Alphonse and approached me. "Why the scowl?"

I did my best to smile. "The sunlight is excessively bright." True, but my bonnet shaded my eyes perfectly well.

"It's your confused conscience at work," he said. "Come, let's walk up the fellside to watch the hounds pass by."

When I hesitated, he gave an entirely unnecessary explanation. "Surely you've seen a hound trail. A horde of dogs follow a trail for miles across the fells. They are admirable creatures, but I couldn't care less who wins, so I refuse to stand at the finish line while their lunatic owners shout themselves hoarse."

"Yes, years ago." I remembered Papa's footman coming home exhausted after laying the trail with the stinking remains of a rabbit, and the shouts and cheers when the hounds arrived at the finish. I didn't like Lance much, but I do like dogs, and a walk would do me good.

He offered me his arm, and I took it, because 1) it would stop me from scowling at McBrae enjoying himself, 2) I wanted to ask how Miranda was doing, and 3) what the deuce did he mean by that remark?

"Confused conscience?" I asked, as we left the green and began the steep climb up the fell, but on a wider path than we had followed yesterday.

He glanced at me sideways. "Come now, surely it's clear. You won't tattle on Miranda, a thief, and yet you can't tolerate the thought of a murderer going free."

"I won't betray Miranda because I feel for her," I said. "I understand what it is to be betrayed by those who profess to love one."

He smirked. "And yet you participated willingly in a *ménage à trois*…or did you? Do you mean to imply that you really were a scorned wife? That you did indeed push the footman down the stairs?"

"I don't mean anything of the sort." And I couldn't possibly explain what I *had* meant.

"Perhaps, but if you really cared about justice, surely you would require her to return all the items she has stolen, not merely your father's pin."

"I'm not a representative of the law. Once I knew she was the thief, I couldn't let her keep my father's pin, but what she does with the rest is none of my business."

"What an elastic moral code you possess, Lady Rosamund. I saw you frowning at Mac. How can you expect him and me, neither of whom are connected with our excellent system of laws and justice, to abandon our enjoyment of these games to unmask a murderer, no matter who he—or she—might be, no matter why he—or she—committed the dastardly deed?"

I couldn't respond, for I knew I was being unreasonable. If they hadn't worked it out yet, it was probably too late anyway. Soon the games would be over and the inquest would take place.

"Fortunately, females will not attend the inquest," he said.

That got my back up. "I have no patience with excluding women. I am perfectly capable of testifying to what I saw." Except that I would have to lie about the appearance of the corpse, I thought guiltily.

We left the beaten path to take a sheep track up the side of the fell. He preceded me, and for a while we didn't speak. A startled grouse flew out of the heather, calling a warning.

Soon we were next to a rushing beck with a waterfall above it. We stood to catch our breath. "It's beautiful," I said. "How much farther?"

"Not much." Again, he preceded me upwards. I hoped we had finished with the subject of my conscience.

No such luck. "You see what I mean by confused? You lied about the corpse's expression because you felt sorry for Miss Gardner. What if you were to unmask the murderer and find that you sympathized with his—or her—motive? Then what would your conscience tell you to do?"

I didn't know how to answer the second question, so I ignored it. "I expect we all would sympathize. Mr. Fence was a horrid man, and for everyone's peace of mind, he is better off dead."

"We agree on that, and yet your conscience still grates that the murderer remains free?"

"Yes, it does." So did the way he kept saying *him—or her. His—or hers*, as if he thought it just as likely that a woman had killed Fence.

My blood ran cold. I stumbled, and cried out as I caught myself.

He turned. "Is the climb too much for you? This waterfall is Bleakwater Force, and the hounds will pass close above here any minute now."

"I'm fine," I bleated, too aghast to think clearly. I scrambled the rest of the way behind him, and we emerged onto the moor. The beck tumbled past, still full with the accumulated rainfall. A few minutes later, we reached the shore of a tranquil little lake.

He gestured at the shimmering water. "Bleakwater Tarn. Come." He tucked my hand in his arm, and I continued obediently around the lakeshore, thinking hard.

Miranda, agreeing that drinking coffee late at night would keep one awake.

Miranda, two nights earlier, carrying a tray with coffee—at midnight. Where was she taking the coffee, and to whom? I had automatically assumed—if I'd even thought about it—that it was for herself and Sir Alphonse.

What if the coffee was meant for Mr. Fence? The powerful flavor might mask any number of bitter poisons. That would explain a great deal.

We had reached the far shore of the little lake. "It's quite deep and cold," Lancelot said. "My friends and I used to swim there as children, but I wouldn't wish to do so now."

What if Mr. Fence was drugged—or already dead—when the trophy fell on him? Or was placed there to hide the true cause of death.

Cold fear clenched my gut. I removed my hand from Lance's arm and bent to pick up a pebble from the shore. I turned it around and around in my hand. Surely not Miranda. I simply couldn't believe it.

"How is Miranda doing this morning?" I asked casually, wandering away from him, back toward the beck.

"As well as can be expected. I reassured her. I told her she needn't fear betrayal. That I would keep her safe."

Safe from me?

"Do you swim, Lady Rosamund?" he asked.

Lance would do anything to protect Miranda, whom he adored.

Including murder? "I learned as a child in Kent." I'd been too afraid then to do more than paddle in the shallows, but now I would learn to swim properly if it killed me.

If Lance didn't kill me first.

"There's a charcoal burner's hut down there." He was beside me again, one hand on my shoulder, the other indicating a dense area of wood on the far slope of the fell. Trying to distract me, before he pushed me in the lake?

"The hounds!" I cried, moving away from him to point. The first of them careened into view, followed by a horde of others, intent on nothing but the trail. He turned to watch.

I picked up my skirts and ran straight for the pack of dogs.

"Stop!" Lance bellowed. "Don't get in their way!" but I ran anyway, and the agile hounds, baying their excitement, poured around me in a stream. I leapt past the waterfall, slipping and sliding down the rocks. Lance uttered a furious oath, and I kept going down, down through the sheep tracks in the heather.

And into the arms of McBrae.

"Thank God!" I clung to him for dear life.

There is something excessively comforting about clinging to McBrae, but it is also most improper. I recovered myself quickly and stood away.

"Lance?" he asked.

"He threatened me," I blurted. Perhaps I wasn't as recovered as I thought. I was panting in a most unladylike way, and my heart pounded in my chest.

McBrae sighed. Didn't he believe me?

"Not in so many words," I protested, "but he said the tarn was deep and cold, and asked if I could swim, and—" I shuddered.

"Lance adores Miranda, but I don't think he would have drowned you when it came right down to it."

Just what I would expect from McBrae—he had already guessed Lance's reason for frightening me. He glanced up the path, but there was no sign of his horrid friend. Suddenly, a volley of cheers and cries of encouragement filled the air. "That's the end of the hound trail." He bent to pick up a sketchbook and pencil. He must have dropped them when I tumbled straight into his arms.

He ripped out a sheet of paper, folded it, and stowed it in his pocket. Before he closed the book, I glimpsed the drawing beneath it – a sketch of the fairy well, with a mischievous little creature helping himself to the cup of ale.

"That's a pretty drawing," I said. "A hobgoblin?"

"Could be. Come, let's return to the village." He motioned to me to precede him.

"I don't think of you as drawing something so fanciful." It was awkward to speak on this narrow path. "What did you rip out?" When he didn't give me an answer, I supplied one. "A new caricature."

"Aye." Which meant he didn't want to tell me about it.

Fine, but I couldn't just let it go. "When I caught you on the landing, you were sketching a group of people looking at the body with the trophy on top of it."

"Aye. I think I'll call it *The Revenge of the Horned God*."

I stopped and turned, as the implications assailed me. "Surely you won't publish that."

The corner of his mouth twitched up. "Why not? There are plenty of well-known people here, so it should sell well. Sir Alphonse and Miranda, your father, Mr. Bellevue… Even Sir Roderick, which has its amusing side, since he is known to be straightlaced and would ordinarily avoid such loose company."

"So would Lady Benson and I. You promised not to caricature her." I had scarcely begun to calm down, and already annoyance simmered within me. I resisted the urge to stomp away. McBrae aroused unladylike instincts which I should know better than to possess.

"I promised not to reveal her pregnancy—which I will not, and any portrait of you or her will be favorable."

"Thank you," I said a little too huffily, "but what about the others?" There—proof that I wasn't a thoughtless, selfish aristocrat. I was thinking of others, not only of myself.

"You can't expect me to choose my subject matter according to your whims, Lady Rosamund."

How dare he? Somehow, I managed not to clench my fists. "It's not a *whim*. What if one of them is a murderer?"

"That's precisely the point," he said. "The coroner's verdict will likely be accidental death. The murderer will consider himself—or herself—safe. Which he—or she—will be from the law, but not from me."

Which was unfair to those who were innocent but would be included in any unpleasant speculation about Fence's death. I told him so, but he just shrugged. "Are you concerned about your father?"

"No, he'll find it amusing," I admitted grumpily, "especially the bit about the horned god, for he and Sir Alphonse have an ongoing disagreement about the subject." We had reached the wider path, and I glanced back. There was still no sign of Lancelot Lewis.

Did McBrae believe Miranda was guilty—hence his odious repetition of *he—or she*, just like Lance?

"He'll come down soon enough," McBrae said. "He's obliged to attend the inquest."

"He's worried about Miranda," I said, "and I made it worse by insisting that the murderer must be caught."

"That's no excuse for threatening you," McBrae said.

"I told him I was perfectly capable of testifying. Perhaps he feared I would force my way into the inquest."

"Ah," he said. "Did you see something that you believe is significant in identifying Miranda as the murderer?"

"No!" I protested, and then, "Perhaps, but I refuse to believe it."

"You'd better tell me," he said.

"It never even occurred to me until Lance began acting in such a menacing way," I said. "But *you* thought of it. Do you believe she did it?"

"She certainly had a motive. She's been stealing to save for her retirement, and that blackguard Fence would have blackmailed every penny from her. I wonder how he knew."

"He seems to have known a great deal about many people," I said, and then wished I hadn't. McBrae also knew too much about too many people.

"Yes," he said, as if I'd voiced my thought. "I admit to being intolerably nosy."

I explained how the first night I'd been unable to sleep and had gone looking for milk, and luckily met Miranda in the corridor. "She was carrying a tray with a coffeepot and two cups. I assumed it was for her and Sir Alphonse, but…maybe not."

"You suspect she intended to meet Mr. Fence and poison him?"

"Midnight is not the usual time to drink coffee," I said unhappily. "If he died of poisoning, the stag's head was a good way to disguise it."

"True."

"And later, when Miss Gardner screamed and ran up the stairs, I peered over the baluster before going down. It was scarcely light, but I saw a woman's form lean over the body and—and push down on whatever was on top of it."

McBrae snorted. And then chuckled—imagine! "Shoving the antlers in good and proper."

I shuddered again. "To make sure he was dead."

"Or perhaps out of sheer relief, even glee." He tutted. "It doesn't look good for her, does it?"

No, it didn't, and what was I to do? What did he intend? I opened my mouth to ask, but he put up a hand. "There are a few difficulties with this theory, apart from the fact that neither of us wishes her to be guilty."

What a relief that we were united in our dilemma.

"Where was she going with the coffee? Where did she intend to meet Fence? If in the drawing room, why did she bring the coffee up an extra flight? If she meant to meet him upstairs, then where? If so, how did Fence end up in the Great Hall? Much as she would have liked to push him down the stairs—a womanly sort of solution to the problem—he showed no sign of injury consistent with a fall."

"It may be womanly," I said, nettled, "but I was not a scorned wife, and I did not push the footman down the stairs." Drat, I shouldn't have changed the subject, but every time I am accused of participating in a *ménage à trois* (or as good as), I become irate.

He snorted again. "If you say so."

Indignation seized me. "Don't you even *care* whether I killed him?"

"I'm sure you did not," he said, which was all very well, but made it clear that although he believed me innocent in that respect, he also didn't believe my denial about being a desperate wife scorned.

I longed to tell him the truth, but it would be far too mortifying, not to mention an entirely improper subject of conversation between a gentleman and a lady. Also, none of his business. Instead, I took a deep breath.

"I beg your pardon," he said softly. "I shouldn't tease. Obviously, it's a sore point with you."

"Your refusal to believe me is the sore point." I hoped that would make him reconsider his unfair conclusion about me. "Back to more important matters. I don't suppose Miranda could easily have lifted that trophy from the wall."

"No. Either she had an accomplice, or our speculations are mere fantasy. We must question her."

"Why? Neither of us intends to accuse her."

"Because if she didn't kill Fence, who did? Maybe there was nothing to find in Fence's room—no documents, no letters, no pleas for more time—because whoever killed him took it all away. If not Miranda, then who?"

"Surely whoever took it would have burned it."

"In which case there would be ashes in a bedchamber grate—unlikely at this time of year."

This was true. It was far too warm for fires, and the grates had likely been swept clean months ago, so ashes would tell a tale.

"I'll have a look round," he said. "As a footman, I can easily check the bedchambers."

We were almost at the green when Lance hailed us. He limped heavily down the path, looking like thunder. He must have fallen in that melee of hounds. I didn't feel the slightest bit sorry for him.

On the other hand, I didn't know what he might do or say. "I'm safe enough now. I suppose I could pretend I ran because the dogs frightened me."

McBrae glanced ahead at the green. "Will your father believe that?"

I followed his gaze to where Papa conversed with a bent and tattered old man—gathering folk tales, no doubt. Had he seen me speaking with McBrae? Quite possibly. I shook my head.

"Nor will Lance." McBrae bowed, and when he raised his head, he was not-McBrae once more. In that soft, Scottish voice, he said, "Thank you for coming to fetch me, my lady."

"Poor Mr. Lewis," I said sweetly, watching Lance approach. "He managed to walk this far, so perhaps it's not such a bad sprain after all."

McBrae gave me a grin, and we retraced our steps to meet Lance.

I admit, I had to suppress a grin of my own at McBrae's pretense of deference: that air of concern, that bow to his supposed master, that murmur which definitely wasn't an inquiry about the injury.

Lance reddened and motioned McBrae brusquely to the side. "My dear Lady Rosamund," he began, far too loudly, "it was most unwise of you to run into the hound trail. You might have been badly hurt."

"Keep your voice down," I retorted. "I have no intention of accusing Miranda, whether privately or in public."

He glared at me, but he did lower his voice. "You could have said so."

"I might have, if instead of threatening me, you had given me the chance."

"But…I didn't *threaten* you." His air of shocked innocence was beautifully done.

"Your acting prowess is wasted on me." I wondered if he had inherited this skill from his mother. "You must pretend that you sprained your ankle, and that I hurried down to find Mac."

"I don't have to pretend, damn you. Ouch."

"Mind your manners." McBrae moved to Lance's injured side and offered his arm.

Lance refused it. "Manners be damned. A lady who tries to identify a murderer—an entirely unladylike sort of activity, if you ask me—"

"Nobody is asking you," McBrae said.

"—Can bloody well put up with being treated like a man."

"You're just miffed because she's not bowled over by your charms," McBrae said.

Lance opened his mouth to retort. I put up a hand. "Hush, you two. I have brothers, so I'm used to both bad language and bad behavior."

Lance snarled. "How would you behave, if you thought your mother was about to be accused of murder?"

That took me aback. I dislike my mother, which is most unfilial of me, so how would I feel? I wouldn't wish such a thing on her—in fact, it was almost impossible to imagine—and yet I hadn't the faintest idea what I would do about it.

McBrae snickered. He had seen enough of my mother to understand.

My father, however… The thought of him being so accused froze me to the heart. "Very well, I understand, but you needn't fret. The inquest is about to take place, and they will surely bring in a verdict of accidental death. Then it won't matter whether or not she killed Mr. Fence."

"She didn't kill him, curse you," he hissed. "She's going to leave us. I already lost one mother. I don't care to lose another."

Oh, dear. Sometimes I wish I *could* lose my mother. "Why didn't Sir Alphonse marry her?"

"He couldn't, because my mother was still alive. She left him when I was a child."

"But she's dead now, isn't she?" I asked. "Why didn't he marry Miranda once he was free to do so?"

"It probably never crossed his mind," McBrae said.

Or Lance's either, judging by his blank expression—until she decided to leave. "Then we should make it do so," I said. "Perhaps Miranda fears his interest is waning. He's paying far too much attention to Miss Ellis."

"Because Miranda wants him to help further her career," Lance snapped. "He's only doing as he was asked."

"A little too effusively last night, but that was in hope of avoiding a murder inquiry," murmured McBrae. "It's plain that he adores Miranda."

This I believed, and I could see why. In her way, she was an estimable woman, and Sir Alphonse spoke of her with affection and pride. She held her head high and acted the perfect lady despite being tolerated only for his sake. Not that this would explain *his* admiration, but it certainly explained mine.

"He will be heartbroken if she leaves." Lance sighed. "As will I."

"We shall do our best to prevent that," I said. "Can you walk as far as the inn? You should put your foot up."

"A tankard of ale wouldn't go amiss." His charming smile reappeared. "Do forgive me, Lady Rosamund." He was far too competent at playing the penitent.

"Very well," I said sternly, hoping he didn't realize that although I would do my best to protect Miranda, I intended to question her first.

The difficulty was finding a way to speak to her alone. As the afternoon progressed, some of us returned briefly to the Grange for rest or refreshment, or to use the necessary in more comfort and privacy than one can expect at a common inn. The servants took turns remaining in pairs at the house to provide assistance when needed, while the others had time off to enjoy the Lammas fair.

The inquest was set for three o'clock, but as it happened, fate intervened in the shape of a cragfast sheep. Fully five of Mr. Johnson's jurors left with ropes, picks, and other equipment to rescue a foolish ewe who had wandered too far along a ledge and now had no room to turn around.

Mr. Johnson muttered a little, but as a countryman he understood that a live sheep mattered far more than a dead man. "Ah, well. The corpse won't get any deader overnight. We'll do the inquest first thing tomorrow morning."

At first this seemed a gift from the heavens. We now had the remainder of the afternoon and evening to identify the murderer.

And then my brother Julius arrived.

Chapter Fourteen

*She feels safe with me. I should be pleased; instead, I am an
ungrateful oaf.*

—From the diary of Corvus

Let me introduce my brother before I proceed. Julius, Viscount
Derwent, is my father's heir and my least favorite sibling. He is a
masculine copy of my mother. He takes all her maxims to heart and
truly believes he and his peers are God's gift to the English people.

He also believes, as she does, that my peculiarity renders me insane, or
close enough to it that I constitute a danger to the reputation of the Medway
earldom. He would gladly see me shut away at home, declared too weak and
ill to see visitors, there to waste away in captivity. No, I'm not jesting. Nor
am I lying.

What the devil—pardon my language—was he doing here in the Lakes? To
his mind, anyplace north of Derbyshire is uncivilized, even barbaric. (And
you thought I suffered from stupid prejudices.) He spends most of his time
in Kent, managing my father's principal seat, but takes frequent visits to
London to transact business and see his mistress.

(Poor girl, how horrid to be at his mercy. I decided, after meeting her a
few months ago, that when he dismisses her, I shall help her in whatever way
I can. Not that he would be likely to leave her destitute; he's an honorable
man by prevailing standards, and will provide for her in some small way.

But his nature, like my mother's, is bereft of compassion.

Or so it seems, but perhaps my dislike of him is colored by his willingness to persecute me.)

Enough digressing. The landlord of the inn had set out tables in the shade, where some of us partook of coffee or the local ale. Miss Ellis sulkily played dice with Mr. Powers; Beaver and Bellevue had wandered off in separate directions. Mr. Johnson and Sir Roderick swapped stories about their hounds, while Miranda, Mrs. Wendell, and Miss Gardner discussed their purchases and pondered one more round of the booths. The Colonel had gone to fetch some cigarillos, while Mrs. Holloway followed the farmers who'd gone to rescue the sheep. Papa and Sir Alphonse peppered McBrae with questions about Scottish banshees as opposed to Irish ones.

Lance, next to me, put his foot up on a stool and glowered into his tankard of ale. I was still rather annoyed, but on the other hand I did understand his fears for Miranda. (Which did not excuse frightening the wits out of me.) I was enjoying McBrae's nonsense about banshees, particularly the one he claimed to have encountered while staying at a friend's house as a child. Apparently, banshees are friendly creatures when not obliged to wail about impending doom.

What a pity no banshee was here to warn us about the doom about to be inflicted on me. Perhaps I should have noticed something was wrong when Sir Roderick suddenly stood, muttering something about checking on his wife, and strode hurriedly away.

I couldn't have done anything to prevent the unwelcome arrival, but I could have worn strict mourning instead of a deep blue gown, and I could have put the new red ribbons I'd purchased at one of the booths in my reticule instead of tying them onto my bonnet. I could have sat anywhere but next to the most handsome gentleman in the party, and I could have stifled my laughter (which was far too immoderate for mother's, and therefore Julius' taste) at one of McBrae's tales. I muffled it soon enough when I spied my brother, completely out of place in this idyllic scene, striding toward our (mostly) pleasant little group.

My first thought, of course, was that he came bearing bad news. Had something dreadful happened to my mother, my sisters, or more likely my other brother, who is a soldier in the Peninsula?

But Julius wouldn't have come all the way here for that; he would have sent Papa an express instead. Besides, he was looking down his nose—his everyday expression—so why?

"Derwent!" Papa said. "This is a surprise. Your mother doing well?"

"As well as can be expected," he said, and clamped his mouth shut. I knew what he wanted to add: *under the circumstances*. The *circumstances* always have to do with me.

Surely not this time, though. I was two hundred or so miles away from Mother. She had no cause for complaint. She should be happy I was safely out of the way.

"Oh? What's to do?" When Julius merely scowled, Papa motioned to McBrae. "A chair and a tankard of ale for my son and heir, please, Mac." Whilst McBrae obliged, Papa introduced everyone, and Julius exchanged polite nothings with Sir Alphonse and Mrs. Wendell, with whom he was previously acquainted.

Miss Ellis commanded Mr. Powers to carry her chair to our table, where she gazed at my brother, transfixed—not by his looks, although he is a reasonably handsome man, but by his wealth, status, and single state. I knew a catty urge to tell her he already had a mistress, since she was doubtless pondering seduction with marriage as her goal. Impossible, needless to say. Julius knows what is due his name.

But how amusing if Corvus put Miss Ellis and her ambitions in a caricature! Then I caught Julius' admonitory glower, and nothing seemed funny anymore.

"So, my boy," my father said, "cough it up, whatever it is, and get it over with. Yes, I know some of these people are strangers to you, but we're all friends here."

Julius' appalled expression showed how unlikely he was to consider any of these people his friends. Stiffly, he said, "Very well, sir. It's public property by now, so every lout in every backwater of the realm will see it before long."

Oh, *no*.

He motioned to his groom, who hovered not far away. The man approached with a folded sheet of paper, which Julius opened and spread upon the table.

I knew what was coming. Well, not precisely what, but who had made the what. It took every ounce of self-control I possessed not to glance at McBrae.

"Corvus' latest effort." Julius spat the words. "My dear mother is prostrate."

Everyone clustered around to take a look. As usual, the drawing was magnificent. Corvus sat bare-bottomed and dejected on a bench, a birch rod beside him, lamenting the departure of his muse. Cynthia and I were about to leave London. Sir Roderick knelt by the coach in tears, pleading with her to stay, whilst I, with one foot on the steps, turned towards Corvus to blow him a kiss.

That made me blush. The nerve of the man!

Meanwhile, my mother was portrayed as a witch with unkempt hair and wild eyes, crying, "One hundred stripes!" while Julius, sneering even more than usual, tried to calm her, saying, 'Leave it to me, Mother. I'll have his head if it's the last thing I do.'

Oh, *dear*, and that wasn't the worst of it. A footman with a cat-o'-nine-tails—far more damaging than a mere birch rod—was refusing the order to flog Corvus, saying, 'Druther not, missus. He draws such lovely pictures.'

I choked on a laugh. A footman addressing the Countess of Medway as *missus*—can you imagine?

"I should have known you would be amused," my brother said austerely.

My father chuckled, rescuing me. "Yes, you should. It's brilliantly done."

There was a relieved sigh all around, and those who had been valiantly holding back their laughter released a cacophony of titters, chortles, and guffaws.

Julius snorted down his nose like a bull. He wanted to lambaste the lot of them, but to do so would show disrespect for my father, and Julius is always rigidly proper.

(Except when he's drunk, or so I have heard.)

"You'll be a peer one day," Papa said. "You'd best get accustomed to mockery."

Julius made a dismissive sound. "I don't care about myself, but for that scoundrel to upset my mother, to insult her in such a way, is intolerable. She has taken to her bed and doubts she will ever recover."

When seriously upset, my mother always becomes prostrate and prophesies that she is about to breathe her last.

"Poor, dear Lady Medway," Mrs. Wendell offered politely.

"Indeed," my brother said. "For a lady of her exquisite sensibilities to encounter such callousness is devastating, and it's not the first time. He has caricatured her twice in the most cruel, unjust way. Who knows when it will end?"

The first caricature, in which she'd helped to persecute an innocent maid, had been entirely justified. This one, however entertaining, was not.

"Most improper of the fellow," Sir Alphonse said. "Deserves the punishment coming to him." Which evoked more laughter and a snarl from my brother.

"Poor Mother," I murmured belatedly.

"Nonsense," Papa said. "Your mother shouldn't take it to heart. Matter of fact, she should take a leaf from your book, Rosie. You're not upset in the least, despite the man's infernal impudence. Blowing a kiss, indeed!"

"True, but he makes me prettier than I am. What lady would object to that, or fail to be flattered at being a muse?" Drat, I sounded far too cheerful.

"That's the spirit," Papa said heartily, but Julius turned so red that I feared he might have an apoplectic fit.

"A muse for that—that *villain?*" he bellowed.

"I may be his inspiration, but I can't control how he expresses himself," I retorted. I would have to remonstrate with McBrae—an unpleasant prospect. Meanwhile, I did my best to placate my brother. "He will have to do without me, though, for I don't intend to return to London anytime soon. I expect he will find a new muse."

Julius opened his mouth to retort, but shut it again. He had already said far more than he deemed proper. It would certainly give the theater people plenty to gossip and jest about.

"If Mother doesn't allow Corvus to upset her, he'll look for another victim," I said. It was *torment* not to frown meaningfully at McBrae.

"Quite so," Papa said. "Can't say I understand why you came all the way here to show this to me, Derwent. What does your mother expect me to do about it?"

Julius' facial muscles twitched, but he said nothing. He couldn't say what he really wanted to, because whatever Mother wished, it was a private matter. A family matter.

In other words, Rosie's madness? My stomach clenched—but it seemed unlikely. I was securely out of the way, causing no scandals. I couldn't help it if Corvus had put me in another caricature.

Papa echoed my thought. "I can't stop the fellow from drawing whatever he wishes. No one even knows who he is."

Julius shrugged and took a long swallow of ale. "Mother ordered me to come to you, so I did."

"You couldn't have arrived at a better time," Sir Alphonse said. "We're having a jolly party here, and we always have room for another guest."

"That's most kind of you, sir, but I must head back to Kent in the morning."

"Nonsense," Papa said. "No point in exhausting yourself. Stay a few days, do some fishing, maybe take a sailboat on the lake."

Longing crossed my brother's face. He'd loved sailing as a boy. He'd been quite a pleasant sort back then, as elder brothers go.

"That settles it," Papa said. "You'll stay."

Which was all very well, but how were we to get through the evening? Last night had been bad enough. As evening drew in, we all returned to the Grange. Miss Ellis, who had made no headway in attracting my brother's attention, swanned in with Mr. Powers. He looked strained and unhappy, but he was too polite to forcibly peel her off his arm.

Miranda waved him in the direction of the billiards room. "The gentlemen are there with a bowl of punch. You must join them as well, Mr. Powers." She detached him smoothly from Miss Ellis, and next rescued Miss Gardner, once more escorted by Harold Bellevue, by shooing him off as well. "Ladies, there will be coffee in the drawing room shortly."

"This place is such a *bore*," Miss Ellis said. "I *loathe* watching rustics."

"I thought it was rather fun," Miss Gardner said. "Mrs. Holloway and I both took a turn at archery. Mr. Beaver, too—he's quite good. I was hopeless, but I'd love to learn."

Miss Ellis rolled her eyes. "Why? You'd never have the guts to shoot anything."

"For the accomplishment," Miss Gardner said. "Fencing would be more useful, though, if I want to imagine that sort of scene in a play."

Miss Ellis laughed. "Next you'll say you want to fight a duel. No, wait—you're too lily-livered to even *watch* a fight." She batted her eyelashes in my brother's direction, a waste of effort as he was deep in conversation with Sir Roderick, who had spent the latter part of the afternoon here with Cynthia. I wondered what lies Sir Roderick was telling Julius about his so-called marriage. I realized now why he had sprung up and hurried away from the inn before my brother saw him. He'd probably felt as much dismay as I about my brother's arrival. What if Julius had expressed surprise and come out with something tactless like, "You married *Lady Benson*?" (After which he would have glared at me as if it was all my fault.)

No, Sir Roderick would explain that he'd chosen to marry Cynthia privately and retire to the country to avoid gossip. Julius, for whom discretion was a religion, would understand that, even if he deplored Sir Roderick's choice of wife.

"I don't like fighting," Miss Gardner said. "It's horrid. People should be polite and kind to one another."

"If you want to write plays that will actually be performed, you'd best learn about the real world." Miss Ellis widened her eyes and assumed an aspect of terror. "Where people are murdered." She drew the word out, just as she had done the other day, and cast a darkling glance at Beaver, who had just walked in the door.

"Enough," Miranda said. "My sister seems to have taught you no manners at all—which you'll soon learn are as important as acting ability in the real world."

"Humph." Miss Ellis flounced away.

"No one was murdered," Miss Gardner said, the tremor back in her voice.

"Of course not," I said soothingly. "Miss Ellis prefers to infuse drama into everything. It's natural for an actress to do so."

Miss Ellis glanced over her shoulder at me, almost pleased, as if she thought this might be a compliment. Any complacency wouldn't last, however. She had merely to drop a word in Mr. Johnson's ear to get revenge on Beaver, and she must have noticed Powers' martyred air this afternoon. Something must be done, and done soon.

Very well—I would kill two birds with one stone.

I turned to Miranda. "Mrs. Tyne, too much sun has given me a headache. Do you by any chance have some laudanum drops?"

Miranda led me silently to her bedchamber and closed the door behind us. "You don't have a headache."

"No," I said. "I want to drug Miss Ellis." When she simply stared at me, I said, "I'm sorry to insult your niece, but she's dangerous. Her admirers are dropping away one after another, and my brother is far too fastidious to join their ranks. I don't think even Sir Alphonse will put up with her much longer. He's only doing so for your sake."

She shrugged, stony-faced. Evidently, this subject was not up for discussion.

"If she mentions murder in Mr. Johnson's hearing, we'll be in the soup," I said. "I believe almost everyone here had a reason to wish Mr. Fence was dead."

There was a silence.

"Stop beating about the bush," Miranda said. "As I said last night, you're observant. It doesn't take a stretch of the imagination to realize that I was one of them. He found out that I was selling jewelry, some of it not my own."

"I'm not accusing you of murder," I said. "But I think you did drug him."

"What choice did I have? He had somehow inveigled a bill of sale from the shop where I sold them." She sneered. "Probably threatened to tell the runners the shop was receiving stolen goods. He was that sort of man."

"You drugged him…so you could search his bedchamber for those documents?"

"Yes. He was hovering in the corridor, waiting for me, when I came upstairs. I said I had to give Alphonse his coffee first—so of course he took it for himself." She rolled her eyes. "He said he had a long night ahead. Maybe the fool thought I would sleep with him—although he usually prefers them young."

"Ugh. What a loathsome man."

"I feigned a tantrum and stomped away, telling him I would bring some money to his room as soon as I could get away from Alphonse."

"What if he hadn't taken the coffee?"

"I had already drugged the brandy in the decanter in his chamber. There was only a small amount in the bottom, so he was almost certain to drink it."

"Thorough of you," I said. Dangerous, though, for if he had drunk everything it might have killed him.

What if it had? What if she had found him dead and run to Lance, who had dragged him downstairs and put the stag's head atop him? I didn't favor this theory, but I tend to think the best of those I like (meaning Miranda, not Lance).

(For example, I should be furious at McBrae, but all I felt about his latest caricature was dismay.)

"I know what you're thinking," she said. "Maybe he drank both, and that killed him. I don't think so—I didn't use an inordinate amount—but we'll never know for sure."

Did this mean she had made certain of that?

"But I didn't drop the stag's head on him. I waited as long as I dared, hoping he would fall asleep, and then Alphonse came to my chamber." Sadness suffused her voice. "He was uneasy and wanted comfort. I couldn't bring myself to turn him away. Eventually, he left."

"And when you went to Mr. Fence's chamber?"

"He wasn't there."

"He'd gone? Where?"

"How was I to know? I was frantic, not knowing where he was or to whom he was speaking. Perhaps I had taken too long and he'd decided to tattle to Alphonse—but the coffee pot was empty and the decanter was gone."

"Where was it?"

"I have no idea. Perhaps Fence brought it down to refill it in the drawing room, and then became drowsy. I thought it wisest not to draw attention to it."

Which made complete sense, but if Fence hadn't removed it, who had? And why?

"I searched the room," she said. "The writing desk was empty. His valise contained a few personal items. I thought perhaps he had hidden any documents for fear of prying servants, but they weren't under the mattress or in his boots, or anywhere else. I went looking for him and at last found him fast asleep in a chair in the Great Hall.

"I don't know why he went downstairs, but evidently the laudanum had overcome him there. I searched him thoroughly but again found nothing, and went up to my bedchamber again, utterly defeated. He must have hidden the bill of sale so carefully that no one would find it. He would wake in the morning and realize I had drugged him. He would demand even more money. I couldn't sleep for wondering what to do."

I sensed that she was well into her role. Not that she was lying, necessarily, but acting was second nature to her.

"And then?" I asked.

"I went to the kitchen to make more coffee, and drank it there, wondering what to do. Eventually, I crept back to the Great Hall to see if he was still asleep. Imagine my astonishment to find him on the floor with that horrid stag's head on top of him, the antlers penetrating his chest. He was dead."

"What a relief that must have been."

"Yes—dead, but not by my hand. The trophy had finally fallen off the wall. Then I saw light coming from the drawing room and backed away before Miss Gardner saw me. She dropped her candle and started screaming and sobbing. You know what happened after that."

Yes, you returned and pushed the antlers even more firmly into his chest. But I didn't say that—what was the point? I believed the essentials of her story, and I didn't blame her for that last little act of revenge.

Lancelot Lewis stormed into the room. "Meddling again, Lady Rosamund? You said you weren't going to accuse Miranda!"

"I didn't," I began, but Miranda rose up, virago-like.

"Lance, where are your manners? Lady Rosamund and I have been having a pleasant chat about the demise of Mr. Fence. We have concluded that although I drugged him, his death was an accident."

"It was?" He looked utterly *bouleversé*. Dear me—had he indeed believed her guilty? Or had he killed the man himself? Or did he accept that we had really come to such an absurd conclusion?

"Yes," I agreed cheerfully, "but unfortunately Miss Ellis is likely to stir up trouble this evening. One by one, her admirers are losing interest. We feel that the only way to get through the evening safely is to drug *her*."

At this precise moment, Mrs. Wendell burst into loud shrieks. We poured out into the passageway and met her as she reached the head of the stairs.

"Someone has ransacked my room!" she cried. "My garments, my jewels, my husband's cravat pins—they're all over the place."

"Was anything stolen?" I asked. We hurried towards her chamber.

"I don't know. How can I possibly tell? It's in such disarray!"

I glanced at Lance, for he had organized the pairings of servants for the day—ostensibly so they could keep an eye on one another in case anything went missing. But since McBrae had suggested it, I suspected he had another sort of theft in mind.

Sir Roderick bounded up the stairs to check on Cynthia. I wanted to detour after him, but I dared not. Instead, I glanced into my bedchamber, and sure enough: my possessions had been strewn about. "Oh, dear Lord," I said, disbelieving. Why hadn't Mary Jane come to tell me? She had returned to the Grange far in advance of me.

"Mmmph! Mmmph!"

My poor maid had been trussed like a chicken, blindfolded and gagged, and thrust behind a clothes press. Choking on tears, I pulled her out and released her from her bonds. "My dear, dear Mary Jane. Who did this to you?"

She shook her head, then winced. Good God, there was blood in her hair! Her assailant had knocked her out. "You didn't see him?" I said.

"No, my lady," she croaked, stifling a sob.

"He must have crept up behind you and hit you on the head."

"Yes, my lady." She pressed her lips tightly together. She was trembling all over and doing her best not to weep, poor dear.

I helped her up and ordered her to lie on my bed, but she refused. "It wouldn't be right, my lady. I'll be fine. I must tidy up."

My dressing case had been broken open. My immediate thought was how fortunate I had brought few jewels, but naturally she took the possible loss much more seriously than I. She hurried forward, then cried out in pain.

"No, you must and shall rest." I guided her forcibly to the sofa, settled her with a pillow behind her head, and brought her a drink of water from the pitcher on the washstand.

"You may be concussed," I told her. "You must remain perfectly still while I gather everything." I gave her a cool, damp cloth to bathe the wound. That should keep her occupied for a minute or two, but she would loathe feeling helpless, so I added, "I'll need you to tell me if anything is missing." Which goes to show that I am not as unsympathetic as many a lady towards her maid.

That didn't keep her quiescent for long, for once I had sorted through everything, she insisted on folding the clothing and putting it away—moving far too slowly and closing her eyes from time to time. When I saw two tears roll down her cheeks, I decided enough martyrdom was enough.

It's not easy to decide what is best for a servant under such circumstances. It was a blow to her pride—yes, thanks to McBrae, I now understand that servants have pride—that she had been so unaware that she hadn't even seen her attacker. She had suffered the terror of waking to find herself bound and gagged, and the ensuing indignity of being discovered in such a helpless state. Naturally, she wanted to return everything to normal straightaway.

But she was too ill for that, and I told her firmly that her health was more important than her pride, and that she was going straight to bed. She didn't appreciate such a blunt truth from me, but fortunately I am the mistress and she is the servant. She grumbled but let herself be led away by Cynthia's maid, Agnes, who returned to help me dress for dinner and promised to make sure Mary Jane was cared for during the night.

It transpired that most of the bedchambers had been searched, with the exception of Mr. Johnson's, Lance's, Sir Alphonse's, Miranda's, and Cynthia's.

The last was easily explained; apart from a brief morning stroll in the garden, Cynthia had remained in her chamber all day, and Sir Roderick had returned periodically to check on her. He must have been with her when the thief was at work, or I shudder to think what might have happened to her.

(Which reminded me that I desperately wished to speak with her, to see if she were happy or merely resigned. I vowed to snatch the first possible chance.)

A number of small items had been stolen, including my diamond drops (but, thank heavens, not my father's cravat pin, which was still in my reticule). Miranda, however guilty of earlier thefts, was innocent this time. Her trips to the house had been few and brief, as she felt it her duty to attend the fair.

What did all this mean? It didn't make sense for a thief looking for items to sell or pawn to go through all one's clothing and sundry possessions. He could only take away a small amount of booty and safely hide it. Was this chaos a way of disguising his true intention—to find an incriminating document? That explained leaving Johnson's room untouched, but not the rest.

Had he found anything? Perhaps not. Perhaps the murderer didn't have any incriminating documents. Either there were none, and Fence's threat to Miranda had been an empty one—or someone else had taken the papers from his room that fateful night.

Or had today's thief found what he wanted and then stopped?

For the first time since my brother's arrival, I caught McBrae's eye. He was cutting lumps of sugar for the coffee, but returned my gaze pensively, nodded slightly, and bent again to his work. Was he posing the same questions?

Well! I must say, I hope McBrae never has reason to drug *me*. Despite my bold suggestion, I was frightfully uneasy, and definitely unwilling to attempt it myself. I assumed Miranda would handle it, but Lance immediately gave the task to McBrae. I tried to keep a surreptitious eye on him whilst not appearing to do so—a sort of subterfuge at which I clearly do not excel. I didn't see him doctor her coffee, but soon after partaking of a cupful, along with several of the cook's delicious lavender cakes, Miss Ellis began copiously to yawn.

"You've had too much sun, my dear," Miranda said solicitously. "A short nap will refresh you. We'll wake you in time to dress for dinner." She herded her niece upstairs to bed.

"That should keep her out of the way all night," Lance murmured to me.

"Did you see him do it?" I whispered back.

Lance sighed. "He did sleight of hand tricks when we were at Oxford. I didn't even bother to try."

Was there no end to McBrae's strange abilities? He shifted between accents, from Eton-and-Oxford to incomprehensible Cockney to broad Scots, with the greatest of ease. He made subtle changes to his posture and features with similar facility, and now he had proven to be a master of sleight of hand. What next?

When everyone, including Sir Roderick, gathered in the drawing room before dinner, I seized my chance to see Cynthia, who had chosen to dine alone in her chamber. It was my duty to check on her, and see if she had come to her senses and wanted my help.

She didn't. "I shall marry Roderick. He has been most kind, and so dedicated to my welfare that I cannot refuse him."

"Kind? He has persecuted you. I don't call that dedication, but rather a horrid kind of obsession."

"It's an obsession known as love," she said, in her placid way—almost like her old self.

I narrowed my eyes at her. "You may have convinced yourself, but you're not convincing me. I can tell that you're still uneasy."

"Everyone's uneasy. Roderick says they're afraid the coroner will try to make the jury rule that Mr. Fence was murdered, and then everyone here will be under suspicion. I hope not. He was the sort of man someone was bound to kill eventually."

I agreed, but her comment surprised me. "Oh, were you acquainted with him?"

She wrinkled her nose in distaste. "We had acquaintances in common."

I raised my brows at this. She doesn't enjoy the theater and rarely accompanies me there. He certainly wasn't in our circle of friends.

With a shrug, she added, "It will all be over tomorrow, and Sir Roderick and I will leave the following day. Just imagine—he brought a special license with him! Once we are wed, he will take me to his estate, where I can await the baby's birth in peace and comfort."

The unbelievable gall of the man. How dare he be so sure of Cynthia that he bought a license before she agreed to marry him!

"Don't be indignant, dearest," Cynthia soothed. "You cannot imagine how relieved I am to have it all settled."

I went down to dinner in a dudgeon.

Chapter Fifteen

I may have to curtail myself where her mother is concerned, but the henpecked brother remains fair game.

—From the diary of Corvus

Miranda's cook outdid herself, treating us to two roast ducks, an enormous char pie, some creamed spinach, and various salads. We were all weary from a day spent largely outdoors. With any luck, I thought, we should brush through the rest of the evening easily and get rid of Mr. Johnson in the morning.

At first, the discussion centered mostly around the thefts. I had lost the diamond ear drops, Colonel Wendell a snuffbox, his wife a brooch, Mr. Powers a ring, and Miss Gardner a silver bracelet. Bellevue had lost nothing but acted as insulted as if he had. Papa had lost nothing and was less indignant than last time, but Julius was so appalled that he was only prevented from retreating to the village inn for the night at my father's insistence—or perhaps because staying at the Grange was the only way to get a chance to pester him further. He had already tried several times to take my father aside, glancing at me as he did so, but Papa always told him, "Later, my boy. Later."

My heart sank lower each time. What was so urgent that he must discuss it *now*? Should I demand to be included? That might displease my father, but with every passing minute, I knew more certainly that it had to do with me.

Mr. Johnson was irate. "You've had thefts, and you didn't tell me?" he roared. Quite unnecessarily, I might add, for no one had searched *his* room.

"Sorry, old fellow," Sir Alphonse said. "It didn't seem important compared to this dashed accident, so it slipped my mind."

"For the second time," my father said drily. "He forgot to tell me, too. The night we arrived, the fellow stole my diamond pin, and the bloody accident hadn't even happened yet."

"Most remiss of you, Sir Alphonse," Mr. Johnson said. "Most remiss. Nothing of the sort would ever happen in my household, I can tell you that. Have you questioned the servants?"

Sir Alphonse explained wearily that because of the earlier thefts, he had arranged for the servants left in the house during the Lammas celebration to remain in each other's company at all times, except when sent on specific tasks, which they were to complete as quickly as possible. "They wouldn't have had time to search so many rooms," he insisted.

"What if they were in collusion?" Johnson said. "Question them separately. Threaten them. Where's that new fellow, the Scottish rascal?"

How dare he? I thought indignantly. Shame at my own thoughtless prejudices did its best to wash over me, but I staunchly ignored it. This was different…wasn't it? I even tried, in my tangled reflections afterwards, to blame my preconceived notions on my mother, which is unfair. I have a mind of my own—or if I don't, I had best acquire one.

Fortunately, Lance came to the rescue before I could blurt out a protest. It would look extremely odd if I stood up for a servant not my own, particularly with his master there.

And particularly when the servant in question was a young, handsome, brawny, et cetera, footman.

Heavens! When had I begun to think of McBrae as handsome? He was rather ordinary looking—or so I had thought a few months earlier. Perhaps the proverb is wrong, and familiarity breeds appreciation or some such.

"Mac is my servant, not my father's. He spent the entire day at the fair," Lance said.

"Lazy fellow," Johnson grunted, despite the fact that McBrae was serving Miranda right next to him. Such lofty indifference was required by my mother, but in a country gentleman it appeared boorish. "The other footman, then. Or one of the maids."

"Next, you'll accuse Mrs. Alderthwaite," Sir Alphonse said. "Or Wiggs." This last suggestion was so absurd that it drew a few chuckles. Fortunately, the doddering butler was not in the room. (There! I thought of a servant's feelings. I'm not doing too badly for the daughter of an earl, et cetera.) "Pray don't concern yourself with this, Johnson. It's a minor matter, and I shall handle it."

"Very well," growled Mr. Johnson. "But you may be sure I shall leave this ill-managed household by noon tomorrow."

Good riddance. I expect we all, including the murderer, shared that thought.

"The instant the inquest is over," Johnson said.

"Inquest?" my brother asked.

"An untimely accident occurred a few days ago, killing one of my guests. Fellow named Fence," Sir Alphonse explained.

"Fence?" Julius knit his brows. "Not...Daniel Fence, by any chance?"

"That's the man," Sir Alphonse said. "Were you acquainted with him?"

My brother sneered—but as he deems almost everyone beneath him, this in itself was no surprise. "A fortnight or so ago, Lord Mayfield brought him into one of my clubs as a guest. Must have blackmailed him into it, if you ask me."

Everyone froze. What rotten luck that my brother knew something of Fence.

Sir Alphonse merely said, "I beg your pardon?"

"Frightful fellow," Julius said. "He was a civil servant in India until five or six months ago, and should have stayed there. He must have had some sort of hold over Mayfield, for why else would he tolerate the dastard? The fellow was soon caught cheating and turfed out. Mortifying for Mayfield. He's gone to the country to rusticate until the scandal blows over."

"What distressing news," Sir Alphonse said. "I haven't known Fence long, but he seemed amiable enough—although he did have a bad habit of chasing skirts, which is all very well in the theater, but no one is permitted to importune my servants. Still, Miranda took care of that. Threatened him with castration, she did."

Julius goggled, Mr. Johnson snorted, and my father laughed out loud. "The redoubtable Mrs. Tyne," he said with a grin. "How did you intend to carry out your threat, dear lady?"

Miranda rolled her eyes. "I haven't the slightest notion."

"Luckily, that trophy fell on him before you were obliged to try," Sir Alphonse said.

At last, the ladies repaired to the drawing room, followed soon after by the gentlemen.

McBrae and the other footman brought in the tea tray and a decanter of brandy. The brandy, I judged, was a mistake, as Beaver seemed to have no head for alcohol, and Colonel Wendell was also drinking too much. However, it was not my place to protest.

Sir Alphonse came up with the brilliant notion of asking if anyone who was writing a play wished to grace us with a short reading. Needless to say, Harold Bellevue was eager to comply.

"Ladies first," Sir Alphonse said. "Miss Gardner, will you read us a scene?"

She blushed and did her best to demur. "I've hardly written enough…"

"How about the birching scene?" Lance said. "Not much dialogue required there."

She blushed even more, poor girl.

"For shame, Mr. Lewis," I said. "There is no birching scene, as it is hardly suitable to a moral tale."

"Not even a tale about a *ménage*?" he asked piteously. "Well then, how about a Billingsgate brawl?"

By which I assumed he meant a fight between two women as shrill as fishwives. "The *ménage* in question has two men and one *lady*," I reminded him starchily.

"I do have a scene with two ladies," Miss Gardner said, "the heroine and her bosom bow." She turned to me. "Lady Rosamund, would you be so kind as to take the bosom bow's part, if I read the heroine's?" She gasped and put a hand to her mouth, realizing what a solecism she had committed. I, as the social superior, must of course be offered the principal role. "I *beg* your pardon. I should have asked you to read the heroine."

"Nonsense," I said at my most gracious, but cringed a little inside. Graciousness is one of those attributes of a highborn lady which my mother insisted upon as a necessary courtesy toward those beneath one—but I'm not sure it appears as courteous as it is meant to be. "I'm not the heroic sort. I shall be happy to play the bosom friend."

Which I was, for the friend, naturally, was far more pragmatic than the heroine, whose ecstasy (alternating between the hero and the seductive stranger) and agony (ditto) would have sorely tried my meager ability. It was an entertaining scene, the friend interrupting the heroine at every turn with excellent advice, which the heroine promptly ignored. I had great fun rolling my eyes—a vulgarity never permitted to Lady Rosamund Phipps, but perfectly suited to an imaginary bosom friend.

Everyone clapped and complimented us. "If this is a sample of your talent, Miss Gardner, you have a bright future as a playwright," Sir Alphonse said.

The sweet child blushed and beamed, and he turned to me. "Lady Rosamund, I hardly know what to say. If I ask if you have ever considered a career on the stage, it will be deemed an insult; if I do not compliment you on your considerable acting ability, it will be an unforgivable omission on my part."

I laughed. "You're too kind, Sir Alphonse. What little ability I possess was honed in London society, where everyone plays a role." I wished my brother, whose frown had progressively deepened during the performance, were a little better at playing a role. He could at least pretend to enjoy himself!

Never mind him, I told myself, and gestured to Harold Bellevue, who was impatiently rustling his sheaf of papers. "Shall we press on?"

Sir Alphonse nodded, and Mr. Bellevue proceeded to bore us—hopefully to drowsiness and an early night. Much as I didn't wish a murderer to go free, I also wanted the inquest over and done.

Mr. Bellevue began with a plea for mercy by a Roman legionnaire wrongly accused of despoiling a princess, followed by her despairing monologue as she is forced to wed the villainous king who betrayed his fellow Britons.

"What about the life and death of Boudicca?" Lance asked, when Bellevue took a bow. "You'll never fit all that in as well. This is supposed to be a *short* play." It also didn't qualify as a ménage story, but I for one didn't care as long as it was over.

"Thank you, Mr. Bellevue," said Sir Alphonse. "Well done."

Johnny Beaver snorted rudely. "No wonder he hired a friend of mine to write a love poem for him."

"What the devil?" Mr. Bellevue rounded on him, purple with rage.

"Now, now, gentlemen," Sir Alphonse said.

"What a shame you didn't read while Fence was alive." Beaver chuckled drunkenly. "Murder by blank verse."

There was a fraught silence, which I hoped Mr. Johnson would attribute to the imminent threat of a drunken brawl.

My father was playing piquet, but he glanced up at me. *What did I tell you about poets?* his expression seemed to say. He said something softly to Sir Roderick, who chuckled.

Heavens. Sir Roderick—chuckling? Unheard of. Meanwhile, my brother…but no, I shan't bore you with my brother. I was avoiding him, so why shouldn't you?

Bellevue advanced on Beaver. "You little worm, I'll have you up for slander. You couldn't write blank verse if you tried."

"You *did* try," Beaver said with a hiccup. "And you didn't succeed at that, either."

"And you'll never sell a play. Your latest effort is a stinking piece of excrement. (He used a far more vulgar word, needless to say.) No redeeming value whatsoever."

Beaver stood unsteadily, fists clenched. "My play is about the *truth*. The timely death of Fence."

Lance inserted himself between them with a sigh.

"Timely?" Mr. Johnson said. "Surely you mean untimely, young man."

"A eulogy—how fitting," Sir Alphonse said. "But you're too far gone in drink to read for us, and we're all weary after a day out in the sun. You and Powers may read tomorrow evening."

"That bastard doesn't deserve a eulogy," Beaver said. "The play is about how he killed my mother."

Lance made a face. "Fence did what? Don't be absurd. Your mother died in her bed last year. I remember perfectly well, even if you're too drunk to do so." He pushed Beaver back into his chair.

"He killed her with the pox," Beaver said. "The Fence Pox." This met with uneasy spurts of laughter.

"It's called the French pox, you fool." Lance huffed. "Beaver's too drunk to know what he's saying. Fence hadn't been in England long enough to kill anyone by infecting her with the pox—particularly not when she's already dead and buried."

"Pity he came back," Colonel Wendell piped up, his speech slurred with too much brandy. "Bloody disgrace. Should have stayed in India."

I glanced about the room. Miss Gardner was pale and unhappy; Mrs. Holloway grim; Mr. Powers worried; Mrs. Wendell alarmed. Sir Roderick and my father were once again oblivious to everything but their game of piquet.

There was another silence. Mrs. Wendell packed up her knitting and said, "I believe it's time for me to retire. Are you coming, dearest?"

The Colonel raised his head. "Shouldn't have brought you with me, Martha. Shouldn't have come here at all. If I'd known Fence would be here, I would have forbidden it."

Mrs. Wendell tsked. "Nonsense, my dear. He wouldn't have pestered an old lady like me. I've had a delightful visit."

"Well, I haven't," the Colonel muttered. "Bad enough with stuffed heads falling all over the place. Worse with that blackguard here, too."

"Only one of them fell," his wife said. "I asked Sir Alphonse to have the others removed."

Johnson said suddenly, "I've been thinking about that. Been wondering how the trophy could have fallen without a little help."

"Help? From whom?" Sir Alphonse demanded. "That trophy's been askew for years and finally gave way."

"A footman, perhaps," Johnson said seriously. "Protecting one of the maids from this Fence character."

I stifled a gasp of dismay. Mr. Johnson had already tried to accuse the servants of theft. As Sir Alphonse had said, he was indeed the sort who couldn't let go of an idea once it had taken hold of his mind.

"Nonsense," Miranda said. "James, our footman, isn't enamored of any of the maids. His sweetheart is the vicar's maid of all work."

"Well then, how about the Scottish fellow?" Johnson asked.

My heart thudded wildly. What if McBrae were arrested and accused of murder? What would I *do*? My eyes flew involuntarily to his.

He shook his head ever so slightly. With difficulty, I restrained myself for the second time from leaping to his defense. My hands trembled. I twisted them in my shawl.

"As I said earlier, Mac came here with me," Lance said, "and he's madly in love with a woman far above him on the social scale. He doesn't dally with maids, for that would ruin his paltry chances with her."

Several times since arriving at the Grange I'd had murderous feelings about Lance, and this was yet another of them. How unkind of him to mortify McBrae.

But at least he had stood up for him again. And really, I needn't have felt obliged to leap to his defense. If necessary, McBrae could reveal his gentlemanly origins, his Eton-and-Oxford education, et cetera, as well as his reason for being here. Apart from being a Scot, he was perfectly respectable.

(I do not mean to imply that Scots aren't respectable. I am completely aware that most of them probably are, so you needn't jump up and shake a finger at me. I am merely pointing out that the long history of conflict between the English and the Scots has resulted in a certain degree of mistrust.

Mutual mistrust, I expect. Not that I can see from the Scottish point of view, but they must have one.)

Mr. Johnson directed his stern gaze at McBrae. "Is this true?"

"Aye, sir," McBrae said. "It's a hopeless passion, but seems I can't help but love the lady all the same."

Mr. Johnson frowned. "Young man, it is both foolish and presumptuous to get ideas above your station. Find a pretty Scottish girl and forget this lady, whoever she is."

"Aye, sir. I'll try my best to do so."

Hopeless passion, my foot! I didn't believe for a minute that McBrae was in love with me. Granted, he found me attractive, and he was kind and protective, but he also recognized my faults and did not hesitate to let me know.

At last we were free to go to bed. However, I didn't intend to sleep yet, for I had important matters to attend to. I must find out what Julius intended to say to Papa, even if it meant barging in on them.

I didn't know where they had put Julius, but I didn't think my father would go to him. Papa didn't seem interested in whatever Julius wanted to say—perhaps would rather not hear it—so my brother would have to come to him. Papa's bedchamber was next door to mine.

I had chosen to wear a comfortable jump instead of my stays (Mother would not approve, but amongst this louche company, I simply didn't care), so I would not need Agnes to help me undress. I went to check on poor Mary Jane, who was fast asleep, and neared my bedchamber again in time to see Julius entering Papa's room.

Should I force my way in? No, for Papa might not wish me to be there. I couldn't bear to be rude to him, and although I felt little respect for Julius, it wouldn't do to rant at him or burst into tears, either of which would upset Papa and give Julius further ammunition for his belief that I am unbalanced and will sooner or later become insane.

I put my ear to Papa's door, but heard nothing. No doubt they were speaking in low tones.

I repaired to my bedchamber. What a pity there was no peephole between Papa's room and mine, for it would be perfect for eavesdropping.

The window! I pushed the casement wide. It gave a dreadful squawk. I froze, waiting, but nothing happened, so I leaned out, listening hard. Papa's window was open too, but only a little way. I heard my father's placid voice, but couldn't distinguish the words.

"This Corvus business is making her ill," Julius said. "He must be stopped." By the way his voice ebbed and faded, I surmised that he was pacing back and forth.

A murmur came from Papa, perhaps reiterating that he couldn't stop Corvus if he didn't know who he was.

"Precisely, sir. The only way to stop Corvus from persecuting Mother is to remove Rosie from Town. Out of sight, out of mind."

I could almost hear Papa now, but it was obvious what he would say. "She's nowhere near London now," or something to that effect.

Julius' next words corroborated my assumption. "She was supposedly going to spend her year of mourning in the quiet countryside, not at a party of low, immoral persons. Good God, sir! The man's hostess is a trollop, encouraging them to write plays about a *ménage à trois!*"

How unfair. Miranda might be immoral, but she was a competent hostess. Furthermore, she had played little part in encouraging the choice of subject matter. I didn't hear what Papa responded, but I hoped he'd stood up for Miranda.

"What's more, I hear he had an orgy here once," Julius said. "How could you expose my sister to such degradation!"

Papa raised his voice. "You forget yourself, Derwent. I am perfectly capable of protecting my daughter."

My brother mumbled an apology.

"It's damned hot in here," Papa said and pushed his window wide. I ducked back in a hurry, hoping he hadn't seen me.

"There will be no orgy," he said sternly, "and I assure you, Rosie has seen enough of the world to weather a week or two with theater people. She did a bang-up job of reading that part tonight. Remember when you all put on Christmas plays as children? She always had a good sense of comedic rhythm."

Poor Julius! I could picture his clenched fists. "We are no longer children. Rosie is a danger not only to herself, but to the Medway name."

"Nonsense. Your mother is a fool, but you should know better. Have some whisky, my boy." I heard the faint trickle of the beverage being poured. "Very well, don't have any, but I certainly shall. I mean to visit Scotland soon. That footman of young Lance's knows of an illicit distiller who makes an even better brew, or so he tells me."

Seemingly, my father had spent quite a while chatting with McBrae.

After a moment, Papa spoke again, a frown in his voice. "I don't see why you came north, Derwent. For all you and your mother knew, Rosie was rusticating comfortably with me."

"That dreadfully underbred Mrs. Wendell told Mother she expected to see you at this damned party. Mother rightly suspected that you would bring Rosie along in complete disregard of propriety and commonsense." A pause, while Julius floundered, belatedly realizing he was being disrespectful, and collected himself by clearing his throat. "Rosie's in mourning, sir," he said more composedly. "I know you and Mother disagree a great deal, but surely a lately-widowed lady should live quietly, not cavort with immoral persons. Today she wasn't even wearing her blacks, and I dare swear you didn't remonstrate with her."

"She's her own mistress. In any event, she looks better in colors."

Julius growled. "I wish Mrs. Wendell had kept her mouth shut, because it's obvious I'm wasting my time here."

"You knew that before you came," Papa said. "You shouldn't let your mother push you around."

"I *care* about my mother," Julius snapped, but that didn't arouse Papa's ire, for we all know—and he frankly acknowledges—that he stopped caring about Mother ages ago. "She sent to me in London, and bloody inconvenient it was to cancel my own engagements. Now that I'm here, I must insist that you let me take Rosie home with me."

My blood ran cold. No, no, *no!*

"I can't do that. Rosie won't want to, and as I said, she's her own mistress." A pause. "I wouldn't do it, even if I could. She's intelligent and fun and an all-round good sport, entirely capable of ordering her own life. So what if she has a taste for footmen? Many ladies do."

"Footmen?" Julius was aghast. (As was I, briefly.) "Do you mean to say she actually *did* push that footman down the stairs?"

"No, no, of course she didn't, but if people choose to believe that sort of nonsense, why should we care? The lower orders enjoy laughing at the peccadilloes of their betters. Sure you don't want to try some whisky?"

"Damn it, Father, I'm trying to discuss an important matter with you."

"Unfortunately," Papa sighed. "I like a quiet evening—one reason I gave up on your mother. If anyone has inherited a taint, it's she. We aristocrats are so inbred, it's no wonder we're not all tottering on the verge of lunacy." He paused. "Might be an interesting subject to study… Hmm."

"Mother is a perfect lady," Julius retorted.

"That's it precisely," Papa said. "She's perfect to the point of obsession, poor soul, and wants Rosie to be just like her. Well, I like my Rosie just fine as she is."

How sweet of my father. Do you see why I adore him? He loves me despite my many faults, and I don't mean my supposed insanity.

But Julius did, and by now he was snarling. "Rosie must be *locked up* before she does something that reveals her incipient madness. We've been lucky so far, but this can't go on."

I knew Papa would stand up for me, but I couldn't help being frightened all the same. Julius is determined to have me confined, and he would agree with Mama that I must be starved into submission. I think, under such circumstances, that I might actually go mad.

And then what they predicted would become the truth.

"Fiddle-faddle," Papa said, and I let out a breath. "You are allowing the superstitious fears of a shy, frightened young girl—which Rosie no longer is—to be magnified by your mother into a diagnosis of madness. If you really want to be useful, Derwent, take my advice. Instead of pandering to your mother's whims and coming whining to me, just don't say anything in public about Corvus."

"I don't!"

"I'll wager you did. In fact, I expect those words on the caricature were a direct quote. 'I'll have his head if it's the last thing I do!' Pah! You were foxed, I don't doubt, and said it to your cronies at your club. You're not a complete fool, but you become indiscreet when you drink too much. Either Corvus heard you, or one of his informers did."

"In a *gentleman's club*?"

"Why not? There are servants everywhere. That sounds exactly like something you would say."

"Perhaps I did say it," Julius muttered.

"He couldn't resist caricaturing you, just as he couldn't when Rosie said he deserved to be birched."

"The dastard," Julius said.

"I daresay, but the best course is to ignore him and tell your mother to do the same." He paused. "You might mention to her, gently of course, that her own behavior is what makes him portray her as a crazed witch." He paused. "No, don't even try. She'd never understand. Off you go now. I'm tired, and I need peace and quiet to read before I sleep."

"Good night, sir," my brother said stiffly. "We'll speak again tomorrow."

Which meant he hadn't finished pestering my father. My heart sank. He couldn't force me to go with him, but I dreaded his efforts to do so, for both my sake and my father's.

It's all very well to be my own mistress, but I know perfectly well that when it comes down to it, I'm not. No woman truly is. There is always some man or other who thinks he must order her life.

My husband was exceptional in that regard. For the most part he let me be. In many ways, it was an excellent marriage—until the last month or so, when everything went wrong.

I pulled my casement slowly to, hoping it wouldn't squawk again if handled gently, which is why I heard a knock next door and my brother's barked, "What is it, fellow?"

"His lordship the Earl asked me to bring him some whisky." It was McBrae. Good God, what if he had overheard that horrid conversation? He mustn't learn about my madness. He simply *mustn't*.

And he *hadn't*, I told myself. Only shouts would penetrate that door, and Papa and Julius had spoken in ordinary tones. I should close the casement completely, as I had no reason to eavesdrop any longer, but I gave in to temptation and listened anyway.

"Asked you to bring some whisky *what?*" Julius said pompously.

"Whisky to drink," McBrae said after a pause.

"To drink *what?*"

"Och, you mean *why,* mister, and that's because it tastes wonderful!"

Oh, dear. Not that Julius wasn't asking for it, but had McBrae no shame?

"Because it tastes so bloody wonderful *what?*" Julius roared.

"Ahhh," said McBrae innocently, as if he were a dim student who'd suddenly understood what the schoolmaster wanted. "Because it tastes bloody wonderful, *sir!*" He rolled his r particularly hard.

I hugged myself trying not to laugh out loud. Julius practically invites people to make game of him. "Henceforth, you must address me as 'my lord,' he pronounced.

Are you rolling your eyes? Even if it's beneath you, feel free to do so. He is correct to expect a proper form of address, at least initially upon each encounter, but insisting on it in that starchy way should be beneath him.

"Aye, sirrrr, I'll do that," McBrae said, and I prayed that my brother would think him merely stupid.

"Let the lad enter," Papa said. "What have you brought me, Mac?"

"A taste of my father's best, my lord," McBrae said.

"Excellent," Papa said. The slamming of the door told me Julius had gone.

This time I shut the casement properly and pulled the curtains across. I couldn't possibly sleep. I was anxious about tomorrow's inquest, particularly since I wouldn't be permitted to attend. What if my brother took offense at McBrae and encouraged Mr. Johnson's suspicions of him? I told myself that it didn't matter, since he wasn't really a servant, but I didn't quite believe myself. Anything might happen. If he were accused, what could I do to clear him?

An idea came to mind, so shocking that I dismissed it immediately. Or tried to, but you know what shocking notions are like. They persist in vivid, colorful images in one's mind. This one, if I resorted to it, would be believed.

I forced my thoughts to other possibilities. What if the coroner wasn't convinced by Miranda's defense of the other footman? What if Miss Ellis said something horrid at breakfast—she would likely have a headache after all that laudanum—and Powers or Beaver came under scrutiny? Not that Beaver didn't deserve it; he should learn either to drink less, talk less, or both.

Again, I told myself it didn't really matter what Mr. Johnson surmised, for he couldn't prove that anyone was guilty of murdering Mr. Fence. However, a verdict of murder by person or persons unknown would lead to far too many awkward questions and might result in the arrest of some unfortunate person. The only way to ensure the safety of the innocent was to identify the real murderer.

Perhaps if I wrote everything down again, I would see a clue that hadn't occurred to me before. I got out paper, pen, and ink, and set to work. After a half hour's toil, all I came up with was a lack of motive on the part of Sir Alphonse and Mrs. Holloway. Just because I didn't know of any, it didn't mean there were none—for example, if Fence had known something to Sir Alphonse's discredit, or if Mrs. Holloway had done something worse than pen scandalous farces.

I'd just written a great deal of useless information—not worth converting into code—but now I would have to hide it. I dithered for a while, looking for a hiding place where I had none, and was almost in tears (which shows how tired and worried I was) before it occurred to me to burn it. Which reminded me: perhaps McBrae had found some telltale ashes. I wished I had had a chance to speak to him about it.

Sighing, I burned my notes and pushed the ashes to the back of the grate. Restless still, I wandered across to the window, parted the curtains, and opened the casement again, breathing in the fresh Lakeland air. It was a clear, calm, beautiful night. The waxing moon was almost full. Very romantic—the stuff of poetry.

A shadow darted through a moonbeam and headed down the hill. I craned out the window, but the shape had vanished.

Going where? Suddenly I knew.

Chapter Sixteen

Damnation. I missed overhearing much of what I suspect was a most interesting conversation. If I knew more about her, I might know better what to do.

—From the diary of Corvus

Oh, very well, I didn't really *know*. It was a guess which proved to be accurate.

Someone was sneaking down to the ice house, where the body of Mr. Fence lay. To do what? I hadn't the faintest notion. No one in his right mind would go to visit a corpse.

Drat. I do try to avoid mentioning madness in any form—it makes me *most* uneasy. Allow me to rephrase that thought. Who would sneak out in the middle of the night to Mr. Fence's corpse, and why?

My imagination threw up some fascinating notions. If Sir Alphonse were the culprit, to perform a Druid ceremony upon it, for example. If Mr. Beaver: to cut off the corpse's privates, if Mr. Fence had somehow given Beaver's mother the pox. (A frightfully unladylike thought, but you won't tell my mother, I'm sure.) Miranda might like the idea of cutting off his privates, but I couldn't see her slipping down to the ice house to do so. Besides, judging by its clothing, that swift-moving shadow was male.

Hmm. What if the murderer meant to plant evidence upon the corpse so as to incriminate someone else? He might feel it to be a clever move, since several people had publicly mentioned disliking Fence.

By now, I had dressed hurriedly, donning a simple round gown over my chemise. I felt dreadfully underdressed, but time was of the essence. Besides, I didn't intend to be seen—merely to observe and report to McBrae in the morning.

(I am aware that *report* was not the correct word in this instance. I was not working for him or in any way subservient. Heaven forbid! And yet, reporting is what it felt like.)

Fortunately, my mourning clothes included a dark grey cloak. I crept down the back stairs and through the empty kitchen, almost treading on a plate with two honey cakes, then narrowly missing overturning a bowl of milk on the floor. I muttered in annoyance, then remembered that they were the hobgoblin's due and whispered an apology.

Yes, I know that's absurd, but what if there really is a hobgoblin at the Grange? Apologizing to nothing is harmless, while not apologizing to someone is impolite—not to mention potentially hazardous where the fae are concerned. Or so my father says, and I expect McBrae agrees.

The door was already unbolted, which meant the murderer had exited here. Heavens, what if he returned unseen and locked me out?

I would just have to risk it. If I didn't rush, he might be gone before I reached the ice house. I hurried down the path, keeping to the shade. The moonlight which had revealed him could just as easily reveal me.

Dear God, what if the murderer was already on his way back and saw me?

A member of the House of Medway does not know fear, I reminded myself sternly. It's nonsense—I have too many fears to count—but it does rather help in sticky situations. (It helps far more if there is someone from whom one must disguise one's fear.)

It was most unnerving creeping down the hill at night. What with odd rustlings here and there and an owl that flew directly across my path, I was trembling by the time the solid stone form of the ice house loomed before me.

What if the culprit emerged just as I reached the door? I crept carefully the longer way around the building, for he would surely leave by the shortest route. Nevertheless, it took every ounce of courage I possessed to round the last corner.

A faint light illumined the doorway. Dare I approach? I must. My heart battered my chest. I wished I possessed a weapon. Even an umbrella would do, and if I had had the sense to go out by the front door, I could have brought one with me.

Such thoughts were useless. I sidled closer, pressing myself against the darkness by the wall, determined to prove my Medway fearlessness.

A soft thud from inside the ice house chilled me to the bone. I shuddered. A louder thud followed. Horrified at I knew not what, I backed away.

A nightjar cried close by, and I stifled a squeak. From nearby came a clinking sound and a curse in a soft Scottish voice.

I let out a breath and trod toward the entrance. "Thank heavens it's only you." I saw what had made him curse. He must have bumped against the dobby stones hanging in the doorway of the ice house.

How strange. Usually, stones with a naturally-bored hole would hang above cattle in a byre, as a charm against witchcraft. "Surely *you* didn't hang the dobby stones?"

McBrae huffed. "I'm not afraid of the evil eye." He took my arm and practically dragged me inside. I scarcely had time to duck to avoid the stones. "What the devil are you doing out here?" he whispered. "And why am I not surprised?"

I crossed my arms, fury swiftly replacing my relief. "I might ask you the same." I thought for a second and added, "About what you're doing here, that is. I *am* surprised. I thought it was the murderer down here."

"You risked your life following a *murderer*?" he hissed. "Are you quite mad?"

For a frozen moment, I could say nothing. It's bad enough when I mention madness myself; when another person does so, it terrifies me.

I knew that wasn't how he meant it—or at least not in the precise way I feared. I gathered what little composure I possessed and hissed right back. "If you must know, I couldn't sleep, and when I looked out the window, I saw someone sneaking in this direction. I thought perhaps the murderer had come to…to place evidence here that would point to someone else." I glared. "What are *you* doing here?"

"Desecrating the corpse," he said irritably. "Not my idea of an enjoyable way to spend a beautiful summer's night, but now that Johnson is suspicious, we have to make it appear that Fence was standing innocently when the trophy happened to fall on him."

I hesitated, realizing with a sick feeling what that thud had been. "You just made a wound on the back of his head. There wasn't one before. I remember—you felt beneath his head, but there was no blood."

He nodded.

"This is what comes of trying to pervert the course of justice," I said self-righteously. "It would serve you right if the coroner had followed you down here."

After a horrid silence, he said, "My sins are not those under consideration."

Dear God, what was *wrong* with me? Not only had my cattiness emerged once again when speaking with McBrae, but he had taken it entirely the wrong way.

"That's not what I meant," I said.

"No?" His tone was chillier than this horrid ice house.

"No." I tried to summon the courage to ask if he had intended my husband to die that night a few months ago, but I couldn't. Maybe I didn't really want to know. I didn't want him to think I was ungrateful, and yet…

I gave up on courage. "I just meant that lies are dangerous, particularly if they lead to more lies."

"True enough. Come away from the door."

Still I hesitated. It was icy cold in there, so the corpse hadn't deteriorated much, but…

"I'm sorry if you're squeamish, but he doesn't smell too bad yet." He lowered his voice further, beckoning. "We mustn't risk being heard."

I glanced about, unnerved at the thought of someone listening, and did as he asked. "I'm not squeamish." I paused. "Didn't the coroner already examine the corpse?"

"He glanced at it but didn't touch anything. Luckily, the nearest doctor is miles away, so no one called him in. A competent medical man would be able to tell whether a wound was inflicted before or after death." He closed the door, shutting us in. "Since we're discussing lies, you'll have to embroider yours a little."

I bridled. "Which lies?"

"If Johnson happens to ask you before the inquest, don't forget to add to your fanciful version of the corpse's appearance that his limbs were askew, as if he'd fallen that way."

Oh. Those lies. "Very well, but I don't think that will help, if Mr. Johnson tries dropping the trophy to see how it would fall."

"I've already put a weight in the head, in the hope that it will drop head first, but I don't know how the rack will affect its fall. I can't try it out for fear of causing more damage."

"Which would show we'd been meddling. Mr. Johnson has already examined the trophy, hasn't he?"

He nodded, seemingly abstracted, and suddenly I knew what he must be thinking (and this time it wasn't just a guess). "He won't want to drop it," I said. "He has coveted it for years. He'll want to claim it as deodand and keep it."

"Aye, we'll encourage that thought, if required," McBrae said, "but hopefully Sir Alphonse's resentment will suffice. Go back to the house, my lady. I'll be close behind but out of sight."

"What about identifying the murderer? Did you find any telltale ashes?"

"No. Nor do I know who ransacked the rooms."

"If we knew that, we might know who really killed Fence."

"Perhaps, but it could just as easily be someone innocent who fears being accused and hoped to find whatever written evidence Fence used to blackmail him."

"Not so innocent, considering he hurt my maid."

"Aye, poor lass." He paused. "If Johnson suspects murder, he may want everyone's rooms searched, not only those of the servants. Whoever did this needed a place to put the goods that won't be traced back to him if they are found." Another pause. "Off you go. We mustn't be seen together."

I huffed, but headed for the door. "It wouldn't be so very dreadful. I don't care what these people think."

"I do," he said firmly. "Not about me, but about you."

"If you cared about me, you wouldn't draw horrid caricatures of my mother," I said. "It may seem amusing to you, but when she is upset, it ends up hurting *me*."

"Aye, I realize that now. It never occurred to me her tantrums would affect you up here."

Did that mean he'd overheard the conversation between my father and brother?

No. He'd been able to conclude that much from my brother's arrival this afternoon.

"I'll leave her be from now on," he said, sounding so wistful I almost laughed. But it was no laughing matter. "Must I spare your brother, too?"

"You would be wise to do so. What if he discovers who you are? He's not terribly bright, but he has men and money at his disposal."

He nodded, looking pensive but unworried.

"Which reminds me," I said, "you are in danger here. If Mr. Johnson were to fix his suspicion on you again, I would have to—to vouch for you." I didn't have the courage to make it any plainer than that.

"You needn't protect me, my lady," he said. "I'll do fine."

"And if you don't? Then it will be my *duty* to protect you." Which was true; he had saved my life. Why shouldn't I save his?

"Lance will say he and I were playing piquet until after the body was discovered."

"I don't trust Lance," I said. "I *wish* I could attend the inquest." When he didn't respond, I added, "It's not *fair*. I can testify as well or better than many men."

"Aye, lassie, I know." He propelled me gently out the door. Did he really mean that? More likely, he was simply being a typical, patronizing male.

Still pondering foolishly—for his opinion did not matter a whit—I returned safely to my bedchamber and fell into an exhausted sleep.

And woke with a brilliant notion. It was still early—light, but not time for the servants to be up. I needn't dress, and I needn't worry about being seen, for everyone was still asleep.

I donned my dressing gown. Fortunately, I hadn't far to go—past Cynthia's room and around the corner, where the three doors led to the Wendells' room, the service stairs, and the lumber room.

I opened the door to the left upon a gloomy jungle of objects, for the sun rose on the other side of the house, and the windows were festooned with cobwebs and coated with grime. No one bothered to clean this room. What furniture mattered was swathed in Holland covers, and the rest was a hodge-podge of old desks, lanterns without glass, an ancient suit of armor, a huge sword, three cracked chamber pots, a jug, some oak planks, and so on. I shan't bore you with a complete inventory of the room.

Where, I pondered, could one quickly hide a few small but valuable objects? I opened several desk drawers, but found nothing. The chamber pots and the jug were empty, and I forbore to peer into the suit of armor. Only a lunatic (I don't mean that literally) would drop jewelry or a snuffbox in there. Finally, I got down on my knees to look under the Holland covers.

I needn't have done so. After finding nothing on two old sofas, I stood and proceeded past a deal table sporting a couple of broken lamps to a chaise longue. There, in plain view on the stiff linen cover, lay a little pile of booty—everything that had been reported stolen.

I was extremely pleased with myself—but confused. Why steal all those items but not bother to conceal them from sight? There were dozens of better hiding places in this room. Believe me, I know all about hiding things.

The sound of footsteps interrupted my cogitations. What if the murderer—or simply the thief—had come to retrieve his booty? I didn't have time to dither. I grabbed the sword and hid behind the open door. The instant I knew who it was, I would dash into the corridor and raise a fuss. (The sword was just in case.)

Someone came into the room—and stopped. Immediately, I knew why—because the door was wide open, whereas before it had been closed. Stupid of me to leave it open, but it was too late to regret that. I gripped the sword and held my breath.

"Whoever you are, come out and help me with this bloody thing," McBrae said. "I assure you, we have the same end in mind."

I gulped with relief. "Oh, thank heavens." I came around the door. He strode past me and laid the huge stag's head carefully on the chaise longue next to the little pile of booty.

"I should have known you would think of this room," he said softly. "You've passed it a couple of times going to the kitchen, and you're the curious sort."

Yes, and I'd been *so* chuffed with my own brilliance until now. "How did you find the goods?" A horrid thought struck me. "Did you already *know* they were here?"

"I did not. Kindly use your clever mind properly rather than jumping to conclusions which are both absurd and insulting. I don't hit helpless maids over the head."

"I didn't mean that," I said. "I meant…" But he was right. I had meant that. I was too rattled to think clearly, but that was no excuse.

"I used old-fashioned, dogged perseverance." He'd probably searched all night; he looked that weary. He removed the sword from my slackened grip. "Go back to bed, Lady Rosamund, and forget what you just saw."

I bristled, because the alternative was to burst into tears, which I absolutely, positively refused to do. "Why should I forget it?"

"Because I asked you to," he said. "If that's not sufficient reason, think about it and you will realize why."

Abashed, I crept back to my bedchamber, where I did shed a few—a very few—tears. I blew my nose, locked my door, and climbed back into bed. For the life of me, I couldn't work out why he had put the trophy with the stolen goods.

So much for having a clever mind.

I was far too upset to sleep, or so I thought. Wrong again, for I woke much later to the soft scratching of Agnes on my door.

"Such a to-do as there's been this morning, my lady," she said the instant I let her in. "We should all lock our doors in this sinful place." She set a tray with coffee and a slice of plum cake on the dressing table. "Immoral persons were bad enough, and now it's thieves and murderers! Thank the Lord my good lady has Sir Roderick to protect her."

I did *not* want to hear about Sir Roderick's supposed virtues. I assumed a baffled expression and asked, "Murderers? Has someone else died?"

"Not yet," she said darkly, "but Lord only knows what's to come next. They were setting up for the inquest, and Mr. Johnson sent for the trophy that fell on Mr. Fence. James the footman and that dreadful Scottish man of Mr. Lance's went to the cellar to fetch it, and it wasn't there!"

By the way she said *dreadful* it was clear she meant the opposite. McBrae's flirtatious nature would be legend before long, I thought grumpily.

"Dear me," I said. "Mr. Johnson must be frightfully upset."

"That's putting it mildly, my lady. He says he needs it for the inquest, but I don't see why. If he must set everything up like it was—which makes no sense to me, for it's just horrid—one of the other trophies would do just as well."

"Not for Mr. Johnson. He wants to confiscate the biggest trophy and keep it for himself."

"Aye, so Mr. Wiggs says. Mr. Johnson accused Sir Alphonse of hiding it because he wants to keep it. Oh, my lady, if you'd seen the look on Sir Alphonse's face! It set my heart a-palpitating in my breast, and so I told my dear lady this morning."

"How is she doing today?"

"Very well, thank you, and ever so contented now that all is settled." Agnes clasped her hands and heaved a tremendous sigh. "Sir Roderick is so tender and kind to her, it brings tears to my eyes. I'm so happy for her."

Perhaps Agnes believed what she was saying, but I certainly didn't.

She prattled on. "Sir Alphonse set all the servants to searching in pairs, with Mr. Wiggs and Mrs. Alderthwaite keeping an eye on them for the sake of appearances, and Mr. Lance and Mrs. Holloway keeping an eye on *them*."

Good grief. All the servants would be upset, and rightly so. One offended servant at a time is tolerable—even convenient, when one wants to be left alone—but an entire houseful of them? There is quite a difference between a proper silence—for servants should not speak unless spoken to—and an offended one. *Most* unpleasant, I assure you.

"That's why I brought you coffee and cake, my lady. Mr. Johnson says the ladies must stay well away from the Great Hall this morning because of their delicate constitutions."

"What rubbish," I muttered.

"Yes, my lady, it's nonsense, but men have their ways, and it's no use fretting about it. Not that I would want to see such a sight, and glad I am I didn't see the real body, like you did, my lady. But this cake will be better than the eggs and whatnot, for they've all gone cold, what with everyone scurrying about looking for that ugly trophy, and you can't be expected to go down by the service stairs and through the kitchen. That wouldn't be right."

I was about to say I didn't mind the kitchen or cold eggs, but then it occurred to me that if I remained here, I could spy on the proceedings from above. If I were careful, the stupid men wouldn't even know I was there.

I thanked her. "Hopefully, they'll find it quickly and the inquest will be over soon." I wondered how McBrae intended to engineer the 'discovery' scene. I was quite out of charity with him.

Please do not assume I am always annoyed with others. For the most part, I'm rather easy-going. I got on very well with my husband, and even the most irritating people don't bother me much. (Except for Mother and Julius, but they persecute me, as you have just seen. And Sir Roderick, but until he arrived at Lewis Grange, I found his hatred of me somewhat amusing.) I enjoy the company of my London friends while recognizing their flaws and foibles. Cynthia and I have been bosom bows for years.

But there is something about McBrae which rubs me the wrong way.

Constantly. I don't understand why. It makes me feel petty, which I don't like at all.

The first day we met, I decided that I disliked him intensely. However, his persistent kindness changed my mind about that, and I gradually came to like him quite well. I would much rather get on with him harmoniously despite his faults, just as I do with others. I don't like to feel that I'm not as pleasant company as I would wish.

Ah, well. I didn't intend to spend any time today thinking about it, as more important matters needed attention. I sent Agnes away to give Cynthia my fond wishes and spent the next little while drinking coffee, eating plum cake, and making a list. If I thought hard enough, I should be able to remember who wasn't in the village in the latter part of yesterday afternoon—or in other words, who might have been here, searching bedchambers?

Colonel Wendell, who had taken a long time to fetch his cigarillos.

Mr. Bellevue, who might or might not have left the fair early, gone to the house, and returned to the village again.

Mr. Beaver, ditto.

Sir Alphonse, who had walked up to the Grange with my brother to arrange his accommodation, leaving my father still talking to McBrae and taking notes.

Lance, who had spied an acquaintance and walked off to greet him. Soon after, I'd seen him going towards the Grange, hardly limping at all.

Mrs. Holloway, who'd followed the farmers. I didn't recall whether she'd been at the Grange when we arrived, but she might have been in her bedchamber.

Every single one of these people was capable of knocking my poor maid over the head. Colonel Wendell seemed the least likely of the men. Soldiers are accustomed to using violent means, but I doubted he would be quick enough to surprise her. Sir Alphonse was more capable but without apparent motive. The other three men had all demonstrated a capacity for violence. Apart from her absence from the village, I had no reason to suspect Mrs. Holloway. Perhaps I should ask her how the rescuers had fared. If she proved evasive, that might indicate guilt. No, she was far too intelligent to get caught in a lie.

What a paltry list!

A shout from the corridor interrupted my sighs of dismay. I sprang up and peered out my door. A triumphant little procession passed me, Lance in the lead. He winked at me. (Unlike McBrae's, that wink did *not* make me blush.) "Mac!" he called. "Up here, on the double."

Behind him came one of the housemaids with a cracked chamber pot containing the stolen goods, and bringing up the rear was James the footman, lugging the stag's head.

Evidently, Mac was waiting close by, for he appeared almost immediately to help James carry the trophy safely down the stairs. I folded my list, stowed it in my reticule, waited until they were all safely out of the way, and hid behind the balustrade.

"It was in the lumber room," Lance proclaimed, "with last night's stolen goods as well!"

"Aha," Mr. Johnson said. "I knew it. This proves my theory."

"What bloody theory?" Sir Alphonse echoed my thought precisely. Such a vulgar word is not in my vocabulary, which goes to show how worried I was. Whom did Mr. Johnson intend to accuse, and what if he chose McBrae?

"You shall see." Mr. Johnson ordered the maid to set the chamber pot on a table and then leave the Great Hall. "Is this everything that was stolen yesterday?"

"I believe so." Lance counted the items off on his fingers. "Eardrops, snuffbox, brooch, bracelet, ring."

"Excellent." Mr. Johnson ordered the jurors, who were milling about with tankards of ale, to take their seats. He directed McBrae to stand near but not quite under the landing and slump to the floor as if he'd been hit by a falling stag's head.

McBrae did a *most* artistic job of it, even assuming an expression of horror just as I had described. However, I could scarcely appreciate that whilst wondering what ghastly conclusion Mr. Johnson was about to spring on us.

He called on Lance to testify that McBrae lay in the same position and attitude as the corpse. "You need not continue to imitate Mr. Fence's death grimace, fellow," he told McBrae testily. "It smacks of disrespect, not that one expects better from a Scot."

I bristled, which was strange considering my habit of maligning the Scots when within McBrae's hearing (although seldom otherwise; I don't really believe they are barbaric. At least, not as much as before).

As for McBrae, he *grinned* at Johnson's insult, as if disrespect were a matter of pride with his countrymen. It may well be so, but I refuse to make myself seem any more foolish with respect to the Scots than I have already done.

Mr. Johnson next called upon James, the footman, asking if he had anything to add to Lance's testimony about the corpse. James did not; he knew which side his bread was buttered on. Or perhaps he hadn't noticed the dead Mr. Fence's calm expression and closed eyes. Or, like the rest of us, he merely wished to get it over with and send Mr. Johnson on his way.

But moments like this made me wish I hadn't invented the death grimace, however noble my motive at the time.

Mr. Johnson gestured irritably to McBrae to "get up now, fool", and proceeded to examine the trophy with a great deal of pomp and posturing. "It is painfully obvious to any man of intelligence that if this trophy had fallen off the wall, it would not have bounced off the balustrade and landed in the Great Hall. It would merely have fallen to the landing. Therefore, it is evident that someone tampered with it." He paused, scowling meaningfully at the jury. "Someone with a fell purpose in mind."

My heart thudded against my breast. *Please, no.* I hadn't the faintest notion who the murderer was, but I was sure Johnson didn't, either. I really, truly didn't want to have to defend McBrae. How mortifying to admit to dallying with a footman!

But I would. I *must.*

"I admit to being somewhat nonplussed by the dent on the balustrade, but that might have happened earlier, or the clumsy fellow who took it might have bumped it against the balustrade. For he *was* a clumsy man, of that I am sure."

Well. McBrae wasn't the least bit clumsy—although I didn't expect Johnson to have noticed that. In any event, his observation proved that it is unwise to falsify the evidence. Both McBrae and I should have left well enough alone.

"And what was his fell purpose?" Johnson asked dramatically. "It's plain as a pikestaff! He meant to steal this valuable trophy. He lost his balance whilst maneuvering it, and accidentally *dropped* it onto the hapless Mr. Fence standing below."

At last, I understood McBrae's plan.

"This nefarious fellow was not only clumsy, but stupid," Johnson said. "He stole a number of other items, but instead of secreting them somewhere safe, he left them in an obscure lumber room—indicating, incidentally, that he knew the house well. Last night, knowing I intended to take the trophy as deodand, he removed it from the cellar and hid it with his other booty, no doubt planning to abscond with everything today. Ha! How could a man with his wits about him expect these items to remain undiscovered?"

He rounded on Sir Alphonse. "I understand this sort of thieving to have gone on at Lewis Grange for some time. It's shameful, sir, shameful that you have so little control over your servants! I expect you to be more diligent in future in your attempts to identify the thief."

How mortifying for Sir Alphonse, but he merely clicked his tongue, wagged his head, and sighed. "Mr. Johnson, you are entirely correct. I am indeed ashamed."

With a nod much like a schoolmaster berating an errant pupil, Mr. Johnson returned his stern gaze to the jury, whose expressions ranged from agreement to disbelief to affront. As in every village, there were differing opinions of the great man of the neighborhood and his household. However, they immediately reverted to solemn acquiescence whilst Mr. Johnson instructed them to bring in a verdict of accidental death.

Chapter Seventeen

I begin to have an inkling.

—From the diary of Corvus

nd that was that—except, of course, that it wasn't. We still didn't know who had killed Mr. Fence.

"Does it matter?" Lance asked, as he and McBrae and I watched Mr. Johnson drive away with the trophy on the seat beside him. We headed across the lawn and down the path toward the boathouse. My brother had gone ahead of us to inspect the sailboat. He seemed in a better mood today, perhaps because I was obediently wearing my blacks and acting the perfect lady.

It was a glorious afternoon. Hot, but with a brisk breeze, clouds sailing in an azure sky, et cetera. It seemed foolish not to enjoy it, and yet...

"You don't object to sharing the house with a murderer?" I demanded.

"I didn't kill him, and nor did my father, Miranda, or any of the servants. The rest of you will leave soon enough."

How callous of Lance, but unsurprising. "I found it shameful that the jury didn't even attempt to deliberate, but meekly did as Mr. Johnson ordered."

"Why would they make a fuss? They had no reason to care one way or another about Fence, but they will have to deal with both my father and Mr. Johnson in the years to come. A verdict of accidental death was the tidiest outcome." He turned to grin at McBrae, who followed us with a jug of ale.

"I thought we pulled it off rather well."

We? As far as I could see, McBrae had done both the planning and the work, except for Lance's 'discovery' of the stolen goods.

"Aye," McBrae said, but he seemed pensive.

I pounced on that. "You don't seem as pleased as Lance. Didn't you get what you wanted? No innocent person was accused." Nor a guilty one, which rankled. "Don't you care who did it?"

"I'd prefer to have the answer to this puzzle."

Was that how he saw it—as a puzzle? I was tempted to protest, but then realized that to a certain extent I felt much the same. I wanted it all sorted out, settled, and left tidily tucked away.

Unlike my husband's demise, about which I still didn't have the entire story—and was far too cowardly to ask for it.

"However," McBrae said, "I care far more about the others—those who are innocent and don't know what happened to whatever written evidence was used to blackmail them. At least when it was in Fence's hands, they knew where it was."

"If it has all been burned, they'll never know," I said.

"I've seen no sign of ashes, so I think it's hidden somewhere. I want to find it and restore it to those concerned."

"Good God, *why?*" Lance complained. "Leave well enough alone."

Which made a great deal of sense, but when I put myself in the place of the blackmail victims, I couldn't help but agree with McBrae.

At the boathouse, Julius and the boatman were already fiddling with ropes, cleats, sails, and so on. Lance settled me and my parasol in a chair on the dock, then lowered himself into the sailboat to take the oars. Soon he and Julius were headed into the open water, where they raised the sail and shot away down the lake. It would be a quick run to the end and a long series of tacks back.

Which meant McBrae and I had plenty of time to discuss what to do next.

And—which was almost as important to me at the moment—time for me to defy my mother and brother and dip my toes in the lake.

Most improper, you say. And in the company of a *footman?* Yes, yes, he's a gentleman, but no one knew that except Lance. And in any event, I shouldn't bare my feet in a gentleman's presence either.

I didn't care. I frequently dip my toes in the lake at Papa's estate. Admittedly, I'm alone when doing so, but to Hades with propriety. I took my shoes off. Luckily, it was far too warm for stockings, because removing them in the company of a gentleman would have been impossible. I am not and never shall be as bold as that.

"What are you up to, my lady?" McBrae asked in a low voice.

"I intend to dangle my toes in the lake," I said. "My horrid brother won't be back for ages, so it's perfectly safe."

"It's also improper," he said stuffily.

"I don't *care*," I snapped, sorely tempted to jump right in and get properly wet. "I am sick and tired of being proper. What is the point, when people believe anything they choose?" I flapped a hand. "I'm not blaming you. A few caricatures are nothing. I even enjoyed some of them. It's my mother and brother who make my life unbearable." Suddenly, inexplicably, I was close to tears. "Why can't they leave me *be*?"

Hurriedly, I dropped the parasol and plumped myself at the edge of the dock. I moved my toes back and forth in the cool, heavenly water. I dipped my fingers and splashed my face to hide my brimming eyes.

McBrae lowered himself to sit cross-legged next to me. "I don't think Lady Medway can help herself. She's incapable of rational thought."

I sniffled. "I know."

"Lord Derwent may be salvageable. He shows all the signs of a man henpecked half to death. Does he plan to marry soon?"

"Not that I know of. Mother henpecks him about that, too. Sometimes I think he persecutes me because if he pleases her in that way, he can put off having to wed."

"A clever wife might detach him from her."

Perhaps, but the sort of ladies Mother approves of are just like her. No wonder he prefers his mistress, who is gentle and biddable. What a pity she is so ineligible—a merchant's daughter is bad enough, but she is a fallen woman, cast off by her family, and therefore wouldn't even bring a fortune to the table.

I swished my feet back and forth. The hem of my dress was getting wet, but I was not so lost to propriety as to expose my calves. "In any event, we have more important matters to discuss, such as where to find the written proof of Mr. Fence's blackmail. This morning I made a list of those of us who were not in the village for a longish while during the latter part of the day."

I hadn't brought the list with me—in fact, I had memorized it, which wasn't difficult as there were only six names—and then burned it. I counted them off on my fingers: Mr. Bellevue, Mr. Beaver, Colonel Wendell, Mrs. Holloway, Sir Alphonse, and Lance. "I can't think of anyone else except servants."

"Only Sir Roderick and his lady," McBrae said.

"Yes, but they don't count. Nor do the servants, whatever Mr. Johnson may think. I mean to ask Miss Gardner if she or Mr. Powers were being blackmailed by way of written proof." She and I had become quite friendly, but she was a little in awe of my station in life, so she might feel obliged to answer my questions. "At the same time, I can find out what she was really doing downstairs at that hour, and if she saw anyone else up and about."

"Unwise," McBrae said. "We don't want the murderer to learn that we hope to identify him."

I bristled, but he put up a hand to forestall my objection, which was effective but most impolite. I am not only a lady, but the daughter of an earl; therefore, a gentleman should defer to me.

But McBrae was no ordinary gentleman, and although he was usually polite and fairly respectful, he treated me more or less as an equal. He completely ignored the difference in our stations—but at the same time, he never condescended to me as men usually do to women. Although I decried the former, I couldn't help but be grateful for the latter.

"Think about it, Lady Rosamund. Anyone who identifies him might go on to blackmail him."

"Now, that *would* be unwise," I retorted. "Having killed once, he may do so again, which is why I wanted to identify him *before* the inquest. I've been thinking about what I saw on the night of the murder, and wondering if any of it might prove useful. For example, when Mr. Powers came out in response to Miss Gardner's screams, he was partly dressed—shirt and breeches, but no coat, no shoes and stockings. Would he have had time to dress between the sound of the screams and when he came out of his room?"

McBrae didn't respond, which wasn't the least bit helpful. I know very little about men's clothing—only that it's far less complicated than what women are obliged to wear.

I answered my own question. "Perhaps, but he seemed tidy for one who has dressed in a hurry. If he was already wearing his clothing…why? Was he in the process of dressing…or undressing?"

Again, McBrae said nothing.

"Then there's Mrs. Holloway," I said. "I don't think she followed the farmers all the way to the cragfast sheep, or if she did, she didn't wait while they rescued it. She arrived here much too soon for that."

At that he smiled. "You're dangerously observant. I got into conversation with a couple of the jurors this morning. It seems she accompanied them for a while, but when she found out how far and how high she would have to walk, she changed her mind."

"That doesn't sound like her. She often takes long walks uphill." I paused before demanding, "What do you mean about 'dangerously observant?'"

"Mrs. Holloway is a determined sort of lady. I wouldn't put it past her to knock someone on the head if necessary."

How sickening. I rather liked her, but I wouldn't anymore if she had hurt Mary Jane.

"I don't want you to risk being knocked on the head as well," he said. "Best to leave well enough alone."

So much for treating me as an equal. "Since we're suspecting people right and left, what about Lance?"

His mouth quirked up. "You really don't trust him, do you?"

"He didn't sneak into *your* bedchamber," I retorted. "He didn't threaten to drown *you.*"

"He's usually not such a bad sort. He wasn't fully dressed, either."

"No, but his banyan could have covered his clothes." I sighed, realizing I was making up reasons to suspect Lance, which was just as bad as finding reasons not to suspect those I liked. "But he looked tousled, as if he had just woken." Aha! "As to that, where had *you* been? *You* were fully dressed."

"Out for a walk, wondering what to do about you."

"About me?" I felt myself flushing—for no reason at all. What could he possibly have to do about me?

"Whether to reveal myself or hope you wouldn't penetrate my disguise."

Oh. That. I glanced about, as if someone might hear. We were entirely alone, except for a curlew calling nearby. "How do you...*do* that with your face?" I whispered.

He shrugged. "I think of myself as another man, the product of different experiences, with different hopes and goals, and my expression changes."

"More than your expression," I said, awed.

Another shrug. "I've been doing it since childhood. When I'm in a good disguise, I become unrecognizable to those who know me."

"So, it really was you acting as a footman in London. At the ball where I jostled the footman, for example."

He smiled. "You guessed."

"And when you restored my cloak to my bedchamber after my husband's funeral."

The smile vanished into a bleak expression. "Which brings us to my indecision about revealing myself here. I feared you might wish never to see me or speak to me again."

"Oh." Well, now. Perhaps that was how I should feel...and perhaps not. This was as close as we had come to discussing my husband's death, and despite the chance he had just offered me, I realized I wasn't ready to do so now.

So I said what little I could. "I shall always be grateful to you."

He shook his head slightly. Deprecatingly. Absurd, considering he had saved my life.

I couldn't think what to say next. The only escape from this embarrassing moment was to change the subject. "Apart from those I have mentioned, only the butler, Sir Alphonse, and Sir Roderick came into the Great Hall. Wiggs was pulling on his coat as he entered, but the other two were fully dressed. Sir Alphonse may have been wakened by Miranda and took the time to dress and comb his hair."

"And Sir Roderick?"

I shrugged. "Cynthia heard the screams and sent him to see what was going on." I paused, but this was no time for embarrassment. "I believe he slept in his clothes. He would never emerge from his bedchamber in dishabille. He is far too proper, or pretends to be."

McBrae raised his brows.

"Forcing Cynthia to see him by pretending she is his wife was worse than improper."

"He felt he had no choice," McBrae said, "and what little we have seen of her indicates that she appreciates and relies on him."

Grudgingly, I agreed. "To do him some small justice, he slept on the sofa—that first night, at least." I flushed. I had tried to avoid mentioning that by saying he'd slept in his clothes. Just because I was fed up with propriety, it didn't mean I would abandon it completely. One shouldn't refer to carnal matters when speaking with a gentleman—particularly while waggling one's bare feet in the lake.

"Did he indeed," McBrae said. "So that's where you went when you left the Great Hall. I wondered."

"It was my only opportunity to speak to Cynthia alone. The pillow and blanket were on the sofa in plain sight." To my chagrin, she'd had to point that out—but I wasn't about to admit it to McBrae. "What about the other possibilities, for the ransacking at least—Mr. Bellevue, Mr. Beaver, and Colonel Wendell?"

"The Colonel's bedchamber was close to the lumber room, so he may have known about it."

"Yes, but can you imagine him dashing from room to room in a frantic search?"

He gave an abbreviated chuckle. "Beaver wandered about the fair most of the afternoon. Bellevue's room is in the other wing, but we know that he resorts to violence, so again, it's best to leave well enough alone."

It seemed to me that we were getting nowhere. "We can't just do *nothing*."

He waited a moment or two before proceeding. I expect he was exasperated with me, but the feeling was mutual. At last he said, "We're not doing nothing. Our goal is to find any documents Fence might have held."

"Therefore, we must work out who ransacked the bedchambers, and whether he found anything."

"Or we must simply find the documents themselves. Where would you conceal papers that you wanted no one to see?"

"Inside a book," I blurted, and immediately wished I hadn't. I had made it all too clear that I did indeed use books for such a purpose, so I added hastily, "As a child, books were my best hiding place, because I was the youngest, and the others had long since read those in the nursery. But that wouldn't be a good choice when away from home. One can only bring so many books."

"There's a small bookroom next to the drawing room. How about behind a shelf of dusty books?"

Another of my usual hiding places—but it suddenly occurred to me that perhaps he hid things often, too. "I hope you haven't hidden any sketches here. Anyone might find them."

"I don't take foolish risks…" Muttering an oath, he leapt to his feet. "With my drawings, that is." I turned, to see him fetching my parasol—and Sir Alphonse and my father approaching the dock.

McBrae tsked. "I shouldn't have let you lure me into carelessness. Shall I hold the parasol over you, like a humble, obedient footman?"

I snatched it from him. "Definitely not, but some ale would be welcome. And I didn't *lure* you."

"You lure me every minute of the day, lass." He poured me a cup of ale and turned as the two men arrived. "Shall I fetch chairs, sirs?" He did so without waiting for an answer, placing them so that I didn't have to skew myself around much to converse.

"Dangling your toes in the water, Lady Rosamund?" Sir Alphonse laughed. "How delightful. I am always pleased when my guests feel free to break the bonds of propriety."

"In innocent ways," my father added dryly, and I cringed.

"Yes, yes, Medway, I'm not advocating orgies, but why shouldn't a pretty woman splash about in the lake? Do you swim, my dear?"

"Yes, and I am sorely tempted to jump in—against Mac's advice. He is as mindful of propriety as my father." Hopefully that would stave off a scold. Drat it, I hadn't been doing anything wrong! We'd been discussing theft and murder, for heaven's sake.

Oh, very well. My mother (and brother) would consider such a discussion unladylike. But it wasn't improper in any other way. I hadn't been *flirting*, for heaven's sake.

Although McBrae had come very, very close to it. *Luring* him, indeed. I am *not* that sort of lady.

Sir Alphonse took a long swallow of ale. "What a relief all that nonsense is over with. I wonder which of us killed him."

Heavens! I certainly wasn't expecting that.

"Does it matter?" Papa asked. "He seems to have been a rotten sort."

"Idle curiosity, my dear fellow," Sir Alphonse said. "I for one had plenty of motive. The dastard tried to steal Miranda from me—not that she would ever leave me, but the sheer unmitigated gall of the man!"

Oh, dear. Here was another loose end, one that I had pledged (to myself) to do my best to tidy up. It would be frightfully forward of me to broach such a subject, but…

I opened my mouth to say…what?

"Don't be so sure," my father said. "If my wife were so kind as to pop off the hooks, I would snatch up your Miranda just like that." He snapped his fingers.

"You wouldn't dare!" Sir Alphonse said.

"Why not? I could use a competent hostess, and she might like to be a countess."

I gaped at Papa, who treasures his solitude.

"Lady Rosamund's not too pleased with that notion," Sir Alphonse said.

"I like Miranda very much," I said, "but if you ask me, she should marry *you*, Sir Alphonse."

Sir Alphonse frowned. "You, too? Lance said the same an hour ago. Never been so surprised in my life. I don't know what got into him; he loves her like a mother, but why should it matter to him whether we're married?"

"Because of thieving dastards like me," my father quipped.

Sir Alphonse huffed. For a while he stroked his side whiskers in silence, and said at last, "If you must know, she won't. I asked her, and she said no."

"When?" I asked.

"Oh, years ago," he said. "Said I'd be happy to marry her once my wife died, but she said I needn't feel obliged. Said she might have a yearning to go back on the stage. As if I would prevent her from doing so! Wouldn't think of it."

"Ask her again now," Papa said.

Sir Alphonse pouted. "I've already allowed myself to be humiliated once today."

"Your timing couldn't be better," Papa said. "If she refuses you, you've got all the humiliation over and done with in the space of a day; if she accepts, it will more than make up for humoring Johnson."

Which was both amusing and true, but not what Sir Alphonse needed. Now that the subject had been broached, I could take a hand. "Do you love her, Sir Alphonse?"

He stared at me. "What a question! Indeed, I do. Couldn't live without her."

"And I'm sure she loves you," I said.

"You think so?" he said dubiously. "I'm a bit of an old bore."

"Nonsense! You're a kind, charming man, but more important, you love each other, and therefore you should marry. It's as simple as that."

Would that life were always so simple. Papa sent McBrae back to the house. Evidently, he didn't believe my assertion that the footman was mindful of propriety. He remained in apparent good humor as we sat on the deck, drinking ale and sunning ourselves, but I know my father. I was in for a scold.

By the time we returned to the house, Mary Jane was up and doing her best to bustle about my room. "That Agnes is all very well, but her standards are not the equal of mine." She exclaimed at my wet gown. "You'll never wear that again. Look how the dye has run."

"That's fine with me," I said. "I'm fed up with wearing black."

She tutted. "Perhaps, but you've no choice but to wear it for several more months. I wish I'd thought to bring more dye from London, but they must sell dye *somewhere* in the North."

I refrained from a sharp retort. She didn't feel well, she knows when she's saying something absurd, and in any event, I was far more concerned about the imminent visit from my father. I wanted to speak to McBrae first, which was well-nigh impossible without either 1) a meeting under cover of darkness, or 2) Lance's help. Since it was mid-afternoon and Lance was on the lake, neither of these options were available. I could send Mary Jane in search of him, but with what excuse? She wouldn't ask why, but she would wonder, and even if she found him, she wouldn't want to leave us alone. She would suspect exactly what my father suspected, with far better reason.

Dear God. What if Papa spoke to McBrae instead? Or as well?

How mortifying. A footman might find it difficult to repulse a lady's advances. He might easily misinterpret the free and easy behavior of dangling her toes in the lake. Papa would consider that I was the one at fault, but he might feel obliged to warn McBrae off anyway.

Drat! I struggled with my conscience while Mary Jane dressed me in another black gown and left grumbling about the wet one just as my father arrived. He shut the door and gestured to me to sit down. "My dear child," he said somberly, "we must have a little talk."

"Yes, Papa?" I sat primly on the sofa and did my best to assume an air of innocence. Well, why not? I *was* innocent. I hadn't done anything wrong.

He sighed and sat next to me. "This is not the sort of conversation I would wish to have with you, but there is no suitable female to advise you, so the duty falls upon me."

"Papa, this isn't necessary," I began. "*Truly* it isn't."

"It is indeed necessary," he said in the stern, fatherly voice which he rarely uses. "I thought that despite your mother's deficiencies as a parent, you possessed commonsense beyond your years and had developed a better understanding of the proper relationship between a lady and the lower classes, servants in particular, but it seems not."

"Papa, you have misinterpreted my actions," I protested. "You don't know why I—"

"My dear child, I understand all too well. You were accustomed to a lively sort of time in the bedchamber—Albert must have been quite a virile man to satisfy both you and Cynthia, but—"

I put my face in my hands and moaned. What a ghastly conversation!

Papa sighed heavily and soldiered on. "Nevertheless, even if you have lured footmen in the past—not that I ever believed that caricature, but there is usually a degree of truth in Corvus' efforts—"

"There was *no* truth in that one," I interrupted hotly. Lured, indeed! He was as bad as McBrae.

With an admonitory frown, he continued. "As I was saying, it is unbecoming of you to impose on a servant. I have noticed you speaking tête-à-tête with Mac more than once, and however charming he may be—"

My conscience and I were battling fiercely by now. "Papa, you don't understand, and I can't explain, unless—" Drat and damn. I had no choice. "Unless you promise to keep a secret."

"I *beg* your pardon?" He was both baffled and annoyed, and no wonder.

It is painful to dispute with my father. With difficulty, I said, "You accuse me unfairly because you don't know the truth, but the secret is not mine to disclose. I would really rather not do so, but nor do I wish to show you disrespect." Knowing Papa, that wouldn't suffice. "May I count on your discretion?"

Now he was hurt. "Rosie, that is unkind. Have you ever had cause to assume me indiscreet?"

Well, yes—he's often too oblivious to be discreet—but he means well. And come to think of it, a secret that was known to Lance wasn't much of a secret.

My conscience gave up then and there. "He's not a footman."

He blinked. "I beg your pardon?"

"Mac is not really a footman. His name is Gilroy McBrae. He's the son of a Scottish laird and a friend of Lance from his Oxford days. I met him in London some months ago by way of Sir Edwin Walters, the magistrate, and encountered him from time to time, as he is friendly with Lord Baffleton and Lord Logan as well."

My father's brows drew together. "Then what the devil is he doing playing at being a footman?"

"Lance asked him to come here to unmask the thief, expecting it would be one of the servants."

"Good Lord, I should have thought the answer was obvious. It took only a few moments' thought, once I put my mind to it. Why do you think I encouraged Alphonse to marry Miranda?"

"It was obvious to Mr. McBrae as well." Which reminded me—I had Papa's diamond cravat pin in my reticule, wrapped in a spare handkerchief. "I've been meaning to return this to you." Knowing Papa, he would have stowed it in his pocket, thereby endangering both himself and Sir Alphonse's valet. He wore only a knotted neckerchief that afternoon, so I put it through his lapel instead.

"That explains Mac's easy manner," he said. "He is invariably respectful, but not in the least cowed. It also explains the assurance with which he invited me to the great house at Loch Tarlaid. It's his home. I wonder when he meant to spring that on me—or if he expected you to tell me." He rubbed his hands together in cheerful anticipation. "I'm sure you'll enjoy visiting there too, Rosie."

I wished I hadn't promised to accompany him to Scotland, but perhaps I could manage to avoid it. "While we're here, you must keep the secret, Papa. If his true identity were to become known, it would cause resentment amongst the servants."

"I quite see that. I shan't say a word, my dear." He stood. "I beg your pardon for misjudging you. Generally, it would be preferable not to display your bare feet and ankles even to a young gentleman with whom you are already acquainted, but here in the country I doubt it will do much harm."

With that he stood and ambled to the door, humming contentedly, then turned. "As for when you *do* consider—" He broke off, shaking his head, mumbled, "Best not venture there," and shut the door.

Heat flooded my face again. What had he almost said?

Taking into account my father's liking for Mac, I took a wild guess. *When you do consider taking a lover, you could do worse than that young man.*

Chapter Eighteen

She has such pretty feet.

—From the diary of Corvus

I would never take a lover. However, Papa didn't understand, and I couldn't possibly explain. I must simply avoid any more mortifying discussions.

Meanwhile, I might as well do as McBrae suggested. I made my way downstairs. The Great Hall was deserted, as was the drawing room; everyone was either outdoors or indulging in an afternoon nap.

No, not quite everyone.

"Give it to me," a man snarled, "or else."

"I will not!" That was Miss Gardner, her voice trembling. "How dare you touch me. Let me go!" Her voice rose to a warbling shriek.

I reached the bookroom just as Miss Gardner boxed Harold Bellevue's ear with the book in her hand. "You bitch!" he bellowed, raising his fist.

"Mr. Bellevue!" I cried. "Have you run mad?"

I know, I know. I don't use that word, but for a moment there, I was my mother. Or perhaps my grandmother, whose absolute certainty that no one dared oppose her had made her quite terrifying to her children, grandchildren, servants, and everyone else.

"Unhand Miss Gardner." I marched forward, and he let her go—but grabbed the book. He turned it upside down and shook it. A paper fell out, and he snatched it.

Miss Gardner hurried to my side. "I don't know what got into him. I had just taken the book down from the shelf and opened it when he stormed in."

Bellevue threw both book and paper to the floor. "This is a damned cookery book!"

"I *told* you it was," Miss Gardner said. "Why would I want any paper of yours?"

"I thought you were different, but you're as bad as the rest," he muttered savagely. "I must find that letter. It's a fraud!"

"Mr. Bellevue," I said with a composure I didn't feel (for I am not and never will be my mother or grandmother), "I believe many were being blackmailed by Mr. Fence, and we all hope to recover whatever damning documents he possessed. Perhaps if we work together—"

"Don't you understand? They're all against me. It's the fate of genius."

Heavens. He truly was mad.

"I can't let it get into anyone's hands—and I *shan't*." He growled that last word and yanked books off the shelves one by one, shaking them for hidden documents and dropping them to the floor. He glared at Miss Gardner. "Don't try to cozen me. You were looking for it because you're jealous."

"Of you? Oh, please don't throw the books about!" She bent to grab as many as she could.

"Either that, or you're sneaking about on behalf of your lover, trying to discredit me," he sneered, tossing another book. It hit Miss Gardner's shoulder. She yelped and backed away with an armful of books.

This was getting out of hand. I went to the bell-rope and yanked it hard.

"I don't have a lover, and I'm not jealous of you, and nor is Mr. Powers, if that's who you mean!" Miss Gardner was in tears. "Why would we be? He's a poet, and I write comedies."

"Because that's all you're capable of." He tossed another unfortunate book. "Where in the bloody hell is it? It's got to be in here. I've looked everywhere else."

Realization struck me. "It was *you* who hit my maid over the head!"

"She was in my way." He huffed. "You needn't look at me as if I were a murderer. *I* didn't kill Fence, although it's obvious one of us did. If I'd meant to do anything so stupid, I would have got the letter from him first."

Enraged, I yanked the bell-rope again. "How *could* you hurt my poor, helpless maid? What did you think to find in my room? I could not care less about your dirty little secret, whatever it is."

"Because all the world knows yours already."

I froze—silly of me, but whenever anyone suggests I have a secret, I become paralyzed (albeit briefly) with horror.

"You really did kill that footman," he said.

Was that all? I pulled myself together and retorted, "I did not. Corvus made that up."

"Corvus." Bellevue spat. On the floor. On top of the books! "Fence threatened me with Corvus."

"He *what?*" I'm sure my jaw dropped.

"He's the one who fed Corvus all that gossip," Bellevue said.

Surely not. Had I misread McBrae? If Fence knew who he was and had threatened exposure, might he have killed Fence to shut his mouth? It would explain his determination to have the murder declared an accident…

No. I didn't believe that for a minute. That was not the McBrae I knew. Or thought I knew…

Oh, for heaven's sake. If I hadn't allowed my mind to panic, I would have seen it for the obvious lie it was. I pulled myself together *again.* "How do you know that?"

"He told me so," Bellevue said.

I shook my head. "He was lying. Corvus started selling caricatures in London well over a year ago, and Mr. Fence returned from India no more than six months ago."

I hadn't considered that before. How had he learned so much to people's discredit in such a short time?

"He must have started helping Corvus as soon as he returned," Bellevue said.

"Not likely. Corvus caricatures the cream of society. Mr. Fence was an insignificant civil servant with no connections to speak of. How could he be of use to Corvus?"

"How should I know?" Another book hit the floor. "My ancestry is as ancient as yours. If he loves the haut ton so much, why doesn't he caricature *me*?"

He will now, I thought. Finally, Lance and Mac had arrived.

Mac and Lance bore the furiously protesting Mr. Bellevue away. "The Holloway female killed him," he protested—although no one had accused him of anything but a temper tantrum. "Must have been. She was searching bedchambers, too."

"How *dare* he?" Miss Gardner said for the third or fourth time. While the men struggled, we had retreated to two comfortable Bergère chairs by the window. "My godmother would never harm anyone."

"I'm sure she wouldn't." (The appropriate response, if not strictly true.) "But she must have had a good reason for searching." Assuming Mr. Bellevue was telling the truth, but Miss Gardner didn't jump to deny *that*.

She picked up a book and dusted it off. "Mr. Fence said he had proof that Mr. Gardner, who everyone believes is my father, died before I was conceived. As I said before, I don't care whether people know I'm illegitimate, but it would reflect badly on my godmother."

"Why?" I stood and began restoring the books to the shelves.

"Because her son is such a prig. He disapproves of her in general—she's a bluestocking and an independent woman, and she breeds pigs and goes fell walking. Not the meek, compliant sort."

"Why do men always want meek women? It sounds frightfully tedious to me."

"So true! That's why I shall never marry." She replaced a few books. "Mrs. Holloway is a friend of my real father, and it was she who helped my mother establish herself as a respectable widow. If her son finds out, he'll forbid her to see her grandchildren, on the score of being immoral and a bad influence."

Good Lord. I shuddered to think what might happen if he learned about the bawdy plays.

"If necessary, I shall examine every book in this room," Miss Gardner said.

I smiled my sympathy. "For documents which may or may not exist."

"Yes, but I must not fail my godmother."

"Or your brother?"

She paled. "He didn't do it! I'm *sure* he didn't."

Which meant she wasn't sure at all. "Does he have a dreadful secret, too?"

"No! Only my secret, and I told him it didn't matter."

"But clearly he thought it did."

"Yes, but—" Her pretty features twisted into a scowl. "He didn't do it."

"I don't suppose he did, so why do you feel obliged to defend him so vehemently?"

She shook her head. "I don't!"

"Tell me, Miss Gardner—why were *you* downstairs in the wee hours that morning?" I put up a hand. "I'm not accusing you. You said you'd gone to fetch your book, but I don't recall that you had one in the drawing room."

"I had to say *something*," she said at last. "I came down because of Miss Ellis."

That surprised me. "I beg your pardon?"

"She's such an idiot," Miss Gardner said. "Believe me, I told her so. That afternoon—before you arrived—she boasted to me that she had arranged a secret meeting with Mr. Fence in the drawing room at two o'clock in the morning!"

"Heavens, why?" Idiot, indeed.

"She said Mr. Fence had offered her a fabulous role. Where, I ask you? Maybe he was blackmailing the manager of a theatre. In any event, she said Sir Alphonse didn't appreciate her nearly enough, so she planned to play him and Mr. Fence against each other."

"She would have got herself ravished," I said bluntly.

"I came down to make sure she didn't." She laughed palely. "It's not as stupid as it sounds. I have a pistol. I brought it with me just in case."

"And what happened?"

"Nothing." Pause. "Well, not precisely nothing. I hid in here, in the dark, and after a while I heard Miss Ellis. She paced back and forth, grumbling, not trying in the least to be quiet. After a while she lost her temper, let out a few choice phrases that a lady shouldn't say, and went away. I didn't want her to know I'd been here, so I decided to wait a little longer before returning to my room."

"And then?"

"I fell asleep! Those chairs are so comfortable, and I was so relieved. I woke with a start, thinking I had heard something. I waited again, for what if Mr. Fence had come late? I did *not* want to confront him on my own. I heard nothing for a while, but as I was about to light my candle, some low, stealthy sounds reached my ears—not from the drawing room, but from the Great Hall. I heard no voices, only a few grunts, and—"

"Grunts? Did it sound like a man or a woman?"

"A man, I believe." Somberly, she added, "It must have been the murderer."

"A very quiet sort of murderer." No altercation, and probably no struggle… because Mr. Fence had drunk the coffee or the brandy or both, and was fast asleep. A single candle wouldn't shed its light far. If he were in one of the massive oak chairs by the wall, Miss Ellis wouldn't have seen him.

"Eventually, there were no more sounds, and it began to grow light, so I dared venture out without lighting my candle." She shuddered. "I saw Mr. Fence on the floor with that horrid trophy on top of him, and I acted like such a ninny!"

I commiserated with her; I've had my share of behaving like a ninny, too.

We returned to the tedious task of looking through every single book in the room.

I spent the hour before dinner working on my moral tale. At first, I was tempted to make Cynthia foolish and helpless—for that is how she was behaving—but that was no fun. I decided to base my fictional Cynthia on her London persona of sultry mystery, which drives men to madness. (It also aroused some spiteful gossip, but Cynthia handled it tranquilly, rarely showing any emotion other than amusement. I do miss her!)

As for Sir Roderick, I tried to do him justice in some ways. He is a fine figure of a man, if you like that sort—tall, broad, and powerful. He would have made an excellent bully, if I'd been sticking to my original plan. I could have made him a spindly little villain, but what challenge would that provide for the hero who would come to rescue her?

Ah, the hero. Here, I was stumped.

But, you ask, "What hero? What about the Druid priestess who comes to rescue him from the heroine's clutches?"

No, *no*, that was just to make Cynthia believe I wasn't writing about her situation. She'd seemed upset when I'd suggested that a lover from her past would rescue my hapless heroine, so I'd invented a lover from *his* past, instead.

Which is why I was now stumped. The lover from her past was my husband Albert, who was now dead and not the heroic sort. He was a politician and a bit of a spindleshanks, too, by what I'd seen of him (purely by accident when he'd emerged from his chamber wearing only his nightshirt, and believe me, I was content never to see more).

In fact, Sir Roderick was far more the hero, for he was rescuing Cynthia and the baby from possible disgrace.

My little tale was not coming out the way I wanted it to.

My father came to my room just as I finished dressing for dinner. He dismissed Mary Jane and asked me to sit with him on the couch. My heart sank. I didn't think he had reason to scold me. I hadn't even had a chance to speak to McBrae—but, surely he wouldn't object to that anymore. So why else would he make a point of speaking to me alone?

"Sir Roderick tells me Cynthia is feeling better and wishes to come down to dinner."

"I'm glad to hear that," I said, unsure quite how I meant it. Naturally, I wanted her to feel well, but I feared she was adapting to Sir Roderick's wishes because she saw no alternative. How could she possibly dislike him one day and passionately love him the next? "But is it really a good idea, with Julius here?"

"I have just come from speaking with him," Papa said. "Sir Roderick had already spoken to him, but I wanted to make it clear to Julius that the utmost discretion is required. He disapproves of Cynthia, but he also respects Sir

Roderick and considers his willingness to take on another man's child to be honorable in the extreme."

"I'm glad you told Julius to behave himself," I said. "I only wish he would behave himself with me. That he would show *me* some respect."

"That is why I came to speak with you, Rosie. Show confidence, rather than anger and defiance, and gradually he will accept you as you are."

"How can I help but defy him? He *wants* to disapprove of me."

"Only because he is unduly influenced by your mother's absurd fears. He is not naturally unkind or critical of others. He doesn't enjoy the role she has thrust upon him, and it has made him an unhappy man."

"I expect that's why he drinks too much."

"Unfortunately, yes, but I believe that sooner or later, he will shake off his shackles and need our support."

Support from my father I could well understand, but— "What sort of support could I possibly offer him? He thinks I am mad. He wants to lock me up and starve me. How can I—" My breath caught in my throat. I hate being afraid. "How can I be confident when he frightens me so?"

"*Starve* you?"

"Yes! You don't know what it's like when Mama comes to town. She puts me on an invalid diet to make me quiet and compliant. That's what they did to old Aunt Edna. She would have wasted away to nothing if the servants hadn't taken pity and fed her proper food."

"Your mother can't starve you in your own house. Instead of defying her, you must stand up to her and eat what you please." He sighed. "Easier said than done, I know. Sometimes one complies just to make her go away."

Which is why my father eventually went away—far, *far* away from his principal seat in Kent, where she prefers to reside. Now he spends most of the year in the north instead.

"Soon you will remarry and be safe from your mother again, but in the meantime, try to be kind to poor Julius."

"Very well," I said. He left, cheerfully assuming he had made all well, but he hadn't. If the only way to escape Mother and Julius was to remarry, I was doomed. One spouse who was willing to leave me untouched was unusual, to say the least. Two such men? Impossible.

I could never marry again.

Cynthia came down to dinner looking quite her old self, with a bloom in her cheeks. Either 1) she was putting on an excellent act, or 2) she had a fever, or 3) my father was correct, and she was happy. Sir Roderick was more cheerful—or rather, less quelling—than usual, but why not? He had got what he wanted.

Surprisingly, I also got something I wanted—to talk to Cynthia. Thanks to the complete lack of formality at Lewis Grange, we could sit where we chose. *Confidence*, I told myself as we trooped into the dining room. I had best begin practicing it straightaway. I wasn't a superstitious young girl any longer.

(Not that those kind words of my father's stopped me from checking my reticule twice before going downstairs, and it had nothing to do with superstition. I believe I could have controlled myself, but the mere notion of remarrying had made me frightfully uneasy.)

I chose to sit (confidently) next to Cynthia despite the looming presence of Sir Roderick on her other side, and she welcomed me with a smile. How lovely to have my friend back! We chatted about innocuous subjects—the weather, the baby's health, her health, recipes to aid with various minor ailments, and so on—nothing to which Sir Roderick could take exception.

As dinner drew to a close, Sir Alphonse rose to make an announcement. He had dismissed all the servants—a pity, for I sensed what was coming and wished McBrae could be here to observe people's reactions. I would do my best, but I couldn't watch everyone at once.

He cleared his throat. "As I daresay we all suspect by now, one of us murdered Mr. Fence."

There was a murmur of protest, and I glanced immediately to my brother. He didn't even blink. Papa must have told him what to expect. What a pity I had wasted my opportunity for observation on my brother. I let my eye fall on my fellow guests in turn, but saw nothing beyond the usual.

Mr. Bellevue was nursing his offended dignity; Johnny Beaver was in high fettle but not yet intoxicated; Colonel Wendell uneasy and his wife thoughtful; Mr. Powers, belligerent; Miss Ellis—

"I knew it!" she cried. "I told you all so." She assumed a pout. "Alas, no one believed me."

"It was not a matter of belief," Sir Alphonse said, "merely of supposition. His death *could* have been an accident, which is why I didn't dispute Mr. Johnson's conclusion, despite being forced to pretend humility."

That provoked a few titters and snorts. Miss Ellis huffed and folded her arms. "Whether or not you want to admit it, I was *right*."

"I have already agreed that that was so, Miss Ellis. Since Mr. Fence was a villainous sort, it is reasonable to assume someone in this house killed him. No one will miss him—not even you, my child, whatever you may believe. I hear he offered you a role in a tableau he intended to present. Believe me, it wouldn't have been an enjoyable experience. He would most certainly have expected you to perform naked."

For once, Miss Ellis didn't put on an act. She paled, retched, and dashed from the room.

I could hardly blame her, so shocking was this disclosure. Miss Gardner clapped her hands to her palpitating heart. (I assume it was palpitating, for mine surely was. I could scarcely believe that such villainy exists!)

I glanced at Cynthia, who looked disgusted but not the least bit shocked. This didn't surprise me much, for she knows a great deal about the carnal behavior of men, whereas I know very little. "Perform where?" I asked, trying to imagine any such spectacle at Drury Lane.

I regretted my hasty words the instant they were out. I'm sure I turned red as a raspberry. My scandalized brother cried, "Good *God!*" and thumped the table, barely restraining himself from leaping to his feet. "Sir, there are ladies present!" He shot me a glare.

"Yes, but best to have it all out in the open," Sir Alphonse said. "I don't want anyone to leave here believing Johnson's ruling was a miscarriage of justice."

Cynthia leaned closer to me and murmured, "At a brothel, or perhaps a private gathering for gentlemen."

How ghastly. I simply cannot understand the workings of gentlemen's minds. Or perhaps it is their private parts which are responsible for such lecherous behavior. I noted with dismay that none of the gentlemen present seemed surprised.

I also noticed Sir Roderick patting Cynthia's hand, as if she needed comfort. I all but snorted at this patronizing gesture. Cynthia is not a helpless woman needing the guidance and protection of a man, however much he wants to believe it.

Julius subsided, muttering his disapproval, and Sir Alphonse turned to Colonel Wendell. "I suspect, Colonel, that having become acquainted with Fence during your time in India, you know what I say about him to be true."

The Colonel reddened. "I would rather not discuss such a subject in mixed company." My brother concurred with a stern nod.

"Come now, Colonel," Papa said. "It's awkward, no doubt, but let's get this over with."

Unhappily, the Colonel gave in. "I believe he tried something of the sort whilst there, but—" He glanced at his wife, who was discussing remedies with Miranda, and lowered his voice to a murmur. "But not with prostitutes."

I suppressed a huff. Why must he persist in thinking of his wife as a hapless innocent?

He harrumphed and raised his voice again. "Nowhere near where we were—it's a vast country—but there were whispers of shameful behavior. It's a wonder no one murdered him long ago."

Cynthia had said something of the sort the other day, hadn't she? Again, I wondered through whom she'd known of him—and then it struck me: it must have been in India, before she returned to England after Lord Benson's untimely death.

"Now that I think of it, I believe someone did exactly that," the Colonel said. "A pothouse brawl in which Fence was gravely injured but pulled through. Pity, that."

I glanced at Mrs. Wendell, but she wasn't listening. Her eyes were on Cynthia. Hurriedly, she dropped them to her plate. *Oh, drat.* She must have recognized the former Lady Benson. (Yes, at the time Cynthia was still Lady

Benson, but it becomes confusing if I insist on calling her by that name, because 1) most everyone believed she was Lady Frockmartin and 2) now she actually *is*.)

Mrs. Wendell raised her eyes again, catching mine now. I brushed a finger to my lips in a plea for silence. There would be plenty of gossip sooner or later about who had fathered Cynthia's baby, but preferably not here and now.

"I'm glad he's dead," Johnny Beaver said.

Lance huffed. "Spare us the yarn about your mother and the French pox. She was never in India."

Johnny huffed right back. "Nor was he at the time. He seduced her in England, before he went to India."

"How can you possibly know that? She didn't *tell* you, surely?" Without waiting for an answer no one wanted to hear—for what mother would confide something so unsavory to her young son?—Lance added, "If he was so damned poxy a dozen or more years ago, why isn't he dead, too?"

Roars of merriment erupted. "I meant dead of the pox," Lance said, laughing as well. I could see, in such moments, why McBrae liked him; Lance could laugh at himself.

There followed a discussion of the pox, including its symptoms and several horrifying examples of its victims, which I shall not repeat. Suffice it to say that not everyone who contracts it dies at the same rate, or even dies of it at all.

Johnny stood and raised his glass of wine. "A toast to the murderer! Who will join me in dancing on Fence's grave?"

"Sit down and behave," Sir Alphonse said, and addressed us all again. "I believe we also realize by now that many among us were being blackmailed by Fence, and that the recent ransacking was not theft, but an attempt by one of us to mask a search for whatever written evidence Fence used in his dastardly business. Unfortunately, such items still remain missing. Today, Mr. Bellevue began the process of checking every volume in my bookroom for such evidence, and Lady Rosamund and Miss Gardner completed this irksome task. However, nothing was found."

Heavens, how diplomatic of him—and Mr. Bellevue, the hypocrite, actually preened a little!

"Therefore, I have a proposal to make. Naturally, we hope to find the evidence soon, but if it is not found before you all leave, we shall continue to search for any missing documents. If found, they shall be given to Lord Medway, who undertakes to return them to their owners."

There was an uncomfortable silence. No one dared question my father's probity, but nor did they wish him to learn their secrets.

"However, I believe someone amongst us knows where those documents may be found. That someone—whether or not the murderer—retrieved them from Mr. Fence's belongings before his body was discovered. I would greatly appreciate it if, before leaving, that someone would place the evidence someplace neutral where it is likely to be found."

Another silence ensued, accompanied by a great many furtive glances.

Satisfied, Sir Alphonse raised his glass in a toast. "To Justice, however she may be achieved!"

(I ask you—if Justice is female, why do we not have female judges?)

Cynthia and Sir Roderick retired immediately after dinner, as they intended an early start the next morning. Others had decided to leave early as well—Harold Bellevue for one, and Johnny Beaver for another. So much for the play-writing contest! Sir Alphonse and Mr. Powers withdrew their entries, making Miss Gardner the winner by default, but I suspect she would have won anyway.

Sir Alphonse then announced his betrothal to Miranda. The banns would be announced immediately, and plans were in train for a wedding in Druid costume. Miss Ellis complained bitterly about how boring it would be, until Miranda ordered her to behave or be sent home immediately by stagecoach.

On the other hand, my sunburned brother had enjoyed sailing so much that he decided to stay a few more days. After one day on the lake, he looked healthier than he had in years.

When we all withdrew to the drawing room for tea, Mrs. Wendell gave me a meaningful look and patted the place next to her on a small settee.

Resigned to what was coming, I sat beside her.

"My dear Rosie," she whispered. "That was Lady Benson, wasn't it?"

"Lady Frockmartin now," I said with feigned cheerfulness. "Isn't it wonderful?"

"I don't know why I didn't recognize her earlier—perhaps because I'm seldom in London, so I hadn't seen her since India, when she was Lady Benson. She and Lord Benson didn't live near us, but they came to spend a fortnight with some of our neighbors." She paused, grimacing. "I knew she had returned to England after the tragedy of Lord Benson's death—although it was less tragic than it might have been."

"Oh?" She had my attention now. I knew very little about Cynthia's past, for she always shrugged off even the mildest of inquiries.

"Lord Benson almost killed a man in a fistfight, or so I heard. He was a big man, so it's not impossible. And then he wandered away, drunk as a lord—unsurprising, I suppose, since he *was* a lord—fell in the river, and drowned. But think how much more tragic if he had lived and his opponent had died, for he might have been hanged, although with a silken rope, of course, and what would have happened to her?"

"Dear me," I said. "How fortunate for Lady Benson that it worked out as it did."

"Yes, she hurried home to England, a wealthy widow, and enchanted all the eligible bachelors, or so I heard. She is still very beautiful and could have had anyone; one wonders why she took up with your husband instead. Even we country dwellers know the gossip about that, thanks to Corvus."

What was I to say? That I'd found Albert somewhat repulsive physically, although pleasant in other ways, so I hadn't the slightest notion why she'd chosen to be his mistress? "He was an easygoing sort of man," I said. "Perhaps she wanted someone who wouldn't get into drunken brawls."

"She has certainly found that in Sir Roderick. He seems a very sober sort of man." She tsked. "She must be six months gone or more. How noble of him to take on another man's child."

"Perhaps it will prove to be *his* child," I said. "He pursued her for at least a year while she was my husband's mistress, but even if it's not his, he's too much in love with her to care."

"Maybe, but there will be a great deal of unpleasant gossip." Mrs. Wendell spoke in a kindly way, not eagerly as so often in London society. "Even if she stays away from London for a year or more, people will talk."

"They would have done so if she had returned unwed with a baby, despite whatever polite fiction she invented." I gritted my teeth—figuratively, that is—and spouted one of the usual platitudes. "She was prepared to manage on her own, but it is *so* much better for the baby to have a father, and for her to have a besotted husband."

"He *is* besotted, isn't he? He would do anything she asked."

Chapter Nineteen

I hinted; she did not respond. Therefore, I am under no obligation to tell her that the puzzle is now solved.

—From the diary of Corvus

That was the horrid moment when it all fell into place. Well, almost all of it. I had misjudged Cynthia quite dreadfully once before, and I didn't care to do so again, so I did my best not to jump to a ghastly conclusion.

But the facts did add up. What if the man Lord Benson had almost killed was Fence? If one took the two stories—the Colonel's and his wife's—and put them together, it seemed likely. Cynthia had never told me the details about her husband's demise, only that he had drowned.

Cynthia couldn't possibly have lifted that trophy, carried it down, and pushed the antlers into Fence's chest—but Sir Roderick could.

I could easily imagine Sir Roderick committing murder, but not Cynthia doing the asking. Nor could I imagine why. It couldn't be to do with blackmail. Cynthia would never have agreed to perform naked, and she'd had a husband to protect her.

What if she'd betrayed Lord Benson with Mr. Fence? Surely not. Cynthia wasn't pure as the driven snow, but she wouldn't have allowed that diseased libertine to touch her.

McBrae thought she might have betrayed my husband with Sir Roderick, but that was a different matter entirely. She wasn't married to either of them.

None of this explained why she might want Mr. Fence dead. She might blame him for her husband's death, but not enough to risk her own life or Sir Roderick's.

Mrs. Wendell wasn't the only one who saw how much Sir Roderick cared for Cynthia. What had McBrae said? A man will do anything for the woman he loves.

Where *was* McBrae? Not serving tea this evening, which was actually a lucky thing, because I couldn't possibly go to him for advice on a matter so dear to my heart.

If only I had suspected Sir Roderick earlier! I had made the logical but flawed assumption that because Cynthia and Sir Roderick were uninvited guests, they had no connection with Fence.

I had to find out the truth. To *know,* because what if Cynthia were innocent? I couldn't let her drive away with a murderer, all unknowing. I dithered over my tea, answering the still maundering Mrs. Wendell completely at random, I'm sure.

Until I had one of my brilliant notions.

"Do excuse me, Mrs. Wendell," I blurted. "I'm a tiny bit queasy. I must run upstairs and take a dose of my special remedy."

"No need, dear child," she said. "I have a paper of stomach powders here in my reticule. I use them frequently, but tonight my digestion is perfectly fine. We'll just shake some into your tea." She pulled open the strings and dug inside.

"So very kind," I protested, hurtling to my feet, "but I'd much rather use the remedy my dearest mother gave me. It has worked infallibly for me since childhood. Just the thought of trying something else seems like—like dishonoring her."

What a lot of nonsense that was. My mother's remedies tend to cause queasiness, not cure it. Mrs. Wendell nodded understandingly, and I grabbed an empty lemonade glass and dashed away.

I was not happy about going against my father's wishes, but I had no choice. This wasn't a case of meddling anymore. It was a matter of life and death.

Well, perhaps not quite that…but it definitely was related to life and death, and Papa need never know.

How horrid. I trust my father more than anyone else in the world. I like to think he can trust me, too.

These thoughts churned in my mind as I lit a bedroom candle and hurried up the stairs, past my bedchamber, then past Cynthia's to the broom closet. I glanced about, took a deep breath, and opened the door.

Someone was already in there. I gasped—and he emerged from the gloom. I should have known.

"Why am I not surprised?" McBrae's whisper echoed my thought. "Come. Quickly. Don't make a sound."

As usual when it came to McBrae, I did as I was told first and thought about it later. He took the lemonade glass, moved me bodily past him, softly shut the door, said, "Quiet, now," and snuffed my candle.

I bit my lip to muffle a protest. It was pitch dark, and— No, it wasn't. A small circle of dim light showed on the right-hand wall, farther into the closet.

Well! Evidently, this peephole at least hadn't been closed.

He put an arm about my waist—which was frightfully improper—and moved me toward the circle.

"Slowly, softly. Mustn't make a sound."

The strength of his hands and his warm breath made my skin prickle. He eased us carefully into position next to the hole. It was cramped and stuffy, and also deathly quiet. Maybe Cynthia and Sir Roderick were already asleep, which would be fine with me, for if so, I could leave. I wasn't afraid of McBrae, but this intimacy disturbed me.

"Remain perfectly still," he whispered in my ear.

I nodded my comprehension. Any quick movement might dislodge something and give us away. His arms encircled me, holding me close, as if he feared I might shift, regardless of his command. Did he think me a complete fool?

Perhaps he did, for it dawned on me belatedly that he was taking advantage of our proximity. Enjoying it. How dared he?

Well, why wouldn't he? He'd made it clear that he found me attractive. I wasn't likely to make an outcry, for two reasons: 1) I was attempting to eavesdrop on Cynthia and Sir Roderick, and 2) I couldn't afford to be found in a closet with McBrae.

I was already known for consorting with footmen, and if I were caught, here was the proof for all to see. I imagined the utter mortification and knew I had no choice but to remain absolutely still.

Not that McBrae was doing anything to me, not really. He was simply holding me still and breathing softly next to me.

Cynthia said, "That Wendell woman recognized me."

"So?" Sir Roderick said. "Why should it matter?"

"Just that she will gossip. I thought she wouldn't recognize me, for she didn't earlier. We had only met once before, years ago in India."

"You're unforgettable, my love." Sir Roderick's voice was soft and indulgent—a tone I would never have believed possible.

"Fence knew me immediately," she said bitterly. I heard the swish of brush strokes on her hair.

"And now Fence is dead." Sir Roderick's voice was now cold as the corpse. I shivered, and McBrae's arms tightened. I shouldn't have been comforted by his hug, but I was.

"Let them talk," Sir Roderick said. "Maybe Corvus will caricature us, too. He's already drawn me on my knees in tears. I think I deserve to be a knight in shining armor next time."

"You *are* a knight in shining armor."

At that, I had to muffle a snort. Behind me, McBrae quivered, too. It was funny—and yet it wasn't. Real knights in shining armor were big, violent brutes who killed people.

"You're not going to tell me, are you?" she asked. "Exactly what…what happened, that is."

"Some things are best left unsaid," came his chilly voice in what, to me, seemed tantamount to a confession. I didn't need any convincing to believe

Sir Roderick had killed Fence.

It had never occurred to me to suspect him. I had assumed…

"Oh, Roddy," she said, "I don't know what I would have done if you hadn't been here."

Roddy? Unbelievable.

"But I *was* here," Sir Roderick said, "and I always will be." Which was frightfully romantic, I supposed, but it's hard to think of a murderer in a romantic light.

Which reminded me forcefully that the man with his arms around me was quite possibly as bad. Cynthia might accept that Sir Roderick would never confess in so many words. I didn't think I would ever be able to do so from the man who had saved me.

"I thought that when you found out, you would abandon me in utter disgust." She set the brush down with a clatter. "You do understand, don't you—why I couldn't marry you? Why I couldn't even *tell* you."

"It wasn't your fault. Your husband was a fool. After subjecting you to such indignity, he was right to drown himself. Here, let me do that." The brush strokes began again. "In any event, it's all over now."

What, exactly, had happened in India? Had Fence somehow obliged Lord Benson to make Cynthia perform naked?

I supposed I would never know. I couldn't just ask her someday while we were having tea.

"Roddy darling, it will never really be over," she said. "Mrs. Wendell may not realize I was the subject of that story her husband told—he didn't seem to know whom it was about—but one of these days, someone who was there will know, and that someone may tell."

"So what? I certainly don't care. I love you, and that's that. I'm disinclined to compliment Lady Rosamund, but you might take a leaf from her book. She laughs off the gossip."

"Yes, she's frightfully brave. I shall miss her. She's my dearest friend, and it will be ages before we see each other again."

I sighed. I would miss Cynthia, too.

How strange that she considered me brave. I was anything but. She was the courageous one, to return from India and rejoin society as if nothing dreadful had happened to her.

"That's up to you, sweetheart," he said. "We shall return to London whenever you wish, the gossips be damned—or you may invite her to stay with us."

Cynthia laughed softly. "I think not. She dislikes you just as much as you dislike her." She heaved a huge sigh, or maybe it was a yawn. "The baby is so active tonight! I'm sure I shan't sleep a wink."

Their voices faded; perhaps she had climbed into bed.

I came to with a jolt. I'd become so intent on the conversation in the next room that I had relaxed against McBrae.

And now I couldn't help but feel a pronounced bulge in his breeches. I stiffened, horrified. It was bad enough for him to enjoy holding me; far worse for him to become sexually aroused. Unfortunately, I had an all too vivid picture of his condition, thanks to that horrid caricature where I was birching his bare bottom, whilst the tip of his aroused member poked coyly from beneath him.

His arms loosened slightly, and then he kissed a sensitive spot where my neck joins my shoulder. At least, I didn't realize until then how sensitive that spot is. The touch of his lips made me shiver—in a pleasant way entirely at odds with my dismay.

My heart beat heavily in my breast, and a flush crawled up my entire body. What was the *matter* with me?

I pushed on his arms. He let me go, and I tiptoed toward the door—and froze. Voices reached us from the corridor: my father and the Wendells.

"I believe we'll leave tomorrow," the Colonel said. "I've had enough of this place."

"If there are any damaging documents related to you, I'll return them," Papa said.

"I can't think what they might be." The Colonel harrumphed. "Appreciate your discretion, my lord."

"Of course, of course," Papa said. "I wonder where my Rosie got to? She must have gone to bed early."

"She felt queasy and went upstairs to take Lady Medway's infallible remedy," Mrs. Wendell said.

"Is that so?" Papa said.

I sucked in a breath. Behind me, McBrae shook with silent laughter.

"It's not funny," I hissed, but that just made him shake even more.

"Her mother's remedy, you say?" Papa knew perfectly well there was no such thing.

"She said it would dishonor her mother if she tried my excellent remedy instead. Perhaps I should see if she is better. If not, she might like to try it now."

"Best let her be," Papa said. "Most likely it put her to sleep. Good night, Mrs. Wendell. Good night, Colonel."

Footsteps approached and passed us…but what would Papa do? What if he looked in my bedchamber, found it empty, and then started searching for me?

"Oh, no," I whispered. "What if he looks in here?"

McBrae got between me and the door. "The time-honored method of preserving a lady's reputation is to block the intruder's view of her. You might have to pretend to kiss me."

He pressed his lips briefly to mine. Like the previous time he'd kissed me, a few months ago in London, it was…pleasant.

And impossible! "That wasn't pretending," I hissed.

"Close enough. It was only half a kiss. It'll be more convincing if you kiss me back."

"I fail to see how kissing you would protect my reputation," I whispered, and then his lips met mine again, more forcefully, almost demanding, and—

Oh, heavens! I found myself responding.

Desperately, I pushed away. "This simply won't do." I knocked something over in my haste.

"Tsk," he sighed. "I'll go first, as if I came to get a broom."

He must be a cat to see so well in the dark, for he recovered my candle, lit it, and found the broom I had bumped into, all with scarcely a sound.

"We must speak to Lord Medway." He opened the door, stepped out, and left it ajar. "Quickly now." He shut the door and hurried me down the corridor toward Papa's room.

"I shan't speak to my father about this," I protested.

He grinned. "No, best not. I'm only a footman."

Oh, Lord—another problem. "He knows you're not a footman. I'm sorry, but I had to tell him, because he worried that I was too friendly with you."

"And what did he reply?"

"Does it matter?"

"To me, it does." My dismay must have shown, for the smile left his eyes. "Sorry. I didn't mean to fall in love with you, Rosie. It just…happened."

"That wasn't love," I hissed. "It was *lust*." And how dare he address me by my nickname!

"Lust is the natural result of love between a man and a woman," he said.

Perhaps, but not where this woman was concerned. "What about your sweetheart in Scotland?"

He grimaced. "An invention to stave off the *lust* of the servant girls. What did your father say?"

"He was relieved, I think. He…" I certainly couldn't tell him that Papa had implied McBrae would be an appropriate lover for me. "He said it explained your ease with him." We were almost at Papa's bedchamber now.

"Wait," I whispered. "What I meant was that I can't tell him about what we just overheard. He asked me not to interfere between Cynthia and Sir Roderick, but tonight, I felt I had no choice. What if Cynthia was about to marry a murderer all unknowing?"

Evidently, though, she did know—just as I knew about McBrae. Perhaps some things really are best left unsaid; but whatever the understanding between Cynthia and Sir Roderick, it wasn't the same between McBrae and me. We weren't lovers and never would be.

What had made McBrae decide to eavesdrop? Along with that question, a realization struck me. "You wouldn't have told me, would you?"

He didn't pretend to misunderstand. "Five years down the road, maybe, when you'd had time to see that Cynthia was happy with him."

I tamped down my simmering anger. He would have let me go *five years* or more, perhaps forever, without knowing who had killed Fence. He was as bad as Papa, interfering but forbidding me to do so. I had been right about Sir Roderick all along—he wasn't a good man. Yes, he had spared her a great deal of humiliation, but he was a murderer all the same. A lucky one, for all he'd had to do was deliver the final thrust of the antlers to a man already deeply asleep.

Well! It was a good thing I'd worked it out for myself, since I hadn't the slightest expectation of continuing my acquaintance with McBrae. In five years, he would be a distant memory.

"We won't mention eavesdropping. We're going to discuss the written evidence." McBrae ducked under the table by the balustrade and pulled out a sheaf of papers tied with a ribbon. He tapped on Papa's door.

"Come!"

I preceded McBrae into the room. Papa stood in shirt and breeches, riffling through the pages of a book. He raised his brows. "Ah, there you are, Rosie. I wondered."

Drat. He mustn't be allowed to think there was more than friendship between McBrae and me, because there *wasn't*.

I gave McBrae a darkling look and said imperiously, "Why, again, are we here?"

He smirked, blast the man. "My lord, I have the missing papers." He spoke with his Eton-and-Oxford accent in open acknowledgement that Papa knew who he was. "Sir Roderick put them in the lumber room."

"You saw him do this?"

McBrae nodded. "I watched from the shadows." He removed folded papers from both his pockets. "I asked Lady Rosamund to come here because I believe she should deliver two of them."

"Very well." He waved us to the sofa. "I'll be glad to get this over with."

There was a letter to Mrs. Holloway's son, revealing her authorship of the bawdy farces, which my father undertook to give her. Next was an invoice to Mr. Bellevue from an impoverished poet whose name I shall withhold, requesting payment for writing a romantic sonnet.

Poor Mr. Bellevue. Judging by the gleam in McBrae's eye, this would soon be the subject of a mortifying caricature.

The sheaf of papers was a draft of a treatise on the horned god of the Celts, written by one L. Barnes.

"A carrot for a donkey," Papa said austerely. "Fence must have promised it to Sir Alphonse in exchange for…what? The invitation, I assume, for although Alphonse is a fool, he would never have agreed to exchange it for Miranda." He tsked. "Barnes and Alphonse are great rivals. I hope Alphonse will not use it in an underhanded way, but that is not my responsibility." He adjusted his spectacles on his nose, reluctantly setting the treatise aside. Knowing Papa, he would stay up half the night reading it.

There remained Miranda's bill of sale, which I agreed to deliver, and a letter addressed to Mrs. Wendell. On his return voyage to England, Fence had encountered the Colonel's illegitimate daughter by a woman in India who had recently died. The girl was being escorted by a respectable widow to school in England.

"Fence must have threatened to send the letter to Mrs. Wendell if the Colonel didn't pay," I said. "What a silly man. She knew about his mistresses, and I'll wager she knew about this daughter, too."

Papa had already lost interest and retrieved the treatise. "It's all settled, then. Off you go. Good night."

I bade him good night and hurried to the door, suddenly exhausted and desperate to be alone, but I couldn't escape McBrae. I didn't want to talk to him, or feel sorry for him, or sorry for myself, or feel anything at all, but he was before me, opening the door, and behind me, closing it.

Without a word, he escorted me to my chamber. He propped the broom against the wall and bowed over my hand, brushing it gently with his lips. "Good night, my lady."

"Good night," I croaked, writhing inside with a dozen kinds of unease and…regret?

He retrieved the broom and strode silently away.

Mrs. Wendell was not only surprised—she was overjoyed, once she got over her annoyance at the Colonel. "Foolish, inconsiderate man! The poor child has been in England for months now, surrounded by strangers, missing her mother and the only place she's known. I must fetch her immediately."

She beamed. "I dearly love my sons, but I have always wanted a daughter." She bustled away to give the Colonel a piece of her mind.

Miranda took the bill of sale and held it to the candle flame. "Thank you. Are you also responsible for the proposal of marriage I received?"

"I believe that was Lance, with a little help from my father," I said.

"I'm grateful," she said a bit grumpily. I sympathized with her. How mortifying when the man one loves must be prodded into marriage. It was partly her own fault—she should have taken him up on his promise to do so when his wife died—but perhaps she'd been too proud.

I understood pride. As the daughter of an earl, et cetera, I was possessed of a great deal of it. I had a feeling it was getting in my way. I should explain myself to McBrae, but I hadn't the slightest notion what to say. Nobody wants to hear a negative sort of truth such as, "It's not because I don't like you."

I *did* like him, and I had grown to admire him, but despite a few—actually, more than a few—pleasurable tingles when he kissed me, I wasn't... I didn't know quite what. I couldn't explain, "I wasn't ready for a lover," because that implied that someday I would be.

Which was impossible, because of my secrets: 1) My virginity, and along with it the conditions of my marriage, and 2) my mortifying tendency to check things. An untouched virgin cannot take a lover, and what man would want a woman with incipient madness?

(Not that I consider myself mad, but what if McBrae did?)

I dithered through the morning and into the afternoon. McBrae didn't serve at breakfast, nor at the light nuncheon. He didn't bring ale down to the dock when my brother and Lance went sailing again.

Where *was* he? I considered asking Lance, in a vague, airy sort of voice which probably wouldn't fool anyone. Pride kept me silent. I trudged upstairs to take a nap.

What was a volume of John Donne's poems doing on the table by my bed? I had left my Donne at Papa's house. A ribbon marked one of the elegies: "Love's Progress." Donne is one of my favorite poets, but this poem is a vulgar one which I dislike. I read the first three lines:

Whoever loves, if he do not propose
The right true end of love, he's one that goes
To sea for nothing but to make him sick.

The poem goes on to equate love with physical desire. Perhaps, judging by some of his other poetry, this one is mostly a conceit, even a jest. Nevertheless, Donne, like most men—like McBrae—had a lewd streak.

Perhaps McBrae was merely stating the obvious—that he loved me, but not enough to do without the physical aspect of love.

Or perhaps he meant that loving me but doing without would make him ill, and therefore he must distance himself.

Or perhaps the ribbon was at that page purely by happenstance—but I doubted it.

Maybe there was a pretty lass in Scotland who would help him to forget about me. For his sake, I hoped so.

For mine…I shed more than a few tears.

Papa and I remained at Lewis Grange for another week—a pleasant one, since the more annoying of the guests had gone. My brother stayed almost as long, but eventually guilt at ignoring our mother became too much for him. A pity, because he became almost human under the mellowing influences of sailing and McBrae's whisky, which he finally deigned to sample.

"Shall we take advantage of Mr. McBrae's invitation and hare our way up to Scotland before autumn?" Papa asked, when we finally arrived back at his estate. "You'd like to see him again, I'll wager."

This wasn't his first attempt to tease me about McBrae. "I daresay I should, but not so badly that I wish to go to Scotland to do it." Then I blurted out the truth. "But in any event, as far as I know he has returned to London." Or so Lance had said when Sir Alphonse happened to ask why Mac wasn't helping to serve dinner.

"Ah," my father said, "another time, then." How exasperating that his visit to Scotland had become linked to my supposed *tendre* for McBrae. I believe Papa expected me to hurry back to the metropolis, so I stubbornly remained several more weeks with him. I did not want him to think I was eager to meet McBrae again—for I wasn't.

Or at least, not really. I felt I owed McBrae some sort of explanation—why, I couldn't say, because I had no intention of encouraging his advances—but I couldn't tell him the truth.

On the other hand, I did like him very much, and I did value his friendship, and if I were another sort of female—not an earl's daughter, not a virgin, and not rather peculiar, I might well have wished for a closer association. But that was impossible, so why dwell on it? Far better, I told myself firmly, if I never saw him again.

Fortunately, fate had other plans.

Acknowledgements

Nancy Mayer, Regency researcher extraordinaire, answered my questions about coroners, juries, inquests, and deodand. Any mistakes and breaking of the rules of the Regency era are mine (although I bet those same rules were often broken back then, too).

Alexander McRae gave me a name for Gilroy McBrae's home in Scotland, fleshed out his backstory, and explained just enough about the history of Scotland that I simply had to learn more and more. Alec's vast knowledge makes me feel like a student with an assignment, which motivates me incredibly well.

About the Author

Rumor has it that Barbara Monajem is descended from English aristocrats. If one keeps to verifiable claims, however, her ancestors include London shopkeepers and hardy Canadian pioneers. As far as personal attributes go, she suffers from an annoying tendency to check and recheck anything and everything, usually for no good reason. Hopefully all this helps to explain her decision to write from the point of view of a compulsive English lady with a lot to learn about how the other ninety-nine percent lived in 1811 or so.

As for qualifications, Barbara is the author of over twenty historical romances and a few mysteries, for which she has won several awards. On the other hand, she has no artistic talent and therefore is really stretching it to write about an artist who draws wickedly good caricatures. But she's doing it anyway, because he's irresistible. To her, anyway. Not so much to the aristocratic lady. Or at least not yet.